F

Darcy's Dice With Fate

A Pride & Prejudice Variation

The Elizabeth Bennet Series Book 3

GILL MATHER

INQUISITOR BOOKS

Published in 2024 by Inquisitor Books, an imprint of
Write Now! Publications

Cover Artwork: Gill Mather

Paperback ISBN – 978-1-912955-55-8
ebook ISBN – 978-1-912955-54-1

To Write Now! and to the Suffolk Writers' Group – Great to be part of a group dedicated to writing

To John – for talking over the difficult bits with me

To Dan, proof-reader supreme

To Ann for fabulous beta-reading

Also to Anita Dow for taking an interest in my work and lots of other people's.

And a special thank you to Dr Maureen Green paper historian and author

ABOUT THE AUTHOR

Gillian ('Gill') Mather has been a solicitor for several decades and at various times has worked in most of the basic areas covered by general practice in England (crime, family, employment, civil litigation, wills, probate and property). Gill ran a small solicitor's practice from her home near Colchester until 2020. She is a member of several writers' groups in Essex and Suffolk, including Write Now! Some of Gill's novels were previously published under the pen name of Julie Langham.

Gill has published eight full-length novels on Amazon, the first five being a series of romantic-cum-crime novels set in Colchester around a fictional law firm and featuring the same main characters over a number of years. The last book in the series is also a paranormal romance.

As The Clock Struck Ten, a crime/mystery/psychological drama about an accusation of sexual abuse, is the sixth novel. *The Unreliable Placebo*, a rom-com with a difference, is the seventh novel. And the eighth novel, *Class of '97*, is a mystery/psychological drama.

There are six books so far in the Roz Benedict Detective Novellas series. Further novellas in the series are planned.

All Gill's novels are available as both ebooks and paperbacks and now on Kindle Unlimited.

Intrigue At Longbourn was Gill's first historical novel and is a *Pride & Prejudice* prequel. *Menace At Pemberley* was the second novel in the Elizabeth Bennet series and is a sequel

Now, *Easter At Netherfield* is the third.

Gillian Mather – January 2024

Also by Gill Mather

(The Elizabeth Bennet Series)
Intrigue At Longbourn: Elizabeth Bennet's Secret Investigation &
Mr Bennet's Audacious Plan: A Pride & Prejudice Prequel

Menace At Pemberley: Darcy & Lizzy's First Christmas:
A Pride & Prejudice Sequel

(Roz Benedict Detective Novellas Series)
Compromised
Cut Off
Conflicts of Little Avail
Conjecture Most Macabre
Le Frottage
Confounded

(Colchester Law World series)
The Ardent Intern
Threshold
Relatively Innocent
Reasonable Doubts
Beyond The Realms

As The Clock Struck Ten
The Unreliable Placebo
Class of '97

DRAMATIS PERSONAE

Mr and Mrs Bennet

Elizabeth Darcy née Bennet
Fitzwilliam Darcy, husband of Elizabeth and owner of Pemberley in Derbyshire

Jane Bingley née Bennet
Charles Bingley, husband of Jane and owner of Netherfield in Hertfordshire

Mary Bennet
Catherine Bennet

Lydia Wickham née Bennet
Lieutenant George Wickham, husband of Lydia

Georgiana Darcy, sister of Fitzwilliam Darcy

Colonel [Jeremy] Fitzwilliam, cousin of Fitzwilliam Darcy

Ernest Fitzwilliam, Earl of Wareham, brother of Colonel Fitzwilliam and cousin of Fitzwilliam Darcy

Lady Catherine de Bourgh of Rosings Park, Kent, aunt of Fitzwilliam Darcy and Colonel Fitzwilliam and the patroness of the Reverend William Collins
Miss Anne de Bourgh, Lady Catherine's daughter

Lieutenant Colonel James Harvey, friend of Colonel Fitzwilliam and suitor of Catherine Bennet

Mr Gardiner, a London businessman and brother of Mrs Bennet
Mrs Gardiner, wife of Mr Gardiner
Their children:
Julia, Anthony, David and Beth

Mrs Philips, sister of Mrs Bennet
Mr Philips, a Meryton attorney and husband of Mrs Philips

Caroline Bingley, Charles Bingley's sister
Louisa Hurst, née Bingley, sister of Charles Bingley
Mr Hurst, Louisa Hurst's husband
Susan and Margaret, Charles Bingley's other sisters

Harriet Layham, Derbyshire friend of Elizabeth Darcy
Sir Peter Layham, an hereditary baronet and Harriet's father
Lady Layham, Harriet's mother

Clara Lang, née Kohler, Prussian lady, daughter of Professor Kohler deceased
Maximilian Kohler, son of Clara Lang

Viscount Cedric Morley, was at Cambridge with Darcy and Bingley, now a friend of Caroline Bingley

Julius Fairweather, scientist, disappeared in 1797 and wanted for holding up stagecoaches
Lady Rose Fairweather, Julius's mother, emigrated to America in 1797
The Honourable Charles Fairweather, an industrialist, husband of Lady Rose Fairweather, father of Julius, emigrated to America in 1797

Adolphus Barrant, a young American gentlemen, correspondent of Mary Bennet.

The Honourable Daniel Barton, cousin of Julius Fairweather and prospective suitor of Georgiana Darcy

Sir William Lucas, a knight and former businessman
Lady Lucas, wife of Sir William
(The Lucases are old friends and neighbours of the Bennets)
Charlotte Collins née Lucas, wife of the Reverend William Collins, daughter of Sir William and Lady Lucas and best friend of

Elizabeth Darcy

Reverend William Collins, husband of Charlotte, heir presumptive to the Longbourn estate and Rector of Hunsford, near Westerham, Kent

William Collins, baby of Charlotte and the Reverend William Collins

Maria Lucas, Charlotte's sister, daughter of Sir William and Lady Lucas

Mr Holmes, owner of Frogmore Mill, Apsley, Hertfordshire
Mrs Holmes, wife of Mr Holmes

Mr Thomas Hollingworth, owner of Turkey Mill, near Maidstone, Kent
Mary Hollingworth, wife of Thomas Hollingworth
Finch Hollingworth, co-owner of Turkey Mill and brother of Thomas Hollingworth
Ann Hollingworth, wife of Finch Hollingworth
William Balston, partner of Thomas and Finch Hollingworth
Susanna Whatman, widow of James Whatman II deceased former owner of Turkey Mill
James Whatman, son of James Whatman II deceased and Susanna Whatman

George, footman at Netherfield House

Bernard Thompson, footman of the Fairweather's London residence

Mrs Penny Pepper, housekeeper at house in Berkeley Square, Bristol and former nurse of Julius Fairweather
Faith, black maid at house in Berkeley Square, Bristol
Adam, Faith's son

The Reverend Andrew Wilde, Rector of Longbourn parish in 1797

"Shall we ask your cousin the reason of this?" said Elizabeth, still addressing Colonel Fitzwilliam. "Shall we ask him why a man of sense and education, and who has lived in the world, is ill qualified to recommend himself to strangers?"

Jane Austen

Pride And Prejudice, 1813

Prologue

THE salon of the large house in a fashionable part of London was hot and stuffy. The furnishings were ostentatious, gaudy to Darcy's taste, and the air was thick with the scent worn by the ladies in the room, and probably the men also. The effect was almost overpowering. The chairs were hard with stuffing and there were so many people in the audience tonight that, should he have chosen to leave the room for just five minutes to cool down, he doubted if he could have forced his way towards the narrow aisle between the two banks of chairs in the crowded room.

They had all come to witness a performance of the violin by a Prussian prodigy, a mere child of nine or ten called Max, who was a virtuoso despite his tender years and was presently astonishing and delighting audiences all over London, including King George, Queen Charlotte and Prince George. It was also said that he had been composing since the age of five. Darcy had never heard of the boy, but one of Bingley's sisters had procured the invitation to this private recital.

Darcy wished he had not accepted the invitation, but it would have seemed churlish to have refused, especially as it was known that he would be in town anyway to see his lawyer about letting his London house and that he was staying in Bingley's London house for the few days' duration necessary to complete his business.

The performances so far had been mediocre. The interval was thus very welcome.

Darcy forced a hand between his neck and his stock in an effort to cool at least a small portion of his anatomy, while Bingley beside him chatted happily with his older sister Margaret sitting on his other side. His sister Caroline sat to the right of Margaret and another sister, Susan, to the right of her.

In truth, both Darcy and Bingley had been happy to leave Netherfield for a few days, Bingley because he enjoyed London society, and Darcy because he was bored with the sudden leisure, having spent the last two months directing improvements about his estate and in particular making plans for his mill. Furthermore, Bingley had amassed no significant library in which Darcy might have profitably spent his time and it would be five or so more days before Lizzy's relations, including her extended family, would be descending on Netherfield for Easter. It was an invasion to which he was bizarrely looking forward, finding that he quite missed the society of the Bennets, the Philipses and the Gardiners who had been at Pemberley at Christmas.

His cousin Colonel Fitzwilliam probably wouldn't be coming. As Darcy understood it, he was hoping to secure an invitation to the home of Sir Peter Layham in Derbyshire, to whose daughter Harriet he was actively paying court. Lieutenant Colonel James Harvey, an admirer of Kitty, might possibly be able to visit Netherfield. He had been invited, but it was not yet certain that he could come.

Darcy would far rather have returned to Longbourn and to Lizzy once he had seen his attorney. Lizzy had preferred not to venture to town. While her husband was away, she had wished instead to stay at Longbourn House with her family, accompanied by Jane and Georgiana. Lizzy's great friend, Charlotte Collins, would be coming to Lucas Lodge, may even be there now with her odious husband, Mr Collins, the heir to the Longbourn estate on Mr Bennet's death. But Lizzy still fervently wished to see her friend.

An expectant hush suddenly descended and Darcy's attention was redirected to his immediate surroundings when the boy Max — presumably that was who it was — emerged from behind a curtain to a roar of wild applause. Darcy had to admit that he was a good-looking boy with his dark curls and sweet face. He smiled at his audience, took up his instrument and started to play.

The boy played for an hour without music. He played pieces which Darcy had never heard before, strong, complicated, tuneful music. The audience was enthralled, as would have been

Darcy, had he not been so hot and uncomfortable and increasingly stiff at the inability to move more than an inch either way.

At last the performance ended. Max took a bow and disappeared behind the curtain. This, Darcy understood, signalled the end of this evening's recitals.

"Thank the Lord for that," he muttered to Bingley, who laughed. The audience was still clapping and calling for an encore.

Please, God, no, thought Darcy as he stared dolefully out of the window. Mercifully, the boy did not return. The audience rose and shuffled towards the next room where refreshments were being served and where the gathering would spend further hours no doubt praising the boy's performance to the heavens.

The glass of wine with which he was served was, at least, welcome and now it was necessary to make conversation with Bingley's sisters. Caroline Bingley wasted no time before addressing him.

"Mr Darcy, how delightful to see you again. I trust you have enjoyed this evening's treat. It was a huge triumph to have secured a recital by Max for my great friend Octavia Brandreth's soirée."

She spoke as though she knew Max personally.

"We are much obliged to you, I am sure, Miss Bingley, for the opportunity to witness such a wondrous performance."

"Indeed, our thanks should go to Viscount Cedric Morley. You will recall him, Charles, Mr Darcy. He was at Cambridge with you. He knows Max's mother and I am honoured to say that she has become a good friend of mine in the short time she and Max have been in town."

Vague misgivings started to stir in Darcy's breast at that point. At Cambridge, Morley had been a known mischief-maker, ready to play a prank or queer anyone's pitch.

"And it is hoped that Max and his mother Frau Lang will come in and mingle with us before the evening is out."

Just then, Caroline Bingley's attention was taken by another of her acquaintance standing nearby and she, Margaret and Susan turned to the woman. Susan introduced her to Darcy and Bingley after which the four women became engaged in close conversation. Darcy and Bingley turned away and Darcy was about to make a plea to leave when movement near a side door caught his attention.

The boy Max came through the door and looked about, followed by a slender, flaxen-haired woman. Bingley noticed too. His sisters and their friend for the time being failed to observe the prodigy's entrance.

Darcy recognised the woman immediately. He looked at Bingley who stood with his mouth open. He, too, knew who she was. It was Clara. At Cambridge, they had known her as Clara Kohler.

"Bingley, how old is that boy Max said to be?"

"I think Caroline said earlier before you arrived that he is between nine and ten years old."

Darcy's eyes met his friend's. Some unspoken meaning passed between them and, his heart racing, he strode away towards the main door, leaving Bingley to make their excuses.

"I AM most truly sorry, Darcy. I had no idea it would be her."

"It is not your fault, my friend. How could you know?"

"I have seen little of Caroline since our arrival in town. I could have visited her before tonight."

At present, Caroline was living in London with another sister, Mrs Hurst, and Mrs Hurst's husband.

"But, Darcy, I have to tell you that Caroline was talking earlier of coming to Netherfield for Easter and, she said, bringing with her a friend and the friend's son. Now, I assume she meant Clara and Max."

Darcy turned and stared at his friend. "Bingley, please tell me you jest."

"Honestly, Darcy, I thought nothing of it. I don't see how I could turn her down. She said that her friend, who is visiting England, would delight in a sojourn with an English family on an English country estate and that her son would benefit and gain from the experience. I thought she was probably talking about an Irish or perhaps an American friend."

"What is Max's surname?"

Bingley dug his hand in his pocket.

"Here," he said. He handed over a playbill which Darcy scrutinised. He saw at the top of the bill in large letters the name 'Maximilian Kohler'.

"I don't believe it." Darcy crumpled the bill and slumped back in his Hackney carriage seat. "How long have you and I been married, Bingley?"

"Four months? A little over?"

"Yes. And this has to happen. You must not let them come to Netherfield, Bingley."

"But that would be very difficult. You know how it is."

Darcy did know. That a son, such as Bingley, would inherit the majority of the wealth, but was expected to provide for unmarried sisters who had to be hospitably housed if they needed it. He himself now had duties to Elizabeth's sisters should they need a home in the future, indeed to her mother, to say nothing of his own sister Georgiana, although she had a fortune of her own. Of course Bingley, married to Lizzy's sister Jane, had the same responsibility towards the Bennet ladies.

Caroline Bingley had thus far failed to secure an offer of marriage. She was not yet an old maid but the fear must always be there. It was somewhat pitiable but at this moment, he could not afford to exercise compassion for her.

They would not be returning to Hertfordshire until the day after tomorrow, when Bingley had completed his own business, consulting a lawyer about the possible sale or sub-letting of Netherfield. Bingley had not wished to consult Mr Philips in Meryton. How would he, thought Darcy, be able to endure another day here?

"Yes, but..." Darcy cast about for some reasonable excuse to turn Caroline Bingley away. What possible credible reason could there be?

He swallowed down his alarm to say: "Can you not tell her that you have received a report that servants at Netherfield have been struck down by some contagious infection so that it is not safe to invite visitors there for the time being?"

"What about Elizabeth's family? Would you put them off to support the fiction?"

"Well, by the time your sister found out that the infection

turned out to be short-lived, it would be too late. Bingley, I cannot subject Elizabeth to three weeks in the same house as Clara and her son. It would be unconscionable. And do you think that Caroline is entirely innocent of the history here? She referred to Morley. You will recall his propensity to play tricks on people."

"Darcy, it was only a few days in Cambridge."

"Bingley, I cannot take the risk."

"Very well. I will see what I can do."

Chapter 1

Thursday 21st March 1799

CHARLOTTE, Mr Collins and the baby had arrived yesterday, and Charlotte had already sent a note to Elizabeth at Longbourn House inviting her to Lucas Lodge today for tea, together with any members of her family who wished to accompany her. Kitty was eager to pay a visit to Charlotte's younger sister, Maria, in particular. Naturally, Georgiana had walked with Kitty and Elizabeth, the baby being an additional attraction for all the ladies.

Georgiana, moreover, had heard much of Lucas Lodge from Kitty and the shared history of the two families, the entail and Mr Collins's entitlement, not to mention the connection with Georgiana's Aunt Catherine de Bourgh, the patroness of Mr Collins the Rector of Hunsford, the Rectory being within the grounds of Rosings Park.

Mary, of course, would not go, saying she had to attend Clarke's library in Meryton. Jane decided to walk to Meryton also. Mary had fairly evidently wished to go alone, but even she could not avoid her sister's offer of company without giving offence.

Mr and Mrs Bennet had no wish to meet Mr Collins; they already saw the Lucases often enough. It was always in Mrs Bennet's contemplation that Charlotte's husband would inherit the Longbourn estate one day and she had no desire to be further reminded of the fact by being expected to dandle the next generation of Collinses on her knee. The very thought of it set palpitations to course through her breast.

The three visitors, therefore, sat with Lady Lucas, Charlotte, the baby and Maria enjoying tea, seed-cake and sandwiches. Mr Collins, happily, was outside with Sir William instructing the latter on some more productive arrangement for the vegetable garden and upon the cultivation of roses to their best effect later in the year. On their earlier approach to Lucas Lodge, Elizabeth had heard the murmurings of the two gentlemen and had ducked behind a thicket.

"Quickly, over here," she had urged Kitty and Georgiana, "or they will see us and call us over."

Kitty had needed no second warning and tugged at her sister's hand. The two girls huddled, softly giggling, behind the shrubbery. Kitty could recall similar attempts to avoid Mr Collins during his visits to Longbourn House in the last two years, first to unsuccessfully seek the hand of one of the daughters of the house, and the second time to seemingly gloat and disingenuously commiserate with them over Lydia's elopement with Wickham, and she quietly laughed all the more. At length, the three of them slipped away to the house.

Lady Lucas and Maria congratulated Elizabeth fulsomely at the news, passed on by her mother, that she was expecting a happy event later in the year.

"I thank you. I am almost over the worst sickness. And Jane as you know will be confined a month or so before me. I am pleased to say that she is in very excellent health also."

"We had hopes of seeing her today, Lizzy."

"Oh, she sends her regrets. She had chores to attend to in Meryton, Lady Lucas. Living at Netherfield, it is not so easy for her to visit Meryton, whereas 'tis but a short walk from Longbourn."

But the baby present today was a fine specimen and soon called for the visitors' attention. They needed no prompting to admire him, tickle him and, in turn, hold him to their respective bosoms where he sought fruitlessly for nourishment.

"Charlotte will take him upstairs directly," said Lady Lucas, looking fondly at her grandson, "for 'tis clear that he wishes to be fed. He has a healthy appetite."

Charlotte smiled. "Indeed, Mama. It will not take very long, but Lizzy, my dearest friend, would you care to accompany me and tell me all your news. And of course assist me."

A change of napkin, Elizabeth imagined. The practice would do no harm.

"Charlotte, I would be delighted."

Kitty, Georgiana, Maria and Lady Lucas were thus left in the parlour to exchange pleasantries.

GEORGIANA gazed in wonderment at Mr Collins and Sir William Lucas who had come in from the garden and joined the ladies.

"Mr Collins," Sir William was saying as they entered the parlour, "your kind advice will, I am sure, quickly produce an abundance of greens for our table. And I have no doubt that Lucas Lodge will be filled with the most delightful fragrance of roses throughout the summer. I will get Brown onto it immediately."

The other hesitated. "Ah, your gardener, of course, Sir William. It is my humble opinion that my own garden flourishes as it does due to my direct attention. I would not trust it to any other hands. You must oversee your man closely to ensure the best results."

"Oh, indeed."

At first meeting, Georgiana found the two men to have a passing similarity, not in appearance, not at all, but in their tendency to unintentionally amuse those around them. She could see that the description she had been given of Mr Collins as pompous was quite accurate. Both men treated the ladies with the greatest deference, but in such an exaggerated, comical way that Georgiana had to stifle a laugh when she was being introduced to the gentlemen.

Mr Collins launched into an appreciation of the fine qualities of Lady Catherine and the great advantages accruing to him of being in her sphere of influence. Though he addressed his comments to the room, Mr Collins's eyes frequently rested on Georgiana so that she assumed that much of what he said was directed towards her. He must know, surely, that Lady Catherine was estranged from her brother and therefore, by association, from Georgiana as well but he seemed not to feel the need to avoid the subject in case of causing affront. Fortunately, Georgiana experienced only mild contempt and derision for the display.

Sir William enthusiastically nodded his agreement to all of

his son-in-law's declarations. Kitty did not seem to notice the comedy being played out. Doubtless, she was accustomed to the ways of at least Sir William.

Georgiana was struck, too, by the number of Williams in the house and associated with the family. She understood that the baby William had been named for his father, the Reverend William Collins. And their host today also bore the name William.

Soon, another William would return to the neighbourhood to reside at Netherfield Park for a number of weeks, her own brother, Fitzwilliam Darcy, often called William for short. And her cousin, the Colonel, bore the surname, Fitzwilliam.

What was Mr Bennet's Christian name? No one seemed to know.

As she mused, Lady Lucas, encouraged by Maria, was telling the gathering that Kitty's sister, Mary, spent an inordinate amount of time at the library. There was indeed, they were told, a very handsome young librarian, though of course he was not a rich man by any means, but learned by all accounts. The inference was inescapable.

Georgiana found herself highly entertained by the insinuations at play in this handsome, if over-ornate, parlour in this fairly ostentatious house in this rural part of Hertfordshire.

Kitty looked on doubtfully, knowing how immune was her next sister to the opposite sex.

The subject was suddenly changed when Maria turned to her father.

"Papa, you did talk of giving a ball while Lizzy and Mr Darcy are here in Hertfordshire…and Georgiana."

"Ahem! Did I?" said he.

"We have not held a ball for ages! What say you, Mr Collins?" continued Maria. "I recall that you are fond of dancing, despite your position as a minister of the Church."

"Indeed, your memory serves you aright, sister. I am far from objecting to dancing."

"You will have to help in the arrangements, Maria," said her mother.

"Oh, of course, Mama."

"But did not Mr Bingley's sisters often stay at Netherfield with him?"

"Well, yes, they lived there for part of last year and the year before last, but now they stay in town, so far as I am aware."

The sounds of a horse could be heard from outside, but there was no knock on the door, therefore Lady Lucas continued:

"I see. But may they not come to Netherfield for Easter, with perhaps their friends? I only ask for the purposes of counting the numbers of persons, if we are to hold a ball."

"I do not know, to speak the truth. Mr Darcy and Mr Bingley will be returning to Hertfordshire tomorrow, I think, and they will know."

Footsteps in the hall suddenly drew everyone's attention. The parlour door was slightly ajar, but the butler, Harding, still knocked before entering.

Addressing himself to his master, he said: "Mr Darcy has arrived, sir. May I show him in?"

"Upon my word!" Sir William looked at Elizabeth, but she too seemed at a loss.

"Well, of course," Sir William told his butler. "Do show Mr Darcy in."

Harding withdrew. After a few moments William entered the room and bowed. Looking around, his eyes alighted first on Elizabeth.

Then, to Georgiana's astonishment, as though he himself was the host, Mr Collins rose from his seat, handed his son quickly to his wife and, walking towards William, he stopped and bowed a few feet from him. Georgiana saw her brother visibly bristle before he looked away, towards Elizabeth again.

Undeterred, Mr Collins began to address William.

"Your servant, Mr Darcy." He cleared his throat. "As you know, Mr Darcy, I have the honour to have been distinguished by the patronage of your aunt, the Right Honourable Lady Catherine de Bourgh, whose bounty and beneficence has preferred me to the valuable rectory of Hunsford, where it has been my earnest endeavour to demean myself with grateful respect towards her Ladyship.

"As such, I flatter myself that, as we dine at Rosings twice a week, we are uniquely placed to know her Ladyship's opinions. She made it abundantly clear last year that she did not look on your match with my cousin Elizabeth with a friendly eye. Indeed, I wrote to Mr Bennet warning against you and her running hastily into a marriage which had not been properly sanctioned. And now I am led to believe that a rift has arisen between your two houses, a grievous divide between a man and his deceased mother's sister. As a clergyman, I feel it my duty to prevail upon you to make overtures of reconciliation towards her Ladyship and forgive any harsh words she may have uttered or written.

"She, of course, cannot be expected to make any approach to heal the rift. Her position is justified. She was most appalled by the behaviour of my cousin Lydia in living together with Mr Wickham before a marriage took place which had become generally known and —"

William's apparent and growing disdain for this man addressing him came to a head.

"Thank you, Mr Collins," said William stiffly. "You have made your feelings eminently clear."

Mr Collins bowed and backed away.

"Mr Darcy," said Lady Lucas quickly, "we welcome you to our home and are delighted to see you, especially as Lizzy says that she did not expect your return until the morrow. Have you ridden straight here from town? Will you not therefore take some refreshment with us?"

Georgiana saw that her brother did indeed appear a little dishevelled, his curly dark hair ruffled and his face ruddy from exertion and the brisk air of late March. He still held his riding crop.

"I thank you, Lady Lucas. I came to briefly pay my respects to you and Sir William. I have been to Longbourn House and was told that Elizabeth, together with my sisters Georgiana and Catherine were here. I would beg your pardon and would not propose to prevail upon your hospitality. I pray you would allow me to take my leave and I hope to see you again very soon."

Thereafter he bowed and left the parlour.

At her husband's departure, Elizabeth stood.

"I too would pray you excuse me, Sir William and Lady Lucas. I will walk to Longbourn House with Mr Darcy. Do not trouble to accompany us Georgiana and Kitty. We will see you there in due time."

And she hurriedly left the parlour. Georgiana craned her neck to watch through the window. A footman held the horse's reins on the front drive, evidently waiting for William. So her brother had not intended to stay. He was mounting his horse when Elizabeth appeared and he jumped down to greet her.

Something was wrong. Something was afoot, Georgiana thought. What could it possibly be?

Chapter 2

DARCY dismounted and they walked together in the direction of Longbourn House.

Elizabeth too had perceived that there was something wrong with her husband. Even before Mr Collins had approached him and had addressed him so insolently with such over-familiarity and in front of the Lucases and the others in the room, Elizabeth had detected that all was not right with her husband. He was often not easy in company, but it was not that. Whatever it was, she hoped he would tell her.

More relaxed, now that he was out of the house, Darcy smiled down at Elizabeth as he led the horse out of the grounds.

"You do not know how pleased I am to see you, Lizzy."

"And I you, Fitz." Fitz was her private pet name for Darcy, agreed upon just before their marriage last year. "And you are a day early which is even better."

Darcy peered around as they came to a deserted lane and stopped walking. Looping the reins over a fence post, he held his arms out to Elizabeth and she fell into his embrace at once.

"Lizzy." He whispered her name more than once. "Oh, Lizzy. I do love you so very much."

She could feel his emotion, hear it in his voice. She drew back slightly.

"Fitz, is there something wrong? Did something happen while you were in town?"

"No, no, not at all. I have missed you. That is all." He hesitated. "I find I like London less and less." He paused.

"And that man, Collins. Of all the nerve! To engage me at all on the subject of my aunt's opposition to our marriage, but to do it so publicly! 'Tis incredible. I will not have him invited to Netherfield while we are there."

"I imagine it will be of little consolation and does not at all excuse his ill-breeding, but everyone in the room is likely to know the full particulars already. Charlotte and Mr Collins are bound to have related every detail to Sir William and Lady Lucas."

"I suppose so." He did not sound in the least relieved.

"As to their coming to Netherfield, I am sure that will not happen," Elizabeth said soothingly, though she was not at all confident as to how that could be achieved if Jane and Bingley did wish to invite the Lucases. And there might be a ball at Lucas Lodge as well as one at the Assembly Rooms which everyone would no doubt wish to attend, with which in mind she posed the following question to Darcy:

"Before you arrived, there was some talk of a ball at Lucas Lodge and Lady Lucas was enquiring whether you and Bingley might be bringing a party of friends with you from London. I could not tell her but—"

She saw that Darcy had suddenly turned pale and looked off into the distance. The question had evidently given rise to more consternation on his part than she could understand and she could think of nothing to say.

At length Darcy recovered sufficient to tell her that he doubted if any of Bingley's sisters or acquaintances would be visiting Netherfield and that *he*, certainly, had invited no one.

Whatever was amiss, she could at least administer love and tenderness.

"I love you Fitz," she said and pulled him towards her again and he willingly submitted. For whatever reason besides Mr Collins, he clearly needed comforting at this time.

DARCY started to feel calmer in his wife's arms. His welcome at Longbourn House had also been a great solace to him. The warmth of the Bennets' reception had surprised and delighted him. Mrs Bennet in particular had greeted him effusively, embracing him like a son and saying that he must stay with them that night before returning to Netherfield tomorrow as intended. Mr Bennet had clasped his arms and patted him on the back and Darcy was pleased to be able to sincerely remark how well his father-in-law looked, having clearly fully recovered from his ordeal in Derbyshire nearly three months ago.

He told himself that Lizzy's chance remark about he and Bingley bringing a party to Netherfield was just that. Pure coincidence. He should not be so uneasy, actually looking for reasons to worry. Indeed, he wished he had not visited Lucas Lodge, had not displayed his disquiet so obviously to Elizabeth at least, causing her unnecessary anxiety.

Before Darcy left town this morning, Bingley had promised that he would make absolutely sure that Caroline would not come to Netherfield, either with or without her Prussian friend and the friend's son. He must trust to Bingley's guile to achieve this.

WHILE Darcy chatted affably to her parents on their arrival at Longbourn House, Elizabeth spent her time combing through the more obvious reasons why her husband might be discomfited. It had to do with London in some way as he had been in reasonable spirits before he left Netherfield with Bingley a few days ago. It seemed most likely to her that it was connected with his London house. Perhaps there was something wrong with the deeds, or with the house itself. That, at least, was the reasonable explanation.

A less reasonable explanation was the possibility of a party arriving at Netherfield with Bingley tomorrow. Why that should cause consternation, Elizabeth could not fathom. She tried to join, with her usual cheerfulness, in the general conversation, but felt an anxiety which drew off her attention. She would attempt to entice her husband into her confidence later when they had gained their own room.

At length, she abandoned her unprofitable musings, excused herself and went to find Mary who had returned with Jane. She had her own theories why Mary spent so much time at the library, handsome librarian or nay. Had not her father complained yesterday that Mary seemed to get through an inordinate amount of paper, an expensive luxury? No one else at the table had taken any notice and Mary had already excused herself and was thought to be in their father's library.

But her father's words had caused a memory to surface, of

Mary, Elizabeth and her friend Harriet Layham in a carriage being driven to the ball at the Assembly Rooms in Lambton on the last Saturday of the year. When Mary would not converse and had explained herself by telling them of a book which she was reading and was constantly on her mind, Harriet had carelessly suggested that Mary should write a book of her own. Elizabeth pictured now the expression on her sister's face, of surprise, of sudden rapt interest. Perhaps the suggestion had been quietly taken up.

The ball had ended in near-tragedy when it became clear that her father had been abducted and panic had ensued. Happily, he had been recovered some days later, but it was a fine-run thing that he had survived his ordeal.

These events and the fortunate conclusion served to enable Elizabeth to forget, for a while, what might be troubling her husband.

So she hunted for Mary and found her eventually in her bedroom.

"May I come in," she asked after knocking on the door. Elizabeth waited for at least ten seconds wondering if, remarkably, her sister would send her away. But that did not happen and she walked in to find Mary sitting at an escritoire which she did not know her sister had.

Mary saw her scrutinising the ancient piece of furniture, though it was attractive enough and appeared serviceable.

"It was in an outhouse. It seemed a pity to waste it."

"Oh, I agree." Elizabeth wondered how to approach the subject of book-writing. It was probably best to be direct. "And I do recall that in December on the way to the ball at Lambton, my friend Harriet talked of you writing a book. I wondered if you might have adopted her suggestion, Mary."

A secretive look overcame Mary. Elizabeth could understand it. If she were to have the courage to write a book herself, she would be bashful, certainly.

"Mary, I will keep your confidence, if that is what you are doing. I would not tell anyone, anyone at all. Well, I would tell William, but he would not repeat it."

Mary's face, never very obviously cheerful or open, took on

an expression of suspicion. Then she seemed to come to a decision.

"Do you promise, Lizzy?"

"Oh, of course."

"You would not tell Harriet, even though she suggested it?"

"Never."

"Or Papa, or Mama?"

Elizabeth smiled. "Most certainly not Papa or Mama. That is unless you gave permission. Papa might be able to help. But I would tell no one without your consent, save for William. And for William to know is just the same as me knowing. He is eminently trustworthy, Mary."

"Hmm. Very well. You recall Julius Fairweather, I expect."

"Of course I do. He was one of the most interesting people I have ever met."

"When he disappeared, what do you think happened to him?"

"Well, I do not know. His parents and sisters soon thereafter left for America. I thought he might have escaped there himself and that they followed him. His mother was distraught at the thought of him being hanged for holding up stagecoaches."

"You know how clever he was."

"Yes, indeed, I certainly thought he was."

"He knows much, of course, about America. And America has universities too."

Elizabeth did not know what to say to this.

"Elizabeth, with his help, I would like to write about life in America. I have written a couple of chapters and have submitted them to newspapers as a serial. The papers are interested."

"Oh, Mary, that is wonderful. And all since Christmas."

Mary smiled, a fulsome smile for her, full of pride and excitement.

"Well, letters to and from America take several months. But we have been corresponding since shortly after...since about the beginning of last year, therefore I already have a number of letters from him. Elizabeth, to speak the truth, most of what I have sent to the papers is about science and was written by Julius. If I write anything myself, it will be at a much more mundane level.

About people and what they do and how they live in America."

"Mary. It sounds very exciting. But...how do you communicate with Julius. How do you receive his letters and reply?"

"He uses the name Adolphus Barrant, but I know it is him. He addresses letters to me at the library, and I have to go into Meryton to post letters to him. And I have written chapters of my own but I have not sent them anywhere yet. Elizabeth, life in America is very similar in many ways to life here. Especially in the place they call 'New England'."

AT the dinner table, the family talked about Darcy's plans for his mill and his estate. Mr Bennet asked a great many questions which Darcy answered as best he could.

"I am minded," Darcy told them, "to sell my London house instead of re-letting it, to help finance the industry at the mill, whatever I decide to do with the mill. I was thinking of paper manufacturing, as it is such an essential commodity and so necessary for communication.

"And," he said with somewhat unnecessary vehemence, "I have become a small matter disenchanted with London lately."

At the mention of paper, both Elizabeth and her father turned to Mary, who concentrated on her plate before her. And Elizabeth wished to but did not look at Darcy who, it crossed her mind, had some other reasons to dispose of his London house than he had admitted.

Darcy spoke further of his desire that his mill should be more than a simple vat mill as most were. Elizabeth knew what this meant from their previous discussions. He had to explain to Mr Bennet that vat mills were small mills in which rags were pulped and frames with wires sewn into them were dipped into the pulp by vatmen leaving a flat piece of paper when the pulp was dry. The mills employed very few people.

"The process is primitive, though at least in recent decades rag engines have been brought into England to pulp the rags. Also, a woven wire mould is now used in the frames producing smoother paper. Nevertheless, it is laborious resulting in low production. There is a shortage of rags and of paper. Much paper has to be imported."

"Oh, I had not realised," said Mr Bennet. "Is there nothing you can do to improve the process?"

"Alas, I have not the technical knowledge. Would that I had paid attention to science and mathematics as a schoolboy. But, it is said that a machine is being invented in France which would use a wire-cloth-covered cylinder revolving in the pulp and producing much longer sheets of paper than the small rectangles now produced."

Mr Bennet laughed. "But does anyone need anything other than small rectangles of paper?"

"Indeed they do, Father," Darcy smiled. "And of course longer lengths can be cut into smaller pieces. The point is that the cylinder would speed up the production considerably and produce about four times the quantity of paper. And we need more paper in England. For now though, no such machine is available. If I want higher production, I will have to build more mills or larger mills and employ more hands."

Elizabeth was happy to see that Darcy had shed his mantle of anxiety for the present in his enthusiasm for his subject. And she noticed his addressing her Papa as 'Father' which pleased her greatly.

Mr Bennet looked somewhat bemused and Darcy continued:

"One of my aims is to provide employment for the men and some of the women on the estate." At Mr Bennet's quizzical expression, Darcy said: "Women would grade the rags. 'Tis a skilled task."

"Indeed!" said Mr Bennet.

"The rag engines introduced from Holland are all very well and produce a pulp more quickly but the resulting paper is not always so strong because the fibres are generally shorter than those produced if stampers are used to pulp the rags. And for me, the advantage of the stampers is that they are powered by a water wheel and my mill has a water wheel, though in need of repair, whereas a rag engine is said to be powered by a windmill and I do not have any windmills. Although there has been some talk of steam power, but that would mean tall chimneys belching smoke and having to purchase coal."

"I see," said Mr Bennet, who looked as though he did not see at all.

Coal made Elizabeth think of children in mines and one of the Reverend Wilde's last sermons before he left Longbourn, decrying the practice of employing small children in any way, but especially in vile conditions in hazardous industries.

"If the paper is to be of good quality when a rag engine is employed, then those sorting the rags, handling the fermentation and the beatermen must be more skilled, whereas my labour force is not skilled. They will learn of course."

"I imagine so," said Mr Bennet.

Darcy smiled. "I apologise for the lecture. All else I would say is that I hope to visit mills in operation in Hertfordshire, while we are here."

"Yes, yes, I understand that there are some."

Mrs Bennet was stifling a yawn. Lizzy and Jane and their sisters also looked tired.

"Well, for now I am sure that you have heard enough. And I see that Lizzy is trying not to yawn. After your excellent dinner, I hope that you will not object to our retiring. And I thank you again Mother and Father for your hospitality today and tonight."

"You are very welcome, William," said Mrs Bennet. "We could not be more delighted to receive you."

A WEARY Elizabeth climbed the stairs with her husband, looking forward, as always, to time alone with him. It seemed odd to be sharing a bedroom with a man in her childhood home. The normally serious Mrs Hill had smiled and chuckled as she supervised the maids to change the bed linen, tidy the room and gather herbs to freshen the room. There was no dressing room. Elizabeth was relieved not to have had to explain that Darcy would share her bed. Her mother was already well aware of their sleeping arrangements from her stay at Pemberley over Christmas and had instructed Mrs Hill accordingly.

Darcy was as affectionate as ever, though not passionate tonight. Perhaps she could entice him later. For now, Elizabeth contented herself with expressions of pleasure at his engagement with her parents and tales of Mary's new-found literary ambitions. He already knew of the exploits of Julius Fairweather, of his disappearance and of the family's abrupt departure to America before Darcy's own arrival in Meryton.

"And Mary thinks that Adolphus Barrant is the same person? How extraordinary!" was Darcy's comment.

"Indeed it is."

"And does Mary use a false name for her articles?"

"I believe so, although she was shy of telling me what it is. I am sure she will in due time."

"Do you know whether Kitty has been corresponding with Lieutenant Colonel Harvey since Christmas?"

"One or two letters passing between them I think. Of course it has not been a long time. I think she still hopes that he will come to Netherfield."

They talked on quietly. She made sure to avoid the subject of Bingley's arrival tomorrow. And by and by she moved even closer to him and he responded.

"And are you full sure that the baby is well?"

"Quite sure. I have missed you, Fitz," she whispered. "I love you so very much."

"And I, you, more than you can imagine."

"Show me, then."

He laughed softly in the darkness, and needed no second invitation.

Chapter 3

BINGLEY'S carriage arrived at Longbourn House in the early afternoon. While tea was being taken, Mrs Bennet questioned Bingley as to whether he had invited a party of friends and perhaps his sisters to stay at Netherfield over Easter. She had received, she said, a note from Lady Lucas enquiring on the subject in view of a possible ball at Lucas Lodge, though it was still to be resolved whether there would be one.

"No, Mother," he replied. "There was some talk of it but it was decided otherwise."

Elizabeth noted that Bingley had adopted Darcy's style of addressing their mother. She noted, too, Darcy's determinedly blank expression as the brief exchange took place. What could be going on here?

But there was little time to worry since the two couples, the Darcys and the Bingleys, were to travel back to Netherfield that afternoon, the ladies including Georgiana in the carriage, and Darcy and Bingley on horseback. Darcy had actually bought a horse yesterday on which to ride to Longbourn, so anxious had he evidently been to leave London. Bingley's horse was already at Longbourn House from an earlier visit.

Elizabeth and Jane bade their parents and sisters farewell for now. Very soon, the four Bennets would be travelling to Netherfield when the Gardiners and the Philipses arrived for the Easter festivities.

THE gentlemen rode slowly together in the growing dusk.

"I was greatly relieved to hear you tell our mother-in-law that there are to be no London visitors to Netherfield. How were you able to dissuade Caroline?"

"I chose to let her down softly to begin with by suggesting that Clara and Max could experience life on an English country estate just as well at the seat of Viscount Morley."

"A splendid idea, I should say."

"But Caroline said that Clara and Max had already spent a short time there. It transpires that they came to England directly from America. They disembarked at Falmouth and Morley had invited them to stay. You will recall that his seat is in Devon. Caroline pointed out that to journey back to Devon now would involve many days' travel and it was not to be borne. Besides which, Morley is in London."

"Yes," said Darcy heavily. Evidently, Max was a much-travelled young man.

"Therefore, I put it to Caroline that some parts of Netherfield House are being renovated since I may sell or sublet the estate and there is little room left to accommodate more than the guests who have already been invited. Caroline became pretty impatient at that."

"I imagine she did."

"She said, well then, put them up in the attics, that Clara had complained to her that when she and Max are touring for him to perform in different towns, they have often had to stay in poor lodgings. A few attic rooms with the servants, Caroline said, would do them admirably.

"Of course she did not speak seriously, hoping I suppose to provoke me into agreeing that suitable rooms could be found for them."

Darcy frowned. "And?"

"So I told her the truth. I had no choice."

Darcy pulled his horse up sharply, as did Bingley after a few steps and Darcy drew level with him. "Bingley, you cannot be serious!"

"What was I to do?"

Darcy's brow contracted. "Oh, no. This is dreadful."

"I told her one truth, Darcy, not your possible version of one possible truth. And, of course, we do not know that what you fear has any basis in reality. No, I told the plain truth about her obvious past disdain for the Bennet family, including Elizabeth, and that the memory still rankled of her complicity in separating me from Jane during the autumn before last and thereafter, failing to tell me of Jane's presence in town. I told Caroline that as Elizabeth is with child, you did not wish to place her in the way of possible distress."

"I see." Darcy considered this. "And how did she react?"

"With angry tears as you may imagine. It was most unpleasant. In due course, she started to plead with me. And she made the obvious point that if Jane, also with child, could tolerate it, why could not Elizabeth? And, of course, that it was you who instigated the move to London away from Hertfordshire and Jane."

Darcy shook his head. "I am so very sorry, my friend, to have visited this trouble upon you."

"Indeed, Darcy. I fear that it may create a rift, although I am sure that Caroline will not spread it abroad that her own brother refused to have her as a guest in his house or the stated reasons for it. She would not wish to be the object of people's pity or for them to know our family's business. In short, her place in society depends upon people having respect for her."

This was a pretty picture indeed, Darcy reflected. And, as Bingley had said, his suspicions may be misplaced.

"I would hope, Bingley, that in the fullness of time, her position will soften. That is often the outcome. People can change. I would hope that what you have said may give her cause to reflect upon her past behaviour and find it wanting. That unkindness towards others is usually without merit and regretted later. That is certainly how I have come to view things."

Bingley eyed his friend. "Aye, Darcy. I see that you have. Maybe you are right at that."

"And you may be right that there is no foundation for the fears which I have raised between us. It is entirely my problem, and yet you have had cause to suffer as a result of it and share it with me. I am immeasurably in your debt for your support, Bingley."

Darcy passed his tongue over dry lips as another idea forced itself upon him.

"Elizabeth and I have always looked unfavourably upon those men who would not take responsibility for their...actions; those who would leave ladies to bear all the difficulties of liaisons formerly embarked upon. I feel strongly that I should try to make some amends."

Bingley's tone was dismissive. "You use the word '*always*'. Darcy, you and Elizabeth have been married barely four months. How can you and she in such a short time have formed firm views on any subject?"

"I know full well what I feel upon the occasion. And I know that Elizabeth thinks the same. To my knowledge, there have been at least two examples of her disgust at men who shun their responsibilities."

"But, Darcy, you were only...what...eighteen or nineteen at the time?"

"I am still responsible."

"What of Clara's husband? She was married when she came to Cambridge."

"Yes, as I only discovered on the day she left. I related to you what she told me at the time, that her English husband lived in India and had taken an Indian mistress. That was why, she said, she was using her maiden name."

"What happened to him? Why is she using her married name now?"

"I have no idea as to either question. Perhaps he died and she remarried. I do not know what his name was but Lang could be either English or Germanic. Perhaps she found it convenient to use her married name at some point, presumably after Max was born though his surname is Kohler, the same as Clara and her father, Professor Kohler."

"Well, I suggest, my friend, that before you determinedly don your hair shirt and assume the burdens of which you speak, or indeed share your fears with Elizabeth, that you endeavour to ascertain whether there is in fact any foundation to your fears."

Darcy was thoughtful as they rode on. America, Bingley had said. Perhaps there was something in the allusion to America worthy of closer consideration.

Chapter 4

THREE days later, three carriages drew up in the drive of Netherfield House, the four Bennets in one comprising Mr and Mrs Bennet with Kitty and Mary, the Gardiners with their children in their carriage, and Mr and Mrs Philips in the carriage sent for them by Bingley.

Bingley's field dogs raced out to meet the party ahead of Bingley and Jane, Darcy and Elizabeth. The children were delighted and begged to be allowed to play outside with the dogs as soon as may be.

"When everyone is settled," said their mother.

And then, most unexpectedly, Colonel Fitzwilliam and Lieutenant Colonel Harvey trotted out of the house and ran down the steps. The visitors were amazed and delighted to see the soldiers and recall the largely happy times at Pemberley at Christmas.

Lieutenant Colonel Harvey handed a smiling Kitty out of the carriage, and then her mother and Mary.

"We arrived only yesterday ourselves," Colonel Fitzwilliam told the latest guests to arrive. "I am hoping, too, that Miss Harriet Layham may be able to join us at Netherfield. Her parents have been obliged to travel to Cambridge to visit an elderly distant cousin of Lady Layham's who is very unwell and has no other living relations. I am to travel to Cambridge to meet her and her parents in a carriage to be generously provided by Bingley and if it is deigned to be suitable for Harriet to come on to Hertfordshire, then she would travel here with me. I hope for a letter tomorrow to communicate the arrangements."

A happy few weeks, therefore, lay spread before them all.

"We have made our own puppet theatre," said Anthony, "and have brought it with us."

"Yes," Julia told everyone, "and our own puppets. And we

have written more plays. We hope to present them over Easter."

"And so you shall," Bingley told them.

"Indeed," said Mrs Philips, "I have not been so well entertained since your Christmas shows about the Prince of Wales and Napoleon, rot him."

Laughter filled the reception hall as they made their way to the salon where refreshments were to be served.

MARY seemed surprised to be approached and engaged in general conversation by Darcy. She had not, Elizabeth realised, ever spoken to him directly before now.

He drew close to her, looked her straight in the eye and whispered that he much admired the fact that she was attempting to write stories, and particularly stories about America. It must, he said, require a great deal of effort to do so. He wondered at the source or sources of her intelligence.

Elizabeth watched them with some amusement. Knowing, of course, how very attractive he was, she was not surprised to see that Mary was affected by his proximity and his earnestness regarding the subject.

Neither was she surprised to see Mary blanche, look about her for escape, smile weakly, gulp and make her excuses to Darcy. Thereafter, she moved towards the piano to strike up a refrain for the general enjoyment of the gathering.

"Fitz," she said, walking over to him and gently chiding him, "whatever it is you think she may be able to assist you with, you should not use your exceptional charm on someone like Mary. She cannot deal with it."

The jolly tune echoed around the room.

He laughed. "Am I so frightful?"

"No. It is just Mary. She is very serious usually, censorious even, and is certainly not in the habit of dallying with gentlemen or gentlemen dallying with her."

"I would not presume to dally, as you call it, with any woman. I simply asked her if she could put me in touch with Adolphus Barrant for any ideas he can provide regarding paper production. He is, I believe you said, an engineer."

"Yes, interested in roads and bridge-building, so he told me."

"Well then, I would think that the very simple process of paper-making would be mere child's play for him. Of course, that communications take at least two or three months in each direction does mean that any intelligence would be painfully slow to be provided. Nonetheless, I think it is worth pursuing."

"I hope it proves to be of some value, Fitz."

"But, Mary did tell me, before she scuttled off to the pianoforte, that friends of Barrant in this country, recently arrived from America, may be able to assist. I do hope so."

"That is very fortunate."

"Indeed, she thinks that Adolphus sent a package to her in the care of one of his friends but she has yet to meet this person. Indeed, it would be difficult for her to do so as he is in London, she thinks. I am minded to facilitate her possession of her package by visiting London after Easter is over."

"Even though you dislike London so much?"

"I would speak to the attorney regarding the sale of my house. If it helps me with my plans for a mill, then it would be worthwhile. And Mary mentioned that there are other friends of Barrant here in gaol it seems. The poor souls in gaol may welcome the diversion. It is widely known that the conditions are harsh."

Elizabeth was pondering on this when Colonel Fitzwilliam joined them and urged them to take to the floor. The Lieutenant Colonel, he said, strongly desired to dance with Kitty and Georgiana had consented to dance with him.

Elizabeth laughed. "It is Christmas all over again," she cried.

THE time flew by. Lieutenant Colonel Harvey was singing a ballad to Georgiana's accompaniment on the pianoforte. Elizabeth sat with Jane sharing their experiences of pregnancy, still relatively early in Elizabeth's case.

"I cannot drink tea, much less coffee," said Jane.

"No, *neither can I.* It is so strange. And I have to eat sweet treats *all* the time or else I am sick. I like some fruits but above all, I *love* dates."

"Oh, as do I, Lizzy. But in truth, I am longing for it to be over, even if the birth is dangerous."

Colonel Fitzwilliam, walking past and shaking his head at the dull nature of the discourse, seized the opportunity to sit with Darcy, presently on his own.

"And how is the brooding father-to-be, Darcy?"

"I assure you, I do not brood. 'Tis far too early for that."

"Oh, I see. So the air of anxiety I detect about you is for some other reason, then."

"What air of anxiety?" said Darcy sharply.

Colonel Fitzwilliam burst out laughing. When he had exhausted his mirth, his brow wrinkled and he stared at his cousin.

"I am sorry, Cousin, if I have accidentally struck a nerve."

"There is nothing wrong with *me* Fitzwilliam. Perhaps 'tis *you* who are discomfited at the prospect of Easter without your intended."

"Ha! I wish she were my intended. Dealing with Sir Peter is like negotiating one's way through a thorn hedge. I wonder, should I ask one of the ladies to accompany me to Cambridge to act as a chaperone. It may be tomorrow. I await a letter informing me of the arrangements. Evidently, Miss Layham could not possibly be safe alone in a carriage with me between Cambridge and Netherfield."

"You know as well as I do, Fitzwilliam, that young ladies are delicate creatures who are obviously at risk from the predatory male."

"Predatory male! Speak for yourself, Darcy."

Darcy scrutinised the Colonel as though the other was able to look into his very soul.

"Darcy, what is to do with you?"

"What in heaven's name do you mean?"

"I have known you for most of our lives and...you are not yourself."

"Look. This is nonsense. I dare say that Lizzy would accompany you to Cambridge as she is Harriet's great friend, and if she did, then I would come too. That is if you wish it and think that it will improve the prospects of Miss Layham being allowed to travel on to Hertfordshire. Sir Peter, I think, has some respect for me."

"If you and Elizabeth would do this, Darcy, I would be greatly in your debt."

"That is not to say, Fitzwilliam, that if Sir Peter is wholly opposed to Harriet coming here, that I would seek to persuade him otherwise. He must freely decide for himself. He would not appreciate my pestering him or trying to take advantage of my position."

"No. Very well. I see that. But I thank you."

THE GUESTS were tired over dinner from their journeys today and most disposed to retire promptly. Elizabeth went early to the rooms assigned to her and Darcy. The gentlemen stayed up later with their port but Darcy soon came to their rooms and folded his arms around Elizabeth, nearly asleep.

"We are going to Cambridge tomorrow," he whispered in her ear.

"Hmm?" she said sleepily.

"We are to go to Cambridge tomorrow with Fitzwilliam in the hope that our presence will help to persuade Sir Peter and Lady Layham to allow Harriet to come here for Easter. Without us, I fear Sir Peter would refuse to allow it."

"Oh," she said. And almost fell asleep again.

"Lizzy, you do wish to see your friend suitably married, do you not?"

Rousing herself, Elizabeth said: "Yes, but...is Colonel Fitzwilliam suitable?"

"Lizzy, he is not at all a bad man. Do not forget that I have known him all my life. And I think he likes her very well. It isn't to say that they will ultimately marry, but we can at least make it easier for them."

"All right then. Cambridge tomorrow."

Chapter 5

A LETTER addressed to the Colonel arrived the next morning. He rushed to the breakfast room where some were already seated, taking kidneys, ham, eggs and warm bread, with tea and coffee.

"Lizzy will be down soon," said Darcy who had risen early. "She is taking breakfast in our rooms."

"The letter is from Lady Layham. At least they wish to see me at the Little Rose in Cambridge," Fitzwilliam told him. "They will arrive early afternoon today, hence I hope that we could set out very soon. I would not wish to miss them."

"I have asked Brandon to furnish the best carriage and horses," said Bingley. "The journey is but forty miles or thereabouts. And 'tis almost a straight road."

"Indeed," said Darcy. He rose from his seat. "I will speak to Elizabeth directly. We will go straight to the hall if you will call the carriage."

Fitzwilliam clasped his cousin's hand in both of his. "I do so thank you, Darcy."

ELIZABETH was dressed and ready and peering out of the window when Darcy entered their room. He went over to her and put his arm around her waist, now expanded to a degree. The Gardiners were already outside, the children frolicking with the dogs, and from the edge of the scene framed by the window, a couple emerged, the girl's arm through the man's. It was Kitty and Harvey, talking and laughing.

It would be but a few months before Kitty attained the age of eighteen years, not so very young to marry. Elizabeth was reminded of the large mansion house and lands in Staffordshire owned by Harvey. If Kitty did marry him, then they would be financially secure.

"Fitz," she said, still facing the window, "if Fitzwilliam and Harriet should marry in due course, where do you think they would live?"

"I confess I have given the matter little thought."

"But he has no house. And at Rosings last Easter, he spoke as though he has no money. What income has he?"

"My love, he is of a wealthy family and her family are modestly rich. I feel sure that they will not starve."

"But where will they *live*?"

"He has a house on his brother's property in Kent. I have never been there but rarely. We have always met up at Rosings. He does not own it of course. His brother owns everything. I would hazard that Sir Peter has one or two suitable houses on his estate."

"They would have little independence on that score."

"Of course, there is the army."

"She would go with him into army accommodation?" At this, Elizabeth turned towards her husband, her eyes wide in surprise. "What would that be like?"

She thought immediately of Lydia, although of course Wickham was only a lieutenant and if Lydia had written to her mother describing her life in the North of England, their mama had forborne to pass the intelligence on to Elizabeth.

"I know little of the arrangements. It must depend where a soldier is billeted. And I recall that when we were at Netherfield for the first time, Colonel Forster and his wife seemed to live well enough."

Elizabeth pictured the ball at Netherfield in the autumn of 1797 which many of the officers billeted locally had attended, including Colonel Forster with his wife. It was his wife to whom Lydia had been a special friend, possibly indeed instrumental in the elopement from Brighton which took place last year.

"You seem unconvinced, Lizzy. But rest assured that Fitzwilliam would wish to negotiate a propitious settlement with Sir Peter by which he and Harriet would live well and be financially secure. But it is his business into which I would not presume to enquire closely.

"Now we must make haste to leave with Fitzwilliam or there

may be no meeting today in Cambridge, no chance of Harriet coming here for Easter, no possibility of any marriage proposal, no financial negotiations. And," he smiled, "you have to admit, she would be far better off with him than with the Earl of Langford."

Elizabeth sighed. Of course he was right in that respect, the Earl of Langford having a preference for young men rather than young women. She caught up her cloak and they left the bedroom to descend to the hall and meet Fitzwilliam.

Darcy had still not told her what was gnawing away at him. He and the Colonel often enjoyed quiet chats. If he had confided in the Colonel, perhaps something would emerge during today's carriage ride.

THEY left Netherfield just after nine o' clock. The journey was not especially uncomfortable but it took over four hours with changes of horses. The men's banter kept Elizabeth amused for all of ten minutes, then she tired of it and tried to read. The jouncing of the carriage was not markedly pronounced but the book was not sufficiently interesting to warrant gripping it tightly and attempting to move it in time with the vibrations in order to stop the lines from blurring before her eyes.

So, after thirty minutes, she gave herself over to speculations about Darcy's unsettled state of mind and whether she should ask Jane if Bingley had told her of any untoward events in London. Would it be fair to do so? If Bingley had said nothing to Jane, then Jane would surely ask him, putting him in an awkward position. He would not wish to lie to Jane, but neither would he wish to break his friend's confidence...if indeed any confidence there was.

She had to consider that her musings were ill-founded, that something had upset Darcy which was not in any way personal to him. Perhaps he had witnessed in London some act of cruelty which had played upon his senses, and which Bingley would not necessarily have been aware of. Maybe a child being ill-treated or even an episode involving cruelty to animals, for example bear-baiting. She knew that her father abhorred such displays, in particular cock fighting, although in his case it was due more to the fact that he was quite opposed to the gambling which supported such sport.

Darcy would probably have deplored the mere sport itself, the unnecessary torturing of an innocent animal. In that respect, he was similar to Mr Wilde, the former rector of Longbourn parish who had railed against unkindnesses of various kinds. Yet if Darcy was troubled by something of the sort, surely he would have been open about it and told her.

Hence, her feelings leaned towards his distress being the result of something personal to Darcy, and hence something that Bingley *would* be aware of. Bringing Jane into the occasion may therefore cause unnecessary discord.

No, then, she would not ask Jane, at least not for now. If Darcy wished to tell her what was troubling him, he would. But it was a sadness to her that he may be keeping from her something which affected him.

She had heard nothing pass between Darcy and his cousin today suggestive of any secrets or subterfuge.

By eleven o' clock, it became warm in the carriage. Gradually, the drone of the men's conversation caused torpor to overcome her and after some minutes, she succumbed and fell into a slumber. She vaguely felt Darcy's arm around her shoulder and leaned into his sturdy, familiar body and thereby the journey passed, for her, more quickly than it might have done.

THEY drew into the yard of the Little Rose at about half past one as had been expected. The carriage and horses were taken away and Elizabeth, Darcy and Fitzwilliam walked into the dark interior where they found Sir Peter, Lady Layham and Harriet waiting for them, apparently having arrived the previous night. The Layham family rose from their seats. They were solemn in Elizabeth's opinion and she wondered what could be amiss.

Felicitations were exchanged and the Colonel in particular greeted Sir Peter and Lady Layham warmly and, bowing over Harriet's hand, expressed his great happiness at seeing her again. Harriet was obviously considerably cheered at this but the parents remained unsmiling.

The Layhams, Elizabeth, Darcy and the Colonel sat down.

Lady Layham leaned forward. "Unfortunately, we have had some bad news," she informed the newcomers.

"Indeed," grumbled Sir Peter, "had we not arranged this appointment with you today, we would have immediately boarded a stagecoach back to Derbyshire this morning. It is most inconvenient."

The word 'appointment' struck Elizabeth as a formal way to describe a friendly meeting. Furthermore, it was not clear whether Sir Peter perceived the inconvenience to have resulted from the bad news, or more the fact that their anticipated arrival from Netherfield was preventing the Layhams making an expeditious return to Derbyshire and that he resented the delay.

Darcy stepped in at that point.

"Indeed, we are sorry that you have received bad tidings. If I am able to be of service to you in this matter, you may be assured of my keenest assistance."

"My wife's cousin died, it appears, three days ago and now the lawyer, Bates, has taken everything in hand and has declared that we are not required. This journey, therefore, has been quite unnecessary."

This, thought Elizabeth with a sinking heart, is unlikely to strengthen the prospects of Harriet being allowed to accompany us to Netherfield.

"My dear," said Lady Layham, a smile hovering around her mouth, "I am quite sure that my cousin did not deliberately expire when she did in order to create annoyance for you. As to returning immediately, I am unhappy to be dismissed by the lawyer so perfunctorily. As Emma's only living relation, I do feel that I must remain in Cambridge to...ensure that her wishes are being observed."

"But it is a confounded nuisance," replied her husband.

"Not really," said Lady Layham. "We were to stay in Cambridge for at least some days if Emma had not succumbed."

Sir Peter shook his head. "I don't know."

"Well, Sir Peter," broke in Darcy, "one way in which we may perhaps assist is to offer hospitality to Miss Harriet at Netherfield, the home of my great friend Mr Bingley, over the Easter period and hence remove her from the sphere of any...unpleasantness."

Sir Peter's brow creased. Before he could respond, Lady Layham turned to Darcy.

"Oh, Mr Darcy, if you would do so, it would be a great kindness."

It was a magnificent move by Lady Layham and Elizabeth saw that Harriet's face was determinedly blank. With a father like Sir Peter, she must be accustomed to having her future arranged for her and being discussed as though she were not present.

"Do you think that is really necessary, my dear?" Sir Peter asked his wife, suspicion clouding his features.

"I fear so. I do not trust the lawyer, as Mr Darcy has already apprehended. I would feel so much happier if Harriet is safely away in cordial company. Do not forget, my dear, that my cousin Emma was a very wealthy woman, and Harriet was a great favourite of hers."

Elizabeth stole a glance at Fitzwilliam, expecting to see a gleam in his eye at such intelligence. What she did see surprised her. If she was not mistaken, he and Harriet were exchanging a secret smile. The pair were apparently in some sort of accord. They must have been corresponding since Christmas. That could be the only explanation. In that case, the auspices for a good match were excellent and her worries for her friend's future seemingly misplaced. She looked forward to witnessing the flowering of their courtship over Easter, that is of course if Sir Peter accepted his wife's recommendation.

Sir Peter shifted in his chair, a movement which Elizabeth hoped also signalled a consequent shift in his attitude. He cleared his throat.

"Naturally, I would wish to ensure that there is no foul play, and yes, Darcy, we should be obliged to accept your kind and hospitable invitation to entertain Harriet over Easter, that is of course if you are sure that your friend is agreeable."

"Oh, indeed, he is very agreeable," said Darcy. "He provided his best carriage and horses, that we may travel here to carry Miss Layham back with us to Netherfield if you so choose. And you will recall meeting Mr Bingley at our shoot at Christmas at

Pemberley."

"Yes," added Elizabeth, "a more amiable gentleman could not be imagined."

Lady Layham smiled. "Indeed, Elizabeth, he much impressed me with his good breeding. I am sure Harriet will have an enjoyable stay with you, her very good friend, and all your relations and indeed the Colonel in such cordial company, while we consult another lawyer here in Cambridge and see what is to be done about that scoundrel, Bates."

"I thank you, Sir Peter, Lady Layham," said Colonel Fitzwilliam. "You may be assured of our every regard for Miss Layham's comfort."

The matter being settled, a light meal was ordered and, before long, Bingley's carriage was called. As Harriet's trunk was being brought down and she and Elizabeth took a stroll along the street, Darcy whispered to Fitzwilliam:

"You did well to keep silent in there before our meal. Lady Layham obviously knows how to handle her husband to best effect."

Chapter 6

Wednesday 27th March 1799

IN HIS absence, a note addressed to Darcy had been delivered to Netherfield and, clutching it, he went next to the saloon.

"I fear," he told the assembled company, "that I must be away again tomorrow. This," he flicked the note with his free hand, "tells me that I will be welcome to attend Frogmore Mill at Apsley tomorrow to witness their paper production and learn more of the new machinery presently being contemplated. It is intended to speed the process and increase production."

Elizabeth had expected that he would have to visit one or more paper manufactories at some time during their sojourn at Netherfield. She knew that, sadly, she would be unable to accompany him. With her friend Harriet so newly arrived, it behoved her to stay at Netherfield. There would be other opportunities when they returned to Pemberley.

"If I could accompany you, William, I would but as you know, I cannot. Will you be gone much of the day?"

"I hope to return well before dusk. It is but eight miles away. The majority of the time will be taken up inspecting the process in detail and talking to Mr Holmes and others about the new process, looking at designs, that sort of thing."

"You amaze me," said Bingley.

"Do you think it is worthwhile?" asked Fitzwilliam.

"That remains to be seen. As I was telling Mr and Mrs Bennet the other day, I wish to provide employment for men on the estate. And there would be jobs for women as well."

"Extraordinary!" said Bingley. "I do not know what Caroline would think."

"Well, she may think what she likes. According to you, she will not be coming here over Easter to express any view."

"True."

"So," said Darcy. "What are we for tonight? Singing? Dancing? Cards, Lizzy, as you became so proficient after the ball at Lambton at Christmas?"

Elizabeth could detect that his geniality was forced and wished that there was something she could do to alleviate his predicament, whatever it may be.

"Interested, not proficient, William. And only for the lowest of stakes. But I would make up a four tonight with anyone who wishes to play whist or quadrille."

"Mary and I have been practising a duet on the piano," said Georgiana. "We were hoping to perform it for you all."

"Yes, we were," Mary nodded. "And it is a lively tune to dance to."

"Will you sing tonight, Lieutenant Colonel Harvey?" asked Elizabeth. "We would all be delighted if you would."

"Yes, indeed," said Mrs Philips. "A finer voice I have never heard in any gentleman. You could take to the stage."

Harvey laughed. "You are very kind, but I think not, ma'am. Tours of duty in the army are more than sufficient for me. To tour with a troupe of musicians would not be to my taste."

"No," said Mrs Philips. "You might garner fame, but a life on the road would be largely without comforts I would hazard."

DARCY looked away, thinking of Bingley's allusion to the disadvantages of touring by Clara and Max. The audience only saw the performance, but behind that, it could not be an easy life.

"As is soldiering, ma'am," Harvey answered. "But we are doing so in the cause of our King and country and with our comrades-in-arms. We rejoice in the hardships which render such gatherings as this and at Pemberley at Christmas all the more precious."

"Hear, hear," said Colonel Fitzwilliam. "Our hard life is softened by such drawing rooms as this and in such cordial company." He glanced with a ready smile at Harriet sitting quite close to him.

Would, thought Darcy, that I had been equally at ease last year when I so hoped that Elizabeth might some day consent to be my wife. But instead, I formed a fence of reserve around myself which the poor girl had to penetrate before I found it in myself to once again renew my addresses and make my feelings known. I was a fool, and yet now we are married in spite of my stupid reserve. So how could it come to pass that some unimagined consequence of innocent, boyish actions years gone by could rear its head to sully our perfect union today?

"Fitz," came the whisper in his ear. Only one person could it be. "Will you not take the floor with me? Georgiana and Mary are starting their duet and everyone is rising to dance."

Was it not he who had asked after the entertainments tonight to selfishly deflect attention from his commercial leanings?

"I would be honoured," he said, smiling at his wife, rising and bowing over her hand.

Chapter 7

DARCY did not return to Netherfield before dusk contrary to his expectations. The mill at Apsley worked a long day and he felt obliged to remain until almost the last vat of fermented pulp had been emptied and the pressed sheets of paper hung to dry. At nine o' clock in the evening, the candles were guttering. The oil lamps were turned down and the hands were allowed to stand down and go home, as were the women who sorted the rags.

By this time he was at the home of Holmes, the owner, who had invited him to take dinner with the family and he felt he could not refuse.

He excused himself as soon as decorum would allow, thanked his host and expressed his hope to return before his party left Netherfield for Derbyshire. Mr Holmes insisted that he return the following day with his wife who Darcy had told him several times was much interested in his plans, but excused her presence today on account of having to attend a friend newly arrived at Netherfield yesterday. The mill would be idle tomorrow, Darcy was told, due to it being Good Friday and it was the ideal opportunity for a lady to be shown how the mill worked. Darcy said that he would come back tomorrow if it proved possible for his wife.

He covered the eight miles back to Netherfield in short order and, on entering the hall, was surprised to find Georgiana waiting up for him with Kitty. The rest of the household appeared to have retired early tonight, after, Georgiana said, some of them had walked to the common and along the River Ver for several hours towards Childwickbury Manor.

"'Tis a chilly day to have taken such a long ramble," observed Darcy. "They will have had to keep up a brisk pace. 'Tis little wonder they were ready early for their bed."

And others, the girls suggested, were tired for...the reason wasn't made clear immediately. Darcy frowned.

He could see that both girls were brimming with excitement, suppressed for reasons Darcy rather dreaded hearing.

"We did not go on the walk," said Georgiana, glancing at Kitty. "William, we received a visit from Caroline today. She arrived after Mr Bennet, Colonel Fitzwilliam, Harriet and Mr and Mrs Philips left for the common. She was sorry to have missed you but had to leave at five o' clock to return to London. And...er...Charles did not invite the party to stay."

"She was not alone then, by the sound of it?" Darcy asked tentatively.

He hoped that the flicker of apprehension which crossed his face would not have been visible to the girls in the gloom of the hall.

"No. She was accompanied by a Viscount Morley who apparently knows you and Charles..."

Georgiana sounded as though she would say more, but stopped and looked at Kitty whose barely contained intensity was pretty evident to Darcy. Kitty bit her lip.

"You will never guess who else she brought with her."

Darcy's heart missed a beat, but he said kindly enough to Kitty: "Well, if you would tell me, Kitty, then I shall not have to guess."

"They brought Lydia with them...I say 'they' because Viscount Morley seemed to know Lydia as well as Caroline. Apparently, Wickham has been posted to Ireland and Lydia has been staying in London with the wife of Wickham's commanding officer with whom she has become friendly. She has become reacquainted with Caroline who said she thought that it would be ideal for Lydia to have the opportunity to see her family."

As was common knowledge, there had been a rebellion in Ireland which had been put down and there was still a military presence there.

"I see," said Darcy, concealing his irritation as best he could. He could not avoid the suspicion that Caroline's motive in coming here with Lydia and Morley was connected with her having been refused an Easter sojourn at Netherfield, rather than the generous gesture alluded to. Doubtless she would be curious.

"Well, thank you, both, for staying up to enlighten me as to to-day's events. Now you should get to bed as I must. It has been a long day."

Darcy wondered what antics could have occurred for those who had not partaken of the walk to have become fatigued nevertheless.

He took up a candlestick and led them towards the stairs, but stopped and bade them goodnight, turning towards the dining room.

"Have you not eaten, William?" asked Georgiana.

"I have. I was handsomely entertained by the mill owner Mr Holmes and his wife. But I would take a glass of port before retiring."

"Goodnight," the girls both said and hurried up the stairs.

Darcy poured himself a large port and sat some moments wondering what further disruption might yet occur at the hands of Caroline, Morley and Lydia.

ELIZABETH stirred as he entered, the lamp still lit, and he could see that she was in fact fully awake. She sat up to greet him and he dropped down on the bed to embrace her.

"Kitty and Georgiana were still downstairs when I arrived and have been thoughtfully apprising me of today's events." He spoke into Elizabeth's thick, dark hair, relishing the feel and the smell of her. "I cannot fathom what Caroline is about, bringing Lydia here. I trust she behaved herself. I mean Lydia."

"Not really. But the whole day was strange."

"What do you mean? In what respect?"

"Well, in the first place, Caroline's attitude. I could not make it out. She was excessively courteous to Mama. And indeed to me. Mama was more than moderately astonished. I suspected that Caroline would break out into some expression of veiled derision towards us at any time, but at length, I had to consider that her good manners, if contrived for some cause I don't know about, may at least have been well meant. But still, I knew not how to respond."

Darcy, of course, could see what Caroline was about; hoping to be admitted into the fold of her brother's hospitality once more. The pathos struck him forcibly, especially as it was all in vain in the present circumstances. He was spared any reply by which his voice might have betrayed him as Elizabeth continued.

She laughed faintly. "Naturally, Mary had a Bible quotation appropriate to the occasion."

"And what of Lydia?"

"Oh, she wanted to play Blind Man's Buff and Sardines in the afternoon. Of course, the children were wildly enthusiastic. Kitty and Harvey joined in to begin with but withdrew when Morley started to chase Lydia round the house. They had the house in uproar for a time. I am glad to say that neither Mama nor Kitty gave her any encouragement."

Elizabeth shook her head. "Georgiana seemed fascinated. She has never witnessed Lydia's excesses before. I was wondering whether Wickham is likely to have told Lydia of his attempted elopement with Georgiana. In Lydia's hands, the intelligence could do much harm."

"I doubt it. I think he would not divulge it unless there was something to be gained for himself, and I would say that even he is above using the intelligence to his advantage by, for example, extorting money to keep quiet. If that was his game, I suspicion he would have approached me. He may perceive that Lydia probably is not to be trusted. He brazenly lied about me to Hertfordshire society yet, where ladies are concerned, I believe he has some standards. At least insofar as public disclosures are concerned."

He paused while standing to remove his clothes.

"And he will likely surmise that I may yet be of some use to him in the future."

"Well, I hope you are right about Wickham's discretion. And another thing, I would not be surprised if Lydia and Morley are engaged in some sort of liaison. Yet Jane whispered to me that Charles thought he had heard somewhere of Morley's marriage."

"That does not stop some people, my love."

"I felt so helpless. Lydia is a married woman. I could not reprimand her as I would have done formerly to possibly some effect, though I did try to speak to her and caution her. We must hope that she is not brought here again."

"I will speak to Charles."

"Yes. And she, Lydia, was mightily interested when Harvey's estate in Staffordshire was mentioned, and she could see how Kitty and Harvey are together. I had the sense that Lydia was envious of Kitty."

"As I say, I will ask Charles to caution Caroline against bringing Lydia here again."

"Indeed, but I cannot help but be concerned that if Kitty and Harvey were to be married and Kitty is left at Brownham Hall on her own while Harvey returns to his regiment, that Lydia may try to persuade Kitty to have her there as her companion. It would be the worst possible thing for Kitty."

"You are right," Darcy said as he wet the cloth in the bowl of water left for him by Lizzy, after she had washed herself earlier. In the water, dried lavender floated, lending its soft scent to the still warm washing water. He patted his face with the cloth and roughly abraded the folds of his ears with it. He rubbed it over his neck and gradually over the rest of his body as he had been taught to do in childhood, stopping from time to time to rinse the cloth in the water and wring it out. He hoped that his naked body was as pleasing to her as hers was to him, the more so now that hers held their baby-to-be, four months on or so, the beginning of their own family. "We must not let that happen."

While he washed himself, he told her of his day at Frogmore mill, in particular about the plans he had been told of for a machine which used a revolving wire mesh which, Mr Holmes said, would be able to make twelve feet of paper in a third of the time it took for the handmade paper to be made. There were no detailed plans; the owner made some rough drawings to illustrate what it was thought the machine would look like and how it would operate. Darcy also mentioned the possibility of using steam to power his mills, rather than wind or water. Elizabeth listened with interest.

"Oh," she then said as she undid the bows tying her nightgown, "Caroline was talking about someone called Clara Lang and her son Max who plays the violin like an angel, Caroline said, and is lauded all over America and England, though Max seems to have a different surname from his mother. Mrs Lang apparently knows you and Bingley from your days at Cambridge. Caroline thought that you and Bingley would wish to meet her."

Darcy, who had finished washing and had taken up a cup holding an infusion of spearmint, was swilling the liquid around his mouth to freshen his breath. When Elizabeth said this, he put a hand over his mouth, coughed and then swallowed the mouthful.

"I recall her, I believe."

"I do not believe I have heard of her son, Max, but they have reputedly spent much time in America and some in Europe."

"So I understand. From Charles."

"You and Charles and his sisters were at a recital in London where Max played, so Caroline said."

"We were." He washed the infusion around his mouth again and swallowed it.

Elizabeth waited, no doubt expecting him to give some reason for his silence on the subject, a subject which he heartily wished she would drop, but how was she to know? After all, a world-renowned prodigy was something to be remarked upon. He sighed and said:

"It was a hot night, or at least the room was hot with too many people. I wished I had not attended and left as soon as I could."

Elizabeth laughed. She knew what he was like and he felt safe again. He washed one more mouthful of the liquid around and through his teeth, then put down the cup and climbed into bed.

I will never, he decided, as he commenced to plant kisses upon her face and mouth, allow anything to come between us and damage our perfect union.

And, he thought, as she responded strongly and as their bodies became one, I would do anything at all to prevent her being hurt in any way.

Chapter 8

"DARCY, you must do something about this Max and Clara business."

Bingley had ushered Darcy outside to, he said, talk over yesterday's events, after finding his friend walking between the library and the dining room and no one else was in evidence. They strode away from the house towards the copse to the east of the trout lake, Bingley urging speed to avoid anyone espying them and hurrying out to join them.

"Do not imagine that my mind is ever free of the subject," Darcy replied.

"Have you thought of *no* solution?"

"Well, I have considered offering her a large sum of money, through a go-between, to leave England and never come back."

"That is, if I may say so, a ridiculous plan. I trust you jest, Darcy."

"You trust aright, my friend. As you know, I fear I may have responsibilities towards the child. And indeed towards Clara. But tell me, Bingley, what occurred yesterday to precipitate this enquiry? I know that Lydia misbehaved atrociously, that she appears to be involved in some sort of liaison with Morley, that Caroline talked of Clara and Max, and that Caroline also appeared to be trying to make amends towards Elizabeth. No doubt in an attempt to inveigle herself back into your favour as a house guest, which of course we know is a hopeless cause at this time."

"It is more than that. In the first place, after the guests departed, Elizabeth was asking Jane if *I* knew what was ailing you and naturally Jane asked me later if I did know. Indeed Jane, too, has detected that you are not yourself. I had to tell her that I was not aware of any cause. I do not like lying to her, Darcy."

"No, no, certainly you do not. Decidedly, I will think of

something, Bingley."

"Well, I would say that a good place to begin would be to obtain a copy of Max's birth certificate."

"No doubt, but how am I to do that when I know not the boy's date of birth, or his place of birth. I know nothing about them. I would have to cause someone to make enquiries on my behalf, which may of course bring its own difficulties. And where would this person start? And who would do this? Morley may know something given his acquaintance with Clara, but he is the last person I could approach."

"We both know that Morley is not to be trusted. Indeed, he made a number of comments about you yesterday which — "

"Did he, by God? What do you mean? Not about Max and Clara, surely? He would not know...what happened. We were very discreet."

"I hope he would not for your sake, and that Clara has not told him. No. The comments were...general. That you are an enigma, that you never cease to surprise. These were actually in relation to your plans to start a paper mill. He poured scorn on the scheme and laughed about it. It was said in a light-hearted manner, meant, I think, for entertainment rather than unkindly, but nevertheless I was heartily glad that you were away for the day. Elizabeth asked Jane if Morley could be the reason for your disquiet."

Darcy shook his head.

"Darcy, something must be done to resolve this situation, with everyone labouring under some false apprehension."

"Of course, you are correct. And that a good place to start would be the child's birth certificate. This go-between could, I suppose, obliquely question Clara."

"I fear not. Caroline told me that Clara and Max are leaving London early next week for performances which are to take place in various towns. By the time we are able to instruct someone to make enquiries, Clara will no longer be in London. Though I believe that his first few engagements are not far from London, including Hertfordshire where Max is to perform before visiting towns farther afield."

"I see." Darcy examined the ground as they plodded on

through the trees, thinking that his quandary seemed to get worse at every turn. "Then the woman who held the soirée in London could possibly be approached. She must know something of Clara and Max to have invited Max to play at her house. Or if not, then she could say how or from whom she heard about Max. I can't recall the woman's name."

"Octavia Brandreth, I believe, though by all accounts, Max is well-known, at least among music-lovers. Of course, she may be able to assist. But, Darcy, I have been pondering on that myself, and I have in mind a person who could both intercede and make enquiries on your behalf. He is the father of a boy with whom I was at school. His life and work has been similar to that of Dr Johnson, though he is much less well-known. He is a writer by profession and a very clever man though he has been dogged by poverty as writing is not a secure occupation and I am sorry to say that his gambling habit has contributed to his penury. His name is Matthew Benjamin."

"Would a gambler be a wise choice, Bingley? Would such a man be discreet?"

"I believe so. He has lived in London for twenty years. His advantage is that he knows a great many people. Of course, he would require to be paid handsomely. I suggest that you and I decide how much to offer him and that I make some arrangements to contact him and put the proposal to him."

"But if Clara is not even in London now, would not that rather hinder Benjamin's ability to find anything out about her and Max?"

"It would seem to me to be better if she is out of the way. However discreet he is, his interest in her could well get back to her. That, I would suggest, is far less likely to happen if she is not in London."

"That is true." Darcy and Bingley paused to push aside some shrubbery. "Bingley, I would wish to meet this man if he is to undertake such a…sensitive task for me."

"I would counsel against any direct contact. Indeed, I think he should be instructed through some other person, say a lawyer, and that your name be not given either to the lawyer or to Benjamin."

"Oh no. I would not be prepared to enlist this man's assistance without at least seeing him."

"Then, if we were to go to London together after Easter, we could no doubt visit some venue at which you could observe him covertly."

"Surely, if this man knows so many people, then he may well be aware of our connection, or may easily find out. Upon my word, we were seen in London together barely more than a week ago."

"I would not contact him directly myself. I would ask the lawyer to withhold my own name. The approach to Benjamin would thus be entirely anonymous."

"Does Benjamin drink as well as gamble, Bingley? If so, he may not be dependable. And how are we to know that he will not make up some untrue story to justify his fee."

"I think he drinks no more than you or I. And as to some false report on his part, do not forget that we will be seeking a copy of the boy's birth certificate."

"And if Max was born in some far off place in Europe or in America, how could Benjamin possibly obtain a copy of his birth certificate? Or indeed, how are we to know that any document he produces is not a forgery?"

"If my memory serves me correctly, Professor Kohler, whom Clara was accompanying when we met her in Cambridge, was undertaking a lecture tour of the country which was to last until the following summer and beyond. There is every possibility that Max was born somewhere in England."

These words, Darcy could not help but contemplate, harboured within them the implication that the very upshot which he so feared to acknowledge was well-founded. If his very best friend thought so, then what were others to think? Failing, in his contemplations, to watch his step, he accidentally stood on a small branch which cracked loudly underfoot, sending a flock of pigeons off their perches, their wings making the characteristic hissing sound as they beat the air during their take-offs. Bingley raised an imaginary rifle and mimed a shot in the birds' direction.

Lowering his arms, Bingley continued, "We could verify any

certificate arising from the enquiries by visiting the parish and inspecting the parish records."

"Yes. If Clara did not part company with her father and remained with him for the whole of his tour. She might instead have returned to Europe, or indeed travelled off to America."

By this time they had emerged from the other side of the copse and were walking along a footpath which was totally obscured from the house.

"Darcy, you are being deliberately obtuse. The fact is, we have to start somewhere. Employing Matthew Benjamin in the fashion I have described is my best suggestion. Or else, you had better make your excuses to Elizabeth's family and travel back to Derbyshire with her and Georgiana immediately. Where you would have to try to rid the episode from your mind, pretend to yourself that you had never heard of Maximilian Kohler, if you think such a thing is possible."

Bingley halted and Darcy too. They stood surveying the vista before them, open fields, some grazed by sheep, perhaps clearing the remains of a turnip crop, others already ploughed and sown last autumn, brown with no green shoots yet beginning to emerge. The men knew well enough that the unseasonably cold weather may result in a crop failure this year with all the hardship which this would produce.

Birdsong filled the silence between them for at least a minute. Then Darcy spoke.

"Very well."

"I believe you have told Elizabeth that you were glad to get away from London. How, then, would you explain another visit so soon?"

Darcy waved away the objection.

"It is no matter. We have discussed my going to town again to recover a package to her sister Mary from a correspondent in America. I must also take some steps to sell my London house to raise funds and also talk to a young man with scientific and engineering knowledge in case he can assist me in my plans."

"Yes," sighed Bingley, "your plans."

DARCY and Bingley were not the only members of the household to have quit the building, seeking the opportunity for re-flection. Elizabeth, having watched from an upstairs window the two friends make off around the trout lake, walked in the opposite direction. She had been more disturbed by yesterday's events than she had communicated to Darcy.

It was Good Friday today, and tomorrow a ball was to be held at the Assembly Rooms at Meryton and her aim was, for the moment, to avoid the other ladies who were anxious to discuss their gowns and other adornments for the ball. Kitty and Georgiana, she judged, were also keen to regale her with their further thoughts concerning the visit by Caroline, Lydia and Morley. Perhaps she would talk to them later or tomorrow but for now she wished to keep her own counsel.

Despite her night-time declaration to Darcy that Caroline's altered manner may herald a genuine change of heart, her own doubts tended in the direction of Caroline having had some ulterior motive. Any genuine sympathy at all on her part for Elizabeth or her mother or any of the other Longbourn ladies for that matter could not be believed for certain and she may be using Lydia for her own purposes.

So far as Elizabeth was concerned, Caroline Bingley was, or at least had been, a spiteful creature. Had she not pretended friendship to Jane, while colluding in Bingley's removal from Netherfield the year before last? Had she not implied to Jane in a letter that her brother was destined to marry Georgiana which was not true? These were unpleasant, manipulative acts.

If Caroline Bingley was ever to be trusted, caution would have to be applied at every turn to ensure that others were not being duped by her, as Jane had been in the autumn of 1797.

Chapter 9

ELIZABETH had never wished for Caroline as a friend or ally, though when Morley had comically disparaged Darcy's plan to start a paper mill, Elizabeth was surprised to witness the darkening of Caroline's face and that she had turned away to, so it seemed, conceal her disapprobation. Elizabeth had always assumed that the very obvious pursuit of Darcy by Caroline which she had previously witnessed signalled no huge attraction to him on the part of Caroline, but rather an ambition to make a match with a man of wealth and position. To have observed from Caroline's reaction and countenance today that the woman liked Darcy for himself, desired him even, was a source of amazement. Indeed that part of Elizabeth which might have been this woman's friend could not help but experience some compassion for this rather strident admirer of her husband.

As to Morley, Elizabeth had him marked out as a man who would toy with women with no serious intent. A rake, a dissolute person. She caught him regarding her more than once with what she judged to be a lascivious eye. Even she, who did not frivolously seek the attention of men, could discern his interest in her. Lydia he treated differently, with open gaiety, like some plaything that was his for the taking and Lydia responded with enthusiasm.

Then again, Caroline he conversed and dealt with almost as though she were a man and it suddenly came to Elizabeth that Caroline, with her hauteur and at times stiffness of manner, was simply not attractive to men. Had there been the least degree of friendship between the two women, Elizabeth knew she would be bound to experience sympathy for the other's plight but, as it was, she felt nothing but coldness towards Caroline who had concealed Jane's presence in London from her brother, while pretending affection towards Jane.

To Morley's jests over Darcy's ambitions, Elizabeth felt obliged to respond in her husband's defence, yet in a nonchalant spirit rather than as though she was offering a reproof.

"Lord Morley," she smiled, "those who wish not to be idle must find a useful occupation for themselves and for those who depend upon them. Many a landed estate has been depleted by idleness and extravagance. Many a titled gentleman has refused to sully his hands with commerce and left the management of his affairs to others and woken up one day to find himself penniless."

She paused. "Though I have no doubt that you wisely remain constantly vigilant in the preservation of your own estate and regard the taking of your pleasures as secondary."

"Madam," he replied, "I assure you that I am rarely inactive in any pursuit which I undertake. I eagerly follow all my inclinations with lust and vigour."

Elizabeth was not impressed. The man was unrepentant and her wrinkled forehead and raised eyebrows expressed her combined amusement and dissatisfaction at his answer.

She sighed. "I imagine so."

One of those pursuits alluded to by Morley appeared to be Lydia. Was her youngest sister, Elizabeth had to speculate, happy with the lot she had been complicit in creating for herself? She seemed to have little control over her life, her husband having been sent off to Ireland and for now living on the bounty of a woman, the wife of Wickham's commanding officer, who had no serious responsibilities towards her beyond any duties imposed by army tradition. Did the woman know how scandalously Lydia was behaving? Would she tolerate it?

She wondered what Wickham's circumstances were. With the money he had received from Darcy, he could have purchased a house and land and provided himself and Lydia with a measure of modest security. Instead, he had preferred the life of a soldier and the excitement and variety it no doubt provided. The chances were that he had instead spent his money on fast living and would continue to do so until it was exhausted.

From all Elizabeth was able to judge, Lydia must be living above her means if her gown and jewellery were anything to judge by. Or was Morley financing Lydia's extravagances in return for her favours?

Elizabeth dreaded to think what would become of Lydia if Wickham would not tolerate her infidelity, if indeed infidelity was taking place, and divorced her. She would have nothing. If her present benefactor, the commanding officer's wife, abandoned her, where would she go? She doubted if their parents would give her a home. Lydia's excesses were unlikely to abate. She was still only sixteen and in all probability her behaviour would grow worse before any improvement overcame her, if it ever would.

Though Lydia had been her mother's favourite and could scarce put a foot wrong as recently as last year, the marriages of Elizabeth and Jane, her parents' growing attachment to Darcy and the shock of nearly losing Mr Bennet in Derbyshire over Christmas appeared to have caused Mrs Bennet to undergo a complete change of heart, nay, attitude. Perhaps it was as Aunt Gardiner had expressed over Christmas, that Mrs Bennet's insecurity was rendered unnecessary now that Elizabeth and Jane were well married.

Elizabeth herself was rather more of the opinion that her mother realised that it would be foolish to displease Darcy or, to a lesser extent, Bingley. Indeed, her future depended on them.

If Lydia were to be rendered homeless and penniless, would Darcy step in to provide some sort of relief? He would be sore aggrieved to have to do so and may well fear that Wickham would attempt to somehow re-engage with Lydia. But Darcy was a man of principle and he may also wish to make the gesture to appease Elizabeth.

Nevertheless, such a development was to be deplored.

As was any revival of the dependence on Lydia formerly displayed by Kitty. She caught Lydia several times staring enviously at Kitty both when the latter was variously laughing and talking with Georgiana, and gazing rapturously at Lieutenant Colonel Harvey as they sat together, walked together arm in arm to the dining room and even when they shared whispers and reproachful expressions as they watched Lydia and Morley flirt with one another.

So concerned was she for Lydia's well-being and the possible outcome of her reckless behaviour that she waited for an opportunity to speak to Lydia, to caution her if possible. Such came when the ladies left the gentlemen to their port in the dining room after their meal during the early afternoon. The meal had been delayed for the walkers who had returned, as promised, by two o' clock.

Elizabeth caught her sister's elbow. "Would you care to come to my room to wash and make yourself tidy before you leave?"

"Oh, thank you, Lizzy." Lydia seemed surprised. Well, they had never been great friends as sisters.

LYDIA gazed hungrily about her as she and Elizabeth climbed the broad staircase and gained Elizabeth and Darcy's suite of rooms. She had been to Netherfield House twice before, once when Jane was ill and confined to bed and the second time during the ball which she herself, during her first visit to Netherfield, had encouraged Bingley to hold. However, on those occasions the year before last, she had seen but a small part of the house.

Now she feasted her eyes on the wide decorative staircase as they ascended to the first floor, the large proportions of the rooms, the high ceilings and chandeliers, the elaborate plaster mouldings, the paintings and rich hangings, the wall-coverings and furniture and the busts and statues. She caught Elizabeth watching her.

"I suppose," she said, almost sneered, "that Pemberley is even grander than this; ten times I suspicion."

"It is in truth a lovely house and beautifully situated, standing well on rising ground, and backed by a ridge of high woody hills."

Elizabeth, almost dreamlike, recalled her first sight of Pemberley.

"In front is a stream, no doubt widened into a more imposing watercourse, but without any artificial appearance. Its banks are neither formal nor falsely adorned. I have never seen a place for which nature has done more, or where natural beauty has been so little counteracted by an awkward taste."

Recalling the present, she smiled kindly on her sister, but her warmth was not returned.

"How very pretty." Lydia's own expression was scathing. "I suppose he, Darcy, gives you everything you want. So I have heard."

From whom, Elizabeth wondered, Caroline perhaps? But she would not dignify the comment with a direct response.

"He is a good and kind husband, indeed. But come, make use of the brushes, creams and powders. And the rosewater and the scents. I will help you dress your hair. Or send for a maid to attend you."

"The grand mistress stoops to provide succour to the fallen sister."

Elizabeth turned away to hide her astonishment at the bitterness in Lydia's voice.

"Lydia," she said, looking out of the window as the grounds became enveloped in the growing gloom, "I am neither grand nor the mistress of this house. And you, I hope, are not fallen."

She gathered herself and faced her sister.

"If you are unhappy with your lot, then I would remind you that no one forced you to run off with Wickham. I would suggest that now it is done, that you strive to make the best of it. He will be returned from his tour of duty in Ireland in due course, and it is to be hoped that his next posting will enable you and he to stay together. Young as you were when you married Wickham, you must have known that the life would not be settled."

These truisms did not appear to placate Lydia. She peered down at her feet with a scowl on her face.

"My dear," continued Elizabeth, moving closer to her sister, "do make haste to dress your hair and neaten your garments. Your antics today, rushing around the house, have caused you to be in some disarray. You are a pretty girl, but you should not appear in public with your hair and garments in disorder. It is not seemly."

To Elizabeth's surprise, Lydia pushed her away with some force. Lydia, she knew, had consumed a quantity of wine, including port wine and sherry. Elizabeth realised that she was the worse for it and worried all the more for her sister's well-being.

She drew back.

"Lydia, please do not. I implore you to desist from whatever liaison you are conducting with Lord Morley. I fear he does not hold you in high regard and merely toys with you for his own enjoyment and entertainment. He knows you are a married woman and that any consequences are unlikely to fall on him. By contrast though, if Wickham were to find out about your...friendship with Lord Morley and objected, and if he was minded to break the bonds of matrimony, he may attempt to divorce you. You would then be left with nothing. How would you then fare?"

Lydia pushed past her, her hair still in disarray and her clothes in some disorder.

"You will not lecture me, Lizzy. I will not submit to your censure."

And with that Lydia left the room.

IN THE grand hall as the guests said their farewells and prepared to leave, Lydia looked neater than earlier, though unhappy, and Elizabeth assumed that she had gone to Jane. She would speak to Jane later, or tomorrow.

As Bingley was talking to his sister and Lydia hung by Jane, Elizabeth found herself beside Viscount Morley who appeared to be still in excellent spirits. Elizabeth judged that it would be worth an attempt on her part to persuade him to leave Lydia alone.

Accordingly, she said: "Lord Morley, I fear my youngest sister does not benefit from your attentions. Indeed you could cause her great harm. Would it not be kinder to leave her be? She is adequately accommodated for now in London, and may enjoy London society without a...gentleman friend to cause tongues to wag. Her husband will no doubt soon return from his tour of duty in Ireland and she can resume her former life with him. Why would you wish to disrupt that most desirable outcome?"

Morley sighed. He brushed his rather long, straight, dark brown hair off his face and fixed Elizabeth with a cynical eye.

"Mrs Darcy," he said with his head on one side, "I fear you mistake me for a man who gives a fig for bourgeois morals."

"You need harbour no fears on my account, Lord Morley, but perhaps you should entertain some fear that Wickham may return unexpectedly and call you out for your conduct towards Lydia. I hazard that he must be a skilled swordsman and handy with a pistol. Or even," she laughed, "a man to be reckoned with in a bare-fist fight."

"From all I hear of George Wickham, Mrs Darcy, he is at far greater risk than I of being forced to throw down the gauntlet, in his case before any number of possible parties whom he may have offended."

This was probably nearer the truth and Elizabeth returned to her previous plea.

"Surely, at least you have some compassion, Lord Morley, for my sister's situation, her reputation. I suspicion that your friend Caroline Bingley would not approve of your behaviour, whatever her opinion may be of my sister."

"Caroline Bingley cannot afford to spurn such a friend as I. Caroline Bingley needs friends."

Elizabeth snorted a short laugh.

"I cannot discern your meaning, Lord Morley. Caroline has many friends. She has survived quite well, I surmise, before your arrival in London."

"You think so? And are *you* her friend, Mrs Darcy?"

"My relationship with Caroline Bingley is irrelevant. She does not need *me* to smooth her social path."

"I beg to differ. I believe that a friend such as you would be of great value to Caroline Bingley just now."

Elizabeth laughed. "What you say is preposterous. I am not afraid to tell you that she has never liked me or my family, and we in turn have been...injured in the past by her ill-bred remarks."

He nodded as though in agreement. Yet his next words greatly surprised Elizabeth and she had to suppress her astonishment.

"Caroline is as yet unmarried with no ready prospects of any offer for her hand. She has no appreciable fortune and is largely at the mercy of her brother to provide for her in her spinsterhood. A brother who refused to allow her to stay at Netherfield this Easter, leaving her to find such shelter as she may over the

Easter festivities."

No fortune! This had not been the impression given when Netherfield had first been taken in the autumn of 1797. The fortunes of most of the Netherfield party had become common knowledge within a short time of their entering the first assembly they had attended. Of Caroline Bingley, it had been said that she had a fortune of twenty thousand pounds, but that she was in the habit of spending more than she ought and of associating with people of rank. The same was said of her sister Mrs Hurst. Both women dressed exceedingly elegantly and never seemed to wear the same gown twice.

Perhaps Caroline Bingley had squandered much of her inheritance and grown increasingly dependent on her brother as a result. Yet, whether that was the case or not, she would no doubt have assumed that her right to spend such of her time as she chose in her brother's home was unassailable, regardless of her circumstances. For him to have rejected her, if it was true, was so strange.

To cover her consternation, Elizabeth looked towards Jane and Lydia. Jane had a resigned look on her face, and Lydia smirked unpleasantly at Elizabeth who turned away.

Morley continued, regarding Elizabeth with a sardonic eye. "I see that the irreproachable Fitzwilliam Darcy has not provided his wife with this intelligence, as surely he must know that Charles Bingley harshly turned his sister away this Easter. She has made the best of it, with some story about Netherfield House being re-decorated. But I see no workmen about the place and it is clear to me that Bingley did not want her here."

Elizabeth summoned up a bland expression and she purposely avoided glancing over towards Bingley and Caroline, much as she wished to do so after Morley's disclosure, to attempt to detect whether their discourse might be tinged with any acrimony or urgency.

Some reply was called for. She would not give this troublesome man the satisfaction of assuming that he may have discovered any mendacity towards her on Darcy's part. She gave a gentle laugh.

"Lord Morley, you have a lively imagination. You are free, of course, to make your own interpretation of events, but not all is always as it may seem to you."

If challenged, she had no idea in fact how she would justify such sentiments but Morley merely smiled pleasantly enough in acknowledgement and bowed to Elizabeth.

"I am very glad to have made your acquaintance today, Mrs Darcy, but must take my leave of you. I believe the carriage awaits."

Elizabeth watched Morley's tall, thin figure as he strode away across the hall, gathering up Caroline and Lydia as he went.

More farewells followed and then, mercifully, the visitors had departed. Elizabeth raised her eyebrows at Jane who came to her and took her arm, guiding her towards the small parlour which Jane had made her own since coming to live at Netherfield. It would be a relief to be able to share her thoughts with her calm and sensible older sister.

Chapter 10

Thursday 28th March 1799

"WHAT, then, do you make of the events of today?" Elizabeth asked Jane as they sat and took cool glasses of cordial, neither in their present conditions wishing to indulge in wine, port or sherry. Jane had called for small cakes to be brought and both women pecked at the delicious treats, mindful of the full dinner to be served later.

"Were you able to talk any sense into Lydia after she left me? I declare, she is not conducting herself to her best advantage. Morley has no care for her reputation, I am sure, especially as you said to me earlier that Charles believes Morley to be married. I suppose his poor wife is back in Devon having to stay in the background."

She was on the point of telling Jane of Morley's disclosure that Bingley had turned Caroline away this Easter, questioning what it might mean. She stopped herself, not entirely sure why, but she did not wish her knowledge, if indeed Morley was telling the truth, to get back to Darcy via Jane and Bingley. Something was amiss with Darcy and spreading more rumour, she instinctively felt, would not assist.

"Lizzy, I think he is not such a very bad man," said Jane, drawing Elizabeth's thoughts back to their sister. "Lydia, you will recollect, is most persistent in her...quest for amusement. Morley may be as much in her thrall as she is in his."

"What you say is possibly true, although he did not strike me as a man who could be charmed by a girl such as Lydia. I would say that, on the contrary, he is almost certainly impervious to her wiles, such as they are. He merely takes advantage of the immediate pleasures she offers and then would cast her aside. Jane, she is only yet sixteen and he must know that in the eyes of the world she is cheapened and damaged by his obvious attentions. As an older married man, he should draw back from a liaison which could cause a scandal, especially if her connection to Darcy became widely known, and it would be Lydia who would suffer, not him. Did you glean from your time with Lydia how far her association with Morley has gone?"

"Not...as such. It is difficult to pose such questions directly and Lydia was...in some state of turmoil. It was as much as I could do to persuade her to neaten and tidy herself in readiness for their departure."

"Well, I attempted myself to persuade her to desist from her liaison with Morley, but she would not heed me. Indeed, she became agitated. Jane, she pushed me away from her. I was sore affronted. She had consumed port or sherry, I do not know how much, but she was not herself, not the merry girl we knew. I do fear that her time with Wickham has not been well spent, that she has learned unfortunate ways from him, from his habits as a soldier."

Elizabeth found herself appealing to her sister and giving vent to more fears than she had intended. Her head down, she admitted to Jane:

"And there is something wrong with William. I know not what affects him. It is since he was in London."

Hot tears, long withheld, forced themselves from her eyes. Jane came over and sat on the couch with Elizabeth. She put her arms around her sister. Her embrace was some comfort.

"Lizzy," Jane said, "I have seen it myself, but do not be alarmed. Gentlemen are not always even-tempered. Did we not always observe Darcy to be a man of moods, liable to be stern and unwilling to talk some of the time? We have observed in the past that he has a tendency to hold his tongue and appear taciturn."

"No, Jane. I know his moods." Elizabeth raised her head. "This is not one of them. It is deeper and more profound. Something very serious is affecting him, but he has not told me what it is. I fear to question him, that it will just result in him withdrawing from me. At least, for now, he is as loving as ever, indeed needing my love more than ever. I cannot risk alienating him."

"Lizzy, try not to upset yourself. I am sure it will pass."

"Jane, do you think it is Morley, or something to do with Morley? I do not mean in relation to Lydia. But something between Morley himself and Darcy. Morley did belittle Darcy, William, earlier. There may be more to their history than I know and, whatever it is, Morley has suddenly erupted into William's life again. It could be that which is discomfiting William in this way.

"And, Jane, that you have noticed William's disturbance means that it is real and not merely my imagination."

"I am not aware of any past enmity or other matter between William and Morley. Indeed, until today, I had never heard of Viscount Morley. Charles described him to me as a very rich man of an ancient viscountcy. But Lizzy, your love will surely overcome this very fleeting unpleasantness."

"I must hope so. You are good and kind Jane and I thank you for your reassurance."

At a knock on the door, Jane drew apart from Elizabeth. It heralded Mrs Bennet to Jane's invitation to enter. After her came Kitty, Georgiana and Mary.

"We hoped that we may come and sit with you for a time, as we are perplexed by today's visitors as no doubt are you."

"Of course, Mama. I will order tea for you," said Jane, ringing the bell.

"I declare," said Mrs Bennet as she seated herself, "that Caroline Bingley seems much altered in her manner."

"Indeed," said Elizabeth, "she was unaccountably on her least insufferable behaviour."

Mary sniffed. "As the Good Book instructs us: 'Forbearing one another, and forgiving one another, if any man have a quarrel against any: even as Christ forgave you, so also do ye.'"

"If it gives you comfort, Mary, then believe it if you must."

"I do not think she was wholly genuine," said Kitty. "She seemed to me at times to look a little afraid of something. I could not say what, but fear might cause a person to be less…unpleasant."

Her future maybe, thought Elizabeth, surprised at Kitty's powers of perception and more disconcerted than ever by the undercurrents which appeared to be at play in this strange new world which seemed to have come about in just the last few days. She wished ardently that it was others more remote who were affected by these sudden puzzling and unsettling quandaries, that she and Darcy might sit back and speculate idly upon them instead of being in the thick of them.

"Afraid of Morley, perhaps?" offered Georgiana.

"Well," said Mrs Bennet, "I would say that Lydia had more to fear from him than Caroline Bingley, although you would never guess it by the way she conducted herself. I believe I heard him relate that he has a home in Devon, a good distance away. 'Twould likely be better for all connected with him if he were to take himself off there and remain there for a good duration."

LATER that night, after Darcy had returned and they had fallen asleep, Elizabeth's slumbers were interrupted by a disturbing dream. She found herself in London, having followed Darcy there. The exact reason for her excursion was unclear to her, something possibly to do with her unease at Darcy's odd mood and the desire to investigate.

Without any clear idea where he would be, if not at Bingley's London house, she wandered the streets, stopping ladies and gentlemen, tradesmen and shopkeepers, asking after the whereabouts of Fitzwilliam Darcy, bearing their sneers and odd looks, ranging from perplexity to disgust that a finely-dressed woman should be walking the streets of London unescorted asking after a man. The scene seemed odd, as though viewed in a hall of mirrors, the people and buildings distorted, ever-changing from wide to narrow, tall to short, hampering her passage through the busy thoroughfares. She swayed as the undulations of the ground beneath her made her lose her balance and stumble, as though on board a ship or pleasure boat or under the effects of some drug.

Everyone she approached turned her away and she began to see that they assumed she must, despite her fine clothing, be a woman of ill repute, drunk and on her way to an illicit assignation. Many beggars lined the roadway, afflicted by divers diseases and injuries, limbs and heads covered in bandages or weeping pustules, hands outstretched, if they had hands, or hats upturned, or grunting or aiming pleading eyes at passers-by, noxious smells emanating from them, able to assault the senses from yards away.

Fearing arrest if she continued to accost solid citizens, she ventured near these poor creatures but enjoyed little response. Walking past a man clearly blind, his eyes bandaged, she was inclined to ignore him, but he loudly croaked a demand for her attention.

"Madam, madam, if you seek a man, I can tell you where to go." He beckoned, turning his head this way and that, unable to see her. "Come closer."

Magically, the distorted mirror effect had disappeared and she saw clearly again and could walk in a straight line. She ventured towards him and bent over him.

"Yes? Where is this place?"

He rasped out some directions. She thanked him and handed him a crown, far too much money but in her state it seemed not to matter. She went towards the next turning as he had said.

AT THE corner she held back, seeing a gentleman entering the house described by her informant. Lo! It was Darcy, his head down. Peering at the building, she saw it was a lodging house. In her dream, she waited for a quarter of an hour before entering the house herself. By this time, dusk had fallen and the hall of the house was dark inside. There was no sound from anywhere.

The ground floor appeared deserted, so she climbed the dark stairs to the next floor, again bereft of activity or sounds. And so to the second floor, feeling her way as she went. From the end of the passage, she heard a groaning and a screaming and some rhythmic knocking noise, faint at first but growing louder as she approached a half open door, her breath quickening for fear of what might lie beyond it.

Cautiously, she pushed the door and peered around the gloomy interior of the small room within, lit only by a few candles. Dark as the scene was, the bed was only a couple of feet from the doorway and a man and woman were on the bed, half dressed, the man groaning on top of the woman and the woman screaming below him. The man held himself up by his forearms, his head turning sometimes so that his face was in profile. The woman's long, fair hair radiating out over the pillow shone in the candlelight. Her face was visible over the man's shoulder, her head thrown back and her eyes closed, her breath coming in short gasps.

With a rush of horror, Elizabeth realised that the man was Darcy; Darcy with another woman, his dark curls ruffled, bobbing up and down with his movements, his profile unmistakeable!

Elizabeth stumbled as she groped towards the man, desperate to stop the proceedings before it was too late, before the crisis was reached. But some strong unseen barrier impeded her progress, her feet immoveable as though sunk in thick treacle, and when she tried to cry out, "Stop, Fitz", she found her throat constricted and no sound emerged no matter how hard she strained. The heavy breathing of the woman on the bed had subsided, though the man's body still rose and fell, his speed increasing. The unknown woman's eyes opened lazily, then wider seeing Elizabeth and she aimed an evil, triumphant smile at her.

Elizabeth's efforts to move and shout were suddenly rewarded as her voice broke into a strangled cry and her body, frozen by sleep, would move again. She took a deep, shuddering breath and turned towards Darcy beside her. Surely he would wake and comfort her, but his own breathing remained strong and regular, fatigued, no doubt, by his day out. He did not wake up, even though she staggered to the privy and vomited. Alone and desolate, still deeply affected by the dream, tears pouring down her face, she relieved herself then cleaned herself with the washing water and climbed back into bed where she lay restlessly tossing and turning but Darcy still slept.

It was, she told herself, just a dream. In the morning she would have forgotten it. Darcy would never go with another woman. She must not let a night terror, brought on by a mere few days' moodiness on his part influence her. She would not be unhappy because of it, fall into a ridiculous decline, affecting all around her, Darcy in particular.

Nonetheless, it was at least an hour before sleep again claimed her shattered senses.

DESPITE her resolution of the night before, Elizabeth felt cold towards Darcy the next morning and could not rid her head of the night vision of him with another woman. It seemed ridiculous. Darcy was the very epitome of honesty and trustworthiness. Had not she asserted to Mary only a few days ago that her husband was eminently trustworthy? It made no difference to the considerable degree of resentment she felt towards Darcy, however unreasonable it was. She tried to suppress it yet found she simply could not. But Darcy failed to notice. He seemed distracted and quickly dressed and left the bedroom. The next time she saw him, he was marching away from the front of the house with Bingley.

Chapter 11

FOLLOWING her own early solitary perambulations this morning, Darcy had come upon Elizabeth in their rooms and invited
her to ride with him to Frogmore Mill. She was glad to see that
he seemed to be more himself. He smiled down at her, taking
her hand. A large part of the frost in her heart began to thaw.
She hoped that by the expedition, she would rid herself of the
discomposure caused by her dream and additionally avoid the
other ladies of the house for much of the day.

"It is Good Friday and consequently the mill will not be operating. During my visit yesterday, Mr Holmes invited me to
return with you today to look around the building and have
some of the processes explained. I told him of your eager support for the venture and the plans for the new machine invented
in France. His own wife will likely join us."

"I would be delighted, Fitz, though you will recall that we are
to have an evening of singing and dancing and piano recitals
with a play from the children."

The children were anxious to entertain everyone. Harriet expressed herself to be very desirous of seeing one of these puppet
plays having heard much of the Christmas plays put on by the
children. Anthony had assured anyone who would listen that
they had been reading the news sheets every day since their return to Gracechurch Street after Christmas and visiting libraries
and had written a thrilling sequel to their Christmas play about
the King and Queen, the Prince of Wales, the ladies of the Court
and Napoleon.

"I have not forgotten, Lizzy. We will dine at an inn and return to Netherfield by the early evening in good time for the entertainments."

Elizabeth was pleased to have a day alone with Darcy whom,
she had already decided, she would not question about Bingley's

exclusion of Caroline. That Darcy, who must know about it, had forborne to mention it to her was disquieting. She feared that there was some significance in both his silence on the subject and in Bingley having refused to have Caroline at Netherfield over Easter if Morley was to be believed. Caroline's less hostile attitude towards Elizabeth, Jane and the Bennet ladies suggested that Morley was correct and that Caroline had been attempting yesterday to appease her brother, though why he would have excluded her at all was a mystery.

It seemed to her to be part of whatever was troubling Darcy since he had returned from London. If she was to discover anything, her instincts told her that it would be by stealth rather than open confrontation. She might delve into some peripheral aspects of this present mystery, pose over their dinner such questions as she judged to be safe to ask Darcy, while skirting round the main matter of concern.

They made good time. The weather was as cold as ever, the air chilly, but they had worn thick clothing and Elizabeth found the exercise filled her with energy and new zeal for the plans for the Pemberley estate. They rode quickly and found themselves laughing together at the exhilaration generated by the horses' brisk canter. Relieved she was that Darcy did not treat her like a china doll due to her condition.

Darcy introduced Elizabeth and Mr Holmes introduced his wife. Mr Holmes was in his their late forties or fifties, Mrs Holmes considerably younger, possibly more Darcy's age. Mr Holmes was a man of medium height, not much taller than his wife, and who dressed rather severely. He might, thought Elizabeth, be working today rather than showing guests round his manufactory. Mrs Holmes was a pretty, fair-haired woman and seemed to have made a particular effort today to dress well, though appropriate to the occasion, not ostentatiously but smartly, her garments well-cut and of good material.

After taking tea, they all walked over to the mill building and were given a tour by the couple. Mr and Mrs Holmes had been effusive in their welcome. Elizabeth suspected that their enthusiasm was as much to do with Darcy's status, of which they appeared to be aware, as their desire to assist a fellow industrialist, or would-be industrialist in Darcy's case. Darcy must have imparted to the owner some particulars of his vast estate in order to receive advice as to the best situation for his operations.

Elizabeth knew he had brought with him from Derbyshire a roll of documents which she assumed included detailed plans of the Pemberley estate and he had ridden off with them yesterday.

And they probably recalled the name of Darcy from his time spent in Hertfordshire in the last two years.

The tour and all the explanations took well over two hours. Darcy was full of questions. Elizabeth listened carefully. To be here brought the whole thing to life for her. Previously, she had tried to imagine what might go on in a paper mill but to see it first hand was an education. She was burning with her own questions, but out of politeness to Mrs Holmes, she chose such moments as seemed propitious, when they were walking from one part of the mill to another for example, to talk to the lady of family matters, her relations and of their stay at Netherfield.

"This is a good day for you to see the mill, Mrs Darcy," said Mr Holmes at one point. "On normal days we could hardly have heard ourselves think."

Elizabeth looked around. Some vats were empty, some full of fermenting rags covered in wooden planks, the rag engines were idle and the moulds into which the pulp was poured were clean, dry and stacked in heaps. The most obvious signs of the production which went on here were the vats still full of fermenting rags and the sheets hung from ropes in the drying loft, left to dry from the previous day, though the waterwheel could be heard still turning tirelessly outside in the flow of the River Gade. Darcy had told her on their journey here that this was one of the few days a year the workers were given time off. The others were Christmas and Sundays. It must be a hard, tiring life for them.

She wondered about the employment of children though Fitz had said that the jobs in papermaking were skilled and not suitable for children, who, if they were employed, would be given menial jobs such as sweeping up spills from the vats to stop the floors from becoming slippery, carrying messages and so forth. Notwithstanding, the children employed might, he said, watch and learn skills which would benefit them later. Papermaking, he insisted, was a skilled job and most of the processes could not be left to amateurs or else the resulting paper would be of poor quality or even completely ruined early on at various stages.

They had repaired to the office where they sat chatting and drinking tea. There was talk of some party in two weeks' time which the couple were holding and how honoured they would be if Mr Darcy and his wife would consent to attend.

"The honour would be all ours, sir, madam, however I would have to consult my friend, Mr Bingley, with whom we are spending the Easter period as to his own plans and I will let you know."

"We will send a formal invitation over to Netherfield House," said Mrs Holmes.

"Yes, please do." So saying, Elizabeth glanced towards Darcy, knowing full well that he would be loath to come to this party. She also saw that he was restless and knew he would be wanting to get off as soon as possible.

"Mr Holmes," Elizabeth said as much to change the topic of conversation as out of interest, "I notice that the paper produced is rather small. Cannot larger moulds be made to produce larger sheets of paper?"

She thought of the newssheets which her family took for granted, often discarded once read, with little thought to the amount of work which must have gone into the production of the paper on which they were printed.

Mr Holmes's reply was directed more at Darcy than at her. "That is a very good question, but the way we produce paper here has been in use for centuries, I would say. 'Tis the span of a man's arms which limits the size. A man cannot safely carry a larger mould. I can show you a double deckle, though we rarely use them here." He paused, as though considering the point. "Have you ever heard of James Whatman? Turkey Mill?"

Darcy shook his head. "I don't believe so."

"Ah, well, Mr Whatman has made large sheets of paper, but it took many men and other equipment. They – "

"How large?" Darcy wanted to know.

"Oh, I do not know." Mr Holmes spread his arms wide apart to indicate presumably a number of feet. "'Tis called...let me think. The word is something like a collector or scholar interested in old scripts and books and so forth. I cannot bring to mind the exact word. His large sheets have been used for important ceremonial documents. Mr Whatman made many other improvements such as sizing the paper with gelatine, but many layers. Famous artists used his paper. And woven mesh instead of wires in the moulds. He — "

"How many men?"

"Men? You mean for the large sheets? Well again, I do not know precisely."

"Where is this place…Turkey Mill?"

Elizabeth moved gradually, hopefully imperceptibly, closer to her husband and leaned in to him. She could hardly nudge him openly, but saw that firing questions at the mill owner was irritating the man. He must by now be tiring of the what was effectively a series of lectures he had had to give on papermaking which must be as familiar a daily activity to him as eating and drinking and no doubt quite tedious to impart to others as a favour. She almost wished she had not asked the question, however, they needed to know these things and others in order to proceed.

She smiled at Mr and Mrs Holmes. "What you have told us, Mr Holmes, is fascinating. My husband and I, as you know, are very new to this industry and hope to discover as much as we can about what is possible. Our knowledge is, I am afraid, elementary and I know that my husband is anxious this Easter to explore any advances which have been made. We are starting afresh in Derbyshire, with a clean slate as it were and have to try to…build into our plans the most recent and, we would hope, the best practices."

Elizabeth was relieved when Mr Holmes returned the smile.

"Yes, indeed," offered Darcy, his expression softening, displaying his more charming side to Mrs Holmes especially. The woman drew back slightly as though to regard him properly and Elizabeth saw something overcome the woman who returned his gaze with sparkling eyes.

Elizabeth's dream suddenly and forcibly returned to her. That Darcy could seduce a woman with one look should not be a surprise to her, but she wished at that moment that it was not so and that she had married a plain man, a man who would not be attractive to women in any common situation.

She swallowed her resentment and fought down the demons of her imagination, her visions of women who might have succumbed to Darcy's charms in the past and the terrible fear that he was involved at this very time in some familiarity another woman. It could not be so, she told herself. Darcy would never betray her in that or any other way. She must put this wild conjecture behind her.

Darcy was still talking, cutting into her musings.

"We are enduringly grateful for your hospitality and for all you have told us."

"We are more than happy to help you in any way we can, Mr and Mrs Darcy," said Mr Holmes. "But the Turkey Mill is not around here. 'Tis in Kent. Maidstone, I think."

"Ah," said Darcy, "I have a...connection near Westerham in Kent. Not so very far from Maidstone, I believe. And another even nearer, if my geography serves me."

He referred of course to his aunt, Lady Catherine de Bourgh, from whom they were presently estranged. The other must be Colonel Fitzwilliam's older brother.

"Ah, well," he said, turning to Elizabeth, "we will have to see if we can get down there before we return to Pemberley."

"Yes, indeed."

"Now, I am afraid, we must take our leave. Our hosts and family members at Netherfield are arranging entertainments tonight, therefore we must make haste, so as to be back in good time."

Mr and Mrs Holmes expressed their regret that the Darcys had to leave so early. It was barely four o' clock in the afternoon. Could they not offer the Darcys a light meal with them before departing?

"I regret not," Darcy replied. "The ride will take us perhaps two hours." He took Elizabeth's hand. "We must pace ourselves. Mrs Darcy cannot ride quickly these days."

They had already told Mr and Mrs Holmes of Elizabeth's condition. Elizabeth smiled at the thought of their exhilarating ride to Apsley earlier.

"Well, of course, we fully understand," said Mrs Holmes. "We do hope to see you again in the near future. If you would come to the house now, we will have your horses brought round."

The two couples enjoyed pleasant conversation until their final leave-taking and Elizabeth and Darcy were soon mounted and on their way.

Chapter 12

Friday 29ᵗʰ March 1799

"I HAVE decided that we should dine at the White Hart at St Albans."

This was typical of Darcy, to decide where they should eat without consulting her. She hoped that the White Hart would prove able to serve a good meal. She was very hungry, having had only tea (at which she had sipped shallowly, preferring cordial just now) and some biscuits since breakfast.

"The inn has been in decline in recent years, I understand, due to the popularity of Dunstable for stagecoaches since improvements in the road. And a new road has been built through St Albans avoiding Holywell Hill, therefore coaches no longer pass by the inn. It's a steep hill up to the White Hart. But your father told me it is still a fine inn, the best in St Albans, and we are only taking a meal there."

"I hope we will be there soon," she said, pulling her cloak around her as the horses trotted along.

"In fact, we are approaching St Albans now."

Within a short time, they were climbing a steep incline and a white building came into view. It was obviously a much older building with a Georgian facade added to the front of it. They rode through the covered passageway to the stables at the rear.

"YOU asked a very pertinent question this afternoon, Lizzy," said Fitz, once they were seated and their meal had been served; plump pullets with greens and fruit with syllabub for after. "If larger sheets of paper can be produced without the need for the cylinder-mould machine of which I have heard much but seen no proper designs, then that would be a very substantial advantage. I think we or I must try to visit this Turkey Mill in Maidstone as soon as may be."

"I have been trying to think of the word for these large sheets of paper. I wonder if he meant 'antiquarian', that is learned men who puzzle over ancient texts and collect antiquities."

"We will find out, I am sure."

"Would you, Fitz, wish to visit your Aunt Catherine and try to mend the breach as Mr Collins implored you to do?" Elizabeth's smile belied her earnest words as Darcy well knew.

"I think not," he said. "The expedition will require an overnight stay, but it will have to be elsewhere than at Rosings."

"Charlotte and Mr Collins will be returning to Hunsford soon after Easter. Would a night at the Rectory be to your taste? If I accompanied you, it might be possible." Since it was unlikely to come about, she felt safe to say this. In truth, Lady Catherine might refuse to countenance their presence at The Rectory at Hunsford.

"I will travel directly to Maidstone. I will go nowhere near Rosings, Lizzy."

One day though, Elizabeth mused to herself, some reconciliation will have to come about. Close relations cannot be cut off forever, and in this respect she speculated that Lady Catherine would in time be willing to heal the breach, though in a quiet way, no doubt, without withdrawing any of the unpleasant sentiments she had expressed.

As to Darcy, the case was more difficult. He would certainly require an apology, probably an open acceptance of his marriage to her and a retraction of the objections and unkind comments made by his aunt both to him in a letter and to Elizabeth to her face before he had proposed to her the second time. For her part, Elizabeth knew she would derive great pleasure to be able to sit in that parlour at The Rectory in which Darcy had bared his soul to her a year ago during his first most unexpected proposal.

A wave of nostalgia assailed her.

Perhaps at some time Colonel Fitzwilliam would be able to intercede with Lady Catherine who would no doubt regard his own marriage to a wealthy baronet's daughter, if it took place, with great approbation by contrast to Darcy's marriage. And he had the advantage that Lady Catherine would scarcely wish to have *him* for her son-in-law as she had wanted Darcy. The Colonel, while not penniless, was certainly not wealthy enough to be a suitable match for Lady Catherine's only child, Anne de Bourgh.

"Oh well," she sighed, "it is likely farther than I would wish to travel, Fitz, therefore I doubt whether I will accompany you. I must stay at Netherfield to be with Harriet and Kitty and oversee their romances."

Darcy laughed.

"Do they need any assistance?"

"Probably not. But they may benefit from a guiding hand."

"Old hand as you are in the realms of love."

She laughed. Then approached a point which may further her cause to discover Darcy's present unsettled state.

"Fitz," she put her head on one side, "what do you think of Caroline Bingley? Do you, for example, find her attractive? I do wonder because I thought that she was very partial to you when we saw your party first appear in Meryton the year before last, and indeed later at Pemberley the following year."

"What has prompted this line of enquiry, Lizzy, for heaven's sake?"

"Nothing as such. But she was at Netherfield yesterday, and I wondered if she still has some sort of...design on you. Or simply hoped to see you."

Darcy examined her face assessingly and she knew that he found her explanation wanting. But he responded evenly enough.

"To answer your question, no, I do not find Caroline Bingley in the least attractive. She is quite pretty in a masculine sort of way, but she has a strident quality about her of determined...arrogance. If I had to counsel her in the art of attracting a husband, I would suggest she should soften her ways, be more kind and gentle. More feminine."

Her thoughts turned to Morley's implied suggestion that she should befriend Caroline, or at least that Caroline might benefit from having Elizabeth as a friend, though whether Caroline would easily accept advice from Elizabeth about how best to secure a husband, she had to doubt. She would consider it further when she had time. Such a move would hardly be a pleasure, but it might have the advantage of bringing her closer to learning what might have occurred in London to upset Darcy.

"And," Darcy continued, "she was very plain in her dislike of your family."

"But so were you, Fitz," she replied, dragging herself back to the present. "You enlisted her support and that of Mrs Hurst for your plan to entice Charles away from Meryton. She freely supported you but it was your plan to begin with."

"Indeed. But I loved you, notwithstanding. Her feelings were borne of some disdain for you and your family and...yes, you are right, probably some partiality towards me."

"I don't know if I have ever told you this, but she wrote to Jane in London of her hopes that her brother would marry Georgiana. It was the utmost cruelty towards Jane at that time, especially as she had made Jane her friend. I must say that there was little overt sign of any special friendship yesterday when Caroline visited, though her major object appeared to be to make some sort of amends to all of us. And indeed, everyone was distracted by Morley and Lydia."

"Lizzy, I cannot change that which has taken place. I would if I could. If I could take us back to the autumn of 1797 and make myself agreeable to you on first meeting and propose to you thereafter at the first opportunity, of course I would. But I cannot. Our path has been strewn with obstacles, many of them, I freely admit, thrown down by me, but nonetheless we have overcome them and, fortunately, now we are at this juncture. Tomorrow during the ball at the Assembly Rooms at Meryton we could, maybe, re-enact our first meeting, turn it into a happier encounter."

At his words, Elizabeth experienced rush of emotion. A frisson passed through her and a gasp escaped her. She knew, of course, that they had been meant for each other from the beginning of time. Nothing could change that. Darcy stretched his hand across the table to take hers and their eyes met, holding each other's for many seconds. She fancied that there were tears in his eyes.

"And I did not then," he said, "and never have had the least desire to make Caroline Bingley my wife." He released her hand and they resumed eating.

"Well, I thought not, but she came to Netherfield yesterday and I must wonder why, if not to try to ingratiate herself with me and Jane and our family."

"Lizzy, did Morley say something to you?"

"About Caroline?"

"About anything which may have discomfited you."

Elizabeth turned the question around in her mind. Morley certainly had put to her a point which she could not fathom, that of Caroline's exclusion from Netherfield this Easter, but it was too close to the quick of the matter.

"Morley says a great many things to discomfit. That is my impression of him. I tried to dissuade him from chasing after Lydia, but I think he is not amenable. But neither, I found, is Lydia amenable to being discouraged from disporting herself in public and encouraging a man like Morley. If Caroline has allied herself to Morley, then I have to wonder why. My estimation of her is that she would not ordinarily approve of Morley's and Lydia's entanglement. Therefore, I wonder why she would do so now, or at least why she would allow it now."

"Lizzy, I cannot possibly say."

"I do wonder also why Charles did not yesterday offer Caroline and her party a bed for the night."

"Did they ask to be accommodated?"

"I do not know."

"Lizzy, we have finished our meal with these musings and speculations. Entertaining though they are, I think we should pay our bill and make haste to return to Netherfield."

SINCE yesterday, the children had made a puppet of a Prussian boy prodigy. He introduced his piece in an exaggerated accent which Anthony presumably thought approximated to German. As there were plenty of Germans living and working in London in various trades and business, especially in that part beyond the Tower, he may well have been right. The puppet had wild black hair and a surly expression and scratched at a toy violin for King George, Queen Charlotte and Prince George.

Napoleon appeared, again depicted with a devil's face as at Christmas, and declared the boy to be incompetent, amid cries of

'"Mon Dieu!" and "Putain!" He compared the boy unfavourably with the French violin prodigy and composer, François Couperin.

"But he is dead," cried the Queen, "this last sixty years. And he played the organ. Far from playing, he is decaying. You have the wrong century, Napoleon."

Bonaparte stomped off.

Then there was the usual chasing of Court ladies by Prince George, more derogatory comments about the English by Bonaparte and a sword fight between Prince George and Bonaparte which the Prince naturally won and Bonaparte ran away. The curtain came down at which the audience applauded extravagantly.

Darcy raised an eyebrow to Elizabeth who smiled. Aunt Gardiner explained that they and the children had seen a caricature of Bonaparte by James Gillray **in** Hannah Humphrey's shop window.

"The puppet is a good likeness. They made it last year even before we saw the plate in Humphrey's window."

Bingley rose as the stage was cleared away and proposed that the singing and recitals, dancing and cards should commence. The day thus ended with entertainments as planned, with more fun tomorrow in the form of the ball at Meryton.

Chapter 13

"LIZZY," said Kitty at breakfast, "will you tell us this morning what you think of our ball gowns for this evening? There is still time to make adjustments. We tried to catch you yesterday, but you marched away outside to the back of the house and then you both disappeared later."

Kitty took Darcy into her last utterance and spoke both for herself and Georgiana. Elizabeth was glad that she had largely absented herself from the company yesterday, as had Darcy, in the form of their visit to Frogmore.

"You know we went to Apsley yesterday, Kitty, to visit the mill. It was immensely interesting."

No one replied. The business of wishing to start a paper mill seemed to perplex most of the family.

"Well," said Darcy, rising from his seat, "I must away to write a letter to Turkey Mill in Kent which I propose to visit soon," he looked around the table as though challenging anyone to make an adverse comment, "and will have delivered to them today."

Bingley, of course, laughed.

"And, if you have no objection, Bingley, I would give them your London address in hopes of a timely reply as we will be there early next week and the post is better in London."

"I certainly have no objection at all."

"Will you visit my brother, Ernest, Darcy?" asked Colonel Fitzwilliam.

"I fear there will not be time, Fitzwilliam."

"Or perhaps our Aunt Catherine?" Fitzwilliam put his head on one side and raised a sardonic eyebrow.

"I think not, as you well know."

With that, Darcy swept from the room.

ELIZABETH knew that she could no longer avoid a session with her sisters. She decided to invite Jane and Harriet to join them, and Mary if she chose, hoping that the weight of numbers would deflect and dilute the worst of the entreaties she felt almost sure would flow from Kitty and Georgiana about Morley, Lydia and Caroline and their own theories concerning the events of Thursday. Mary declined, saying she had some writing to do.

Indeed, her mother and Aunt Gardiner joined them. Aunt Philips, they were told, wished to walk the dogs with the children, Mr Gardiner, Mr Philips, and Mr Bennet. The soldiers were outside too, practising their swordsmanship, as they often did.

Darcy? Where was Darcy? With Bingley presumably, perhaps having another of their long chats. Did these discourses concern London maybe, or Caroline? Or Morley?

Mrs Bennet wasted no time sharing the news that she had, today, received invitations to a ball at Lucas Lodge in two weeks' time and everyone at Netherfield was included. The announcement was greeted with great enthusiasm by the ladies, in particular by Kitty, Georgiana and Harriet.

"Mary will be pleased," said Elizabeth, "it will give her the opportunity to play for us as she loves to do, as we all know."

Thereby, a pleasant few hours were passed by all, discussing tonight's ball and the ball in a fortnight's time, spreading out their gowns for inspection, examining fabric, lace, petticoats, slippers, brooches, earrings, necklaces and divers other adornments, sewing gems and pearls onto gowns and suggesting improvements and enhancements. Workbags were brought down to Jane's parlour and boxes and collections of trinkets to be sorted through, loaned and gifted.

Attracted by the laughter and chatter, Anthony put his head around the door just before lunch and asked whether they were planning to hold a rummage sale. He hurriedly ducked out before a number of cushions hit the door.

"Aunt Gardiner," said Elizabeth, "you have a clever son, with his teasing quips and his satirical plays."

Aunt Gardiner sighed. "He is to be sent away to school soon. We have mixed feeling about it and hope that his ingenuity will flourish under a school's regime."

Elizabeth, who was already quite satisfied with her own gown, put the finishing touches to a reticule she had been able to fashion during the morning to match her gown, liberally embellished with beads and tassels.

"Lizzy," remarked Aunt Gardiner, "I have made this observation before. You are such a neat seamstress, decidedly professional. I am sure you put the rest of us to shame. I could never make anything half so professional."

"You are too kind, Aunt."

"Yes, indeed," cried Georgiana. "I would love to have such a bag."

Others said the same.

"Well," said Elizabeth, "when I am confined later this year, I will certainly take commissions to make bags for you all during my lying-in. I am sure I will welcome the diversion."

MINDFUL of Darcy's words over their dinner yesterday at the White Hart, Elizabeth could not avoid glancing frequently at the door of the Assembly Rooms.

"Do not fret, Lizzy," advised her mother. "I am sure they will arrive soon."

All the ladies and the three older gentlemen had travelled in Bingley's two carriages and the Bennet's carriage. Darcy, Bingley and the soldiers were riding to the Assembly Rooms but seemed to be taking a long time. Riding would ordinarily have brought them earlier to the event than travelling by carriage. The children had begged to be allowed to attend but were firmly refused and had been left in the care of a nurse, Theresa Kirke, who had already been engaged in readiness for Jane's confinement, being now five months on. It was early, Jane admitted, but Charles wanted to be prepared for contingencies. Several maids were helping her mind the children.

On hearing of the nurse earlier, Mr Bennet had immediately recommended that Jane be attended at the birth by Dr Daniel Baldwin, whom he said he held in high regard, having expertly assisted him after the death of his farm manager two years ago and on occasions since.

Kitty and Georgiana had rushed off to speak to the Lucas

party and were being introduced to a number of young men by Sir William. As they watched, Kitty appeared to have declined invitations to dance, but Georgiana was taking the floor with a dashing gentleman in a dark green brocade coat, his hair drawn back and tied by a ribbon of the same colour. Charlotte's sister, Maria, was dancing with another of the young men.

I wonder who Georgiana's partner is, thought Elizabeth absently, and whether Darcy would approve. She was beginning to become alarmed at the non-appearance of Darcy, Bingley and the soldiers. When at last the gentlemen appeared, the soldiers in their uniforms drawing inquisitive looks, a wave of sentimental emotions assailed her. Many of course recognised Darcy and Bingley.

Elizabeth met Darcy's eyes, recalling his first entrance into the Assembly Rooms eighteen months ago. The first impression which drew the attention of the room was of his fine, tall person, handsome features and noble mien, His purported income of ten thousand a year was remarked upon. The gentlemen pronounced him to be a fine figure of a man, the ladies declared he was much handsomer than Mr. Bingley, and he was looked at with great admiration for about half the evening.

Alas, his manners had soon given a disgust which turned the tide of his popularity; for he was discovered to be proud, to be above his company, and above being pleased; and not all his large estate in Derbyshire could then save him from having a most forbidding, disagreeable countenance, and being unworthy to be compared with his friend.

At the time she had found his hauteur rather ridiculous. The unfortunate impression he had made on the company, indeed his own harsh words about Elizabeth within her hearing, now filled her mind and her senses for a moment with a deep wistfulness. She soon cast this aside as Darcy, brushing his hair down with his hands and patting down his coat, came straight over and the others followed.

"Our apologies at our dilatory progress this evening. Harvey's mount cast a shoe, therefore we all had to return to Netherfield for him to change his horse."

Colonel Fitzwilliam greeted Harriet first then bowed to the

Netherfield party as a whole.

Addressing himself to the Colonel, Harriet and Lieutenant Colonel Harvey, Mr Bennet said: "Allow me to introduce you to Sir William and Lady Lucas," and the whole party were led over to the Lucases.

Mrs Bennet had sent a note to Lucas Lodge earlier thanking Lady Lucas for her kind invitation and accepting on behalf of everyone, who were all now able to individually express their gratitude to the Lucases. Thereby, in the ensuing chatter, Mr Bennet managed to omit the Collinses from the introductions.

"Alas," said Mr Collins heavily, "my dear Charlotte and I cannot attend the ball so generously to be given by my esteemed mother and father, as we are for Hunsford on Tuesday. Lady Catherine, I know, will be anxious for our return."

A number of insincere expressions of regret followed this pronouncement. Darcy rolled his eyes.

The next dance was about to begin. Georgiana remained on the floor with her partner and Darcy turned to Elizabeth. She thought he would enquire as to Georgiana's partner but instead he bowed to her and said:

"There is only one woman in the room handsome enough to tempt me. Would you do me the honour, Lizzy?"

Elizabeth blushed as Harriet smiled her puzzlement, not knowing the history of her friend and Darcy's first few meetings. The others could guess. Harvey raised an eyebrow to Kitty.

Bingley laughed.

"You see," Darcy said to him, "it does not take a kingdom."

More confused looks accompanied Elizabeth's reply that she would be honoured and followed them onto the dance floor.

"I have it from you," he said as soon as the dance allowed conversation, "that it would look odd if we were entirely silent for half an hour together. So, shall you be the first to say something, or should I?"

"Oh, sir, on this occasion, certainly it should be you."

"Very well. I shall comment that this public ball is to me no less pleasant than will be the private one to be given in a fortnight. There, how do you respond to that?"

"Yet how much more pleasant will be the private event when

we are deprived of the society of Mr Collins."

"That is a good point. I would now move on to observe that I was told by Sir William Lucas during our first dance together, which you will recall was at Netherfield, that in the sphere of dancing, it was evident that I belonged to the first circles. Such praise in such language is unusual, would you not say? Should I have been flattered? No one else has ever remarked on my dancing skills in such a manner."

"You have unusually accurate recall, sir."

"I remember everything, because I was on the verge of falling in love with you. It is all seared on my memory."

"Then you will recollect that the next compliment offered was that I, your partner, did not disgrace you."

"And neither did she, nor has she, in any way at all since. You went on to compare us as having equally taciturn, unsocial dispositions, with which of course I disagreed as to you. We subsequently indulged in a little light verbal sparring. You talked of trying to make me out. I hope that after these months together, you have found me somewhat satisfactory."

"Eminently, Fitz, which we can explore in more detail later, if you please." She smiled and he laughed.

"On another matter, I wonder with whom Georgiana is dancing. Two dances so far. If they stand for a third, I shall think there is cause for enquiry."

Elizabeth glanced surreptitiously over at her sister. Georgiana did indeed seem taken with the young man. He appeared to have charm and wit in addition to his good looks since Georgiana was laughing at what he was saying.

"I do not know. Perhaps Jane and Charles know of him, or my parents, though the Lucases must be acquainted with him."

"You know, I rather hoped that, given a few years, she and my fellow magistrate, Terence Standing, might make a match. Perhaps I should have said something sooner, but I thought she was too young and Standing, as I told you, avoids society if he possibly can."

At this point, they had to go down the dance and when they were reunited, Darcy told her that he and Bingley intended to visit London next week so that he could recover the package sent to Mary from America and if possible talk to one of the young engineers about his proposed mill. Elizabeth's heart lurched. She had put to the back of her mind the suggestion, made earlier in the week when Darcy had spoken to Mary. Now, after her dream and in view of Darcy's uncertain moods this Easter, she could not avoid the suspicion, however ridiculous she knew it was, that Darcy was going to town to meet another woman.

He had not invited her to accompany him as he had the first time. She had not then wished to go to London, preferring to stay at Longbourn and visit Charlotte Collins. Now, she forced a smile and a degree of levity into her voice.

"Upon my word, I rather fancy a few days in London myself, Fitz."

Was it fear, consternation, which she saw very briefly cross his face? Concentrating on his steps, he said dismissively:

"I am sure you would find it a tedious expedition, Lizzy, on this occasion."

"Why is that? And what of Charles?" she said as evenly as she could. "What reason does he have to return to London so soon?"

"As before, to do with his letting or selling of Netherfield. It is merely exploratory on his part. But I am seriously considering selling my London house. Building a decent-sized, modern mill, Lizzy, will take a great deal of capital and the proceeds of the London house will help. It will be all lawyers and agents. And my attempts to garner such engineering information as I am able from young Fairweather's associates."

"I see."

They stood at their places as the dance finished.

"On the way here, Colonel Fitzwilliam made it clear that he would like to speak to me. Will you save some later dances for me, Lizzy? I must go and find him now."

ELIZABETH in her turn decided that a chat with Harriet was called for and sought out her friend. She saw that Harriet and Colonel Fitzwilliam with whom she had been dancing were drawing apart. She waylaid Harriet and they took seats together at the edge of the room.

"Harriet, I hope you are enjoying your stay with us this Easter. We have certainly enjoyed your company."

"Oh indeed, Lizzy. Upon my word, I could have been bored to death in Cambridge or Derbyshire but instead I am here amongst the most cordial of company. I am most grateful to you and Mr Darcy for interceding with my parents."

"The pleasure was and is all ours. And it is certainly true that a large party adds to the enjoyment and social opportunities."

"Yes. And another ball in two weeks. I am being spoilt with social opportunities. I did also hear from Jeremy that we may be attending a concert at the Shire Hall next Friday or Saturday."

That Harriet and Colonel Fitzwilliam were on first-name terms so quickly was a surprise, as was the news of a concert.

Elizabeth raised her eyebrows. "Oh, I had not heard that."

"No. I believe it was only raised by your father when the men were outside this morning. It seems there is some urgency to obtain tickets which are selling out quickly. Perhaps your father does not want to disappoint by mentioning the event but then we cannot attend. It is some famous young violinist, I believe, from Europe."

Darcy presumably did not know of it either, having been off somewhere with Bingley this morning, perhaps planning their trip to London next week. Elizabeth's pulse quickened. Anything connected with Caroline Bingley, as was the boy prodigy, could also be connected to the present vexation attending Darcy.

"Would it be the boy, the prodigy, Caroline Bingley alluded to on Thursday?"

"Possibly. I may have been out on our walk at the time or changing for lunch. I did not hear of this prodigy. I am bound to say that if it is him, then it would be an event not to be missed. Seeing Mozart or Handel while they were still alive would have been essential."

"I suppose so," Elizabeth replied faintly. "I will ask my father."

To take her mind off the prodigy, London and Caroline Bingley, she glanced over at Darcy and Fitzwilliam. Turning back to look at Harriet, she said:

"Well, I wonder what the two gentlemen are discussing so

earnestly," though she could guess.

"Oh, Lizzy, I am so excited. I am dying to tell someone, but we must keep it a secret until the arrangements are made. Jeremy has asked for my hand and wishes us to be married as soon as possible before he has to return to his regiment. He hopes to travel to Cambridge tomorrow in order to seek an audience with my father. We will have to make some excuse for his absence. My parents are still there. My mother said in a letter to me which I received on Thursday that they expected to remain in Cambridge for at least three weeks to try to resolve the legal matters to do with her cousin's estate."

All the questions Elizabeth had asked Darcy about such a match came to the fore in her mind once again, most particularly, where the couple would live. She could hardly ask outright, so she said:

"I congratulate you, Harriet. That is excellent news. Of course, you are of age I believe, therefore the consent of your father would not be strictly necessary, though I can understand that it would be desirable for you."

And without it, would they receive any financial support from Sir Peter Layham? Elizabeth knew that this happy news should be greeted with ecstatic expressions of joy, not enquiries upon the practical aspects. She was not after all discussing a marriage of convenience with the likes of Charlotte Lucas, as she had been those long months ago. This was a love match, hopefully, though she could not overlook the fact that, for the Colonel, it may well also be a matter of some convenience. Harriet took the point in good part.

"Oh yes, Lizzy, you are right of course. I do not legally need my father's consent, but I should like to have his blessing all the same. Indeed, Jeremy has an aunt in Kent and hopes that we may visit her. He is sure that she would approve the match. I think..." Harriet looked down at her hands and bit her lip. Again Elizabeth could guess what her friend was about to say or may be finding it difficult to voice at all and she decided to save her the trouble.

"I don't doubt that the Colonel has told you that his Aunt Catherine was violently opposed to Darcy's match with me."

"Yes, Lizzy, he did. I hope you do not mind him telling me and I am so sorry that that was the case."

Elizabeth laughed. "Darcy's Aunt Catherine is not an…easy person, Harriet. I can well do without her approbation or her support in any other way."

"I understand that she is quite overbearing. Something of a harridan. Jeremy's word, not mine."

"That is certainly one way of describing her. But in any case, Harriet, Darcy's estrangement from his aunt is no great secret, so of course I do not mind you knowing. It is simply something we barely ever talk about now."

"Lizzy, you told me last year of a Mr Collins whom you refused to marry and then he married your friend Charlotte, you said. I must assume that the very Mr Collins spoken of is the gentleman here this evening with Sir William and Lady Lucas." Elizabeth nodded. "Upon my word! You must be very relieved indeed to have escaped such a match. And he is the person who is to inherit your father's estate."

Elizabeth nodded again.

"The story is highly entertaining, Lizzy, if it were not rather unfortunate. But you have Darcy instead. A thousand times more satisfactory, I would say, than Mr Collins."

"Eminently so, Harriet." Elizabeth no longer felt it ill-judged to ask Harriet where she and the Colonel would go immediately after their marriage.

"To his house in Kent, I think. And I must meet his older brother the Earl of Wareham. Jeremy's house stands in the grounds of the Earl's home. 'Tis a very grand place I understand. In any case, my parents will not have returned to Derbyshire by then. If our plans are realised, we would marry under licence in Meryton. Whether my parents would be able to attend, I do not know."

"How sad if they could not."

"Indeed it would be. But there is a small manor house within my father's estate which I think was always intended for me on my marriage until I inherit the estate, and we would of course hope to spend some of our time there. Lizzy, it is all rather rushed, I know, yet we…Lizzy we love each other."

Elizabeth took her friend's hands in her own. "Harriet, it is excellent news and you have all my love and support. Of course I will keep your confidence until you are ready to disclose your engagement to everyone. I wish we could put on a celebration for you, but maybe we can tomorrow after Colonel Fitzwilliam has seen your father."

And I do wonder what will happen if Sir Peter will not give his blessing, Elizabeth thought. Would they marry in any case or would the Colonel simply abandon the marriage plans, indeed abandon Harriet too at the end of the Easter sojourn. She could not pose this possibility to Harriet, of course. The poor girl would be devastated if the Colonel would not marry her without the prospect of Sir Peter's fortune at some point. She would ask Darcy what he thought about it later.

For now, she asked: "Will…Jeremy remain in the army?"

"I think he will to begin with, but will sell his commission soon, I fancy."

"I am sure that would be for the best."

At this point, she saw Darcy and the Colonel making their way towards her and her friend. The two couples took to the floor immediately. Harriet was positively glowing. Elizabeth so hoped it wouldn't all go wrong for Harriet. If it did, she would feel partly responsible having incidentally facilitated the meeting of the couple in the first place at Pemberley over Christmas.

There was no obvious reason why Sir Peter would not approve the match, unless he was still hoping for a titled person for his daughter, or a man of fortune or both. That apart, the doubt rested on Sir Peter's own character. From all that Elizabeth had seen of him, his immediate reaction to most suggestions was to deny his approval. It was her instinct that Sir Peter would need time to consider such a weighty matter and make a decision.

If Sir Peter refused his consent, then would the couple go ahead anyway? It would be almost like eloping, very romantic but not necessarily the best outcome.

Chapter 14

Saturday 30th March 1799

"LIZZY, William, allow me to introduce the Honourable Daniel Barton. He is a cousin of Julius Fairweather whom you knew Lizzy, on Julius's mother's side."

Georgiana had rushed over with her partner as soon as an interval in the dancing took place.

"He is down from Oxford for Easter."

Near at hand, Mr Barton was younger than Elizabeth had imagined him to be, fresh-faced and eager-looking. Further introductions followed. The gentlemen bowed to each other and Daniel Barton bowed to Elizabeth who curtsied.

"Mr Barton," said Elizabeth, "I wonder if you have any news of Julius. He certainly brightened up our gatherings before he disappeared."

She had never told anyone, not even Darcy, that she had recognised Julius as one of the highwaymen who had held up the stagecoach in which she was travelling with the Gardiners and the Philipses on their return from Buxton eighteen months ago.

"I regret not, Mrs Darcy."

Elizabeth wondered if this was true. The young man's gaze held something, a glint of interest, of knowledge unspoken perhaps.

"Well, if not Julius, then his parents, Lady Rose and Mr Fairweather."

"Yes, of course they are in touch with my family, and well set up, I understand, in Boston. I believe, Mrs Darcy," he continued, "that you have a sister, Miss Mary, who was a good friend to Julius."

"Yes. She…I…believe she has been in communication with a friend of his, Adolphus Barrant."

The knowing look returned.

"And Mr Darcy hopes to make contact with an associate of

Julius in London next week."

"That is very interesting. Mr Darcy, I may be in town myself next week."

Darcy drew two cards from his pocket. "Please look me out if you are there. I will be staying with my friend Charles Bingley at his house in London." He handed over two cards. "The second card is Bingley's with his address."

"I am much obliged," said Daniel.

"Shall we go and take some refreshment," suggested Elizabeth and they all walked to the supper room where many of the rest of their party were seated already, as well as Maria and her parents and, unfortunately, Mr and Mrs Collins.

Daniel was acquainted with Maria's dancing partner and, excusing himself and Georgiana, went over to them whereupon Harriet and Colonel Fitzwilliam joined Elizabeth and Darcy. The four of them were talking in low tones in general terms of the marriage plans, avoiding the most obvious impediment, that of Sir Peter Layham's blessing to the match, when they became aware of the approach of Mr Collins. Charlotte remained with her mother.

"Mr Darcy," Mr Collins said loudly, bowing.

Darcy returned the bow. "Mr Collins."

"I feel that since we shall probably not meet again this Easter, Mr Darcy, I must ask you whether you have given any more thought to my suggestion a week ago that a conciliatory approach to Lady Catherine would be most appropriate in the circumstances. It would be my most fervent wish to be able to deliver your good tidings to Lady Catherine on our return —"

"Mr Collins," interrupted Darcy, "no doubt your intentions are well-meant, or I hope they are, but you would do well, sir, to refrain from meddling in other people's business."

"Mr Darcy, as a man of the cloth, it is incumbent upon me at all times to have to the fore those sentiments whose object is to smooth —"

Darcy took an ominous step toward the clergyman. The volume at which Mr Collins had spoken, as though from a pulpit to a captive congregation, had attracted some attention about the supper room and the room had grown quiet. Darcy was almost quivering with rage and Elizabeth was afraid he would hit Mr Collins. He appeared to be controlling himself and said:

"Mr Collins, would you please do me the favour of leaving me alone, or I will have you thrown out."

A deep, collective intake of breath could be heard from the company close at hand. Sir William Lucas looked aghast, the rest of the Lucases and Charlotte most anxious. Such a threat constituted an obvious challenge and, had Mr Collins not been a clergyman, could lead to Darcy being called out. Perhaps it could still happen. Duels were often hushed up. Mr Collins was younger than Darcy and she had certainly witnessed his bad humour when she had refused his offer of marriage the autumn before last.

In truth, a duel was very unlikely, Elizabeth assured herself. Mr Collins would lose his incumbency and never work again as a clergyman. It was the words spoken by Darcy which would do the harm, so violently threatening were they. She knew it would be pointless to try to encourage Darcy to move away. He would stand his ground no matter what. This impression was strengthened when Colonel Fitzwilliam also moved closer to Mr Collins in a menacing fashion.

Mr Collins leaned backwards away from the cousins and appeared to be floundering. "I...er...well..."

At length, he raised his chin and said coldly, "Just as you wish." He turned and, with such dignity as he could muster, he walked back to his wife and her parents.

Oh dear, thought Elizabeth. The Colonel had, only last Easter, received hospitality from the Collinses at the Rectory at Hunsford. She assumed such would not be extended again the next time the Colonel visited Rosings. For that matter, she and Darcy would not now be likely to be welcome at the Rectory, a huge sadness to her. She could only hope that the bad relations did not extend to Sir William and Lady Lucas. They were, after all, due to attend the ball at Lucas Lodge in two weeks' time. It was something of a disaster.

Indeed, how would the Colonel be received at Rosings when presenting his new wife to Lady Catherine? But she doubted, on balance, whether the story of this public argument would be repeated to Lady Catherine. Mr Collins had been effectively humiliated. He would not wish to spread it abroad.

Elizabeth felt a hand on her arm. It was her father.

"I always knew that idiot would be trouble, Lizzy," he said.

Harriet took Elizabeth's other arm.

"This Easter grows more interesting by the second," she whispered in Elizabeth's ear.

THE remainder of the evening mercifully passed without incident. The Collins episode had put rather a dampener on the evening, at least for Elizabeth, and Darcy was in a foul mood, that is to say she could barely get a word out of him, and they did not dance another dance. Of course it was no one but Mr Collins's fault, but she had to wonder if, at other times when Darcy was his normal cheerful if restrained self, he would have reacted so violently to Mr Collins's inappropriate importunings and would instead have been able to shrug off the obvious rudeness with a smile and a shake of the head. An eminently simple reaction would have been to just walk away leaving Mr Collins in mid-sentence. Alas, not so tonight.

Georgiana remained with Daniel Barton. Harriet and Colonel Fitzwilliam and Kitty and Lieutenant Colonel Harvey danced the evening away. Mr Bennet, Mr and Mrs Philips and Mr Gardiner went off to the card room. Jane and Bingley danced several times and spoke to a number of acquaintances.

No one else came near Elizabeth and Darcy apart from Mrs Bennet and Mrs Gardiner who were sympathetic but said little of the incident, understandably not wishing to risk fanning any remaining embers to life.

Elizabeth was conscious that Lady Lucas in particular was regarding her from time to time in between conversation with her family, probably wondering how to phrase a letter telling them they would no longer be welcome to attend their ball, or even cancelling the ball altogether.

She wanted nothing more than to bring the evening to an end and to go back to Netherfield and to bed. In an effort to be alone for a time, she went off to the ladies' room and made a pretence of going through the pockets of her cloak, thankful that very few women came in. She was just deciding that she must return to the hall when the door was pushed open and Lady Lucas entered.

"Oh Lizzy," she said quickly, "I hoped I would find you in here and that you are not leaving just yet. Lizzy we cannot leave things like this. We are prevailing upon William to apologize to Mr Darcy. He is our son-in-law but Mr Darcy is quite entitled not to have his linen washed in public.

"Our families have been friends for years, Lizzy. You are Charlotte's oldest and still her best friend. She is most awfully upset and is endeavouring to quell her tears until we can be out of here. We must mend this quarrel before a breach becomes permanent. I do not care how William excuses himself, the pressure of new fatherhood, the strains of his situation as a clergyman, but he must apologize. I hope that he will come to Mr Darcy soon, and beg his pardon.

"Oh, Lizzy."

And Lady Lucas caught her in a quick embrace and was then gone before Elizabeth could respond.

She was a little more cheerful on returning to the hall, although the evening was still ruined for her and not only by Mr Collins. There was Darcy's refusal to take her to London with him, not that she really wanted to go but she was testing him by asking. There was the worry that Harriet's marriage plans would go awry. And, of course, there was Darcy himself and the puzzle of what was troubling him. She could not be happy until he had recovered his equilibrium.

She found Darcy with Harriet and Colonel Fitzwilliam and drew him aside. She told him that Mr Collins was probably going to apologize.

"Is he, by God! Well, he can drop dead."

"William, I hope that does not mean that you will refuse to listen to him."

"Listen to him! The man is an abject fool. You heard him today and a week ago. He has no idea how to conduct himself. I've no intention of letting him anywhere near me."

"William," she hissed furiously, "it is my wish that you accept his apology. The Lucases are our friends, my parents' friends, my sisters' friends. Charlotte Lucas is my very oldest friend. I cannot tolerate a rift between us all. Would you think of your family on this occasion. 'Tis more than possible that my parents and sisters will lose the society of the Lucases altogether. You must therefore hear Mr Collins and if his apology is sufficient, then you must accept it."

Darcy stared at her in astonishment, astonishment seemingly that she could contradict him. Then he sighed.

"Lizzy," he said taking her hand. "Yes, of course I will do it for you."

"Thank you," she said somewhat stiffly.

AT LAST the evening was over and their carriages were being brought round. No approach had yet been made by Mr Collins. Everyone stood outside, stamping to keep warm. The Lucases and the Collinses at last emerged from the hall.

Elizabeth surmised that maybe Mr Collins's game was to express his apology in front of all these people and thus come away from the evening as the charitable man, willing to step down from an argument and make amends. If so, it mattered not to her. She wanted a resolution to the unpleasantness.

Darcy turned and nodded to Mr Collins, his expression blank.

Heartened, apparently, by this, Mr Collins came forward.

"Mr Darcy, I have come to realise since our altercation earlier that my entreaties to you were inappropriate. I therefore apologise and beg your pardon for any offence caused."

"That is very good of you. I thank you, Mr Collins."

The two men bowed and Mr Collins started to walk towards his family. He stopped midstride, evidently noticing Colonel Fitzwilliam.

"And I have no quarrel with you, sir," he said rather pompously. "You are welcome at the Rectory at Hunsford at any time."

Thus it was over, the broken vessel of friendship mended as well as it could be.

Chapter 15

COLONEL Fitzwilliam must have risen early and Elizabeth, on herself waking not long after dawn and pulling back a curtain, saw him riding away in the gloom, the noise of hoofs upon gravel faintly reaching the bedroom. A thin, waning crescent moon hung near the tops of the trees. Frost glistened on the grass.

Yesterday evening, he had asked Darcy to make his excuses for his anticipated absence today. As to the exact reason, would Darcy say that he was delivering a letter from Harriet to Sir Peter and Lady Layham who had requested that they be kept informed of Harriet's well-being, which indeed was truthful enough. She returned to bed. Darcy had already been up, lighting the fire as was his habit and ringing for tea to be brought to them.

For once, Elizabeth found herself at a loss what to say to him. Last night they had barely spoken on returning to Netherfield, and then and now his mood seemed impenetrable. She herself felt subdued.

Unable to go back to sleep, she took up a novel but found she could not concentrate. Largely for want of something to do, she decided to try to strike up a conversation with Darcy despite his dour expression, and the most obvious subject was the prospective nuptials of Harriet and the Colonel.

"That was Colonel Fitzwilliam riding off," she said by way of an opening.

"He must then plan to catch the Layhams at church," he said.

Whether this was meant to be a joke, she could not discern.

"I wonder what the prospects are of Sir Peter agreeing to the marriage."

"Around fifty percent I would say. That is to giving his opinion today about an early wedding. He seems to like to vacillate before making any decision, especially where his family is concerned. Given a few weeks, I would say there is a good chance he would approve. Today, I think it unlikely, even if Lady Layham supports Fitzwilliam which she probably would for fear of losing her daughter."

"So they would not be married then, not yet."

"Oh, I think they would. The Sir Peters of this world cannot expect to dominate everything from their front parlours."

Elizabeth was surprised that Darcy had been willing to be drawn into a discussion. If it was an effort for him, then he did not show it.

"But Harriet and the Colonel would be poor."

"I think not. According to Fitzwilliam yesterday, on Harriet's marrying she comes into a trust under which she would receive a healthy income, two thousand or thereabouts. He similarly would also receive benefits on marrying after the age of thirty years, which he now is. And he has his house in Kent."

Two thousand pounds a year, she understood, was about the income generated by the Longbourn estate which had provided sufficiently for the Bennet family all these years. She was not sure how she was aware of the amount but it seemed to be general knowledge amongst her family, probably put about by her mother during one of her emotional outbursts.

"Oh. So that would explain why Colonel Fitzwilliam has never married."

"In part, though I do not know whether that is the reason. Perhaps he has never met the right woman. The provision would not, of course, have prevented him from marrying before the age of thirty."

"Harriet did not tell me yesterday of her trust. I have been worrying that without her parents' support, Colonel Fitzwilliam would not marry her."

"You believe his motives to be entirely financial, then?"

"It had crossed my mind." She thought about it. "And at Rosings last year he was remarkably open to me that a younger son could not marry where he liked. He implied that he would have to pay some attention to money. I flippantly mentioned the sum of fifty thousand pounds and he just as flippantly referred to double that amount. We were not being serious but my impression is that he would be seeking substantial wealth. Two thousand a year is certainly adequate, but it is hardly a fortune."

"They are not going to be exactly poverty stricken, though. He wants to marry her, Lizzy, for better or for worse. He even has his mother's engagement and wedding rings with him to give to her. He tells me that his brother approves of the match."

"I see. I believe you once told me that his older brother is not yet married either. So he is able to have the rings."

She mused for a moment that if the older brother was to die childless, that the title and presumably the estate would pass to the Colonel.

"Well," she continued, "tomorrow we must give them a party. I assume they will announce their engagement this evening."

"We will have to wait and see."

They were both sitting up in bed and he put his arm around her. "It means I cannot go to London immediately as I would prefer, since he will wish me to act as his second bondsman for his licence, and then as his groomsman at the wedding. I will have to fit my trips in between."

"Trips?"

"I will have to combine my trip to London with one to Kent to see the Turkey Mill. Bingley and I will go to London first. Then he will return to Netherfield and I will travel on to Kent. Fortunately, I have left some clothes at Bingley's London house."

Elizabeth turned away so that he should not guess her dark thoughts.

"It sounds as though you will be away for nearly a week."

"I think from Tuesday until, probably, Saturday or, more likely, Sunday."

Elizabeth was silent.

"Lizzy, what is wrong?"

Still facing away, she said, "There is seemingly some possibility of a concert at the Shire Hall on Friday or Saturday. It sounds like the boy, Max, whom Caroline mentioned on Thursday."

Darcy made no immediate answer to this, saying eventually, "Well, it looks as though I will be unable to attend."

"How convenient," she said on an impulse, not actually having any particular reason to suppose that Darcy would wish to avoid another performance by Max.

"Lizzy, what the devil do you mean by that?"

The vehemence of his tone surprised her. Had she by chance hit upon something to do with Darcy's troubled state of mind? What could she say in response?

"You are away so much this Easter. I do not know what to make of it."

"You perplex me, Lizzy. What should you make of it?" He spoke surprisingly sharply. "I want to go to Turkey Mill, you know that. I want to speak to Adolphus Barrant's associates if possible and you know why that is. I want to explore the sale of my London house. I did not think you would find these things unnecessary. You are able to be here with your family and your friend whom you so wanted to come to Netherfield this Easter. I did not realise that these would be hardships for you."

What he said was plausible. He was always so clear-headed, able to make an argument. Should she tell him of her fears, that there was another woman involved? He would probably laugh in her face, probably deservedly. She took refuge in her condition.

"Fitz, I do not feel well. I think I may spend some of the morning in bed. You carry on with whatever it is you wish to do today. I will ask Jane to come and sit with me later."

"Look at me, Lizzy," he said and she had to face him. He brushed the hair out of her eyes and scrutinised her face. "You do look a little pale, Lizzy."

He took her in his arms. "I'm sorry if I've upset you. I don't know how, but I'm sorry."

Don't know how! she wanted to scream at him. *You've been very unsettled since you returned from London and you won't tell me why, what happened to you; you must know that Bingley would not allow his sister to spend Easter at Netherfield but you have never mentioned it to me, or why he may have done that which you must also know; you are off to London again and will be away for five days and would not countenance my accompanying you. Now there seems to be something about a child violin prodigy which you find disturbing. I feel that you are not being honest with me and that I have to peer through frosted*

105

glass to try to find out what is going on.

She could hardly blame him for her dream, but surely anyone in her position would suspect some infidelity.

"Lizzy, my love, you are becoming overwrought, I can see. You are tired. We should perhaps not have ridden to Frogmore. You must take more care of yourself. Yes, stay in bed this morning. I will order your breakfast to be brought up and arrange for Jane to come and see you."

Yes, she thought, so that you can have more scheming meetings with Bingley.

This had been a mistake, her having told him she was unwell. It gave him the opportunity to shut her up here, while he was up to no good. The last thing she really wanted was to stay in bed. She wished she had ignored her urge to start a conversation with him about her friend's marriage or anything else and had left the pair of them to their individual thoughts.

She jumped out of bed. "Fitz, I no longer feel unwell. Whatever it was has passed. Would you mind getting washed and dressed in your dressing room, so that I can call for Evans to help me dress and dress my hair. It is at least half-past-seven now. We must get ready for church."

In an exasperated gesture, Darcy put his head in his hands, sighed and shook his head.

"Very well," he said, facing down at the counterpane, "if you are sure."

Chapter 16

Sunday 31ˢᵗ March 1799

THE whole Netherfield party decided to walk to Meryton Church this morning, save for Darcy, Bingley and Lieutenant Colonel Harvey who travelled on horseback. The day was cold but thankfully not wet, the ground hard beneath their boots and the horses' hoofs. They set out in good time and, before long, Elizabeth found herself walking alongside Harriet as she had hoped.

"So, Harriet, do you think we will be able to arrange an impromptu party for you and Jeremy tomorrow?"

"I would like that but I cannot say until Jeremy returns. We will need to discuss our plans."

"William is under the impression that you will marry regardless of your father's opinion."

"I am sure that would be the preference of both of us, but I feel it is wrong to dwell too much on it until we know my father's opinion."

"I understand," said Elizabeth, although she did not really. Surely Harriet wanted this marriage enough to be able to consider it a certainty sufficient to privately discuss with her friend a small celebration for when the engagement would be announced tomorrow.

"You think it odd, I can see that, Lizzy. But so much depends upon my parents' blessing, in particular the house on the estate in Derbyshire where Jeremy and I could live part of the time. I would so love to be near you at those times, not many miles away in Kent all of the time. And if Jeremy returns to his regiment, as he must in the first place, I think I would be lonely in the house in Kent. I have been thinking about it. I might rather live on our estate, or indeed with my parents. Though I know that we must go to Kent first.

"And on an announcement of the engagement to the household, I would like to be able to tell people with some certainty what is to occur regarding our residence."

"Yes, I see better now, Harriet. You are very wise to think this through."

Kitty, Georgiana and Mary caught up with them, and there the discussion had to end.

It appeared to Elizabeth that the wedding may be delayed if the Layhams did not support an early marriage. She was surprised that Harriet seemed to be retreating from her enthusiasm yesterday to marry as soon as possible, even though Darcy thought that the couple would be modestly financially secure, come what may. If anything, she had imagined that it would be Colonel Fitzwilliam who would postpone the wedding if the inheritance of the Layham's estate might be in doubt.

If Harriet did defer the wedding, she wondered how the Colonel would take the news. Would he be upset, angry even? Or would he readily accept the practical approach? Even be relieved, perhaps, if Sir Peter's reaction was to reject an early wedding.

Well, she had enough to occupy her thoughts, without worrying about her friend's future.

So she gave herself over to consideration of her conversation with Darcy this morning. She was amazed at the extent to which she had found herself distrusting Darcy. Darcy, her fine, upright, honest husband. How could things have reached this pass in the ten days since he had walked into the parlour at Lucas Lodge, returning from London a day early? That was when it had all started.

Though they sat together in church, they might as well have been in different buildings, and as soon as the service had finished, Darcy strode out, collected his horse from the waiting groom and rode off.

OVER THEIR mid-day meal, Mr Bennet announced that he was proposing tomorrow to try to obtain tickets for Friday's performance in Hertford by the Prussian violin prodigy and was very hopeful of being able to secure enough for all who wished to attend.

"How did you find out about it?" everyone wanted to know.

"Utterly by chance. I brought my March copy of the Gentleman's Magazine with me from Longbourn and had read some of it, but had thrown away the envelope in which it was delivered. Some boys had come to the back door yesterday collecting old rags and paper. The under-butler noticed the envelope and brought it to me in case I wanted it. As you know," he addressed the whole table, "advertisements are printed on the envelopes, not in the magazine itself. I had a quick look and noticed the concert."

The ladies liked to read the magazine as well as the gentlemen and were quite aware of the magazine's practice in this respect.

"That is very fortunate," said Mrs Philips. "Your under-butler is to be commended, Mr Bingley. I hope you are able to secure these tickets, Mr Bennet. One day, it may be as though we had seen Mozart perform as a child." Similar to Harriet's sentiments yesterday evening.

"I was reliably informed by the rector today that there are tickets for sale at the Pheasant Inn in Meryton and, though it is a fine inn, the regular custom is not minded to take up the opportunity to see a performance of the violin some fifteen miles away, hence there are many tickets remaining. After tomorrow, the unsold tickets are to be placed elsewhere."

"Are we going to be able to come?" said Anthony. "After all, we did include Max in our play on Friday and you all laughed. And I am probably the same age as Max if not older. And Julia must be at least two years older than he is. And…and it is not as though it is a stupid dance. Why, Mozart was…a genius. Wasn't he?"

The other children all strained forward eagerly.

"Well, I don't know…" Mr Bennet looked round the table for assistance, his gaze landing on Aunt Gardiner.

"I recall that you all wanted to attend the dance last night well enough," she said. "Perhaps we should make a list of those adults who wish to attend and then add the children and if there are enough tickets…what do you think?"

She addressed Mr Gardiner.

"My dear, I am sure they would benefit from the culture, do not you think?"

"Yes, but it is extra people to travel the fifteen miles to Hertford and back."

Mr Bennet took out his pocket book.

"I will write down the names now of those wishing to attend and we will see."

He went round the table. The only person who shook his head was Darcy.

"My regrets, but on Friday I expect to be away at the paper mill in Kent, and will probably not return until some time on Saturday or Sunday."

"Well, I am sorry, William," said Mr Bennet, "but the Pheasant only evidently has tickets for the Friday performance."

Elizabeth tried to catch Darcy's eye but he steadfastly avoided her.

"I assume Colonel Fitzwilliam will wish to attend?" Mr Bennet addressed Darcy as the Colonel's cousin, rather than Harriet as his prospective wife, of which Mr Bennet would have been unaware.

"I imagine so," said Darcy shortly.

Mr Bennet started to count the names.

"Well, I make that fifteen adults and four children. So I must obtain nineteen tickets, if I possibly can."

A discussion then took place as to the number of carriages required. Bingley had two. The Gardiner's and the Bennet's carriages were at Netherfield, as was Darcy's.

Darcy said he and Bingley would travel to London on Tuesday on horseback and then of course he would also ride to Kent and back.

"Yes, we should have enough carriages," confirmed Bingley.

Everyone was in high spirits, the unpleasant incident last night forgotten. Anthony and his brother and sisters were ecstatic.

THE REMAINDER of Sunday and the following day passed cordially enough. Walks were taken, some piano playing, singing and dancing took place. Colonel Fitzwilliam returned from

Cambridge and no engagement was announced, though Darcy and Bingley did not bring forward their plans to go to London due to Darcy no longer needing to act as the Colonel's second bondsman.

Mr Bennet rode into Meryton on Monday and obtained nineteen tickets for the concert on Friday at the Shire Hall at Hertford.

The children clapped on learning that they would be able to attend

Elizabeth cornered Harriet who said she and the Colonel were both agreed that the abandonment of the marriage plans this Easter was the best thing. Her father needed more time to consider Colonel Fitzwilliam's proposals. And her parents were much engaged concerning the complications of her mother's cousin's estate.

It would all be dealt with during Jeremy's next leave.

Elizabeth found herself disappointed. Her own experience had been that, once they had decided to marry, she and Darcy had both wished to do so as soon as possible. Of course, there were no financial implications in their case. She knew people had to be practical, but she was almost sure she would have married Darcy for a far lesser amount than his ten thousand a year.

Would she not have?

But, she recognised, there would have been no estrangement from her parents had Darcy been less wealthy. That was the thing. If Harriet and Colonel Fitzwilliam went ahead and married under licence against Sir Peter's wishes, there may never be a reconciliation. The money, she therefore hoped, was secondary to both Harriet and Colonel Fitzwilliam. It seemed so and she respected them for it.

What Darcy thought, he didn't say.

Chapter 17

DARCY left for London with Bingley. Elizabeth watched them ride away. He had not kissed her goodbye. She did not wave to him. How it could be, she did not know. They had spoken little since Sunday morning. She had never known him so unaccountably distant since their marriage. Certainly over Christmas at Pemberley he had been withdrawn after Mr Bennet's abduction, but there had been a reason for that. There seemed to be no good or clear reason for his present malaise.

Moreover, she sensed that he had somehow lost confidence in her. When she did catch him regarding her, it was with a doubtful expression, as though he wondered whether he could trust her, found her unpredictable perhaps, which seemed the very height of unfairness when it was his own uneasiness that had precipitated the difficulties.

He and Bingley certainly had many quiet chats together. What were they discussing? Caroline's exclusion from Netherfield? Viscount Morley? Lydia? Elizabeth's state of mind? The violin prodigy and his mother? Were these their topics of conversation and if so, what was the significance?

She had no firm idea.

Accordingly, she took refuge in her usual recourse at times of anxiety. She donned warm clothing and, leaving the house by a side door, made off along the same path at the back of the house along which she had walked four days ago and which led to a stream through a meadow and thence to woodland.

April had brought no increase in the temperature. Cold weather was reported all over England, worse in Scotland, and Elizabeth clutched the collar of her cloak more closely around her throat. She had no alternative but to stride rapidly along the path beside the stream, and gradually her hands and feet ceased to be frozen. The exercise calmed her down a little and made her appraise the events of Easter at Netherfield and try to decide whether her relationship with Darcy was permanently damaged.

Was it her imagination that Darcy had been looking at her askance? Could it be possible that he thought she had become mentally unstable? On Sunday before church he had certainly tried to persuade her to stay in bed. Why would a husband do that? To keep her out of the way?

And without warning it occurred to her that a husband conducting a liaison with another woman might well find it convenient for his wife to take to her bed. In a sudden rush of succeeding ideas and suspicions, she was reminded that Darcy had known Max's mother at Cambridge, which would have been what—nine or ten years ago? As night followed day, inevitably these deliberations led to an inescapable conclusion.

Was it possible that Max was Darcy's child?

The notion hit her with such force that she felt faint, her legs failing to support her. She quickly cast about for a seat of some kind, a fallen tree or a tree stump, but there was nothing. She staggered to the nearest tree and leaned against the broad trunk, breathless and dizzy, her heart hammering frantically. She slid down the tree trunk, sinking to the frosty, hard ground.

She had not been listening very attentively last week when Caroline had described Max. She had been more intent on watching Lydia's antics and wondering whether, and if so how, to intervene. Something about an attractive boy with dark hair. She shook her head, trying to picture the various portraits of Darcy at different ages ranged around the walls of Pemberley. His hair had been dark certainly as it was now, but also curly in all of them, as it was now. Caroline had not said that. Had she?

A number of events fell into place, like the dissected puzzles she had seen the children play with, making a complete picture. Sitting against the tree, she counted off the incidents on the fingers of her gloved hand. Darcy had clearly been upset on his return, a day early, from London. The mention of Bingley bringing a party to Netherfield for Easter caused him some obvious disquiet. Viscount Morley had told her that Bingley had refused to have Caroline to stay at Netherfield over Easter.

Caroline during her visit had mentioned the violin prodigy

Max whose mother had known Darcy and Bingley at Cambridge, implying that she, Caroline, had herself forged a great friendship with the boys' mother. It must be a possibility that Caroline had wished to bring Max and his mother to Netherfield for Easter, leading to Bingley's rebuff, presumably to protect Darcy.

The boy was a musical genius, so it was said. Did such abilities run in families? Darcy had no interest in music, but his sister Georgiana was an exceptional pianoforte player, better than anyone else she had ever heard.

Darcy had denied her request to go to London with him for the second time. Darcy was making sure he could not attend Max's performance at Hertford on Friday and he had reacted fiercely when she had suggested that he had contrived so to do. He was going away again with Bingley, with whom he seemed to be in frequent discussions, and was to be away five or six days, though the exact day of his return had not been stated.

He seemed to be withdrawing his love and respect for her.

She fancied that he was seeking to get away from her or get her away from him. This was pure speculation on her part she had to admit, but from it arose another terrible thought. She had earlier in the year, when her family had departed from Pemberley after Christmas, passed some time reading Mary Wollstonecraft's unfinished novel: 'Maria: or, The Wrongs of Woman' published the previous year. It had not made happy reading.

In the book, the heroine, Maria, had been condemned by her husband, a man called Venables, a *libertine*, to live in a lunatic asylum. He had attempted to pay a friend to seduce Maria so that he could leave her for being an adulteress. The attempt failed and Maria left him but he tracked her down, took her new-born child and her fortune left to her by an uncle and had her imprisoned in an asylum.

There the book ended. But it was enough to now form the niggling suspicion in her mind that Darcy could, if he wished, take similar action against her.

The reasonable side of her rejected the idea. While she knew that wicked husbands would and did treat their wives so, Darcy was not wicked. He was a good man. However, he had become distant towards her twice since their marriage, reverting to the cold stranger he had at first presented to the world on first coming to Meryton.

The first time was within a month of their marriage after her receipt of a letter from the Reverend Wilde warning of danger to her and her family. Darcy had apologised the next day, admitting that he had been jealous.

The other time was over the Christmas period after the abduction of her father from the ball at Lambton, when it appeared that her father would not be recovered and would probably die from the cold. Darcy had blamed himself for being unable to rescue Mr Bennet. The unpleasantness had lasted the several days until news of Mr Bennet's survival had reached them.

So she knew that Darcy was capable of treating her coldly, even if the episodes did not last long and were regretted by him. Another woman, however, would not be something which would go away quickly. And in any case, she could not tolerate his having a relationship with another woman.

Her strength had returned by this time. She wished that she could unburden herself, share her fears with someone. At one time it would have been Jane. But now Jane was married and would tell Bingley who would in turn tell Darcy and it would not do. Similarly, Harriet would probably tell Colonel Fitzwilliam and, in any case, she did not feel that Harriet was a good enough friend just yet to disclose to her such a sensitive matter. Even Charlotte she might once have confided in but no longer, apart from the fact that Charlotte was returning to Kent. A small sob escaped her in her isolation.

She recollected herself and struggled to her feet, resolving to confront Darcy as soon as he returned and, until that was possible, to keep her thoughts to herself and try to refrain from the wildest or even any speculation. It was only about five or six days until his return. She must control her thoughts and her emotions until he was here and could tell her the truth.

"PAPA, I hoped that I would find you in here."

On returning to the house, after discarding her cloak, gloves and boots, Elizabeth went straight to the library. The door was ajar and she walked in, forcing herself to smile and greet her father warmly. A fire blazed in the grate and she held her hands against it.

"Lizzy, my love, you look pale."

"'Tis freezing outside, Papa, but I do love to ramble. And Hertfordshire is far less wild and open than Derbyshire. I sometimes miss its leafy lanes, the little hamlets and frequent farmhouses and cottages."

"But you are happy, I hope, at Pemberley?"

"Oh yes, Papa. I am looking forward to going back. But one cannot help comparing the picturesque nature of Hertfordshire to the grandness of the Derbyshire landscape."

"You have seemed a little out of sorts, Lizzy, in the last two or three days. So, I must say, has young Darcy."

Her father missed nothing.

"I dare say being away from home is a mite unsettling—for both of us. And then there was Lydia turning up with that man Morley."

"He upset you, I think, Morley."

"He would upset anyone, Papa. As would Lydia at the moment."

However much she longed to offload some of her misgivings on another and receive advice from a sensible, sympathetic quarter, she could not tell her father what troubled her. He would be appalled at the very thought, the mere possibility of Darcy philandering with another woman. She must turn the conversation to some other topic and so she posed the question she had come here to ask.

"Papa, do you still have the Gentleman's Magazine and the envelope in which it was delivered. I had a fancy to see the advertisement about the concert we are to attend on Friday."

"I believe so. I left it..." he stretched towards a side table. "Here it is. Take the whole thing, Lizzy, magazine and all."

"Thank you, Papa. I will take it to my room and probably read some of the articles too."

She kissed her father on his head, took up the periodical, neatly re-inserted into the envelope by her father, and tripped out, with more bounce in her step than she actually felt like employing.

THERE was little additional intelligence of any great interest to be to be gleaned from the advertisement. It listed the towns at which Max Kohler would be performing throughout the month of April, the first being Cambridge tomorrow evening. The next was Hertford on Friday as they knew. After that there was a break of about a week, then the performances were to take place every two or three days on a route which would take Max in a westerly direction towards Oxford and then beyond.

Elizabeth could see that the itinerary would probably be gruelling, although the distances between the towns were not great.

She searched the magazine for any article about the prodigy himself, but there was nothing. Somewhat frustrated, she leafed through the magazine trying to find any article which might interest her. Wherever her eyes alighted, she was unable to concentrate and eventually abandoned the attempt, set the periodical in its cover aside and made ready for lunch which would be served anon.

TWO of their company, Bingley and Darcy, were going to be away for some days. Hence, it fell to Jane to put forward ideas by which the company might be entertained until the concert on Friday. She proposed singing and dancing tonight. The children were desirous of staging another of their puppet plays to which Mrs Bennet and Mrs Philips clapped their hands.

"We have many more ideas," said Anthony. "The news sheets have been full of scandal."

"Anthony!" chided his mother.

"How thrilling!" enthused Aunt Philips.

Aunt Gardiner sighed. Mr Gardiner looked on complacently.

"And tomorrow," said Jane, "Would everyone like to play cards and other games later in the day? In the morning, I have a fancy to walk to Kimpton if enough of you are agreeable."

"We would, Cousin Jane," said Colonel Fitzwilliam, "but Harriet and I have a mind to travel to Cambridge for the day tomorrow in order to meet Harriet's parents. We would be most obliged if we could take one of the carriages."

"Oh, but of course," said Jane. "I will ask Seaton." Seaton was the head coachman.

"We are most grateful, Cousin Jane. We should be returned for games in the evening."

The aims and plans of Harriet and Colonel Fitzwilliam seemed to change by the day. The last intelligence from Harriet had been that the marriage would take place during the Colonel's next leave. Now it looked as though a further attempt was to be made to secure Sir Peter's immediate support.

Cambridge, Elizabeth thought, was where Max's performance was to take place tomorrow at the Black Bear, notable for the excellent concerts given there. He would be in the town with his mother. She had considered attempting to meet Frau Lang on Friday at Hertford before, during or after the performance.

Perchance she could meet Frau Lang at her lodgings tomorrow instead. Indeed, Max and his mother may even be staying at the Black Bear or, if not, the inn would surely know where they were lodging. Before she could stop herself, Elizabeth addressed Colonel Fitzwilliam.

"I would accompany you to Cambridge, tomorrow, if you please."

Her parents and Jane looked at her in astonishment.

"I would...visit the Wren Library. And...read the *Cambridge Intelligencer*, stroll among the colleges. I would like to see the Walkerian Botanic Garden. And the apple tree which inspired Isaac Newton — or a descendant of the tree."

There was silence, and therefore Elizabeth continued.

"As William is away, I would welcome a diversion. And," she turned towards her Aunt Philips and then her Aunt Gardiner, "you will recall, Aunts, how pleasurable it was to visit the Physic Garden in Oxford. I should like to compare it to the garden in Cambridge."

Mrs Philips looked at Mrs Gardiner who looked at Jane who looked at Mr Bennet.

Elizabeth turned to Colonel Fitzwilliam.

"You can drop me near the Little Rose and I would meet you there later."

At last there was a response.

"Lizzy," said Mr Bennet, "if you wish to wander around the centre of Cambridge, then you should have a chaperone."

"I do not know why that should be. I have walked many times alone to Meryton and to Lucas Lodge."

"Lizzy, Meryton is a small town where we know everyone. Cambridge is…a strange place. And much larger."

"But the Garden is hardly any distance from the Little Rose where Colonel Fitzwilliam and Harriet will be. Nor far from Trumpington Street. Everywhere is near Trumpington Street. Including the Wren Library and the Garden and the Little Rose."

She had noticed these places on the recent trip to Cambridge just a week ago with Darcy and Colonel Fitzwilliam, the latter of whom had hoped at that time to persuade Sir Peter to allow his daughter to come to Netherfield for Easter.

The Black Bear was also no great distance away according to its address on Market Street, and she had all day. No doubt Colonel Fitzwilliam and Harriet would haggle with Harriet's parents incessantly.

"But why, Lizzy? Why, when you could go for one of your rambles around the estate here?"

"I wish to go to Cambridge, Papa. And the Colonel and Harriet are to go there tomorrow. Why cannot I?" She tried not to raise her voice petulantly.

If I were a man, she thought, no one would object, but it would be pointless to say this.

"Then send a footman with me, if it must be," she said instead, hoping that she could lose the man if necessary.

"I don't know," said her father, shaking his head. This was often a sign that he was relenting. In truth, he had no power over her. She was a married woman and her husband was away.

She looked at Colonel Fitzwilliam and Harriet. "You have no objection, I suspicion?"

They could hardly decline, staying as they were in someone else's house, enjoying his fare and using his carriage.

The Colonel turned questioningly towards Harriet, who nodded.

"You would be most welcome, Cousin Elizabeth," he said.

Harriet smiled.

She senses some intrigue, Elizabeth thought. I know that expression.

She might, she decided, confide in Harriet. She must talk to someone. The need to do so was brimming over.

"Well, Lizzy, if you are set on visiting Cambridge with your cousin and your friend, then I suppose there is no great harm in it," her father said. "Which footman do you suggest, Jane?"

She thought for a moment. "George, probably."

It was a good choice. George was a tall, handsome young man about a year older than Elizabeth. The maids' eyes lit up whenever he was near at hand. She had even noticed Georgiana glancing at him with admiration. He was always immaculate in his dress, his coat fitting like a glove. Elizabeth could imagine the maids vying with each other to sew on a button, brush and sponge down his coat, launder and iron his shirts, polish his shoes. In his speech, he could have been a member of the gentry. One had to wonder where he had learned such pretty manners. No doubt he would rise to the position of butler one day.

She reflected on the inequalities which kept in his place a young man who could have moved in the upper echelons of society had he been more high born.

At least George would not show her up and she amazed herself at the sudden thought that if Darcy was consorting with another woman, she could do worse than form a liaison with young George. A few days ago, the very notion would have appalled her. How far had she come down the road of the theoretical acceptance of licentiousness. Her cheeks grew warm as her imagination expanded to encompass an actual act of intimacy with the young man. It was something she would have to firmly cast from her mind tomorrow as he escorted her around the streets of Cambridge.

Chapter 18

Tuesday 2nd April 1799

DARCY peered around him, wondering at the area to which his friend had brought him. They had alighted from the hackney carriage somewhere near Tower Hill and Darcy had followed Bingley in what he thought was an easterly direction through a warren of streets and lanes which had gradually grown narrower and darker.

"Bingley," he said at last, "are you sure that this man Benjamin is a gentleman if he has to resort to establishments such as those we are passing to indulge his passion for gambling?"

"He has sunk quite low in fact," answered his friend. "His credit is not good. He is not sufficiently well-placed to gamble at such clubs as Whites or Brooks where vast fortunes are won and lost. That does not mean that he is any less reputable. He must join games at private houses whose owners' business it is to arrange games with some refreshment and other diversions."

As to the 'other diversions', Darcy had to exercise his imagination.

"Lately, he has partaken of hazard. You will know that it is almost impossible to win at hazard. The bank is almost always held by the owner of the gaming house."

After a few more paces, Darcy observed, "I suppose that since gambling is illegal, the more remote is the gambling house, the safer it is from the law."

They had arrived in London at midday and Bingley had wished to get on and ascertain where Benjamin was due to play today and then proceed straight to the gambling den so that Darcy could witness the man at the table and form an opinion. Bingley was anxious to return home as soon as possible and pleaded urgency so that if Darcy approved, tomorrow he could instruct a lawyer who could agree a fee with Benjamin and the investigation could begin.

Furthermore, he wished to leave London quickly so as to lessen the chances of Caroline or any other of his sisters or acquaintances or friends finding out that he was in town. Apart from visiting a gambling den, he had every good reason to be in London, as did Darcy, but he was not used to intrigue. Darcy knew that his friend would be discomposed by having to lie by omission as to his real purpose for being in London and visiting a lawyer.

For Darcy's part, he had to meet up with young Barrant's associates which was a nuisance, he had decided. Though these young men were scholars of mathematics, there was no reason why they would know anything about paper making. Once this business with Benjamin was over and done with, he wanted to travel as soon as possible to Maidstone and see the Turkey Mill, stay there for as long as he could to learn something useful.

On arrival at Bingley's house in South Street today, he was delighted to find that a letter from Mr Thomas Hollingworth of Turkey Mill awaited him, applauding his interest in papermaking and warmly inviting him to the mill as soon as he was able to journey there. Before setting out on this mission to glimpse Matthew Benjamin in his natural habitat, he had hurriedly written a short letter to Mr Hollingworth saying that he hoped to set out for Kent tomorrow. He had business to attend to in London and could not be sure when he would be able to leave, but he was hopeful of arriving at Turkey Mill on Thursday. Forthwith, a footman had been despatched with Darcy's letter to the General Post Office in Lombard Street.

Perhaps, when he had secured Barrant's package for Mary, he would hand it to Bingley to take back with him to Netherfield in advance of Darcy himself returning which might not be until Sunday or even, he now thought, Monday.

They continued to plod along the filthy passages, strewn with noxious, noisome waste of all kinds, ignoring the pleadings of beggars, or contriving to do so in Darcy's case. He threw pennies here and there as he went. The importunings of street ladies were of no interest to either gentleman.

Darcy's thoughts were of Elizabeth as they ventured deeper into this unwholesome neighbourhood. He had left her this morning with no affection. It was heart-breaking for him, but he so dreaded that he might break down and blurt out to her his fears about Max Kohler. He had to ascertain the truth before admitting anything to her.

On Sunday morning, she had overwhelmingly given the impression that she had some intelligence regarding the boy. But how could that be? Surely she could not have read his moods so accurately. Surely he was not so transparent. She was not a mind-reader. So how had it come about that his trip to London and Kent had caused her to conclude that he was intentionally avoiding the concert in Hertford on Friday evening?

Indeed, attending the concert would have been awkward for him, but he certainly had not contrived to avoid it. He, Elizabeth and Georgiana only had a few weeks left in Hertfordshire and would then have to return to Pemberley. Therefore, having found out about Turkey Mill, he must visit it while the opportunity existed. Had he had no reason to visit London and then move on to Kent, of course he would have attended the concert with the rest of the party and taken his chances. He would have sat in the audience with others and then left and taken the carriage back to Netherfield. The possibility existed, of course, that some of the party might wish to meet Clara and Max after the performance, that is if they were available. In that case he would have made the best of it, kept a low profile and said as little as possible. He suspected, though, that the Netherfield party would wish to get on their way since the journey home would take a couple of hours.

But Elizabeth's words, *How convenient*, had jolted him. He had reacted more strongly than he would have wished. That alone may have caused Elizabeth to be suspicious about Max. But even then, why would she be?

Had someone said something to her, and if so who?

Morley?

But what did Morley know? Or Caroline? Or, for heaven's sake, Lydia? Much as he distrusted Morley, he felt that the culprit, if there was one, was far more likely to be Lydia. Lydia was a wild card. She wouldn't need a reason to create discord and disruption. If she had found out something, or just suspected it, then she would heedlessly spread it abroad.

And what of Wickham? Although he had been at Cambridge at the same time, he could not have known anything. They had moved in different circles.

And yet, he was undeniably an attractive man with a most engaging manner. Might it be that he had knowledge springing from some more intimate association himself with Clara Kohler as she had then called herself? Perhaps Clara had spread her attentions more widely than he or Bingley ever suspected. Perhaps even...my God...perhaps Wickham was responsible for Max Kohler being abroad today, entertaining society in England with his musical skills.

"You are very thoughtful, my friend," said Bingley at last.

"I continue to think about Max. You know it has just occurred to me that Wickham could be responsible for Max's existence, just as well as me. Or even Morley."

"Hmm, to the best of my recollection, it was only you she was interested in. You and she seemed to spend all your time together."

Thinking back, Darcy had to accept that this was so. During the few days Clara had been in Cambridge, his allowance being generous, he took a room at an inn where they could meet at all hours. They must have returned to the college at some times, but his memory was hazy on the subject.

"She went back to the college at intervals to visit her father. She hired a carriage from the inn which of course I paid for. And there was a party one early evening. I came back for it but then decided against it because the host was Morley. I couldn't say whether Clara attended."

Instead he had collected some clothes and books and spoke to a Fellow on a paper he was producing. He had been away for several hours.

"I gave it a miss as well, Darcy, for the same reason. I suppose Wickham might have been there."

"I've been wondering whether Wickham at least befriended Clara in Cambridge and she might have obliquely alluded to me in conversation in such a way as to ignite suspicions. If so, he might have said something to Lydia more recently after Clara and Max had turned up in London. I know he is away in Ireland now, but before he left, he could have fed Lydia a web of rumours concerning me, Clara, and now Max."

Except that such conjecture may not be false at all.

"Or," Darcy said, "they may have corresponded after he left. I am worried that she or someone else may have said something to Elizabeth."

"Why do you say that?"

"We have not been in accord in the last few days. I think she suspects something. I mean something other than me being more taciturn than usual."

Bingley did not reply as they walked farther on.

Yet if Clara could have met Wickham in Cambridge and fired up suspicions of a liaison between Darcy and herself, then equally she could have met Morley with the same result.

"Bingley, you told me that Clara and Max had stayed with Morley in Devon when they returned from America. That must mean that they have remained in communication with one another over the years."

"I could ask Caroline the next time I see her."

They walked on and Darcy resumed his deliberations.

What was it he had said to Elizabeth last Thursday? "...he will likely surmise that I may yet be of some use to him in the future." This being his opinion why Wickham was unlikely to have told Lydia of his attempted elopement with Georgiana. The same could well apply to any tales Wickham might otherwise have spread about Darcy and Clara.

Now, Morley was different. He would have no expectations of Darcy. Elizabeth might have been told something by Morley directly, or via Caroline, which Elizabeth's fertile mind could have worked upon until she came to the conclusion that...

No! It was unthinkable! He told himself that these speculations were very tenuous indeed, and more the product of his troubled mind than any serious beliefs.

Darcy's heart again quickened at the enormity of his trouble, which was that until he knew the truth about Max, his speculations could be endless. Nevertheless, with all his musings about Max, an emotion he could only describe as affection for the child was beginning to steal into his heart. He pictured the boy's face, his sweet smile, his skilful young fingers deftly moving quickly up and down the fingerboard of his violin. If it transpired that he had to admit to Elizabeth that his own blood ran through Max's veins, then the situation would have to be managed. It simply would have to be.

"We are here." Bingley recalled Darcy to the immediate purpose of their journey to this most undesirable of destinations.

Darcy took in his immediate surroundings and the house in front of them. It appeared to be in good order.

"How do you know," Darcy asked, "where Benjamin is gaming this afternoon?"

"I told you. I was at school with his son, with whom I remain in contact."

"That hardly answers the question, Bingley."

"Happily for him, my friend has married an heiress and did not inherit his father's predilection for gambling."

"I am still none the wiser, Bingley."

"Well, Benjamin may not be here. If he is not, then I am wrong. But...shall we go in?"

Darcy had little option. A pretty maid answered Bingley's knock and the pair of them were admitted to an anteroom, dimly lit by candles.

"Please wait here," he said to Darcy.

Darcy rolled his eyes but did so. There were a number of doors leading out of the room and a set of thick curtains. Bingley walked through the curtains and Darcy could hear him warmly greeting another man.

At length, Bingley returned.

"Was that the son?" Darcy asked. "Because if so — "

"No. If we meet anyone, neither of us is to call the other by name, remember. Follow me."

Darcy was taken through one of the doors which led into a dark, narrow passage with various twists and turns in a roughly anti-clockwise direction so far as Darcy could tell, interspersed with several short flights of steps going upwards. They reached a corridor with a number of doors to right and left. Bingley opened a door to the left and they walked into the room beyond.

It was windowless, in complete darkness. Bingley shut the door quietly.

"Bingley," Darcy whispered to his friend, "how the devil do you know your way around this place?"

"If you must know, I had something of a problem with gaming myself at one time."

Darcy peered in his friend's direction but could see nothing of his face in the pitch black of the room.

Bingley took his arm and steered him to the wall opposite the door. A pinprick of light was visible in the wall. In fact slightly bigger than a pinprick, and then Darcy realised.

He placed his eye to the hole. Bingley, he felt sure, was at a similar spy-hole farther along the wall.

"And keep very quiet," Bingley told him in hushed tones. "No coughing, no sneezing."

DARCY had never witnessed such intensity at a gaming table. He had only ever played for pennies, and for the pleasure of the game. Not to profit from it. It was whist, so far as he could tell. Bank notes were passed across the table. And silver and gold coins.

"Which one is he?" Darcy said in as quiet a voice as he could muster.

"Can you not tell?"

They were looking down on the scene from their eyrie, hence people's faces were difficult to see. Darcy assumed that the main purpose of such an arrangement was to observe whether any cheating was taking place.

"I regret not."

"Well, obviously, he is Jewish."

"Well, obviously, not having come from a family in trade such as yours, Bingley, I am not easily able to distinguish a Jewish man from any other, especially from above, unless he is very evidently so."

"He is the third man to the left of the dealer at the moment, wearing a purple cravat."

"Thank you."

They watched the game. Benjamin was very conspicuously

losing. The pile of cash in front of him diminished by the minute and eventually was gone. He then wrote notes, presumably I.O.U.s, and the game continued. He drank occasionally from a glass of what could have been wine or port. He frequently mopped his brow.

Darcy watched intently. After about half an hour, he felt a warmth on his right ear and flinched. He realised it was Bingley.

"Have you seen enough?"

They moved away from the wall.

"I would like to hear him speak."

"I do not think that is possible."

Darcy's attention was drawn by another spot of light in the wall to their left. He went over, and gave a small chuckle after a few seconds.

"An example of one of the other diversions, if I am not mistaken."

"No doubt."

They placed their eyes once again to the peepholes over the gaming room. After a short time, they saw Benjamin rise, bow to those around the table and disappear through a set of curtains. Darcy wondered if he had gone to partake of one of the 'other diversions' or would be making his way home.

"Perhaps we can now leave ourselves," said Bingley. "It should be dark outside by now."

"I suppose so. It is a pity we could not hear anything."

"Have you not read any of Benjamin's articles in the Gentleman's Magazine? You could surely gauge his intellectual abilities from that."

"I am sorry. I have never noticed. Have you read any?"

"Well, no, but… I think there are a stack of the magazines at my house. We can spend the evening working through them. We shall have nothing better to do since we cannot go out anywhere."

Chapter 19

THE carriage rattled over the roads and through the towns and villages which had started to become familiar; Hitchin, Baldock, Royston, Harston and at last Trumpington, meaning they were nearly there.

The usual number of stops to change the horses afforded opportunities to stroll outside. Elizabeth took Harriet's arm several times but there was never long enough to discuss any subject in detail. Elizabeth gleaned from Harriet that if her parents, or more correctly her father, had grown amenable to an early wedding, then she and the Colonel would start to make the arrangements immediately, hoping for an early return by Darcy so that he could act as second bondsman.

Harriet understood, however, that the licence could be granted, if necessary, the very day of the wedding. They would wed in Meryton and thereafter travel straightaway or soon after to Jeremy's brother's house Pakeleigh Abbey in Kent and, during the course of their stay, try to visit Lady Catherine at Rosings who, Jeremy thought, would be likely to make a substantial marriage gift to Jeremy as, of course, would the Earl of Wareham added to whatever dowry her father would offer.

"So you must have reason to believe that your father has changed his view since Sunday."

"My mother sent a messenger with a letter which I received yesterday before lunch telling me to try to go to Cambridge with Jeremy as soon as may be. She thinks that a little further persuasion from both of us will secure his approval. She greatly favours the match. She knows I long to be married and she is looking forward to having grandchildren. She would have liked more children herself, but it did not come about. I therefore sent a short note back by return saying that we would try to travel to Cambridge today."

During their further stops, Harriet became expansive on the subject of the furnishings they would order for Jeremy's house on the estate. Although she had yet to see the house, she could picture it all, she told Elizabeth. There were also many family portraits in the main house which they would be likely to receive for their new abode. Elizabeth had no need to enquire of the size of the house.

"'Tis a large house, Lizzy," she was told. "Much larger than any rectory. Indeed, it is hardly smaller than Grinstone Hall."

Grinstone Hall was the seat of Sir Peter Layham, the house in which Harriet had been brought up, though Elizabeth had never been there.

"And it is set in one thousand acres with magnificent gardens and many servants. I shall not have time to be lonely or bored while Jeremy is away. There will be so much for me to arrange."

Elizabeth admired her friend's ability to regard the gift of marriage with such a practical eye to the financial and material benefits to be derived from a match which carried the approbation of both parties' families, it was to be hoped. Of course, there was nothing wrong with this. She reminded herself that Darcy had not needed anyone's approval or financial blessing to their own marriage. He was entirely his own master. It was a happy position to be in.

Elizabeth was finding it difficult to get used to the Colonel being referred to as Jeremy. He had always been Colonel Fitzwilliam to her. To her, he didn't look like a Jeremy. He was not fat, but rather thickset, probably strong and muscular under his fine clothes and uniform, as a soldier doubtless needed to be. The name Jeremy suggested to her a person of slighter build.

"Oh, and I hope my parents will be able to travel to Kent soon to meet Jeremy's family."

Which would include Lady Catherine, Elizabeth presumed. She wished she could be there to witness Lady Layham's impressions of Lady Catherine. And no doubt her efforts to contain her mirth at the other's preposterous pomposity. Sir Peter, she decided, would almost certainly approve of the aristocrat's attempts to dominate those around her and use her position to assist her in such an aim. Between them, they could probably create enough pointless and unwelcome interference to discomfit a whole county. They should do very well together.

As the two women hurried back to the inn at Trumpington, Elizabeth hoped that her friend's wishes and plans would come to pass. A wedding, with the attendant celebrations, would be a pleasant culmination to this Easter at Netherfield which had otherwise presented such a disturbing mixture of surprises, for her at least.

IT WAS already quite late when Elizabeth and the footman George were deposited outside the Walkerian Gardens; at least one o' clock; this after Elizabeth offered, as courtesy required, that she should first enter the Little Rose and greet Harriet's parents. But Harriet and Colonel Fitzwilliam both assured her that it was unnecessary; some opportunity would be bound to arise later, they said, and they insisted on taking her on to the Gardens in the carriage and then doubling back to the Little Rose.

The walk to the Black Bear, her real destination, was some further distance. Making a decision, she said to George:

"There is an inn I would visit, George. I will return to the Garden later. The inn is in Market Street. A reputable place where concerts are frequently held."

"I know the street, ma'am."

"Then please escort me there."

"It would be my pleasure, Mrs Darcy."

He walked a couple of paces behind her, as his station demanded. She found that she was not exactly sure of the way.

"We should turn right here, Mrs Darcy," said the footman, stopping and, with a half-bow, extending his right hand.

"Thank you, George."

Another minute found them outside the Black Bear.

"Would you wait outside, George."

The young man hesitated. Clearly, he knew very well that his task today was to ensure her safety.

Elizabeth indicated the benches either side of the front door.

"I will have a pot of their best ale sent out for you, George. And a plate of their finest fare."

He lowered his head and frowned, but he could hardly argue

with the mistress of Pemberley House. Everyone had heard of Pemberley and its master Mr Darcy. If he upset the mistress and therefore Mr Darcy, he might very well lose his position. It was unfair, she knew, but had to exercise her authority to achieve her aim. By any reasonable standard, she would not have to submit to an escort today or resort to demeaning the man by offering him a meal in exchange for her freedom. Because that is what it amounted to.

"Thank you, ma'am."

WITHIN the dim interior of the inn, she ordered George's ale and meal to be sent out to him as soon as possible. She asked for it to be speedily dealt with. If he was kept waiting too long, he might venture in to investigate. She was hungry herself, increasingly so these days as her girth increased and the child grew within her.

A bill outside had announced the performance tonight of a foremost musical prodigy, Max Kohler. She sat and ordered the same meal for herself and had no alternative but to order weak ale to accompany it. She would not trust any cordial in an inn to be made up with boiled water.

As a maid served her, she produced from her reticule a handbill advertising tonight's performance, having taken up an abandoned bill from another table. The maid would surely know if Max Kohler and his mother, Mrs Lang, were staying here. And so she asked the maid if it was possible to see Max's mother now or later in the day.

"She is not here, ma'am," said the serving maid.

"What do you mean?" Elizabeth looked at the bill. "The performance is going to take place in six hours. If they are staying in this inn, they must be here by now."

"I do not know where they are staying, but they are not here."

Elizabeth sighed and produced her card and handed it to the girl.

"When they arrive, would you please inform Mrs Lang that Mrs Fitzwilliam Darcy of Pemberley House in Derbyshire wishes to urgently speak to her. I may be found at the Little Rose on

Trumpington Street. Would you send a messenger there.

"And, pray, as to where they are staying tonight after the performance, whom should I ask?"

"You could leave a card with Mr Scarborough, ma'am. He arranges the musical recitals."

"And where would I find Mr Scarborough?" asked Elizabeth, finishing her meal.

"In his office on the floor above. Where the recitals are held."

"Thank you."

AS ELIZABETH ascended the stairs, she looked out of the window and saw George on the street below pacing up and down and peering alternately into the ground floor windows and in both directions along the street. He had the pot in his hand and so was at least enjoying his ale.

She soon located the room where performances must take place, a large area with velvet-covered chairs lined up facing a dais at the head of the room. Chandeliers, yet to be lit, hung overhead. At the back of the room, tables had been laden with glasses and plates, but as yet no food or wine.

With six hours to go before the performance, Elizabeth had to wonder whether Mr Scarborough would not still be at home with his family, enjoying a meal with them. Or catching a few hours of sleep.

Leaving the concert room, she almost collided with a man coming out of a door opposite.

"I beg your pardon, ma'am," he said. "May I help you?"

"I am looking for Mr Scarborough, sir."

"Well, you have found him. I am he."

About forty years of age, he had a kindly face and was well dressed. Elizabeth was immediately reassured.

"I am hoping to speak to Mrs Clara Lang, whose son Max Kohler is performing here tonight. I thought that she and her son may also be staying here at the inn."

"I regret not, Mrs...?"

"Oh, I am sorry. I should have introduced myself. I am Mrs Fitzwilliam Darcy of Pemberley House, Derbyshire." The name seemed to mean something to the man. "My husband and I are staying over Easter at Netherfield House near Meryton in Hertfordshire."

She produced another card and handed it to Mr Scarborough who scrutinised it.

"Well, I am sorry to tell you, Mrs Darcy, that Mrs Lang and Max Kohler are not staying here. I expect them at about six o' clock if that is any help to you. They were here earlier in the company of a gentleman when Master Kohler practised with a local pianoforte player, but they are not here now."

Elizabeth frowned. "Then, do you know where they are staying in Cambridge?"

"I regret not, Mrs Darcy."

She must have looked very crestfallen, for he shook his head and said, "Performers often stay elsewhere, Mrs Darcy. The more prominent the performer, the more splendid their accommodation."

"You alluded to a gentleman who was with them. Do you know who he was?"

"I regret not. A tall, dark-haired gentleman, that is all I can tell you."

Elizabeth's heart lurched. Clara and Max and Darcy? Could it possibly be? Behaving like a family?

She turned away abruptly, unable for now to face Mr Scarborough, to face the possible truth which had been staring her in the face for days.

A LITTLE earlier in the day as Elizabeth, Harriet and Colonel Fitzwilliam were still being driven through the high roads of Hertfordshire, Darcy was exploring an area of London with which he was not completely unfamiliar. This morning on rising he had glanced for the first time at the folded piece of paper on which was written, so he had been led to believe, the address where he might find one of Adolphus Barrant's friends, and was surprised to see that it was one of the most exclusive addresses in London. Mr Hurst, the husband of one of Bingley's sisters, had a house in Grosvenor Street, but Barrant's friend's address was actually in Grosvenor Square itself. Presumably it was his parents' house.

Darcy's own house which he was now hoping to sell when the present tenants vacated it was in Upper Grosvenor Street, similarly close to his destination. It was hardly any distance from Bingley's house in South Street to Grosvenor Square. There was barely any point even in taking a hackney carriage, but at Bingley's insistence he did and also ordered the driver to take a circuitous route to the young engineer's home to lessen the possibility of being seen by either of Bingley's sisters or Mr Hurst or any of their friends who knew him.

It seemed faintly ludicrous to Darcy, but Bingley was adamant that he desired no contact with them which might lead to his having to explain himself. He made it clear that he was sick and tired of the subterfuge of the last two weeks and did not want to add to it by any further departures from the truth he might have to make, however minor. Of course, Bingley was only here to help him, therefore Darcy had to accede to his friend's wishes.

His knock on the door was quickly answered by a footman to whom Darcy presented his card. His position was slightly difficult since he did not know the name of the friend of Adolphus Barrant or indeed anyone at the house and he began to regret coming when the footman looked at him askance. He gave such information as he was able.

"I am calling on behalf of Miss Mary Bennet of Longbourn, Hertfordshire to collect a package sent to her from America by Mr Adolphus Barrant whom I understand is associated with your master."

It sounded far-fetched to him as he said it.

The footman scrutinised Darcy's card and led him to a day room facing onto the gardens.

"Please wait in here, sir."

The room was richly decorated and appointed as one would expect at such a prestigious address. He looked out at the ornate scene of ladies and gentlemen walking and horses and carriages driving over the paved area surrounding the central plantings of tall trees within the railings, hoping that he had not been noticed stealing, his head down, between the hackney carriage and the door of the house by anyone familiar with him.

Tiring of the view, he paced impatiently around the room, wondering how Bingley was faring with the lawyer. Benjamin was to be paid in coinage rather than notes to preserve anonymity. He was to be offered a small advance payment of eighty pounds. The total to be offered was three hundred pounds however, Darcy and Bingley had agreed that double or even treble these sums may well be required and the lawyer was to be given room to negotiate. Darcy wasn't at all sure that their highest offer would be a large enough sum to tempt a confirmed gambler to make extensive enquiries on behalf of some unknown person, but he was not prepared to lay out any larger sum than nine hundred if it came to it, on top of the lawyer's fee, especially since the creeping admiration had begun to overcome him of a boy who could play so expertly at Max's age.

But, he decided, it was as much a mistake to harbour tender feelings for the boy as a morbid dread of the consequences if Max should turn out to be—

He paused there as always, reluctant to address his principal fear and at that moment he was saved the trouble of suppressing his thoughts as the door opened and a tall young man entered the room and bowed to Darcy who returned the gesture.

It was none other than the Honourable Daniel Barton whom he had met just days ago at the ball at Meryton. Darcy smiled through his surprise and slight embarrassment, given that Barton had so recently watched him nearly attack a man publicly over mention of a family falling-out. Barton looked amused as well he might and smiled even more broadly as he said:

"I most enjoyed the local Meryton ball on Saturday, Mr Darcy. I hope that your lovely sister Miss Georgiana is well and that I may have the pleasure of meeting her again in the not too distant future."

Darcy assured Mr Barton that his sister was indeed very well. He disliked the use of extravagant sentiments and, using such sober language as he could summon, he said: "I am sure that the pleasure of the event was heightened for my sister by taking the floor with such an agreeable partner on Saturday."

"My family frequently entertain here and if you are to come to town again soon, Mr Darcy, I pray you would bring your family and you would be most welcome to attend one of our soirées."

Nothing could be clearer than Barton's desire to pay court to his sister. It was certainly not something to which he was averse, especially as this young man, who could be no more than about twenty-two, was as self-possessed as anyone he knew and clearly of a wealthy family. At the moment, however, he had other objects more close to his heart and his ambitions during this trip to London than to seek to advance a romantic attachment for his sister.

"That is most gracious of you, Mr Barton. I think unfortunately that it is unlikely that I will return to London again before our departure for Derbyshire in a few weeks' time. And before I even go back to Hertfordshire on this trip, I have business to attend to in Kent which will take me several days. I hope to leave for Kent tomorrow, perhaps even today."

He was itching to get on with the expedition. If he left today, it inevitably meant that he would be unable to take any steps towards the sale of his London house, but so be it.

"Several days? Oh, that is a shame. However," Barton rallied, "perhaps we will see you all again at the ball to be held soon by Sir William and Lady Lucas."

It was only narrowly possible, and no thanks to him, that they would be attending and Darcy assured Barton that they would be there.

"Now," he said, "I believe you have an associate of Adolphus Barrant staying with you at this address and that he has a package for my wife's sister, Miss Mary Bennet, from Mr Barrant. I have been told that Mr Barrant has been corresponding with her from America."

"Yes. He is looking it out. He is most anxious for Miss Mary to receive his documents and writings as soon as may be. And I think I hear him coming now."

Footsteps sounded in the hall outside and another young man strode through the open door holding a thick package tied with string. He stopped after a few paces, placing the package on a side table while at the same time appraising Darcy. Darcy in his turn took in the other's appearance. He had an intense, rather predatory expression and reminded Darcy of nothing so much as a bird of prey, his eyes piercing and his nose aquiline, hooked, though not unattractively so. His lustrous, thick, reddish-brown hair was worn to the nape of the neck and was swept back from his face.

Rather incongruously, he sported a full black beard.

Darcy felt that he should somehow recognise the man, while yet convinced that he had never met him before in his life.

"Good morning, Mr Darcy. Allow me to introduce myself. My name is Adolphus Barrant." He advanced further into the room and the men bowed to one another.

"Ah. I had expected to see a friend of yours, but I am delighted to meet you, sir."

"I am lately come from America and am soon to return." Mr Barrant's voice indicated some urgency.

"Mr Darcy," said Barton to his guest, "is not to return to Hertfordshire for some further days." He sounded anxious.

"But," said Barrant, aiming his piercing gaze at his host, "'tis a new moon tomorrow."

Darcy began to grow a little irritated, nay alarmed, at the turn of the conversation and the seriousness with which it was delivered and wondered whether to tell these men that Bingley would most likely return to Netherfield tomorrow and would deliver the parcel, whatever was in it, to Mary. Of what significance, he wondered, was its most urgent delivery?

"Perhaps," he said, "you will enlighten me as to why my sister Mary should receive this parcel with such alacrity. I was assuming that she was to receive some writings from you. How can it be so pressing? And what have the phases of the moon to do with the whole thing?"

He assumed, in fact, that Barrant wished to catch a boat presumably at anchor in the Pool of London and that a new moon heralded a high tide enabling the vessel to sail. However, what had this to do with Mary?

The men frowned at one another and did not reply immediately.

"Mr Barrant," Darcy sighed, "if you wish to board a ship within the next few days, then that is your business. But I cannot have my wife's sister become embroiled in some possibly dangerous enterprise. If," he indicated the bundle on the table, "this is merely a literary offering, then I imagine that Mary will survive quite well without it for the time being."

"It is just a draft novel, Mr Darcy," said Barrant, "from which Mary was intended to benefit."

"Then show it to me."

"Very well."

Darcy approached the table, watching as Barrant pulled at the bow tying the string around the poor quality wrapping paper and drew the paper apart with his long fingers. On the middle finger of his right hand was a silver signet ring, the bezel of which was decorated with some sort of family crest.

Darcy took up the item within. It was of good quality paper, the pages sewn together to form a hand-written manuscript. It bore the title 'A Boston Story: The Life and Times of Edward Saunders, An English Scientist'.

He flicked through it, but it was a thick document. Barrant could have secreted anything within these pages. And what he had heard here suggested that he might have.

"Very well," he said, "my friend Mr Bingley is to return to Hertfordshire tomorrow, and he will take this with him to Miss Mary Bennet. I hope that it proves to be of value to her."

"Indeed, I am sure that it will."

Barrant re-tied the bow and handed the package to Darcy.

"Gentlemen, I must be on my way if I am to make arrangements for my journey to Kent. I bid you farewell, Mr Barton, Mr Barrant," said Darcy, nodding to them in turn.

"I thank you, sir," said Barrant, "for assisting with the delivery of the manuscript to Miss Mary and bid you good day."

"Good day, Mr Darcy," repeated Barton.

The men bowed and Barton showed him out of the house. Darcy walked to his waiting hackney carriage, his head down as before, clasping the package under his arm.

His journey back to Bingley's house in South Street took hardly any time. Bingley was not yet at home. He swept into the drawing room where a fire was blazing. His first instinct was to hurl the package into the flames but he stood back and reconsidered. To his mind, there was no urgency in Mary receiving the manuscript nor any necessity for it to be destroyed if it contained only harmless fiction.

He was pretty saddle-sore and if he took a carriage or stage-coach instead of riding, he could read the manuscript on his way to and from Maidstone and give it to Mary at the weekend if he adjudged it to be suitable. Therefore he took it upstairs and squeezed it into his portmanteau packed in readiness for his journey.

He decided on balance to travel by carriage. Stagecoaches with others were usually unpleasant; the close proximity to others, the odours, the coughing and sneezing, the non-stop prattle of some people. One of Bingley's footmen could drive the carriage for him, while he read inside. If Bingley needed a carriage, then he would hire one. The journey would be likely to take seven or eight hours and if he set off soon, he could make it to Maidstone by this evening, though an overnight stop en route if it was necessary would not be a huge hindrance. He started to will Bingley to return home in short order so that he could set off.

Coming again downstairs, he searched through the news sheets Bingley left in heaps in the library with no care to arrange them in any order. His friend might as well throw them out as keep them like this. It took Darcy nearly half an hour to locate the papers for September 1797 and thereafter and sort through them and eventually he found what he was looking for.

Two young men of high birth had been arrested and charged with offences relating to the holding up of stage coaches and were languishing in gaol awaiting sentencing, thought to be the gallows. A third had turned King's evidence and was charged with assault and would likely be deported. A fourth had disappeared. An artist's sketch of this fourth man depicted a sharp-eyed character with a hooked nose and full lips. Julius Fairweather, the article claimed, was the ringleader of a gang of rich young men seeking to increase their fortunes by holding up coaches and stealing the passengers' valuables.

The sketch, despite the exaggeratedly hooked nose and rubbery lips, bore more than a passing resemblance to Adolphus

Barrant without the beard. A reward of eighty pounds had been offered for information leading to the arrest of Julius Fairweather, whose whereabouts were unknown.

Elizabeth had told Darcy that she thought that Julius's aim and that of his friends was to raise funds to experiment on galvanism because his rich industrialist father would not finance him. No stagecoach passenger had been hurt, she said.

Darcy chuckled. No wonder the young man wished to put distance between himself and the British mainland as soon as possible.

But still, however worthy were Fairweather's aims, Mary must not be endangered.

It was nearly midday and Darcy called for a meal and wine so that once Bingley had arrived home, if all had been suitably arranged with the attorney, he would leave immediately for Kent.

"WHAT do you think? Do you think he will give it to his friend to take it?"

Back at the house in Grosvenor Square, the cousins debated whether Darcy was to be trusted, by them at least.

"No, I do not. He is a good fellow," said Barrant, "but he is most concerned for his family. Yet I know what Mary wants, what is ultimately in her best interests. He does not."

"He is no doubt concerned that she may fall into danger."

"Well, she does not have to agree with it herself, does she?"

"No, indeed. Do you have another copy of the manuscript and the other document?"

"Yes, of course. I am a scientist. I think of everything. He is merely a land-owner."

"Well, we can send it to Mary by a special messenger."

"Or better still, I could take it myself."

"No, you cannot be seen on the highways and in the towns and villages. I would go myself, but if I take it, Darcy will never let me near his sister again. I am sorry, cousin, but the package must appear to have come from you. You will have to send a footman from your parents' home in London. And, if Mary doesn't come, notwithstanding you must catch the packet to

Falmouth when it sails. You must get away from here."

A DISAPPOINTED Elizabeth had spent the rest of the time available to her walking disconsolately first to the Wren Library and then to the Walkerian Garden, feigning an interest she did not feel. To pass the time, she wandered to the Garden via the Colleges, admiring the architecture. George trailed behind her. They were due to leave Cambridge at four o' clock, hence there would be little possibility of meeting Mrs Lang. It was immensely frustrating. *Someone* must know where she was staying.

Just in case Mrs Lang might have come back to the Black Bear, she led the patient George to the inn and again obliged him to wait outside while she made her enquiries within and left a third card with the manager whom she insisted on seeing, admitting to herself that it was absolutely pointless.

Her traipse around Cambridge did, however, give her a chance to reconsider the probably foolish notion that Darcy was here in Cambridge with Clara and Max. He was bound for London yesterday to collect a package for Mary and to make more enquiries about the sale of his house. Thereafter he was to travel on to Kent to the paper mill. Bingley had left Netherfield with him and would have had to partake in the deceit if Darcy's true destination had been Cambridge and Clara. Elizabeth did not regard Bingley as a man capable of such dissimulation.

And had not Darcy given his card to the Honourable Daniel Barton on Saturday inviting Barton to look him up at Bingley's house? He would hardly have done so had he known that he was not going to be there.

There were many tall, dark-haired men in the world. Common sense told her that Clara Lang must have some assistance in arranging Max's itinerary, their accommodation and means of transport, hiring halls for his performances, suitably advertising engagements, having bills printed and distributed, collecting and banking the money and many more tasks. It would take organisation. Mr Scarborough had alluded to a local pianoforte player to play with and support the young musician. Clara would doubtless need a secretary to ensure that everything ran smoothly.

And Clara was a woman essentially alone in the world. A secretary would serve the duel function of providing an escort.

None of this convinced Elizabeth that Darcy was not embarked on a liaison with a woman, merely that he would probably not be in Cambridge today, yet it was some comfort.

In a state of greater composure, Elizabeth arrived at the Little Rose. She found the Layhams, Harriet and Colonel Fitzwilliam and made desultory conversation with the Layhams, mostly with Lady Layham. They sat in a small private parlour which the Layhams had taken. Lady Layham wanted to hear full particulars of her explorations of Cambridge and she was glad that she had taken some notice of the exhibits at the Wren Library and the plantings in the Garden, since Lady Layham seemed to have visited these places and more herself.

She could see that Harriet was bursting with happiness. Lady Layham, a twinkle in her eye, related the news that her daughter and Colonel Fitzwilliam were to be married very soon. Sir Peter nodded. It was the most one could expect of him. She and Harriet's father, Lady Layham said, were desirous of attending the wedding in Meryton next week. Would Elizabeth deliver a letter which she had already written to her sister, Mrs Charles Bingley? Yes, of course she would be honoured to do so.

Elizabeth entered into the spirit of the happy news with such apparent pleasure as she could summon and admired the diamond and ruby engagement ring already on Harriet's finger. It fit her perfectly. It suddenly occurred to her that, apart from Colonel Fitzwilliam and Harriet, only she and Darcy were aware of the possible impending nuptials. She had no doubt that the rest of the Netherfield company would be delighted at the news that a wedding was to take place and would see the couple off with every blessing and good wish for their future together.

On their return to Netherfield, Harriet could indulge herself and entertain the company by repeating all the details to which Elizabeth had been treated that morning. But she must insist on Harriet giving her time to explain things to Jane before the rest of the company were told.

Having resolved only yesterday to share her unhappy burden with her friend when the opportunity arose, she now hesitated.

Should she risk marring her friend's happiness with her own unsavoury suspicions regarding Max Kohler's paternity? Perhaps she still could. Harriet appeared to love gossip and scandal. She might well relish the tale Elizabeth could tell. Even though it cut Elizabeth to the quick to think of her most bitter apprehensions becoming a source of guilty entertainment for her friend, her need to discuss it with someone was overwhelming.

She cast a quick glance at Colonel Fitzwilliam. He sat close to Harriet, occasionally touching her hand, an indulgent expression on his face, still no doubt too uncertain of Sir Peter's blessing to venture to express his own sentiments. If she was any judge of people, Colonel Fitzwilliam was a happy man, very satisfied with today's outcome and not only for financial reasons. She hoped he did love Harriet and would be a good husband to her.

Chapter 20

DINNER at Netherfield had been delayed for the return of Elizabeth, Harriet and Colonel Fitzwilliam and was then further delayed for Elizabeth to seek an audience with Jane who took her to the small parlour and gave instructions that they were not to be disturbed.

"Jane, it is, I am sure you will agree, the best news that my friend Harriet and Colonel Fitzwilliam are to be married next week in Meryton. I have known of it since Saturday, but Harriet did not wish to marry without her parents' approbation, even though she is over the age of consent and did not legally require her father's consent."

"I am sure she would not wish to marry against her parents' wishes, Lizzy. It is very wise of them to await her parents' pleasure. Their whole future may depend upon their family's support. I am sure neither you nor I would have wished to marry if our parents had objected."

"No indeed, though our cases were full different. Both of our husbands are wealthy. Had our parents opposed our matches, then it would have been a very eccentric position for them to have adopted in the absence of some deeper family or personal objection."

"Luckily there was no such impediment for us. Poor Harriet, to have such a father as you have described to me who would seemingly put impediments in the way of his daughter's happiness out of, so it seemed, a petty habit he had fallen into of protesting at anything without thought or consideration." Jane smiled in her calm manner, so familiar to Elizabeth. "But it is all swept away now. I am sure that Sir Peter is a good man at heart. Tell me Lizzy, her parents will surely wish to attend the wedding. I must therefore write to Lady Layham with all speed to invite them to stay here. And we must put on a celebration for them. The Colonel, I suppose, will have to take a room at an inn in the days preceding the wedding."

"Well, I hoped you would wish to invite Harriet's parents here, indeed so that Harriet should be married from here. As to an inn, I suppose Colonel Fitzwilliam, Jeremy, could stay at Longbourn House, which would mean that William, as his groomsman, would have to stay there too, but I will have to ask Mama and Papa and also of course see whether Colonel Fitzwilliam would be agreeable — and William, naturally." The last three words came out rather harshly and Jane raised her eyebrows.

"'Tis nothing, Jane. I am only tired from today's trip to Cambridge."

"Do you know when he will be returning?"

"No, not exactly." Her irritation was impossible to hide from her most perceptive sister. To avoid further enquiry, she hurried on: "And Jane, before I forget, I have here a letter for you from Lady Layham. I do not know what she says. Most likely I think it is to thank you for your hospitality to Harriet thus far and no doubt express her happiness at the news."

Elizabeth rose and smiled weakly down at Jane. "Now, I must quickly go and tell Harriet that you are aware of her situation and that you would invite her parents to come here. Then of course I must change for dinner. I will see you in the dining room shortly, Jane."

Elizabeth hurried to the door and left the room, Jane peering anxiously after her.

WERE it not for the news of the wedding next week, the company over dinner would have been reasonably muted with the two principal gentlemen still abroad. But the congratulations of the ladies and Lieutenant Colonel Harvey filled the room. Elizabeth did her best to join in the gaiety for a second time today. Messrs Bennet, Gardiner and Philips smiled benignly. The children were ecstatic at the prospect of a party and yet another chance to put on one of their plays.

The party was set for Sunday when it was hoped that Darcy would have returned. Bingley was expected tomorrow, though in the event, he returned late that night.

Everyone wanted to know about the wedding arrangements in more detail and from their short discussion earlier, Jane and Elizabeth were able to tell the company of the invitation to Sir Peter and Lady Layham to reside at Netherfield for the duration so that Harriet would be married from Netherfield. Colonel Fitzwilliam expressed the hope that Darcy would return swiftly. He proposed to visit Meryton Rectory tomorrow and put in hand the necessary licence and arrange a date for the wedding next week.

Harriet was eloquent in her recital of their anticipated movements for the immediate period after the wedding as already recounted to Elizabeth, though Elizabeth was glad to see that she refrained from mention of the financial rewards which the couple expected, though she did comment on the size of Jeremy's house and the thousand acres which accompanied it.

She once again extended her hand that the engagement ring might be admired.

Elizabeth decided that it would be more suitable to discuss with Colonel Fitzwilliam in private the offer of Longbourn House as his residence immediately before the wedding and that of Darcy as his groomsman. Of course, she had to speak to her parents first on the subject in any case. Her opportunity came sooner than expected as everyone passed from the dining room to the saloon.

"Lizzy," said her father, coming alongside her, "I can see that you are still not yourself. Would you not come away with me into the library for five minutes to tell me what it is that ails you?"

"I...yes indeed, Papa." Elizabeth smiled up at her father and quickly agreed to the request largely to avoid the questioning looks of others if they perceived some minor drama unfolding in their midst.

His reassuring hand guided her away from the gaggle of people, into the hall and to the library, where a fire was still burning.

"I asked for it to be made up today," said Mr Bennet. "I spend much time in here as you know, despite the paucity of the literature on offer. There is usually something of interest."

He drew up a chair in front of the fireplace, close to his own.

"Come sit with me, Lizzy," he said, patting the chair.

She did so and, anxious to forestall the questioning she anticipated, she launched into her denial before any accusations had been made.

"Papa, I do so appreciate your concern. It is most kind and considerate of you. But, Papa, nothing ails me. As I said to you before, I am away from home. A good deal of travelling by coach and carriage has taken place and it is tiring and vexing. That is all."

"And yet today you chose to go to Cambridge, four hours in a carriage and four hours back, when you could have rested here at Netherfield and walked the lanes and pathways which you expressed to me yesterday you so loved in their contrast to the landscapes of Derbyshire."

"As I said yesterday, Papa, if you recall, I especially wished to visit the Wren Library and the Walkerian Garden. We shall be gone from Hertfordshire all too soon, Papa, and I wanted to see these places while the opportunity still existed."

"Lizzy, you are only yet twenty-one years of age. You have decades left to explore places of your choice."

"And what of you, Papa?" she said, growing angry, "What further places would you like to explore before you expire? Or are you settled in Hertfordshire, to moulder away here until you die and Mr Collins moves in?"

She regretted the words immediately. There was no cause at all to abuse her good father for kindly enquiring of her low spirits, obviously very evident to him.

"Papa, I —"

"Do not trouble yourself, my child. I understand. I may seem to be a shrivelled old relic to you and the rest of my daughters, a museum exhibit almost, but I do retain the vestiges of human feeling. I believe that my years on this Earth have imbued me with some insight into human behaviour, Lizzy. And I can discern when one of my daughters and her husband are for some reason at odds with one another only five months after their marriage which seemed so happy. An ideal union made, it seemed to me, in heaven, to which I and your mother, I am sad to say, could never aspire. And yet now it appears so damaged. You are my daughter, Lizzy. I love you. I only want to help you."

Elizabeth crumpled under his short speech. Her hot tears coursed down her cheeks and with them sobs escaped her.

"Papa," she wailed, unable to voice her worst fears and he of course took her in his arms and she leaned on him

Her father said no more and minutes of silence ensued. Eventually, he broke the silence.

"I see from the Gentleman's Magazine that the child prodigy Max Kohler is to perform in Cambridge tonight. Would that have anything to do with your journey to Cambridge today?"

Elizabeth's sobs redoubled but she did not reply.

"Lizzy, though I may be getting on in years, I am not an idiot."

Elizabeth looked up at her father through her tears. "No, Papa, I know of course you are not."

"I am as capable as you are of leaps of imagination, of stitching a number of facts together and reaching a conclusion."

He was again silent for a time, then said:

"Now, Lizzy, are you ready to tell me what it is which causes you such pain and grief? If you really do not wish to do so, then of course I will respect your privacy in this matter and leave it be."

At length, Elizabeth moved away from her father and sat up straight, despair wrought heavy across her face. She swallowed and gathered herself.

"Papa, I think that Max Kohler may be his child from a liaison with Mrs Lang ten or so years ago when he was at Cambridge, or I think at least that William is afraid that this may be the case."

"Well, I have been thinking that this possibility may be one reason for the disquiet which you and he seem to be experiencing."

"You have discerned this and yet you do not even know about Caroline Bingley's exclusion over Easter from Netherfield."

"No, Lizzy, I know nothing of that. I do not understand that

149

and I will let that pass. But tell me, Lizzy, does Darcy know of your doubts?"

"No. He has never said anything of the sort."

"So it may not be the case? It may not be what he thinks at all?"

"Papa, I am fairly sure that it is. And now he is off for days to London and elsewhere. He would not let me go with him. I fear he wishes to distance himself from me. He —"

"Lizzy, I would caution you not to let your imagination run away with you. A child from an association when he was a very young man is one thing. A thing, I am sorry, which you would have to bear if it be the case, and actually a not terribly unusual event. But to extend that into some sort of entanglement he may now be having is a mistake, Lizzy, pure and simple. He would naturally be discomfited at the thought of a child he heretofore knew nothing of. But that is probably as far as it goes. If he is off somewhere at the moment, then it is probably to try to find out about Max's parentage, to achieve some certainty on the subject. Not to be unfaithful to you if that is what you were thinking."

Elizabeth peered into the flames as though they may hold the answer.

"Papa, until I know everything, I cannot be happy. That is the truth. I am sorry that this coincides with Harriet's engagement. I do not wish at all to cast any pall of misery over her happiness and have been trying to keep my worries to myself. You know now, but I trust you will keep my fears to yourself.

"I must address you on another matter, though. May I now ask you, would you agree to Colonel Fitzwilliam residing at Longbourn House immediately before the wedding and also William as his groomsman, otherwise they will have to take a room at an inn?"

The sudden adjustment from the theoretical to the practical seemed to take Mr Bennet by surprise and for a moment he looked blank.

"I...well yes, of course they may stay at Longbourn. I will send word."

"Thank you, Papa. I will tell Colonel Fitzwilliam, and of course Mama. And William when he does return."

"Which I am sure will not be too long. Where is it that he has gone?"

"To a paper mill in Kent, Papa, where they manufacture large sheets of paper, far larger than elsewhere."

"That seems reasonable, I must say. And think you that he will visit his aunt in Kent while he is there and endeavour to reconcile with her as Mr Collins so hoped that he would, sufficient to cast a shadow over last Saturday's proceedings?"

"I think not, Papa. Any such reconciliation will have to wait."

"I see."

"Papa, as you have raised this subject with me, would you assist me on Friday evening to attempt to meet Mrs Lang, Max Kohler's mother, so that I may endeavour to ascertain from her Max's paternity? I had hoped to meet her today at Cambridge as you have guessed, but I could not find her. She was not staying at the inn where the performance was to take place tonight and no one knew where she was staying."

"Then, yes, of course, Lizzy. I will assist you in any way that I can. And I, too, will of course speak to your mother of the arrangements for Fitzwilliam and Darcy to stay at Longbourn next week. Now, we had better go to the saloon and continue with the jollity.

Chapter 21

Wednesday 3rd April 1799

AS HE quitted the attorney's chambers, Matthew Benjamin pulled his coat more closely around him, not only against the cold, but in order to conceal the bag of coins which the attorney, Blake, had handed to him at the end of their lengthy encounter. The writer suspected that the lawyer's motive in arguing so strenuously for a lower fee was directed mainly at keeping as much cash for himself as possible rather than to minimise his client's outlay. He had never trusted lawyers.

Benjamin had tried his hardest to trip Blake up and cause him to accidentally disclose the name of his client or something about him, but, garrulous as Benjamin knew most lawyers to be, the lawyer had been tight-lipped on the subject of who this anonymous person could be and why he or she wished to ascertain the paternity of a boy violinist. Even the sex of the person had not been disclosed, Blake referring repeatedly to 'my client'.

The writer had likewise been unmoveable as to the methods he would use and whom he might approach to assist in his enquiries.

On first arriving at Blake's office, he had not the least idea why he had been summoned. He had assumed that it must be in connection with one of his more pressing debts. But not so.

"Do take a seat, sir," the lawyer huffed and puffed as he lowered his bulk into his leather-covered chair and offered Benjamin a glass of port. Benjamin declined.

"Oh, come man. 'Tis too tedious to drink alone. What sort of a Puritan refuses a drink after six o' clock? And from all I hear, Mr Benjamin, you are no Puritan."

Benjamin decided not to waste time arguing the point.

"Perhaps you would tell me first, Mr Blake, why I am here."

Blake poured himself a large glass and settled back in his chair, passing an appraising eye over his visitor, a vague smile crossing his ruddy features.

"Very well. I have asked you here, sir, in the expectation that with your wide knowledge of London society you will easily be able to assist my client who wishes to know the paternity of the boy musician, Max Kohler, who has lately been gracing the saloons and concert halls of the city. You have no doubt heard of him."

"Indeed I have. And who is your client and what is his interest in this child prodigy?"

"Naturally, as an attorney, I am not at liberty to disclose my client's identity nor even whether it be a man or a woman. As to the reason for the enquiry, in all honesty, sir, I do not know myself. Neither is there any necessity for me to know, much less you. I have an offer to make to you and that should be more than sufficient. My — "

"I have undertaken enquiries in the past. I am frequently asked to do so. But this relates to a child. I ask, of course, about your client, Mr Blake, because if your client's interest in the boy is of an unsavoury nature which may lead to some harm befalling an innocent child, then I cannot partake of any investigation which may assist your client."

"I had no idea, sir, that you were a person of such scruples." Blake laughed.

The words and the mirth were, Benjamin determined, uttered with the object of undermining him, no doubt to secure a lower fee and reduce him to a lesser state in which he might go ahead with the commission regardless of the possible outcome to the boy but he would not be intimidated. It was not unknown for children to be borne off and used in nefarious ways. Quite why this particular child might be of interest to anyone who wished to exploit him, apart of course from his musical gifts, Benjamin couldn't speculate. But he would certainly not partake of any plan which may bring the boy into danger.

"Sir, are you able to vouch for this client of yours as a reputable man…or woman…whose interest in the child is purely…perhaps one of family connection and not otherwise."

"God, use your imagination, man! As I have said, I have not been told why the paternity of this child could be of interest to someone, but it would not be without the bounds of possibility that a gentleman may think that Max Kohler may be his child or that a woman may suspicion that he may be her husband's natural child.

"And, I would say, sir, that I do believe my client to be a person of substance, an upright person who would no doubt be indignant at your insinuations as to his or her character."

"And why is that, Mr Blake; that you believe he or she to be a person of substance?"

"I can say no more. I have said enough, I hope, to reassure you. Now, may I put to you my client's offer, that we may not be here all night debating inconsequential and wholly unnecessary points and can get on with the negotiations proper?"

Benjamin sighed. He, too, wished to see what reward may be on offer. If it be a paltry sum, he would walk out.

He had not come initially prepared for a round of negotiating but the preamble between the two men had quickened his interest and stimulated his senses. He had laughed out loud at the first offer of an advance payment of eighty pounds.

Eighty pounds!

This client, this man, because he was sure it must be a man, would have to be a simpleton to seriously offer such a miserly sum. Therefore, he decided it was merely a first offer and that far more could be extracted, as turned out to be so in the end. He would, he told Blake, have to grease palms in order to set any enquiries in motion.

His debts were very pressing and he had taken the lawyer as high as he dared go.

On several occasions he had made as though to walk away when it appeared that no more money was to be offered. The risk of having his false show called out caused him to become breathless and his heart to palpitate though, with his gambler's impassive expression, no outward sign would have been visible to most people. In truth he would have accepted half the sum of money on offer, but the risk-taker in him sensed a rich person behind this enquiry and, eventually, he had secured an advance of two hundred guineas, the amount now clutched to his chest, and a total sum of eight hundred guineas plus a further one hundred to cover his honest disbursements.

As he walked away from the lawyer's chambers in Holborn, having not consumed a drop of port himself, the church clock struck seven. It was late to commence an enquiry, but this was not the first time he had been asked to wheedle out intelligence of one sort or another. His circumstances were well known and thus his constant need for remuneration above what he could make from writing which, sadly, was very little.

Used to being ever vigilant at the card table, he kept his eyes and ears open at all times and was confident that within the hour he could discover where Mrs Clara Lang and her boy had lodged while recently in London and press the appropriate people for such particulars as may shed light on the issue he had been asked to investigate, without if possible saying outright what it was he wanted to know. It would be difficult, he knew, and others may well guess what his goal was but he was nobody's fool. He would not put power in the hands of others who might thwart his aims and assume the benefits of finding out what it was he wanted to know.

And as to the lawyer's request for the boy's birth certificate to prove his paternity, Benjamin laughed to himself at the foolishness of Blake and his client. He had said nothing to the lawyer, but such would never be possible. The child might have been born anywhere, indeed was said to have come from Europe, from Prussia.

Clara Lang and Max Kohler had different family names, which was because, Blake had said, she was married at one time but he had no other information about that. Well, if it was relevant, Benjamin mused as he walked along the dimly-lit street, he would just have to find out.

"MRS PETTIGREW, it is a great pleasure to see you again. I have missed our little discourses and am sorry that our paths have crossed so infrequently in recent years."

"Indeed, Mr Benjamin, but since I do not frequent the gaming houses, it is hardly surprising. Tell me, how is your boy? Well, I trust?"

"Very well, I am pleased to relate. Casper married the daughter of a merchant. They live in Liverpool and have three children. His father-in-law has all manner of interests in the North-West, therefore I hardly see them, but we write frequently, or at least I write to him. I receive a reply about twice a year."

"Well then, you should take yourself off to Liverpool. London does you no good. I told you so five or more years ago."

"And you, Mrs Pettigrew? You appear to be doing well." Benjamin looked about the well-appointed parlour in the house near Covent Garden. "You still let out apartments, I understand, and act as housekeeper to the tenants. 'Tis a good business."

"As a poor widow-woman, I have had to make the best of it."

She looked far from poor to Benjamin.

"I believe that on occasion you let out the house as a whole."

"You are well informed as ever Matthew. If needs be, yes I do."

The use of his Christian name reminded him of their close connection for a short time some years ago, from which she had withdrawn as his gambling habit had become yet more serious. A widower for many years, he had enjoyed several other liaisons since then which had all gone the same way.

Still, he reflected, better in some respects being a gambler than a drunkard. And very fortunate indeed it was that the person who possibly held all the intelligence he needed on this occasion had turned out to be this lady he knew of old and thus he was not having to carve out an understanding with a stranger. Though as the lawyer and no doubt his client surmised, Benjamin maintained a wide circle of acquaintance.

"Mathilda, I need some information for which I am prepared to pay."

She shrugged. "You must have had more luck at the tables than hitherto, if you have money to spare."

Her fishing exercise got her nowhere.

"Do you have any lodgers at the moment?" he said. "I assume that the whole house is not presently let."

"How much are you willing to pay, Matthew?"

Benjamin smiled. "If I am as well-informed, Mathilda, then you are as astute as ever."

"I have to make a living and as you have observed, the house is not let at the moment." She pursed her lips. "I could have had a whole year's lease but had already let to a person who only wanted it for two months so I lost the longer let."

Then she looked angry with herself for having given anything away.

His face remained blank, while he was thinking that two months sounded about right.

"I will pay you sixteen pounds if you can tell me about the last few tenants to whom you have let the house or apartments. For, say, the last six months."

And then he entered his second round of haggling that day. They settled on twenty-five pounds. To toast their accord, she rose, went to a cabinet and returned with a decanter and two glasses.

"I hope you will take a glass of canary with me, Matthew."

"Thank you. Just a very small one for me."

She poured the wine, both large glasses despite what he'd said, and he sipped at his while she took a mouthful.

"So, Mathilda, tell me about your tenants for the last half year."

He well knew already the layout of the house which could be split into two separate apartments by locking some of the connecting doors. Also that there was a much smaller third apartment in which Mathilda herself lived if the whole house or both apartments were let and she acted as the tenants' housekeeper.

"Show me the money would you, first, Matthew."

"Of course," he said, producing the coins and placing them on the small table between them. Twenty-three guineas, a half sovereign and seven shillings to make up the twenty-five pounds. Mathilda eyed the money with evident satisfaction.

He had taken a hackney carriage home after leaving the lawyer's chambers and there had locked most of the guineas away, coming out again with eighty guineas and some individual coins.

"What is so special about the tenants of *my* house?"

"It is not your tenants in particular, Mathilda. Those who have visited London during the period I mentioned, wherever they may have resided, are of possible interest to some. I can say no more, so please do go on."

She seemed satisfied with this very general explanation. She then proceeded to list a ten month let of the whole house which ended in December, four short lettings of two weeks each of the two apartments in January, and then the two month let of the house for February and March which was to have ended just before Easter, but then the lady wished to stay on and only quitted on Sunday this week.

"And what about the tenants? What were their names and what were they like? How many in each party and what were they doing in London?"

A great detail of dreary detail followed. Benjamin resisted the urge to yawn and took some notes regarding the earlier lettings. One never knew what might be useful in the future though it was all very tedious. He asked appropriate questions about the earlier people and continued in the same vein with respect to the last letting to Mrs Clara Lang which had ended only three days ago.

He was told that the lady had a son, a famous violinist who was only nine or ten years old with engagements all over London, that Mathilda suspected Mrs Lang had a lover though they were so discreet she hardly got a look at the man, and that it was thought that she was a Roman Catholic.

Benjamin carried on with his notes and nodded sagely as these particulars emerged.

"I am surprised, Matthew, that with your gamblers brain you need to write things down."

"Believe me, Mathilda, I would make notes during a card game if 'twere possible, though there is a good deal of mathematical logic in card games. There is very little logic of any kind, I would say, in most people's behaviour and movements."

"I can certainly agree with you there." She took up the bottle, pouring herself another glass and allowing the bottle to hover over Benjamin's glass. He put his hand over his nearly-full glass and shook his head, returning swiftly to his questioning.

"Now, Mathilda, if Mrs Lang hired your house for February and March, then she would not have left until Sunday in any case. But you say her letting should have ended before Easter."

"Well, I was talking simply. Yes, she rented and paid for the whole of March, but she told me she would be leaving about three or four days before Easter. Then suddenly about a week before Easter she said she would not leave and would stay over Easter. It was most inconvenient. People had enquired to hire the apartments over Easter and I had almost settled terms with them. I would have charged extra over Easter."

Mathilda looked at Benjamin defiantly.

"Once she had given up the house and left, I would have been quite entitled to let it to someone else notwithstanding she had paid to the end of March. 'Tis the law."

"Of course, Mathilda," he said soothingly. "You are quite right. And how is it that the man who visited Mrs Lang could do so without being seen?"

"The child Max was out performing almost every night and they did not return until very late. I cannot stay up until dawn for my tenants. I would hear noises and sometimes looked out of the window and saw a man with her and the child by the light of their carriage lights or the oil lamps in the street but they throw a very poor light. I could not see him clearly other than that he was tall and well-dressed, I think. And he was gone by the morning which is why I said they were discreet. Not like the lady who visited once or twice. She brought men to the house and made a great deal of noise."

"Was it the same man as visited Mrs Lang?"

"No, I do not think so."

"How do you know? What did she look like? Did you get her name?"

"Only the chamber maid saw her in the mornings, once with a man. It gives the house a bad name. I asked Mrs Lang not to have her here again. The maid said the lady was very young, genteel apart from her loud behaviour. 'Tis all. But the tall gentleman continued to visit Mrs Lang."

"You said Mrs Lang and her son and the man came here by carriage at nights. Was it a hired hackney carriage?"

"No. 'Twas a private carriage. It also came to pick them up earlier on, but without the man."

A shame, thought Benjamin. Had it been a hackney carriage

he could have made enquiries of drivers.

"I assume the carriage did not stay parked in the street all night."

"No, it was driven off. Whether it came back in the morning or the gentleman took a hackney carriage, I could not say. I heard no carriage, so he might have walked away and caught a hackney at the market."

So, there lay some possibility of further enquiries.

"Regarding Mrs Lang's proposed departure before Easter which she postponed, where do you think she was going to stay over Easter had she left here as planned?"

"Exactly where, I do not know. I think it would have been somewhere in the country. A great estate somewhere."

"Very well. And the suspicion of Roman Catholicism? How did that arise?"

"Again it was the maid who saw a statue of the Virgin Mary and a rosary. Oh, and another thing, she was attended by a doctor during her stay."

"Why was that? Was she ill? Who was the doctor?"

"She did not seem ill. But I can tell you who the doctor was."

Benjamin wrote down his name. He knew of the man and would visit him for any information he might provide, confident that a financial reward would loosen his tongue. As to a Catholic priest, there were several secret places of worship of which he knew. He would look them out tomorrow.

But he was no nearer to discovering who Max Kohler's father was. Would that he had received this commission while Mrs Lang was still staying at the house, then Mathilda, or perhaps the maid, could have been prevailed upon to search Mrs Lang's documents while she was out.

"Do you think that the man who visited Mrs Lang was Max Kohler's father?"

A reasonable question, he thought.

"I regret that I have no idea."

"Well, he would most probably be her husband, would he not?"

"In my experience, husbands do not flit about in secret to visit their wives."

"No. I expect you are right," he said heavily, realising that he was finding out little of any value. "Did she leave anything behind, any papers? Letters, old bills, notes, news sheets, maybe artefacts to do with her religion or where she worshipped? A Bible, say, or a book which may have been inscribed?"

He immediately regretted the reference to documents. It demonstrated a special interest in Mrs Lang. A knowing smile spread over Mrs Pettigrew's face.

"She left nothing behind to my knowledge. But I think I see now what it is you are seeking, Matthew."

He shrugged carelessly, but said nothing.

"So, you are working for an organisation spying on Roman Catholics, ensuring that they are not exceeding their rights."

Benjamin had not anticipated this and, while not readily agreeing with her supposition, he did not either suggest otherwise. It certainly suited his purpose if this is what she suspected rather than the true object of his enquiries.

"Then did you or the maid see any of her papers while she was here? I know how curious maids can be." He did not include housekeepers in this observation.

Mathilda appeared to be thinking.

"I could possibly ask Hattie, but she would need to be paid."

"Is she here now?"

"No. Her mother is ill and as I have no tenants I have given her leave to visit for the evening."

"She is a maid of all works I take it."

"Not entirely. I have a cook and a scullery maid. And a boy who runs errands, does jobs, sweeps the yard and so on. But Hattie does a large part of the work here."

He wondered whether he might ask to see the principal areas of the house occupied by Mrs Lang in order to carry out a search. No, he decided, that would be going too far, and in any case a mother and son who spent most of their time moving from town to town according to the boys' engagements would probably travel very light.

To deflect any suspicions that he had a particular interest in Mrs Lang, he went back over some of the points concerning the other tenants. It was all very tiresome. Then he asked a question intended to embrace anything which his previous interrogation may somehow have missed, hoping he would not be deluged with trivial details about the other tenants.

"Is there anything else you can think of which seemed out of the ordinary with any of your tenants?"

"Well, since you ask, though I thought nought of it as she is a foreign lady, it seemed that Mrs Lang may have recently been elsewhere than England."

"What do you mean? Where?"

"Well, I am not a woman of the world. I know little of the world beyond Covent Garden, London even, still less the country."

"Tell me, then, why you think Mrs Lang had been elsewhere."

"It was a coin she had. I asked for payment for some extras goods she ordered and she offered this strange coin. She said it was a Spanish dollar and was accepted all over Europe and America, but I had never heard of it. She said it was worth at least five shillings. I was too suspicious to accept it so the next day she paid in English coins. I thought that the man must have given them to her."

"You said she was foreign. Why did you say that?"

"It was the way she spoke. I could not say exactly. She spoke quite clearly, as though she had been in the country a long time. I had no trouble understanding her but it sounded a little harsh. The boy spoke differently. More like an Irish."

The Spanish dollar. He had certainly heard of it. America was the most obvious place for her to have been, especially as the boy spoke 'like an Irish'.

"Mathilda, you have been a great help and I thank you." He hesitated, smiling at her and remembering the several months which they had spent in each other's company. He may as well express what was on his mind. "You are still as pretty as ever, Mathilda." Indeed, she was. "May I perhaps call upon you again?"

"Nothing would please me more, Matthew, if I thought you would give up the gambling houses. But I doubt you are capable. 'Tis a wicked affliction. Worse than a disease, the pox, say.

162

'Twill kill you in the end, one way or another, I feel sure. In the debtors prison; at the hands of a creditor; by your own hand even; God forbid at the end of a rope if you were to take to stealing to pay your debts. I have buried one man, through drink in his case. You are too good a man to lose, Matthew."

She put her hand over his. He swallowed, knowing what she prophesied was true if he continued with his present way of life. Trying not to appear too bleak, he smiled again his gentle smile.

"I must take my leave of you, Mathilda." He rose and made to bow.

"And the gambling?"

He shook his head. He had tried before. He may try again. With the money he was now earning, he could pay his debts with some over and then try to stay away from the tables. Perhaps visit his son in Liverpool.

He patted her hand and left the room, left her house. Out on the street, he could feel his flimsy resolve already ebbing away. He flagged down a cab and, patting his coat to feel the reassurance of the remaining coins, he gave the driver the approximate address of Mrs Lang's physician. When he was dropped off, he would find the place on foot.

AFTER AN hour and a half with Dr Anstruthers, he was thirty guineas poorer (a doctor valued his time and knowledge rather more highly than that of a landlady) and no nearer to the answer of his primary question of who might be the father of Maximilian Kohler. But the intelligence secured from the arrogant doctor who assured Benjamin that he was absolutely sure of his facts, confusing though it was, meant that he had an answer of sorts.

There was little point in spending many more hours trailing around the various locations of secret houses of Roman Catholic worship on the slim possibility that Mrs Lang had attended one of them during her two months in London.

He would probably visit the market tomorrow. One of the hackney drivers might be able to tell him whither a tall, well-dressed man picked up at the market early in the mornings of February and March had been taken. To know who the man was could be useful, but in his estimation it was unlikely that a present-day, secret lover would be responsible for the fathering of a child now aged nine or ten years.

He decided to go home straightaway, avoiding the gambling dens for tonight. He was tired. He would write a report to Mr Blake tomorrow and a second copy for the lawyer to provide to his client but would not submit it yet. He would wait several days. He would not reveal his sources to be visited and harassed by Blake or his lackeys. That he had earned his commission in one evening would have to be concealed from Blake and his client. A few days would add more substance to his findings.

Someone had determined that he, Benjamin, was the man to make these enquiries and had trusted in his ability to establish the truth. That would have to suffice if Blake took issue and refused to hand over the rest of the fee. He, Benjamin, would in turn refuse to supply his report and would suggest to Blake that he consult his client who, Benjamin felt sure, would have confidence in him and would instruct Blake to complete the deal.

A good evening's work had left his purse considerably fuller, but his heart heavier. He pictured Mathilda's face, now plump but, he thought, the prettier for it. He might well, he decided, take a stagecoach to Liverpool next week and spend a month playing with his grandchildren. If anything, it would be their sweet, innocent faces which could persuade him to abandon his present life. His heart thumped at the prospect of quitting the gaming tables. If he could just hold firm until next week, he might be able to achieve his redemption.

Chapter 22

Thursday 4ᵗʰ April 1799

"LIZZY, I have ordered the rooms in the west wing to be aired and made ready for Sir Peter and Lady Layham, and others in the east wing for Harriet and Colonel Fitzwilliam after their wedding in the event that they do not travel directly to Kent. The latter would have been offered to you and William had you wished to remain in Hertfordshire for a time after your marriage."

Elizabeth nodded her approval. For Harriet and the Colonel to be at the opposite end of the house from Harriet's parents seemed eminently sensible. They were out for a walk together now. They spent a good deal of their time out walking. She smiled, recalling her walks with Darcy at Longbourn before they were married, affording an opportunity for some degree of privacy and intimacy. Likewise Kitty and Lieutenant Colonel Harvey were also walking. She had seen them leave the house, her arm through his, going in the other direction from the Colonel and Harriet.

Courtship certainly provided ample cause for exercise to be taken. Fortunately, the grounds were extensive or they could have become rather crowded once the Gardiners, their children and the dogs had also taken to the fresh air, indeed the Bennets or the Philipses!

Jane had invited her sister to the small parlour after Elizabeth offered to assist with all the arrangements for the next couple of weeks. Not everyone was outside it seemed. Some of the men must be in the billiard room. She had heard the sounds of cues striking balls on her way to the parlour.

"We must hope that William comes soon so that a date can be arranged for the wedding and the celebrations." Jane sounded anxious. "Charles said he might not even return until Monday. I hope it is sooner."

Charles had arrived home late yesterday evening. Normally cheerful and pleasant of countenance, he had appeared to Elizabeth to be in equally as dour a mood as she had ever seen Darcy.

"William told me it would be Sunday at the latest. I am sorely aggrieved to now hear that it is to be even later. And he cannot have handed Charles the package from Adolphus Barrant for Mary. Mary told me this morning that she had asked Charles about it after everyone else had left the breakfast room."

That Darcy had not secured Mary's package to be brought to Netherfield added to Elizabeth's suspicions that he had not been in London at all but she would have to think about that later.

"A package for Mary? From whom?"

"Yes. From Adolphus Barrant."

Elizabeth decided that, despite her promise to Mary, if Charles knew of Mary's communications with Adolphus Barrant, then Jane could be told as well.

"Jane, little has been said about it and I promised Mary to tell no one of her most recent accomplishment which is to write stories which she hopes to have published. Can you promise me that you will keep it to yourself? I assume Charles knows something of it as he has been in London with William and I rather assumed that Charles would bring the package here as William was to travel on to Kent."

Jane's furrowed brow expressed her confusion. "I do not understand any of this, Lizzy."

"Mary has been in communication with a young man named Adolphus Barrant who lives in America and may or may not be a friend of Julius Fairweather," which, Elizabeth thought, may be an over-simplification if the truth be known. "There are young men who studied mathematics and engineering with Julius and who are in London. William was hoping to speak to one or more of them about his plans for a paper mill, but also he offered to bring back a package for Mary which an associate of Adolphus Barrant had brought from America for her. It was some sort of scientific information or possibly a story about life in America, perhaps a manuscript. I do not know exactly."

A slow smile spread over Jane's face and then she laughed, causing Elizabeth much relief.

"Our sister has some eccentric ways, Lizzy. No, I will talk to no one about it, apart from Charles of course — "

A sudden knock at the door interrupted Jane.

"Come in." And to Elizabeth, "I hoped we would not be disturbed."

The footman George entered and bowed.

"I apologize for the interruption, Mrs Bingley. Miss Caroline Bingley is here asking to see you."

The sisters locked eyes in surprise and there was a moment's silence.

"Is she alone?" asked Elizabeth.

"Yes, ma'am."

Jane shrugged and after a moment told George to ask her in. He disappeared and about a minute later he opened the door and Caroline entered looking as regal as ever.

Jane rushed forward to greet her guest and the two embraced warmly with expressions of pleasure that they were meeting again so soon. Jane moved back to accommodate Elizabeth who found that even a smile was difficult to summon but was obliged to move towards Caroline and the two women gave slight curtsies to one another.

"Eliza, I am delighted to see you."

"George," said Jane, "would you take Miss Bingley's cape and bonnet. Oh, and have some refreshments brought to us. Tea and coffee and biscuits. And cordial and some fruit."

To Caroline: "You will stay for luncheon, I hope?"

"Indeed, I would be much obliged."

Then to George. "Tell Mrs Pumphrey that we have a guest for lunch."

George thus dismissed, Jane invited Caroline to sit down and all the women did so. The parlour being small, they were seated fairly close together.

Elizabeth's eyes followed George from the room, noting that the hooded ivory cape which he bore away was of fine, heavy material against the cold, the trimming of which matched perfectly in colour Caroline's yellow netted cotton gown with ribbon beneath and the bandeau she wore extravagantly trimmed with feathers and flowers. Caroline's bracelets, brooch and necklace sparkled with small, exquisitely mounted gemstones. The whole was excessively elegant. Caroline loosed from her wrist her highly embroidered, beaded reticule and placed it on the couch beside her.

Elizabeth's thoughts returned to her reflections a week ago that Caroline was possibly overspending. What would she do if her money ran out? Demand to live with Jane and Bingley? The other contemplation was the unfathomable matter, or so it seemed a week ago, that Charles Bingley had refused his sister's request to spend Easter at Netherfield.

Chatter then filled the room. Caroline had been brought here by her sister Susan and Susan's husband who were visiting his brother at his estate in Buckinghamshire and would return for her later. She was most excessively disappointed to miss Mr Darcy again when told he was away on a matter of business. She looked forward to seeing Charles.

"I think he is playing billiards at the moment," Elizabeth informed the others. "And I must tell you, Caroline, that my friend Harriet Layham whom you met last week is to marry Colonel Fitzwilliam shortly, though the exact date is to be set. But it must of course be before he has to return to his regiment."

A shadow passed over their guest's face. "How very pleasant," she said, then rallying, "And how is dear, sweet Georgiana? I do so miss her."

"Very well," replied Jane. "She and our sister Mary are presently practising together on the pianoforte."

"They must be of a similar age, I think. I am so pleased for her that she has now the friendship and society of sisters."

"In fact," said Elizabeth, "Georgiana and our sister Kitty are nearer in ages and are particularly attached to one another."

"Catherine, though, I think, has a young suitor, so I observed last week. It must draw her attention away from Georgiana which must be a sadness for Georgiana."

Elizabeth had always fancied that Caroline was a person to whom jealousy was no stranger and was not surprised that she obviously viewed Kitty's courtship as a reason for a slackening off of her friendship with Georgiana. A short silence followed during which Elizabeth resolved that she would not delve deeply into her family's business for Caroline's benefit. Caroline was obviously waiting for an answer, so she said:

"The one does not necessarily bring about the other, Caroline."

Caroline took a deep breath and turned to Jane.

"And your parents are well, I hope?"

"Yes, indeed, Caroline. Though they have not come far, they are enjoying a change of scene away from Longbourn House for a few weeks. My father is happy in the library here and is enjoying advising Charles on books he might acquire to enlarge his collection."

"And your other relations? Your aunts and uncles? I trust they are well. They appeared to be enjoying a cordial time last week."

"Likewise my relations. They both value this time in the country as they both live in towns, London in my Aunt and Uncle Gardiner's case."

Yes, in whose house you were uncomfortable when visiting Jane due to it not being in the best part of London.

Over half an hour had passed, yet no clue had been given as to why exactly Caroline had called on them. Elizabeth doubted that it was purely due to the opportunity having arisen. Maybe it was to catch a glimpse of Darcy.

The chatter continued. Caroline's talk turned to the subject of her dear friend Clara Lang via the subject of Lydia.

"As you know, I have crossed paths with your sister Lydia. I did not of course anticipate that when we brought her here last week, I and Viscount Morley, that she would become so…lively. I know it has been difficult for her in London. The society can be…demanding, unkind in many ways. And she is so young."

This is leading up to something, Elizabeth thought. She surreptitiously glanced at Jane. Jane was always placid and could give the impression that no significant emotions troubled her. But Elizabeth knew her sister well and could sense behind the impassive expression that disquiet was building up within her too.

"I saw that she was in London," continued Caroline, "not far from her family, but without any plans to visit her family and apparently not often in communication with her family. I hoped that seeing her family again would be good for her."

How could anyone respond to this? Most of it was probably largely true, but what did Caroline wish them to say?

"What I am trying to convey is that Lydia, I am sure, needs her family. She has called on me and Louisa which is all very well but, Jane, she would not leave. It was extremely difficult. Eventually, Mr Hurst had to take her by hackney carriage to an inn and pay for her to stay there for the night. This happened earlier this week. And I know she persuaded my dear friend Clara Lang to let her stay at Clara's rented house in London a few times, but there was trouble and Clara's landlady complained and Clara had to ask her to leave and not return."

"I am very sorry, we are very sorry to hear this, Caroline," said Jane faintly. "I assume she is still living with her husband's commanding officer's wife?"

"I regret that I do not know Jane. I am...doubtful of that. Jane, what I wanted to ask is whether you and Charles might be prepared to invite her to live with you for a time. At least until Mr Wickham returns from Ireland and then she can return to live with him wherever he is billeted. Unless of course it is possible for her to go to Ireland now to be with Mr Wickham but I do not know if it is. I really do fear that if she stays abroad in London, that she will come to some harm."

This seemed all very fine, but what Caroline didn't say, Elizabeth thought, was that if Lydia was removed from London, then she could no longer be an embarrassment to Caroline through their connection by marriage.

Jane was frowning and looking about her. She clearly had no clue how to respond.

"Jane," said Elizabeth, "you must speak to Charles."

"Yes, yes, of course." And Jane rang for a servant.

ELIZABETH sat on the couch in her bedroom alternately trying to read and gazing out of the window, whilst also wishing that Darcy was here. He usually had the answer to everything, or had until his change of demeanour a couple of weeks ago. Once Bingley had come to the parlour, had greeted Caroline and had the request and the reason for it explained to him, she had judged it proper that she should remove herself from the discussions and, for the moment, leave the issue of Lydia to Jane, Bingley and Caroline.

She could only thank the Lord that no request had been made to accommodate Lydia at Pemberley. Of course, Caroline would not wish to involve Darcy. She had once told Elizabeth that Darcy could not bear to hear George Wickham mentioned, though she did 'not know the particulars' save that George Wickham had 'treated Mr Darcy in a most infamous manner'. Elizabeth trusted that Caroline was still ignorant of those particulars.

Without having a shred of sympathy for Lydia, her heart nonetheless went out to her sister, poor misguided creature who seemed unable to manage her life properly. Thus far until recently, Lydia's appalling decisions had not caused her any major disadvantage. But it was like card-playing, gambling with what you had been dealt and trusting that everything would go your way. What Lydia failed to appreciate was that there were others in the world who would take such advantage as they could at the expense of anyone else to get what *they* wanted. That seemed to include her husband, who had left her in London, ill-equipped as she was.

What Elizabeth had so feared a week ago when imploring Morley to leave Lydia alone appeared to have come about. It sounded as though Lydia was homeless. Was she the only one who could have foreseen this?

Perhaps Jane and Bingley, and Caroline and her father Mr Bennet if called upon, would between them be able to arrive at a solution.

It was still only twelve o' clock. Lunch would not be for another two hours. As she had not taken in a word passing before her eyes and since the weather looked to be calm outside, if probably not at all warm, she decided to don outer clothing and tramp about the grounds, trying to avoid others and clear her head.

Within ten minutes she was outside, striding away around the trout lake towards the copse on the other side, having noted which way the two couples had gone and walking in another direction.

Before she rounded the lake, she took a last look at the house and, to her horror, a figure was at a window gesturing to her. From the vivid yellow of the woman's dress, she adjudged it was Caroline Bingley and the gestures said: 'Wait for me!'

Her heart sank. Her only reason to wait for Caroline was that the other might have some intelligence of interest to impart. She thought for a moment and then beckoned to the figure at the window who nodded, as far as she could tell at this distance, and disappeared. Not long after, a tallish woman in an ivory-coloured cape was hurrying round the trout lake towards her.

THEY had come through the copse, relatively overgrown, and emerged on the other side to see the open fields before them; still no green shoots. The fields would probably have to be ploughed again and re-sown. The seeds already planted would have died and rotted due to the cold, thought Elizabeth, daughter of a gentleman farmer who oversaw a working farm. Caroline Bingley took no notice of the brown fields before her.

"Come this way," urged Caroline. "There is a folly not far from here where we may sit and talk."

"You have the advantage of me," replied Elizabeth, "having lived here before." She had already noticed Caroline's eyes wandering around the small parlour in the house of which she had formerly been effectively the mistress. At the least, it must be uncomfortable for her to have to defer to Jane.

Yet Caroline continued in reasonably cheerful spirits. "It attracts such sun and warmth as may be had at this time of year in this part of Hertfordshire."

"Please, then, lead the way," said Elizabeth, resigned to whatever it was that Caroline had to tell her.

It was indeed warm in the sheltered parts of the folly which Elizabeth had never seen before. In her condition, the walk had tired her already and she sank down gratefully onto the wooden seat.

Without delay or preamble, Caroline revealed the second purpose of her visit. "I wanted to say, Eliza, that I hoped we could be friends. In the past, I am sorry that I have been less than cordial towards you. I hope that I can make amends."

Perhaps, if you desisted from calling me Eliza, a name I rather dis-like, then we might be friends. The Lucases have always called me Eliza but they are friends whom we have known for many years.

"That is most generous of you, Caroline."

If her response was less than encouraging, then she had not sought this approach and it had been Caroline who had always created the ill feeling in the past.

"And your concern for Lydia is very affecting. Of course, I am most concerned for Lydia myself, but I asked your friend Viscount Morley a week ago to stay away from her and he simp-ly laughed me off."

"Morley is a better man than you probably think, Eliza."

"He is a dissolute character so far as I could see."

"He has been a good friend to me, Eliza, and I assure you that your sister Lydia is the one who creates a bad impression for herself, not Morley. She will not stop chasing after Morley and other men. That is why I think her family should take her back under their wing."

Perhaps there was truth in what Caroline said, and the latest events as described by her earlier were most disquieting. As Jane had suggested, Lydia was always avid in her quest for amuse-ment.

If the other two women were right, then she must reconsider Morley's character. It was a pity that Morley had responded so flippantly to her entreaties to him, refusing to either admit or deny some liaison with Lydia. If he was indeed good and kind, then he had apparently deliberately set out to create the opposite impression. Maybe it was something to do with Darcy, whom he had derided as being 'irreproachable'. Morley had perhaps de-cided that she and Darcy were cut from the same cloth and he would not appear to be subdued at her insistence.

"What did Jane and Charles agree to do?"

"They gave no immediate answer. It seems as though they wish for Mr Darcy to agree to any resolution."

"I see. But William is not here and likely will not be for sever-al more days. My opinion is that Lydia should go to Wickham in Ireland if that is possible. I know not how it has come about that she was living with Wickham's commanding officer's wife in London. I feel sure if William were here that he would broker a solution, possibly talk to the army and try to get Lydia back under the direct protection of the military, whether in Ireland or here on the mainland."

"I understand, Eliza, that Lydia was not willing to go to Ireland with Wickham and I assume could not be forced to do so now."

"But would she either come to Netherfield? She was quite…hostile when I spoke to her last Thursday. She cannot be forced to go anywhere against her will."

Unless to an asylum, Elizabeth could not help thinking, but of course did not voice this possibility.

"I take it that my father was not approached this morning."

"Not as far as I am aware. But I do not think I can do any more on the occasion myself. I felt that I should bring Lydia's plight to the attention of her family, that is all. And, as I said, I hoped to extend the hand of friendship to you, Eliza. That was my other main reason for visiting." She smiled. "You made a very good impression on my friend Morley. He considers that you are a woman of great spirit."

"I assure you, Caroline, that I did not set out to make any impression, good or bad, merely to plead Lydia's cause, though doubtless she would not approve of my interference herself."

"Well, Lord Morley may appear to make light of many things, but he is a kind man at heart. It was good of him to invite Mrs Lang and Max to stay with him and his family in Devon when they first came to England from America in December."

"How did he know Clara Lang? And what was she doing in America."

"As I understand it, Lord Morley was at Cambridge when she was there for a few days with her father, a professor of mathematics, a decade or so ago. Clara remembers Mr Darcy and Charles from that short time she had in Cambridge. And Morley spent some time in America himself which is when I think he met Clara again. He has only been back in the country for about six months himself, since he gained his title on his father's death. As far as I know, Max was studying in America and also performing."

"And you became acquainted with them both in London, then, I take it."

"That is right."

Caroline leaned back against the wooden seat and sighed. "'Tis wonderful to be back at Netherfield even for just a day. Though Charles had spoken of acquiring an estate somewhere probably in the North of England, while we were here, I felt very settled here. Now, I am settled nowhere."

Elizabeth wondered what to say and could think of nothing.

"Eliza, you are so very fortunate as is your sister Jane to have made good marriages. And indeed so is your friend Harriet. All my sisters are married. I see Catherine being courted by a genteel, apparently very suitable young man. I see she wears an eternity ring. I cannot help but wonder how these matches come about, yet I seem destined to remain a spinster."

And also Georgiana has attracted a good-looking young man apparently of wealth and character, of which Caroline was ignorant. What would she say if that budding romance be added to the list? Her quandary would seem even more hopeless.

Such a private disclosure Elizabeth had not expected. Was Caroline asking for her advice? If so, should she give it?

Caroline looked at Elizabeth and gave a rather hollow laugh. "Do you have any hints, Eliza, for someone like me?"

So the surprising but anticipated question was out. And had not she only last Friday discussed with Darcy what his impression was of Caroline Bingley? How, though, could you tell a woman that a man, a man indeed towards whom Caroline had been obviously attentive, had described her as masculine; that she had a strident quality of...'determined arrogance' was the phrase used.

"Well," Elizabeth said hesitantly, "in most cases people simply fall in love and are powerless to resist."

"You were able to make Mr Darcy love you. Why will no one fall in love with me?"

"I assure you that I did nothing to attempt to secure his affection. I grew to love him when I knew him better and I think...I think he loved me almost from the first.

"May I ask you, Caroline, have you ever fallen in love with anyone. Apart, of course, from Darcy?" Caroline stiffened. "Yes, I know you were in love with him, Caroline. You made it very plain."

Caroline's face expressed all the emotions which Elizabeth might have expected, the chief amongst them resentment and hurt. "Then, why would he not love me in return."

"I imagine that you made your feelings *too* plain. A little subtlety may have helped. You referred to Lydia chasing after men as though it is an unattractive feature. People may feel trapped and run in the other direction."

Elizabeth paused before posing another possibility.

"Or, I regret, you simply fell in love with the wrong person, someone who would never love you."

Caroline shook her head as though not understanding. Should she tell Caroline what Darcy had actually said, that she should soften her ways and be kinder and more gentle? More feminine?

"Caroline, if I could speak a little more plainly, your conduct towards me and my family demonstrated very clearly that you held us in low esteem. Some of the things you said were scornful. It is a form of cruelty and, I would submit, not an obviously attractive feature. A man observing you might well be repelled. Of course, I have not made a close study of you. I have had no cause to. But you may have similarly treated others and therefore unwittingly portrayed yourself as unkind or appeared so in the eyes of others.

"There. I am sorry if you have been injured by my words. I hope you will consider them in the light in which they are intended. To help you."

If Caroline had burst into tears she would not have been astonished. She saw only a little watering of the eyes and was relieved there was no out-pouring of anger and indignation. She seemed to be doing all the talking, so she asked:

"Would you consider falling in love with a poor man, or would you stop yourself or simply never even consider someone who was not very wealthy, even if he was charming and handsome and had some living if only small?"

Caroline opened her mouth in astonishment. "Upon my word, I have never considered such a question."

"Well, then, perhaps you should. At least, try to look at the world differently. Love simply drops out of the sky unsolicited, but you will never notice it if you restrict your sights to just a few narrow criteria."

She would not tell Caroline to change her demeanour in any distinct way, to smile more, laugh more, act frivolously. It was her opinion that any such displays could appear obviously artificial and have the opposite effect to that intended. She had said enough and Caroline was quiet, appearing to consider what Elizabeth had said.

At length, Caroline suggested walking on a little farther and then turning back. Elizabeth agreed and was glad to stretch her legs again.

"Eliza —"

"In truth, I would prefer you to call me Lizzy."

Caroline appeared surprised and rather moved.

"Oh, that is extremely kind of you...Lizzy. I hope it means that you are willing to set aside any past differences."

The two women walked on.

"There is something else, Lizzy. I hesitate to say, but Mr Darcy was seen walking into a gaming den in a poor part of London, and Charles too. I think it was on Tuesday."

Could this be the remnants at least of the conniving side of Caroline which Elizabeth had suspected would not be easily eliminated? Why openly hesitate to say something, make it clear that a difficult subject was in contemplation, and then say it anyway? Why not simply keep silent if there was no intention at all to cause consternation?

"The servant of a friend of mine recognised Charles and told my friend and described the man with him and it must have been Mr Darcy. I thought I should tell you, though it is hopefully of no importance and there is a reasonable explanation."

"Oh, is this servant quite sure? William does not gamble."

"As told to me, the servant seemed pretty certain. In fact, Charles did once play cards so perhaps Mr Darcy was merely accompanying him. Or they were meeting someone there who does frequent such places."

The intelligence made her uneasy, as was perhaps the motive for imparting it. What could Darcy have been doing in a gaming house in a poor part of London, or a gaming house anywhere for that matter? Elizabeth suspected that prostitutes too worked out of gaming houses and was reminded of her dream. But at least it must mean that Darcy was in London.

"We should turn back," she said to Caroline, refusing to show that Caroline's story had affected her. And indeed, it was just one more curious piece to try to fit into the dissected puzzle of Darcy's strange behaviour and the oddments she had learned in the last two weeks.

Chapter 23

Thursday 4ᵗʰ April 1799

AS ELIZABETH was struggling to make sense of her new and uncertain friendship with Caroline Bingley, Darcy was happily being shown around Turkey Mill by one of the partners, Mr William Balston. He had left London far too late yesterday to get to Maidstone that day. Bingley had been held up by the attorney and had not returned to his house in South Street until five o' clock. The attorney had been immensely awkward, he said. Normally cheerful, Bingley grumbled and fretted about wanting to return to Netherfield as soon as possible.

Darcy had got as far as St Mary Cray last night and had had to stay at the Mary Rose Inn. It had been too dark in the carriage to read the manuscript handed over by Adolphus Barrant.

He left early this morning and assumed he would have to arrange a room at an inn near the mill. However on arriving at the Turkey Mill, still not having read the manuscript, and before being handed over to Balston, Mr Thomas Hollingworth one of the owners had insisted that he should reside at the house for the duration of his stay. He lived in Turkey Court, the residence built by a former tenant, George Gill, Darcy was told. It would save time and travelling to and from the mill each day and Darcy had readily accepted.

He listened to all that Balston said with rapt attention. He began to feel that he had been born to take part in the commerce of the country, that sitting around in parlours making polite, inconsequential conversation, something which he had never been very good at in any case, was a great waste of time. Had he not spent many hours as a boy admiring the work of the old smith at Pemberley who, as well as making horse shoes, managed to fashion complicated, decorative shapes from strips and slabs of metal?

He watched now, fascinated, as two men inserted a metal

pivot positioned in the middle of the shorter sides of a large mould into rings at the bottom of rigid metal rods hanging down each side from the ends of a heavy wooden frame. The mould was thereby suspended over the large vat beneath of pulped and fermented rags, which Balston called 'the stuff'.

The heavy wooden frame was pivoted further along on two upright poles. The frame, by this arrangement, formed a classic lever with another man, the bellows man, at the other end who could, by lowering or raising a round bar fixed between the stout beams of the frame, cause the frame to tilt up or down at the vat end.

The mould for Antiquarian-sized sheets of paper, Darcy was told, was too heavy and too large for one man to hold. It was nearly fifty-eight inches by nearly thirty-six inches, a normal-sized mould being a maximum of forty-four inches. In fact, the whole operation to make a sheet of Antiquarian paper took eleven men for all its many stages.

The two vatmen then held the mould above the vat by one of its longer sides, and tilted the mould towards them. As the bellows man lowered the heavy frame, the vatmen simultaneously supported and guided the mould into a horizontal position and drew it towards them as it sank to a shallow depth into the stuff. Then they manoeuvred the mould so that the stuff ran to the other end of the mould. The bellows man pushed the bar of the frame down thereby raising the mould above the vat, and the two vatmen swung the mould backwards and forwards a few times which resulting in the stuff reaching all edges of the mould and, Darcy was told, causing the fibres to interlock and the water in the stuff to drain off through the wove-wire surface of the mould.

"The stuff on the mould closes into a sheet," said Balston. "The vatmen must correspond precisely in all their movements so that the sheet has exactly the same thickness and texture throughout. It is extremely skilled."

Darcy had of course witnessed the same process at Frogmore Mill for the making of smaller sheets which involved similar skill in the shaking of the mould to settle the pulp on the mould and cause the fibres to knit together. The major complication with

Antiquarian-sized sheets seemed to be that several people had to be ready to perform their tasks flawlessly at the right time.

A fourth man then assisted the vatmen to support the mould while they released the pivots from the metal rods. The mould was then swung onto a copper table and a fifth person, the 'ass boy', raised one side of it to an almost vertical position to enable it to drain further.

Two more men passed a second mould to the vatmen for the process to start again. The same two men cleaned the rectangular border of wood, known as the deckle, now removed from the first mould to enable it to be re-used.

The first mould was inverted onto a layer of moist felt by two couchers and the mould lifted off. The sheet of paper left on the felt was covered in another layer of felt. Gradually, a post of 65 sheets would be built up, each covered by a felt.

"It takes six men to move the post over rollers to the hydraulic press."

Darcy could believe it. Again he had witnessed all this in a smaller way at Frogmore. The speed of the operation at Frogmore had astounded him. The process of dipping the mould, shaking and settling it, inverting the mould and building up a post for pressing had proceeded uninterrupted for hours it seemed.

"Two thousand sheets a day are produced," Mr Holmes had told him.

Of course, the delicacy with which these much larger sheets had to be handled slowed down the operation, but it was still a remarkably efficient operation.

After the sheets were separated from the felts, they were pressed again in a pack of one hundred and thirty sheets.

"Antiquarian sheets require more pressings, but other than that, they are finished in much the same way as the smaller sheets and sized similarly, though they need more time in the drying loft and longer stacking to complete their consolidation."

Darcy nodded.

"I believe Mr Darcy that you have come here especially to see the Antiquarian sheets made, but in truth our major business is the normal, smaller sheets. The Antiquarian tend to be made to order for special purposes, often ceremonial. And there is a higher failure rate."

"I see. Yet what you do here is magnificent."

Balston appeared troubled and turned to Darcy. Over the noise of the operations in the building, he said:

"Mr Darcy, I must say this. I think it would be a mistake for you to imagine that you can just have a mill building put up for you and suddenly start making quality paper. For one, a paper mill has to be properly designed. As to the papermaking, 'tis a skilled job and takes years to learn. I have been here twenty-five years since becoming apprenticed to James Whatman, the son of the first James Whatman. 'Twas he, the son, who invented the method you see here."

"I understand, Mr Balston. I expect to have to undergo some training in papermaking myself. I know that it would not do for an owner to be remote from the work force and know nothing of the crafts being practised by his workers. Restoring my own small derelict mill and extending it will take some time which I hope to use profitably in various ways including learning the skill."

"Well, that is certainly a good principle to start with." Balston seemed moderately reassured.

Darcy was not in fact in the least deterred. He was already forming plans in his mind and knew he must start small, employ suitable people. Lizzy was enthusiastic. She would help him, probably be far better at the delicate job of papermaking than him. It would be hugely diverting for both of them. He would need an architect or at least an experienced builder to design and build his mill building. The building would have to be similar to the Turkey Mill, different parts of it accommodating all the various processes. His men would have to learn building skills some of them, while others would learn the skills of papermaking.

He would have to cultivate relationships with stationers, printers and publishers and others.

His worries of the last two weeks fell away. The Turkey Mill was vast and there was so much more to see. While he hoped that, in due course, he would be able to acquire one of the wire-cloth-covered cylinder machines invented in France, yet to reach

England, to produce longer sheets of paper much more quickly, the method used here to make the Antiquarian-sized sheets of paper, should he find a market for them, was already in existence and would be a good place to start.

In any case, it may be sensible to wait and see how the cylinder machine fared in the first place, before rushing to acquire one. In its infancy to begin with, other better machines may quickly follow.

"What of James Whatman now?" he asked. "Is he still alive?"

"I regret that he died last year. He suffered an apoplexy nearly ten years ago and I managed the Mill after that. He lived on the other side of Ashford Road in a house called Vinters. He brought me up as well as trained me and I lived there until his death. Now I live nearby in a house at Poll Mill. Of course his widow is still at Vinters and his son James when he's down from Cambridge as he is now for Easter for a few more days."

Balston lowered his head and addressed the floor. "Mrs Whatman is a very kind woman and I help her in any way I can. I was taken from the Writing School of Christ's Hospital in London and on first coming to the mill, I was put into lodgings in Maidstone. It was Mrs Whatman who had me brought to the house to live with the family. Mr Whatman and his first wife had two daughters, both now married."

It was an affecting story. Darcy knew of Christ's Hospital, a boarding-school founded by King Edward VI over two hundred years ago for fatherless children and the children of poor men to be cared for and educated. He wondered at Balston's parentage but would not ask. Balston may not himself know.

"Oh. I am sorry, sir, to hear of Mr Whatman's illness and death. And the Hollingworths? When did they become involved?"

Balston's reply was vague.

"A few years ago. Shall we continue with your tour?"

And Balston, extending his arm, indicated the presses. Darcy determined to come back later and look at the lever system more closely, the way the moulds were lightly and quickly shaken to settle the stamped and retted pulp and cause the fibres to knit together and the liquid to drain through. He would draw diagrams and take measurements, while appreciating that he may never make these large sheets in the end.

He could well see how the whole delicate process required extreme skill and that clumsy handling could ruin sheets of paper.

TURKEY Court was immensely grand although, as it adjoined the factory, there was a faint but definite odour even in the house, redolent of the boiling of animal parts to make gelatine for sizing the paper. He already had a home, Pemberley House, which he had no intention of leaving, but would have to build houses near his manufactory for workers of various levels of seniority.

He would certainly need a manager or foreman, no doubt an overlooker, and probably a partner with commercial experience, preferably in the sphere of papermaking. The mill would be some distance from Pemberley House and a second house of his own near the mill would be desirable. What he would not do, Darcy decided, was build residences for himself and his senior people within his mill building or very nearby. James Whatman had, after all, moved to a house on the other side of the road and it could be seen several fields away!

The workers would also need to be housed nearby. It occurred to him that if his mill expanded and he employed enough people, he might have to provide a shop for them from which they could purchase basic goods. Derbyshire differed considerably from Kent, the latter being well-populated, at least this part of it. The same could not be said of Derbyshire where villages and towns were scattered some distance apart with vast, wild, unpopulated areas in between. People working at a mill some distance from any village or town would have nowhere nearby to purchase the necessities of life.

He had heard of workers being exploited by some mills in some parts of the country paying them partly in tokens which they had to spend in the shops provided by the mill owners, with the goods being of a poor standard and more expensive than elsewhere. Paying in tokens or vouchers was often necessary due to coinage being in short supply, but he would not, he vowed, exploit his own workers.

Little could he know that his comparisons between Derbyshire and Kent were very much akin to Elizabeth's comments to her father two days ago, the day he left for London, contrasting Derbyshire with Hertfordshire, citing the grandness of the former's landscape and the latter's leafy lanes, little hamlets and frequent farm-houses and cottages.

The house in which he was staying was built in the time of Queen Anne. James Whatman had considerably extended it with the addition of a West Wing comprising two large rooms, a dining room and drawing room for entertaining. He was sitting that evening at the huge dining table, used, he understood, by James Whatman for council meetings.

He was being entertained by Thomas Hollingworth and his wife Mary who lived at Turkey Mill, by Thomas's brother, Finch Hollingworth a co-owner of Turkey Mill who lived nearby, and his wife Ann, William Balston and, to Darcy's surprise, Susanna Whatman, widow of James Whatman II, and her son, also named James Whatman.

Being a partner only and not one of the owners, Balston must be, Darcy assumed, somewhat subordinate to the Hollingworths, though they would surely still be fairly dependent on Balston being the most experienced papermaker.

The partners looked about the same age, William Balston and Finch about forty years of age, Darcy adjudged, and Thomas a little younger, perhaps mid-thirties. James was twenty-one and, it was explained, was home from Cambridge for Easter. Beyond commenting that he had been at Cambridge himself, he fervently desired that he would not be drawn at any point into conversation regarding Cambridge, much less expected to regale the company with any jolly tales of his time at Cambridge which, at present, he very much wished to forget.

This seemed unlikely. James was quiet and pale and his mother asked him a few times how he was feeling, though there was nothing obviously wrong with him.

In case of Cambridge being utilised as a diversion from James's possible state of health, Darcy turned the conversation to his connections with the county.

"I have both an aunt and a cousin in Kent. My aunt lives at a place called Rosings near Westerham. My cousin's residence is near Wrotham Heath."

Some of those around the table exchanged glances. They obviously knew of Rosings and suspected who was the relation near Wrotham Heath. Darcy realised that it would seem odd, ridiculously coy, if he did not voluntarily expand upon his relations and their titles. He could hardly say that his aunt was the housekeeper and his cousin a footman!

"My late mother's sister, Lady Catherine de Bourgh, lives at Rosings and my cousin, Ernest Fitzwilliam resides at Pakeleigh Abbey." Should he enquire if the Hollingworths, Whatmans or Mr Balston knew either of these relations? He decided not. They would doubtless make any acquaintanceship known without being asked. "Er, my other dear cousin, Colonel Fitzwilliam, the younger brother of the Earl, is staying with us at Netherfield over Easter."

"Will you be visiting your aunt or cousin during this trip, Mr Darcy?" enquired the Mrs Whatman, an elegant woman, not much older than Finch Hollingworth and William Balston.

"Unfortunately not. I have not the time. I must return to Derbyshire a little after the middle of April, and there are matters to which I must attend and certain engagements before quitting Hertfordshire."

Possibly the marriage of Fitzwilliam and Harriet Layham if it took place. He understood that Fitzwilliam had not given up hope, but he could hardly spread abroad his cousin's private aspirations and fears and the reasons for them.

He had said as much as he wanted about himself and sought something of the history of the mills owned by the Hollingworths. There was much for him to be told. It seemed that Turkey Mill was a fulling mill originally in the sixteen hundreds and a corn-grinding mill for a brief period, converting to a paper mill by the end of the seventeenth century.

"Turkey Mill is an unusual name," Darcy observed.

"Yes," Balston volunteered. "It may either come from the Indian corn which was ground known as Turkey wheat. Or maybe even further back when Turkey red dye was used in connection with the fulling."

Darcy nodded.

They fairly obviously wanted to know more about him and he told them about his wife Elizabeth and that they were expecting their first child.

"I dare say that you hope for a son, Mr Darcy," Mrs Whatman said pleasantly, "to carry on your enterprise."

"I really have no preference, Mrs Whatman. My wife is one of five daughters and very lively and varied they are. A son would be delightful of course, but so would a daughter."

"That is very enlightened of you, Mr Darcy. Do your wife's family also reside in Derbyshire?"

"No, no. They are mainly in Hertfordshire where my friend Charles Bingley resides, with whom we are all staying over Easter. When I say 'we', I mean my younger sister, most of my wife's family including aunts, uncles and children, as well as my cousin who is a colonel in the army, a lieutenant colonel accompanying him and a friend of my wife. It is a very jolly gathering."

"Your wife, if you are both in Derbyshire most of the time, must miss her family, Mr Darcy."

"A little perhaps. The whole party I have mentioned also stayed at Pemberley over Christmas and I am sure will wish to come to Pemberley again. Charles Bingley is married to my wife's older sister. Indeed, he hoves from the North of England, as do I, and may well move back there in due course.

"And I hope that we, my wife and I, will be much engaged in the advancement of the mill business for the immediate future. And we have been engaged setting up a school for children on the estate that they may improve their lot and get a good meal each day."

The Hollingworths regarded him with amused puzzlement, Mrs Whatman with approval.

His love for Elizabeth increased with every word spoken of her. She was everything to him. He must resolve this other business as soon as possible.

WHAT he really wished to see during this visit, apart from more

187

of the papermaking process and the other mills, were some books of account to provide a flavour of the economics of the manufactory, just what raw materials and equipment were necessary and what they and other expenses cost. He could hardly blurt this out over the dinner table. He would try to speak to Thomas Hollingworth alone later and perhaps he could spend some time tomorrow or on Saturday in the office near the main entrance to the house.

But before the evening ended, it appeared that piano recitals and singing were obligatory for the entertainment of their guest. Darcy would quite happily have foregone this, for him, doubtful pleasure. He had to suppress yawns as the two Hollingworth wives vied with each other for time at the piano, turned the pages of the music for each other, and gave solo performances of merry songs and a couple of duets.

He took several glasses of wine to get him through the evening which eventually broke up at half-past-eleven and he was left to have a final glass of port with Thomas Hollingworth when he raised his request to see the accounts, monthly, weekly or however they were kept.

"I will not say no, Mr Darcy, but feel that I should give you fair warning that papermaking has become far less profitable of late for a number of reasons."

So, he was about to receive his second warning that day.

"Oh, yes? Pray do go on, Mr Hollingworth. Your intelligence on anything to do with the industry would be invaluable to me. I am not afraid of being told the worse, if that be the case."

"Well then, you will be aware of the civil unrest in recent years and the fear of revolution in this country, indeed fears of an invasion. People, workers, have grown bold as a result and have been seeking higher wages. Kentish manufacturers have been forced to raise their wages.

"The journeymen have been particularly demanding. We hope for the Combination Act to be passed as soon as possible to make these practices of men banding together to demand higher wages and improved working conditions illegal."

Hollingworth used some choice, unrepeatable words and phrases to express his disdain and disregard for these griping working men whom he regarded as a threat and as having not the least entitlement to have their demands met.

Darcy held his tongue. He could hardly cross verbal swords with his host, these people who had shown him such hospitality and encouragement. But he knew how hard life was for most people; near-starvation, living in hovels, wearing rags, freezing in the winter, uneducated, unable to improve their lot in any way, the destitute being consigned to workhouses where they frequently died. When they did have work, the hours were long, the work arduous and the conditions dangerous; children of four and five forced to do a man's work for almost nothing, for a place to sleep and inadequate food.

How could you blame a few, if they wielded some power, to claim more money to support their families and shorter working hours, less harsh circumstances?

Did Balston, Darcy wondered, support this wish to keep the working man down and in his place, when he himself had been poor enough to have been sent to the Christ's Hospital? He was fortunate of course to have been sent there, given the consequences for him.

"So," he said, "what other causes are there for papermaking to be less profitable?"

"All our major expenses. The price of rags continues to rise. We ever fear a rise in Excise Duties. It depends on the war. We have to raise our prices, and buyers accordingly reduce their orders. So far as I can see, the situation is likely to get worse, not better."

IT WAS not until he was in his bedroom that night that he pulled from his portmanteau the manuscript handed to him by Adolphus Barrant and, despite his fatigue after a long day, settled down to skim through it. He had no intention of reading it word for word tonight. It was far too bulky. It turned out to be a mixture of scientific material, accounts of academic life in New England, and anecdotes about Boston worthies and ordinary residents. What English news sheets would make of it to form the basis of articles, he had no idea.

Perhaps Mary, if she was a skilled writer, could weave a novel out of the disparate material sewn together within the vellum covers. In fact, it was the back cover which eventually caught his attention as he was yawning, his eyelids drooping, and eyeing the inviting-looking bed.

He could not help but examine the paper used which must have been made in America. So far as he could see, it was of good quality. If he could make as good himself to begin with, then he would be happy.

His thoughts kept drifting back to his intended new business, the planning of the buildings, the recruiting of workers both from within and outside his estate, the needs of those people.

The paper made at Turkey Mill was watermarked. The shape of it was made out of thin wire bent as necessary to create the design which was then carefully sewn onto the wove-wire surface of the mould. He would have to design his own watermark. Suddenly he thought of Georgiana, so skilful at drawing and painting, of her beautiful calligraphy, of Lizzy whose sewing was so flawlessly, effortlessly neat. Both, he hoped, would help to design and make his watermark. How proud he would be of his first sheets of paper to be made and sold with his own watermark.

It had also seemed to him during the evening that, although William Balston no longer lived at Vinters, indeed probably had to leave for propriety's sake after Mr Whatman's death, he was still closely concerned with all the affairs of the house and estates in all manner of ways. It must place a strain on his energies in addition to his duties at the mills. He wondered at the relationship between William Balston and Susanna Whatman, and concluded that, in view of what Mr Balston had told him, then in the absence of some intimate relationship, William Balston was treated more as an adopted son to Mrs Whatman.

The cautionary warnings of William Balston and Thomas Hollingworth should not be taken lightly. It would be foolish indeed to lose a great deal of money by undertaking this new proposed venture. But neither should he be scared away. All parts of industry must be vulnerable to the demands of workers, to the resistance of customers to price rises, to the vagaries of the government increasing duties and taxes dependent on the course of the war. And the fact was that paper was and would always be a necessary commodity. He could not imagine a time when it would become unnecessary. What could possibly replace it?

It must be the case that the partners of Turkey Mill, in providing him with so much information and assistance, perceived him to be no threat to their business. His own estate was of course many hundreds of miles away and he expected that his customers would largely be from the north rather than London and the south. Yet Turkey Mill had customers all over the country. It was a chastening thought that the partners' real opinion may be that his ambitions amounted to merely the plaything of a rich man which could do them no harm whatsoever and would probably never get off the ground!

Of course he did not wish to cause any disadvantage to his kind hosts, but he was determined to make his enterprise work and certainly not bankrupt himself in the process.

So absorbed was he that he almost overlooked the fact that the back cover of Barrant's manuscript felt thicker than it should be. Very fine stitching edged the cover. Similar stitching edged the front cover as well, but the front cover was thin, two layers only, held together with this stitching. Darcy was sure there was something inside the two layers of the back cover. More documents, perhaps?

He took out his pen knife which he used to trim a quill and snipped at the stitching.

"Good God!" he exclaimed aloud as he read the letter to Mary within, another to Mr Bennet and the document accompanying it. Yet he could not help but smile to himself. "The audacity of the fellow!"

THE mill was vast and Darcy was relieved that he had allowed himself several days to tour the whole place, despite Elizabeth's rather suspicious attitude which he still found puzzling, even after speculating that some untoward intelligence had reached her concerning Clara and Max. Had he bowed to her inference that he was trying to avoid Max's concert, then he would have charged back to Hertfordshire early tomorrow in time to join the party as they left for the Shire Hall in Hertford. Or he could have travelled straight there.

It would not do, he told himself. He must seize this opportunity to gain all he could from his visit to this well-organised, highly-functioning, world-renowned paper mill. He would leave, as planned, on Sunday, and even that would be a wrench. He knew that the Hollingworths owned three other mills, Poll, Loose and Hollingbourne Mills. A look at those might be profitable. They would be smaller, possibly more akin to the size of mill he would have to start off with and extend later as necessary.

Yes, he would make the very best of tomorrow and Saturday.

Chapter 24

HARRIET and Colonel Fitzwilliam were clearly aggravated by Darcy's continuing absence. So indeed was Elizabeth, though for a different reason, and she was privately irritated by their assumption that Darcy should be here at their convenience. He clearly had every right to pursue his own ends during this visit to Hertfordshire and further his own business, visit a mill if he chose and look to the sale of his London house.

Indeed, Harriet would not even be here at all had she and Darcy not accompanied Colonel Fitzwilliam to Cambridge to support his hope that Harriet would be allowed to come to Netherfield for Easter. They should be thankful for Darcy's intervention in particular. Her recollection of the meeting was that it had been his logic and his powers of tact and persuasion which had led to Sir Peter relenting.

She said nothing of her chagrin but, had she done so, would have garnered little support either from Jane and Charles. They, too, made it clear that they looked forward to Darcy's prompt return. They made no secret of Caroline's appeal for Lydia to be offered a home and hoped that Darcy would somehow be instrumental in resolving the matter. The whole subject was debated over the midday meal.

Mr Bennet was tight-lipped.

"Understandably," he said, "Mrs Bennet and I are mindful of Lydia's predicament, but we are older now and not inclined to have our lives disrupted by her unruly behaviour."

Elizabeth took this to mean that Lydia would not be welcomed back to Longbourn in a hurry.

"I am afraid that Lydia should be made to face the consequences of her actions for once. Perhaps then, after a period of discomfort, she would realise the error of her ways and settle down as others have to."

What he didn't seem to apprehend, thought Elizabeth, was that Lydia's downfall if she persisted in her wild ways could be so ruinous that no one would ever want her back and that she may be placed in danger, of her life even.

Mrs Bennet twisted her handkerchief between her hands but did not say anything and did not at least burst into floods of hysterical tears.

Kitty's face expressed her great disquiet.

"Well, what do you say, Kitty? Do you wish for your sister to be brought back into our house to create havoc?"

"No, Papa, no," she cried. "I wish Caroline Bingley had never come here with tales of Lydia's misfortunes, but she brings them upon herself."

Lieutenant Colonel Harvey patted Kitty's hand and she looked at him gratefully.

"That is very much my view, Kitty," said her father. "One day, I hope that she will realise that causing disorder and living according to no reasonable rules will not benefit her. But for now, she has no such sense and must, I think, profit or fall by her own hand. It is unfair that you, my dear," he addressed Kitty, "should once again have to be subjected to her unsuitable influence. You have so lived for long enough already."

"Well, Papa, Mama, she could have lived quietly with the wife of Wickham's commanding officer until Wickham returned. And she could still have played some part in London society but…"

Kitty trailed off, her brow furrowed in her consternation.

Mrs Bennet nodded. Elizabeth was glad of that.

Elizabeth watched Harriet and quietly sighed. Harriet was clearly intrigued by these family airings of areas of dispute. Not surprising as she was the single child of a rather conservative father and a mother who had to negotiate a difficult path to maintain her husband's approval at the same time as creating a cordial ambience. Harriet must have been brought up with little or no interaction between family members since there were hardly any. It would probably be a delight to her to have been able to be part of such turmoil as the Bennets sometimes appeared to be able to produce.

Mary's view had not been sought. No doubt it would be censorious but, Elizabeth noted, Mary appeared much distracted. She was taking hardly any note of the opinions ebbing and flowing around her, though the consensus was not in favour of Lydia. Indeed, if Elizabeth was not mistaken, Mary was much agitated.

That morning, a package had been brought addressed to Mary by a footman claiming to be from the London house of Lady Rose and Mr Fairweather.

"I thought they had sold all their property in England," Elizabeth had said to Mary. "I had no idea they maintained a house in London."

"Well, evidently they do," Mary said, bearing the package away. The impeccable footman George was passing. Mary stopped and asked him to request that the Fairweather's footman be detained so that she might write a short response to the sender of the package.

"He is in the servants' hall, Miss Bennet, taking refreshment before his journey back to London. And the horses are being fed and rested. I will see that he knows of your request."

Elizabeth had watched, dismayed, as Mary hurried away. *Horses!* He must have come in a carriage. How strange!

Harriet had watched this earlier exchange too and had raised an eyebrow to Elizabeth, but Elizabeth was mystified and did not wish to engage with her friend as to the meaning of this. If she discussed it with anyone, it would be Jane. At the time, she had smiled at her friend, shrugged and walked away towards the stairs to go to her room to change for the dining room shortly.

But she must speak to Mary.

DURING the afternoon, Elizabeth washed and then called for Evans to assist her to dress and dress her hair in readiness for tonight's performance in Hertford. They were to take their carriages and leave soon. She would travel with Georgiana, Kitty and Lieutenant Colonel Harvey. She had not spoken to her father today. She hoped that, after the trouble earlier over Lydia, he would still be willing to assist her to seek an audience with

Clara Lang before, during or after Max's performance tonight.

There was very little time before the carriages were to be called when a loud argument started to issue from the library. Certainly it was not Jane and Bingley. It sounded like Mr Bennet and a female. Mr Bennet was shouting. The female voice was also raised with some passion, high-pitched in what sounded like pleading and the beginnings of loud sobs.

Elizabeth had come downstairs to retrieve her reticule from the small parlour intending to take it to Hertford. The library door was slightly ajar and the noise had attracted others; Kitty, Georgiana, Lieutenant Colonel Harvey and Jane. Could it possibly be Mary inside with her father, Mary who never displayed emotion over anything? Now Harriet and the Colonel were approaching, and Mrs Bennet was coming from another direction. Consequently, the female within must be Mary. It certainly was not either of her aunts.

If Mrs Bennet was here, then Elizabeth decided that she should take her mother into the library as it would be her business too. In any case, everyone could hear Mr Bennet shouting, "No! I will not allow it!" and Mary wailing, "But you must sign it!"

Sign what? She caught Jane's eye, and then Harriet's. Both had their mouths open in surprise. If Harriet was enjoying this further evidence of the Bennets' ability to create dramas, then she had the grace not to show it.

"Mama," said Elizabeth, "I think you should go in and see what is amiss. I will come with you."

"I...yes. Thank you, Lizzy." Mrs Bennet's eyes were open wide in shock and consternation. She looked back. "Jane and Kitty, you had better come in as well."

With her hand on her mother's back, Elizabeth guided her mother around the wide door and into the room, leaving the door open for her sisters. The row inside was becoming even more heated. Mr Bennet was pacing the floor and Mary's arms were stiff and her fists were clench. She stamped one foot on the floor. The sisters were too astonished for any of them to think of closing the door.

"What is it, Papa? Mary?" Elizabeth asked.

"Mrs Bennet," Mr Bennet stood still and turned to his wife, "I would be obliged if you would please tell our daughter that she cannot run off to America with a young man."

Mrs Bennet's hand flew to her breast.

"Mary! What have you done?"

"Nothing, Mama. It is not as Papa says."

"Who is this young man? Do we know him? Will he marry you? And why America?"

"Of course he will not marry me," Mary said, a little calmer now. "I have this…"

She flourished a document.

"…but Papa refuses to look at it."

"Indeed I will not." Mr Bennet resumed his pacing.

"Not marry you!" Mrs Bennet's voice was shrill. "Then indeed you cannot go away with him, whoever he is."

Elizabeth walked towards her father. "Papa? Would you object to my reading it?"

"Lizzy, please do so if you must. It will be totally worthless I am sure."

"Mary? May I see it?"

"Here, Lizzy. It is a Deed of Guardianship. Adolphus Barrant would act as my guardian. I do not need to *marry* him."

Mary approached her mother and sisters. "But I must go *now*. With the signed Deed. It was a new moon only yesterday."

This verbal skirmish was starting to make sense. The Fairweather's carriage still waiting to depart, a new moon signalling perhaps a high tide. By heaven, Mary was expected to be borne off to London this very afternoon taking with her a signed Deed of Guardianship in favour of Adolphus Barrant!

Her father was no fool either. He probably knew about the carriage. As to Adolphus Barrant suddenly appearing in Mary's life with some plan to bear her off to America, he made the same connection as Elizabeth.

Before either of them could voice their reasonable suspicions, Mary was speaking again, her voice raised once more in anguish.

"If I have to stay here, I shall suffocate and *die*,"

With the last word, her teeth clenched, her shoulders drew

back in a sort of spasm, her arms grew stiff and her hands formed fists again.

Could this be their disapproving, humourless sister, seeming sometimes devoid of any feeling? Passions obviously did rage, though, beneath her apparently unyielding exterior.

"Mary," said Elizabeth, "what is so much better in America than England?"

"Life is free there. Women will soon be able to attend colleges and universities. I would be able to have a proper education."

"Mary, you can write in this country if you wish to do so. Look at Fanny Burney, Mary Wollstonecraft, Ann Radcliffe."

"I know. But I am not interested in writing scenes set in drawing rooms, carefully thought out conversations between rich people with nothing better to do. Or impossibly improbable novels set in far-off exotic places. I want to learn too. And not just from the feeble literature available in the Clarke's library. With Adolphus Barrant as my guardian, I would be able to learn about science, astronomy, physics, galvanism. I would be able to have a valuable future."

"So, are you saying, Mary, that Adolphus Barrant is actually here in England?"

"Yes. Or how could he become my guardian so that I could travel with him?"

Mr Bennet came forward at that point.

"Let us not fool ourselves here," he said, "that Adolphus Barrant is a real person. If I sign that thing..." he pointed towards the document in Elizabeth's hands which she still had not looked at "...it will be, as I said before, worthless."

"But why, Papa?" said Kitty.

"Because, my dear," he whispered drawing closer to them, "Adolphus Barrant does not exist. The person who calls himself Adolphus Barrant is none other than Julius Fairweather, wanted for eighteen months for holding up stagecoaches, a hanging offence." Elizabeth wished that he had not said that and ardently hoped that it had not been audible to those outside. "This person wants to bear our daughter away to a far-off land and an uncertain future by means of a hazardous sea-crossing and we will never see her again."

"Well," retorted Mary, also more quietly as those within the library moved closer together, "is that so much worse than Lydia running off with an army lieutenant and then marrying him. If she had conducted herself as she should, she would not have others now pleading her case to be reinstated at Longbourn House or with Jane and Charles here at Netherfield. If I land safely in America, I can assure you that I would grasp the opportunities there and lead a useful, profitable life."

"Lydia, as we all know, made a very rash choice to elope with Mr Wickham," said Jane.

"Yes. But my argument is," said Mary, in a near-semblance of her normal self, "that Lydia was allowed the freedom to make that choice and if it has turned out badly for her, it is her fault entirely. And yet I am being prevented from taking a course which, while it may seem no more sensible to you, would be my choice for a life which I choose with open eyes. I doubt if Lydia gave the least consideration to the possible consequences of her actions in running off with Wickham, and yet she was given every opportunity to do so."

"My dear Mary," said Mr Bennet, "if I had my time over again, then I assure you that Lydia would not have been allowed to go to Brighton. But even so, America is a rather different and extreme proposition to Brighton, I think even you will acknowledge."

"So, what is your answer, Papa? The carriage is waiting. What are you going to do?"

"I am sorry, Mary. I will not sign that document and I do not agree to you going to London, and thence to America. You are nineteen years old now. If you still feel the same after your twenty-first birthday then you must do as you please."

Mary collapsed onto the floor in a heap, sobbing. Elizabeth felt terribly sorry for her but could not see that her father's decision was wrong. It was impossible to let her go.

She and Jane helped Mary to her feet and led her, weeping and limp, from the room and through those assembled in the hall outside which now included Bingley, Mr and Mrs Gardiner and Mr and Mrs Philips. The children, no doubt, were still getting ready, chaotically slowly in their excitement at the prospect of an outing. As Elizabeth and Jane bore Mary away to take her up to her bedroom, Jane glanced back at Bingley. He and the others muttered amongst themselves.

Mary would not agree to accompany everyone to Hertford. Mr Bennet came up after them with George and two other footmen who were instructed to keep watch over Mary's room. Elizabeth and Jane had quickly to settle Mary since it was time to leave for Hertford. When they left the room, they found Mr Bennet waiting outside with the footmen.

"For propriety's sake," said Mr Bennet, "and given Mary's condition, it is my opinion that one or more ladies should remain at Netherfield and, I am sorry, forego the pleasures of the concert. Lizzy, I know you are desirous of attending the concert tonight. What say you, Jane?"

"Papa, I would happily stay at home tonight. I would just as well do without the carriage ride. I believe that Mama, too, would prefer to stay here. There has been much disturbance today and she is tired and out of sorts. A quiet evening would suit her very well, I think."

"Very good. Would you go to her then, Jane, and I will inform Bingley.

Upon my word, thought Elizabeth, first Lydia, now Mary. Could anything else intervene today to upset my father and render it less likely that he would assist me in my endeavour to meet Mrs Lang?

And she silently willed Adolphus Barrant to get away from London and England as soon as possible.

Chapter 25

Friday 5th April 1799

THE day was dull and cold as the party bound for Hertford climbed into their carriages. There was no sign of the Fairweather carriage. Elizabeth hoped that this meant that it had already departed. She peered out of the carriage window at the house before the coachman shook the reins to urge the horses to a start. Some windows were lit but Mary's room was at the side of the house so there was no point trying to see if she might be watching the carriages leave.

The carriage lurched as it got under way and Elizabeth and Georgiana were thrown back in their seat. It would not be dark for a couple of hours, but it was still too dim in the carriage to read therefore Elizabeth watched the passing scenery which looked bleak to her today. She wondered why, just a few days ago, she had been describing to her father picturesque leafy lanes and frequent cottages and farmhouses. Today, everywhere appeared empty and dull. Elizabeth wished desperately to take her mind off the troubles which had arisen today but could not stop thinking about them.

Lydia's plight was troubling but largely her own fault. It was Mary who attracted most of her sympathy. If she really felt stifled by her life in Hertfordshire and found her escape route closed to her, then she was to be pitied. To go to America with a handsome, fascinating young man in search of intellectual fulfilment would be a rare adventure to be sure. That Mary was prepared to leave her family apparently without regret was difficult to understand, although Lydia had done so last year, indeed with evident glee. Yet they were very different characters.

Mary had always been a difficult person to understand, where Lydia was transparent. Perhaps the fault lay not with Mary, but with the family, paying too little attention to her, ignoring her comments, even treating them with thinly-veiled scorn, leaving Mary to feel unappreciated and increasing her reserve.

During the summer nearly two years ago when Elizabeth had danced with Julius Fairweather at a ball in London, he had provided Elizabeth with some insight into her sister which she had never before considered; essentially that Mary noticed more than she was given credit for but kept it to herself. At the time, Elizabeth had felt that Julius understood aspects of Mary which her family did not, and now she decided that that must be the case. Granted, Mary tended to expound on moral virtues but beyond that she never ventured any opinions about her sisters or parents or the world at large. She did not chat like other people.

By contrast, Georgiana and Kitty were leaning forward towards each other chatting away, naturally about today's events but also the forthcoming concert. Elizabeth glanced over at Kitty and Harvey. Their cloaks pooled over the seat between them, and Elizabeth was almost sure that they were holding hands beneath the cover provided by the garments. She smiled. It was immensely sweet that he was prepared to wait until Kitty was a little older before pressing his suit. Thus, for the time being, they could be genuine sweethearts.

If Colonel Fitzwilliam decided to sell his commission, then maybe Harvey would buy it and become a colonel himself. Perhaps it would make it easier to marry while remaining in the army if he became a higher-ranking officer, until he was ready to settle at Brownham Hall, his home in Staffordshire which they had visited in January. She started to recall the building and the grounds and what they had been told by the couple who looked after the house.

These were far more pleasant musings than speculation about Lydia and Mary and thus she managed to get through the journey to Hertford in a reasonable spirit.

BY THE time the Netherfield carriages drew up outside the Shire Hall, darkness had fallen and as usual for such events, a festive air was created by light pouring from the windows, braziers burning on the streets outside, oil lamps hanging from brackets on the walls of the building and lively music emanating from the triple arched doorway.

They all gathered in the lobby with the milling crowd showing their tickets and taking glasses of the wine from trays held aloft by footmen. Chatter filled the lobby as everyone waited for some time during which Harriet managed to get Elizabeth alone.

"Lizzy, I do not know quite how to say this. I know this Easter has not been easy for you one way and another. I have sensed some difficulty about Mr Darcy but I know not what it is. And today, not one but two of your sisters have presented what must be terrible dilemmas for your family. And yet, I know this will sound absurd, but I have never enjoyed myself so much in all my life as during my times with you. At Christmas as well. I feel so selfish when you have these burdens to bear.

"And, of course, now I am so happy to be marrying Jeremy soon. He is the man of my dreams. My parents have agreed to it. Lizzy, I have been made so happy, and it is all thanks to you."

Harriet's eyes were misted with tears and Elizabeth wondered if she had had one glass of wine too many, but she was not holding a glass now. Had they not been in a public place, Elizabeth would have hugged her friend and had to be content with putting her arm through Harriet's.

"You are not selfish at all, Harriet. You have made us very happy too. I am so pleased to see Col...Jeremy so joyful." She looked over at him laughing with Bingley. "It gives me so much pleasure to know you are enjoying your stay and that you both have a wonderful future ahead of you."

"Thank you, Lizzy. You are the very best of friends."

Whereupon the welcoming music ended and those gathered in the lobby were asked to ascend the spiral staircase to the first floor Assembly Rooms.

Elizabeth had been here before of course but still found herself casting her eyes around the ornate room, with its five domed semi-circular bays, Doric columns and elaborate moulding. Taking their seats, Elizabeth managed to sit next to her father. She whispered to him how or who they should ask to meet Clara Lang.

"I will make enquiries at the interval," he replied. "Hand me a card of yours."

She discreetly foraged in her reticule and surreptitiously passed over her card.

They sat through a number of short pieces by Mozart, Handel and Vivaldi.

When the interval came, refreshments were served in a side room and Mr Bennet walked away to, he said, find the manager. He was gone for about ten minutes and Elizabeth was becoming anxious when he re-appeared in the refreshment room. The second half was due to start soon and people were pushing their way back into the concert hall.

"I handed over both our cards," he said, "and was told to go and find the manager later. It did not seem very certain." He smiled. "At this rate, we may have to queue at the stage door with all of Max's admirers."

Elizabeth could not return the smile. She had invested much hope and expectation in the prospect of talking to Mrs Lang tonight and the thought of being unable to realise the hope filled her with disappointment.

She settled in her seat to try to enjoy the performance and suddenly Max Kohler was there on the stage with a string quartet to wild applause. He bowed, smiled and started to play straightaway and the effect was magical. So transfixed was Elizabeth that she waited twenty minutes before pulling out her spyglass to get a better look at Max's face. Could he be Darcy's child? He was certainly a handsome boy, just beginning to show signs of the man to come. But, she had to admit, he could be anyone's son.

Her father, she knew, was watching her scrutiny of Max. So was Bingley. It was all too public and she put the glass away.

The performance seemed to pass quickly and before long the music had stopped and Max had made a low bow and left the stage to more ecstatic applause and calls of 'encore' but he did not return. The music seemed to have washed over Elizabeth and she felt slightly dazed. Even the details of Max's face through her spyglass seemed hazy. It must be the strains of the last couple of weeks and her suspicions about Darcy. The audience were kept in their seats for another ten minutes by the string quartet which carried on playing. Was this so that Max and Clara could get away from the Shire Hall, away from her perhaps?

The quartet ceased to play, took a bow and were also gone. The Netherfield party rose and followed the audience downstairs. Mr Bennet was scouring the entrance hall, but appeared to have no luck seeing the manager or anyone else in charge.

"I am sorry, Lizzy. I think that is as much as we can do," he said, coming up to her.

"Do not worry, Papa. I am resigned. I just want to go home now."

"Yes. It has been exhausting, what with one thing and another."

SHE fell asleep in the carriage. So did Kitty and Georgiana, and even Lieutenant Colonel Harvey appeared to be nodding off. The journey thus passed very quickly. When they reached Netherfield, she was suddenly wide awake again. She went with her father to Mary's room. A sleepy George was still guarding the door.

"Miss Bennet asked for some tea about an hour after you left and Mrs Bingley went in and was with her for a time but that is all. Mrs Bennet, I think, had retired for the day. There has been no noise, no disturbance. Miss Bennet must have gone to sleep."

"Well, we had better let her sleep on. You must ask another man to relieve you. Indeed, I will ask someone to come," said Mr Bennet.

"Come along. Lizzy, you must go to bed. You look exhausted."

"Yes, Papa." She yawned.

An unsatisfactory day had ended. No one thought to enquire after the Fairweather carriage.

Chapter 26

Saturday 6th April 1799

AS USUAL these days, Elizabeth woke early. There was no Darcy of course, as there had not been since Tuesday, to make up the fire or call for tea and, despite her suspicions, she missed him terribly. If Max Kohler turned out to be Darcy's son, then she would tolerate it with equanimity. It would be far better than not having Darcy at all.

She felt restless without him and was unable to go back to sleep again. Oh, that he could be here now, so that she could share with him the events of the last few days and hear his own news in return. She tried to picture what he was doing now, up and about already probably, making the most of his time in Kent before his journey back to Hertfordshire, hopefully tomorrow.

It was cold, so she rang for a maid both to order tea and ask for the fire to be lit. The maid seemed to be a long time coming and when she did, the girl was flustered. She curtsied and asked whether she should make the fire or bring the tea first, glancing all the time at the door she had left open.

"What is the matter?" Elizabeth asked, dread clutching at her heart.

"'Tis Miss Bennet," said the girl, on the verge of tears.

"Yes? What of her?"

"I b'lieve she is not in her room, ma'am."

Elizabeth flew out of bed, seized her dressing gown and pushed past the maid, asking for the fire to be lit as she did so. She ran along the landing, struggling into her dressing gown at the same time, turned a corner and found Mary's door open and her father, Bingley and Jane within, likewise in their dressing gowns. Mr Bennet seemed lost for words.

"Elizabeth," said Bingley, "This is a huge disaster. A game-keeper found a ladder thrown into the woodland on the east side of the house and reported it to Price in case there had been some attempted burglary. He — I mean the gamekeeper — did not know about Mary of course but Price did."

Mr Price was the butler.

"The window is part open as you see."

Elizabeth, turning in that direction, saw that the curtains were only partly drawn and fluttered in the breeze from outside.

"Who came in first to check if she was in here or not?"

"I did," said Jane. "It was the first thing we thought of when Price came to our room to report the ladder. A maid had already been in to light a fire but reported nothing amiss. She cannot have noticed the window or that the room is pretty cold."

"I might as well shut it," said Bingley crossing the room and doing so. "We can look outside when it is lighter."

"The maid can't be blamed. I saw myself that there appeared to be someone in the bed, but when I drew the covers back, it was a mound of clothes. Mary appears to have packed a trunk but it is still in here." Jane pointed to a corner of the room where a shape could be seen in the gloom. "The trunk was open with clothes taken from it to bulk up the bed."

The room was still dark with only the light from the fire.

Mr Bennet seemed to come to life.

"The devil of it! Not one but two daughters running off in the night with young men."

Elizabeth was trying to piece the events together. "The maid who has just attended me told me that Mary had gone. How did she know? Or you, Papa? How did you find out?"

"If it was Dotty," said Jane, "then she was about lighting fires and after I had been in here, I asked her to go and fetch our father. She was very upset. I told her it was not her fault."

Bingley walked over to the fireplace. "A succession of footmen were outside this room all night," he said. "The last one, this morning, told us that neither he nor any of the others heard or saw anything during the night. I sent him away to get some breakfast and a few hours' sleep."

He took up a spill which he lit from the fire and went round the room lighting candles.

Mr Bennet turned to Elizabeth. "Lizzy, do you know any more about this business?"

"Not a great deal, Papa. Mary confided to me at Longbourn before Easter that she was writing stories. Also that she was in communication with Adolphus Barrant in America who supposedly knows Julius Fairweather. He sent letters to her at the library and she posted letters to him. He was helping her in some way, about life in New England and with more scientific material which she might be able to have published in a newspaper. You will recall that she corresponded with Julius Fairweather when he was in London before he disappeared. It seemed innocent enough."

Elizabeth bit her lip. Was she now to be blamed for all this coming about?

Jane came instantly to her sister's rescue. "Yes, Papa. When Lizzy told me about it this week, I simply thought it was an example of Mary's eccentricity. And," she turned to Bingley, "you knew about the package too, did you not?"

"Package?" said Mr Bennet. "What package? The one which turned up yesterday with that spurious legal document in it?"

"Well, no," said Elizabeth. "William was to go to London and hoped to talk to associates of Adolphus Barrant, young scientists, engineers, regarding machinery for papermaking. Whether he did so or not, I do not know. But Mary knew that Adolphus Barrant had sent from America a manuscript or some such which William was to collect from one of these young men from an address in London. He was either to bring it here himself, or give it to Charles to bring here. But you did not bring it back, did you, Charles?"

"No. Darcy decided against it, and took it off with him to Kent. I do not know why. He referred to it being some sort of manuscript. I was late back from visiting...my lawyer and we spoke very little. I wished to return here as quickly as possible and Darcy wanted to leave to go to Kent. That was on Wednesday. He took a carriage of mine and a footman to drive it. I think, possibly, he hoped to read the manuscript en route and bring it back himself when he left Kent."

It was a lot for Mr Bennet to take in. "Why on earth would he want to read a pile of worthless rubbish?"

"I cannot say, Father," Bingley answered him. "Perhaps to

see if it was suitable before handing it to Mary."

This seemed reasonable but Mr Bennet was frowning. "Why was I not told any of this? Why did not Mary come to me about her writing ambitions? I could have helped her."

"I think, I am sorry, Papa, that none of us took it seriously," said Elizabeth. "Mary herself did not wish me to tell anyone of her writing ambitions, though I told Jane when Charles did not have the manuscript with him on his return from London. I assumed that Charles knew about it and therefore Jane. William had talked about giving it to Charles after he had collected it himself."

"Barrant must have had another copy of the manuscript or some other package containing the Deed of Guardianship which he sent with the footman yesterday," Bingley offered.

Elizabeth was walking around the room now that it was easier to see, opening drawers and looking in the wardrobe and the open trunk; peering under the bed even.

Knowing how all this came about, she mused, did not tell them what to do about it. She was feeling under the pillows when Mrs Bennet entered the room, demanding to be also told what had been happening. Everyone but Elizabeth turned to her as Jane gave her an abbreviated, rather garbled account, assisted by Bingley.

Elizabeth, meanwhile, had found something under a pillow. A folded piece of paper, not sealed, but addressed on the outside to Mama, Papa, Jane, Lizzy and Kitty. She opened it and saw that it was a short note by Mary to her family dated with yesterday's date. It said very little:

"I am more than sorry to be the means of making any of you unhappy, but I cannot stay in Hertfordshire in my present situation. I would that Papa had been willing to sign the Deed of Guardianship so that my departure might have been more orderly. As it is, please God that I reach America safely and I will write to you therefrom as soon as I am able. As you will apprehend, that will probably be some months away, and some further months for a letter to reach you.

I remain, forever, your loving daughter,

MARY"

"Mama, Papa," Elizabeth turned to them, holding forth the letter, "A letter from Mary."

"Let me see it." Mrs Bennet came forward and unfolded the paper.

She made a small noise of exasperation. "Lizzy, read it to me. You have the best eyesight."

Elizabeth took it back and did so, after which Mrs Bennet voiced the question Elizabeth had been asking herself.

"Well? What are we going to do about this? She must be found and brought back."

Bingley sighed. "I could of course send a footman to London, but do we know where the Fairweather's house is?"

Elizabeth looked up from the letter. "No. The address was written on a piece of paper which William took to London with him. But William went from your London house to collect the package, did he not, Charles? Do not you know where he went?"

"I confess I do not know the exact address, other than that it was very near my house."

"So, did William walk there, Charles?"

Bingley was evidently uncomfortable. He swallowed. "In fact, he took a hackney carriage."

"But why, if it was so near?"

"I..." he stopped. "Well, the fact is I did not wish either of us to be seen by a friend or acquaintance. Or indeed my sisters. Louisa and Mr Hurst live nearby and Caroline is staying with them."

Elizabeth found herself examining Bingley's face and she saw even in the poor light of the candles that he grew pink under the scrutiny.

"Darcy wanted to get off to Kent as soon as possible, and I wanted to come home. I did not wish either of us to be detained by invitations or other distractions therefore I suggested he travelled in a hackney."

This sounded odd indeed to Elizabeth and she continued to

stare at her brother-in-law. There was the mention of Caroline again, and had not Caroline told her of Darcy and Bingley visiting a gaming house in a rough area? She would have to leave it for now, but it was very perplexing.

"Well, I for one," Mr Bennet interjected, "do not intend to go charging off all over that part of London trying to find someone. I had more than enough of that only last year when Lydia ran off from Brighton with Wickham."

"But yesterday," Mrs Bennet said, "did not you declare, Mr Bennet, that Adolphus Barrant is really Julius Fairweather, wanted for holding up coaches? A hanging offence, you said. We must get the law onto it. He must be caught and put on trial."

"No! No, Mama," cried Elizabeth, suddenly in great distress and all turned to her. Attempting to calm herself, she continued, "Papa only thinks Adolphus Barrant might be Julius. But if he is, then consider his parents, the Fairweathers, our friends. We cannot possibly set in motion a course of event which may result in Julius being hanged. We cannot.

"I very much hope," she said, "that we can keep to ourselves the possibility that Julius Fairweather is in this country. I pray that you will all refrain from spreading this tale, for tale it may be, to others in the household outside this room who will not have heard it already. And we do not want the servants to get hold of any rumours to that effect either."

She fixed her family with a firm expression. "Well, will you promise me?"

The others muttered, and then more loudly expressed their agreement.

"Very well." Mr Bennet.

"Yes, Lizzy. It seems to be for the best." Jane.

"Agreed." Bingley.

"If it must be, then yes, I will say nothing," said Mrs Bennet. "But is he, this Barrant, not now guilty of kidnapping, another grave offence? He cannot be allowed to continue to flout the law, causing havoc."

"All the evidence is that Mary went of her own accord, Mama."

"Then he must be made to marry her, as Wickham married

211

Lydia."

"And look where Lydia is now. I would remind everyone that Wickham had to be paid a large sum of money by..." Elizabeth hesitated, "someone. Adolphus Barrant is already rich. A few thousand pounds would make no difference to him."

"That may be so, if he is really Julius Fairweather. But as you said, he may not be. Adolphus Barrant may be poor."

Bingley coughed. "If Mary left with the Fairweather footman soon after tea was taken to her last night, then they could have been in London by midnight. I heard Mary talk about a new moon yesterday. That would tend to suggest that a high tide is anticipated and a ship setting sail, probably from the Pool of London, if Barrant is in London. The ship may already have sailed."

The room fell silent at that. At last Elizabeth spoke.

"Mama, Papa, we know that Mary wanted to go. Whereas Lydia was barely sixteen, Mary is nineteen and much more sensible. Of course, if we had been able to stop her yesterday, that would have been the best thing, but we were not, and now she is gone. My feeling is that we should not seek to impede her any further."

"But we must do something," said Mrs Bennet. "At least send someone to London."

It suddenly occurred to Elizabeth that the Lucases may be able to help.

"Last Saturday," she said, "at the ball in Meryton, I think that Georgiana was introduced to the Honourable Daniel Barton by the Lucases. The Lucases, therefore, may know where Mr Barton lives and he told us that he is a cousin of Julius Fairweather."

"Did he, by heaven? You did not tell us that, Lizzy."

"No, Papa. There were other distractions that evening. It slipped my mind."

The door creaked as it was opened wider. Georgiana entered the room.

"I know where Daniel Barton lives," she said. "Grosvenor Square."

Chapter 27

Saturday 6th April 1799

AS HER family were discussing the problem of Mary, the subject of their deliberations found herself on a narrow country path near a place called Farringdon, sitting on a fallen tree trunk eating bread and cheese and drinking some weak ale which tasted disgusting but she drank it anyway.

"We are about half way there," said the young footman who had told her his name was Bernard. "Are you tired? I hope not as we should press on."

They had been riding all night since she had crept into the woods of Netherfield with Bernard after climbing down the rickety ladder from her bedroom window, with his assistance.

"I thought you had brought a carriage", she had said to Bernard at the time.

He had shushed her until they had reached the outskirts of the estate where a couple of horses were tethered to a fence. Then he had told her that he had travelled from London with another footman who now had the carriage and was taking it back to London, to inform Mr Barrant that Mary's father would not sign the Guardianship Deed.

"Are we not going to London?" Mary had asked.

"No. My orders were to take you to Bristol if your father would not sign the Deed making you Mr Barrant's ward. Mr Barrant will meet us in Bristol, not London. It is possible that when your family find that you are gone, they will send a search party to London. Therefore we are to go in the opposite direction."

"I am tired. And very sore," she said now.

"You said you could ride."

"Yes, side saddle."

"That would have been too slow as I told you."

"Well, riding in the way that men do has been easier. But I do not think I could travel the same distance again. You said we are half way to this place, Bristol. I need to rest soon."

"We are resting."

"I mean a proper rest, a proper sleep in a bed."

"You just wait until we are on a ship bound for America. You will be lucky to get any sleep in a hammock, the ship being violently tossed and being sick. Unless you are fortunate and do not suffer sea-sickness."

"Are you coming to America too?"

"I must. I could be arrested and tried for kidnapping. I'd be hanged or transported."

"Then I owe you a debt of gratitude for risking such a fate to take me to a place where I can board a ship for America."

"No matter. I have always wanted to go to America. I can make my fortune there."

"What is Bristol like?"

"I have never been there. I have heard tell that there are a deal of blackamoors living in Bristol, but then so are there in London in some parts."

"You have a map. I hope it is reliable."

The young man had it spread on his knee and moved it so that she could see it. He pointed to Hertfordshire and then Farringdon. His finger then traced a line down to Bristol.

"See?"

"But Bristol is not near the sea."

"Neither is London but many ships sail from London. They are both on estuaries."

The young man scratched his head.

"Though you have made a good point. Bristol is six miles from the sea and it also suffers from very high but also very low tides. Ships become beached and cannot move until the tides come in."

"Oh," she said, not really understanding, trying to recall the geography books she had read and the pictures she had seen. "Does that mean it will be difficult to find a ship to take us to America?"

"It may, although the new moon may bring a high tide. But come on, get up. We must get going."

"I cannot. I hurt too much all over and I am cold and I think I will fall asleep on the horse's back."

"When we get to Marlborough, I will think about finding us a seat on a stagecoach or a mail coach for the rest of the journey. You could sleep on the coach. We will have to travel as brother and sister. Common people following some trade. I am common anyway. I would be a carpenter. You? What are you good at?"

"I read a lot. And write sometimes. And I practise the piano."

"That does not help. What paying job could you do?"

"A librarian?"

He passed his eyes over her and shook his head.

"Well, you look bedraggled enough after the ride, I suppose, to be a maid. You will have to say you are a housemaid but you must change the way you speak to that of common folk."

"I could be a music teacher."

"Perhaps."

It had been raining some of the night and no doubt she did not look neat and tidy any longer. Bernard had refused to let her take any spare clothes with her in a bag and made her put on several layers under her cloak. He said it would be cold. He had been right about that.

"Come. It is some miles to Marlborough. 'Twill take us at least three hours —"

"Three hours!"

"While we ride, think about what names we can travel under. And in the stagecoach, do not speak to anyone. People on coaches are bored and will often try to engage others in conversation and ask them questions. Some may think it strange that we have no luggage. If there's any word out about a girl being abducted by a man, people may be suspicious. Just go to sleep and if you find that you cannot sleep, then look as though you are sleeping."

Mary thought that at least she should be able to comply with the last request, to go to sleep. Just thinking about it made her eyelids droop.

She peered at the map. "Why must we go to Marlborough? Can we not stop sooner?"

"No. Marlborough is on the main stagecoach route from

London to Bath and Bristol. Many coaches stop there. And we are going slow enough as it is with all the stops we have made. At least the horses have not tired so fast as they would have if we had galloped non-stop."

He folded his map and stowed it in his knapsack with the rest of the food and ale. Then he helped her up off their makeshift seat and into the saddle. Mary groaned. Bernard ignored her and, quickly climbing onto his own horse, dug his heels into its flanks. Mary sighed and did the same, trying to tell herself that this was the adventure she had sought. The hardships would have to be borne. Many months of them so it seemed.

Chapter 28

BINGLEY was about to leave for London with Lieutenant Colonel Harvey when a letter arrived for him by special messenger. He paid the man and was walking towards a side door with the letter when he met Jane, Elizabeth, Kitty, Georgiana and Mrs Bennet repairing to the small parlour as was their habit immediately after breakfast.

"I believe it is from my lawyer, whom I mentioned this morning. I am going outside to read it," he explained and walked on, calling over his shoulder: "Tell Harvey if you see him that I will be a few minutes."

The ladies made themselves comfortable. Considering the events of yesterday and today, they were in reasonable spirits. Knowing that something was being done seemed to have satisfied Mrs Bennet, and Elizabeth was relieved that there were no immediate plans to inform a magistrate that Julius Fairweather may be in England.

"Will he really let or sell Netherfield?" Mrs Bennet asked Jane.

"To tell the truth, I do not know. We have been happy here. It is a beautiful house and estate, though there is not much land. Charles, I know, would like a larger estate. But he also likes being near London."

"And does not William find it convenient to come here on occasion in order to visit Kent, Lizzy?"

"He certainly did, Mama, but as you know, there is less need for that. Although Colonel Fitzwilliam's home is in Kent, where my friend Harriet will also soon reside. *And* William's other cousin, the Earl of Wareham. But as Jane implies, nothing is settled. I think there is no need for you to worry, Mama, at the moment."

Elizabeth rose from her seat and approached the window,

thinking that it was odd that Charles had taken his letter outside to read it. To the library or his small study would have seemed more suitable. She watched Charles walking up and down on the gravel, reading and apparently re-reading the letter. He raised his head then lowered it, turned his head to look this way and that, smacked the letter with his free hand once or twice. She couldn't quite see his face, whether his expression was disgruntled or amused. Was it bad news or good? Though neither was exactly something one would associate with a solicitor's letter. His demeanour simply did not suit someone scrutinising a business communication.

Elizabeth was struck again by the strangeness, too, of Charles's attitude this morning over the matter of Darcy's having taken a hackney carriage on Wednesday to travel just a few streets in London in order to avoid contact with Bingley's friends and family.

Mrs Bennet's voice cut into Elizabeth's speculations.

"You know, Lizzy," she called, forcing Elizabeth to turn from the window, "'Twould have been better, perhaps, if your father had signed that confounded Deed of Guardianship. Then people would not think that Mary had run off with a man. Of course, an older man would have been better to act as a guardian. As it is, we will have to say that Mary is going to America to study with a learned scholar. And now, I suppose, it is less of a problem than it was with Lydia. You, Lizzy, and you, Jane, are married. And Lydia too.

"Kitty? I hope that you do not feel that a terrible scandal has been created, affecting your marriage prospects. It is not an elopement after all. And everyone of our acquaintance is aware of Mary's bookishness."

Elizabeth resumed her seat, uncertain whether their mama was trying to convince herself of the lack of a scandal in Mary's case or really believed what she was saying. The contrast between her attitude today and her pitiable state last summer when Lydia had run away with Wickham was astonishing. Perhaps Mama did believe that there would be no major consequences of Mary leaving — at least not for the family. For Mary there may be considerable danger, but it was the choice she had made.

"Do I think," Kitty said in reply, "that James will abandon me because of this? I think that is highly unlikely. He will go to London with Charles, of course, in the manner of a duty or favour. Not to try to rescue me from a future as a spinster."

"I am comforted to hear that, Kitty. You are a good girl." Mrs Bennet, sitting next to Kitty, patted her knee.

"Though if I behaved as Lydia does, I believe that my marriage prospects to James or any other reasonable man would be negligible."

Bingley entered the room, walked to Jane, bent over her and kissed her on the cheek, taking her hand. They smiled at one another, in perfect accord, thought Elizabeth.

"We had better leave now. We should be back by this evening with any news."

If I know Julius, there will be no news.

Had he not been able to disappear leaving no trace a year and a half ago?

PRESENTLY, Mrs Philips entered the room, having been late down to breakfast and having only just heard from the Gardiners the news of Mary's defection. She sat down, full of questions as to what had happened, of course, which the others did their best to answer as quickly as possible.

"Climbed down a ladder!" she exclaimed. "'Tis scarcely ladylike. But Mary always was an odd girl, burying her head in books all the time. And what is known of the young man?"

She would hopefully be unaware of the theory that Adolphus Barrant was really Julius Fairweather the highwayman, that is if everyone in Mary's room this morning had kept their word. Immediately after leaving Mary's room, Elizabeth had hurried straight to see Kitty who *had* heard yesterday of the possible alias, told her of Mary's disappearance and had sworn her to secrecy regarding Julius Fairweather.

"Very little, Aunt," said Elizabeth, "other than that he is a scholar whom Mary wishes to study under…in America, and that they had been in communication over help he was giving her to…follow her calling as a writer." It seemed best not to expand upon this very basic statement. One thing might lead to another.

"Study! Writer! What was the girl thinking of? Surely her reading and constant piano practise was quite enough."

No one answered and Mrs Philips grew pink in the face, perhaps offended, perhaps feeling that the other women were deliberately excluding her from some intelligence. To try to forestall any further outburst, Elizabeth shrugged.

"It was her wish, Aunt."

"Well, I must say I am perplexed. It is as though you have all accepted the situation, with no thought of punishing her for her waywardness or making her behave."

It seemed to have escaped Mrs Philips that her suggestions were impossible of realisation since the bird had flown.

"Well, Aunt, Mr Bingley and Lieutenant Colonel Harvey have just left for London to try to seek her out."

Mrs Philips harrumphed and sat back in her chair, lifting her shoulders and placing her hands together in her lap. Perhaps in order to try to secure some reaction from Mrs Bennet, she said:

"Well, if she were my daughter, I would not tolerate it. I would have her apprehended and put away."

If Darcy had been here, even in another part of the house, Aunt Philips would probably not have voiced her opinions so freely. Elizabeth found that she could not bear this line of talk any longer and wished to remove her mother for the time being from her aunt's sphere of influence.

"Mama," she said, "would you come to my room with me. I would talk to you in relation to Harriet's wedding; in the matter of…" she searched for something suitable "…William and Colonel Fitzwilliam staying at Longbourn House before the wedding."

"Oh, yes of course, dear." And she and Elizabeth rose and left the room, Elizabeth in the expectation that others would do likewise and that Mrs Philips's tendency to make much of any given occasion would be stifled by the lack of an audience.

Chapter 29

THE COACH rattled into Bristol in the evening, slowing down in the heavy traffic and waking Mary from her slumbers. The journey from Marlborough had taken no time since she had immediately fallen asleep, her head against the side of the seat with Bernard's knapsack as her pillow. Bernard had seated her next to a window and taken up the place next to her. She had only awoken briefly at every stop to change horses. The chatter of the other passengers had washed over her. If Bernard had spoken to others, about himself or herself or anything else, then she hadn't been aware of it.

Her memory of Marlborough was faint indeed. The place was bustling with people, horses, animals, market traders and their customers, carts and wagons, those waiting to board coaches. But she took in a small fraction of the goings on, wishing only to settle down to sleep.

Bernard left her for at least twenty minutes to sell the horses. He sat her down on a bench outside the coaching inn from which he hoped they would leave, telling her not to speak to anyone, and she watched his lanky figure walk away, leading their horses. She was dozing sitting up, even before he returned with a small bag of coins.

BERNARD studied the girl as the carriage raced doggedly along the fairly straight road. The route took in Beckhampton, Calne, Chippenham, Marshfield, Wick, Kingswood, and thence Bristol, missing Bath of course, the other main destination for coaches passing through Marlborough.

The names he had given the coach company were Brian and Marie Saunders, a carpenter and a music teacher, brother and sister travelling to Bristol where he hoped to obtain work in the ship-building trade. They had decided on these details during their ride from Farringdon to Marlborough, though whether the girl would remember much of it he had to doubt, for she was practically asleep in the saddle. As it turned out, the false names were largely superfluous so far as their fellow passengers were concerned. Fortunately, they had not had to enter into any discourse with two fat, be-wigged lawyers who sat opposite each other leaning forward ignoring everyone else and whispering between themselves, and an elderly husband and wife who faced away from each other.

She wasn't bad-looking, Miss Bennet, but certainly not beautiful, not the sort of elegant, high-born girl his master would normally be interested in, so he had to wonder what was the attraction of this rather dowdy maiden from a genteel, though not very wealthy, Hertfordshire family.

Admittedly, his master's taste in girls may have changed in the eighteen months he had been away. And the girl was not ugly. The worst you could say of her was that she was plain. She had a healthy, country, rather rosy-cheeked appearance which some may find appealing. And she had certainly borne up well to the rigours of her departure from the large house in Hertfordshire and the journey which followed. She must have some spirit, and she must want to embark on this uncertain undertaking.

But it was not for him to speculate.

The sea-crossing really would be uncomfortable and hazardous and even the most hardy of girls would be frightened out of their wits. The harshness of sleeping in a hammock was the least of it. The seas could be very rough. If the ship was wrecked, then they were done for.

The Bristol Channel itself, he had heard tell, was a dangerous stretch of water with fast currents, strong tides, hidden rocks and constantly shifting sand bars. With few havens on the north Devon and Somerset coasts, ships were often wrecked.

And on the open seas, there were still privateers, vessels which carried letters of marque from hostile governments enabling them to take a ship which they had captured, resulting in fierce fighting. The flying of false flags, a common practice, rendered sea crossings even more dangerous.

Worse, there were pirates with no official status who would

take any vessel they deemed vulnerable and worth the taking.

No, he would not trouble Miss Bennet with the prospect of death on the high seas or even before they left the Bristol Channel.

Eventually he fell into a deep sleep himself, untroubled by the stops to change the horses and was only jolted awake when a coachman yelled that they were at the Bush Tavern, Corn Street and the other passengers started to struggle out of the carriage, groaning and grumbling at their stiff joints. He turned quickly to the girl, but she was there safe next to him. He peered out of the dirty window and saw that dusk was fallings. Through the now open door, he saw that the large clock on the Corn Exchange opposite showed a time which he reckoned to be a little earlier than it would be in London at this time of year with daylight fading.

He shook the girl who gradually moved and stretched before opening her eyes and then started as she realised where she was. The sights and sounds must appear strange to her indeed, having spent most of her life buried in rural Hertfordshire.

"Up you get, now," he said, leaning past her to relinquish his bag. The coachmen were shouting for the last two passengers, them, to make a move and Bernard all but picked the girl up and carried her out of the carriage, depositing her on the cobbled street where she stood swaying from the sudden awakening and having to stand on her own two feet again.

"Come," he said, steadying her, "we cannot stand here all evening. We have a little walk ahead of us."

"But there is an inn just here. Should we not refresh ourselves before doing anything else?"

"No," he said shortly.

"But I must use the…"

"All right. But quickly."

He escorted her into the building and to a privy at the rear, finding another for himself out in the yard. While he waited for her, he paid a potboy to bring him a jug of ale, drank some of it and poured the rest into his leather flask. Where they were going, he expected that they would get a meal and a bed for the night but in case the plan went wrong and they ended up sleeping in an outhouse, it would help to have the ale to wash down the rest of his meagre food supplies.

"Where are we going now?" came her voice from behind him.

"I will show you."

He had no intention of blabbing the address of their temporary lodgings for all the ogling fellows in the taproom to hear. Taking her by the elbow, he hurried her out onto the road.

"Where will we stay tonight? I would prefer not to spend another night sitting up."

"'Tis a little uphill," was all he would say.

The girl kept pace with him and seemed for all the world refreshed by her sleep. They walked towards the setting sun, the last golden rays falling on the hills above the town.

Walk west towards Brandon Hill he had been told. Being unfamiliar with the town, he knew nothing of Brandon Hill, but they were certainly going in a westerly direction judging by the sun and there was certainly a steep mound ahead of them. The place he was supposed to find was called Berkeley Square. He imagined it to be similar to the squares in London and so it transpired, although it was less grand than the London squares. There, he understood, his master's family had a friend who would offer them refuge to await the arrival of Mr Barrant himself before they could book a passage to America. When he at last found it, it was a terrace of respectable, new-looking houses.

Rapping on the door of the house he decided was the right one, he turned and looked behind him at the Brandon Hill. There was nothing much to see, no monument or statue adorning its modest summit. Pathways laced the grass covering the hill and he decided that it must be a place on which people walked. If they had to wait very long in the house for his master to appear, he must keep the girl's curious eyes away from the windows; similarly, away from the rear windows overlooking what he presumed to be a central grassed area in which the residents no doubt strolled at their leisure.

His knocks were eventually answered by a young man Bernard judged to be a footman, of similar status to himself. The man looked at them with no trace of recognition. Of course, Mr

Barrant would have had no time to alert the owner to the possibility of their coming. He had better, Bernard decided, announce himself and Miss Bennet.

"Sir, I am Bernard Thompson, a servant of Adolphus Barrant, come from Grosvenor Square in London. I believe that your master is well acquainted with his family and that the two families have assisted one another in business and other matters on occasions. The lady is an acquaintance of Mr Barrant."

The young man scrutinised Bernard and Miss Bennet in a worryingly disinterested way.

"My master is from home, sir. I know not when he will return, but it may be some months."

This was an unexpected eventuality. Bernard hoped to God that the house had not been sold on since Barrant was last in the country, or leased to another.

"Is there someone more senior to whom I may speak?" he said.

"There is not." The footman made a gesture plainly intended to take in the house.

"'Tis but a small house, as you can see. The master is often from home and accordingly leaves only a small number of servants to manage the house."

Bernard was at a loss. Possibly he would have to find a cheap inn for them and scour the streets by day for when Mr Barrant turned up.

But the young man was speaking again.

"If you would wait, I will ask the housekeeper, Mrs Pepper, if she has any forewarning of your coming. She has been here for the longest time."

Housekeeper! Mrs Pepper? Could he mean Mrs Penny Pepper, whom Mr Barrant had described as having been at one time the next thing to a mother to him?

"Thank you," Bernard said, feeling a little better in spirits. "I would be much obliged to you."

The footman shut the door on them and they waited. Bernard turned away from Miss Bennet, not wishing to witness the probable confusion in her expression on finding closed to them what she had no doubt hoped would be a refuge and an end to the first part at least of their journey.

It was almost dark by now. Servants would soon be lighting the oil lanterns hanging from wall brackets. The minutes passed. Very evidently, Mrs Pepper, whether she was Adolphus's old nurse or not, would have no forewarning of their coming. She must be advanced in years by now. Would she remember young Adolphus, or rather Julius? Should he have used the Fairweather's name instead? He wondered how long they should wait before abandoning the cause of being admitted to this house and provided with sanctuary.

Bernard felt his tension building up. It was not helped when the girl suddenly hissed:

"Perhaps we should leave. That man might alert a constable."

"I hope not," he said lamely.

"Well, so do I! But that is not the point. After coming all this way, I do not want to be forced to go back."

"Huh! All this way! You have an ocean yet to cross, Miss Bennet."

He was becoming fractious; the worry was making him so. He was immensely tired and just wished at this moment to find a place to lie down and go to sleep. But he knew he must keep his temper. At this late stage, it would be a great mistake to appear rude and boorish to the folks in this house who might still help them.

WITHOUT warning, the door was flung open again, causing Mary to start, and there stood an old woman, her ample frame covered in a neat plain grey dress and her head in a mop cap from which a few strands of white hair escaped and curled round her plump, pink face. The young footman stood behind her.

"You are come from Adolphus Barrant?" she said, peering at them short-sightedly. She stuck her head out of the door and looked up and down the street. "Is he here?"

"No, ma'am," answered Bernard. "He is to come here soon. I was charged with bringing Miss Mary Bennet here to meet him. We have just arrived in Bristol after a long journey."

"A long journey. Oh dear." She looked them over, seeming to

take in their dishevelled appearance for the first time. "Well, you had better come in."

She bustled ahead of them to what was clearly a servants' room, the housekeeper's room by the look of it, at the back of the house down a flight of stairs, where a fire blazed in the hearth and a maid sat drinking tea at a small table. She stood at the entrance of the visitors and eyed them curiously.

"We are most grateful to you, Mrs Pepper," said Mary, making a slight bow to the older woman. At her words, the servants stood about awkwardly. Mary supposed it was because they discerned that she was of the gentry. She wished that her presence did not cause them such discomfort. All she cared about at the moment was getting something to eat, having a wash and going to bed.

"I am that sorry," said Mrs Pepper, who spoke with what must be a West Country burr, "but the good rooms are not ready with the master being from home. We usually get word a day or two before his arrival, and have time to air and ready the rooms and light the fires."

"It is no matter, Mrs Pepper. We are glad of your hospitality."

"Well, if Master Adolphus is coming soon, we must ready the house in any case."

Mrs Pepper turned to the maid.

"Betty, start taking the covers off the chairs and pictures. Light fires and dust in all the rooms above stairs and the bedrooms. Get Faith and the boy to help you."

"Yes'm," the girl said, making to leave the room.

"And tell Mrs Blazer to serve dinner in here for Miss Bennet and me with some good wine." To Mary she said: "Your footman will eat in the kitchen."

"Yes'm." The girl stood there.

"Well, go on then." And the maid scuttled off.

"We wish to cause you no trouble," said Mary, wishing that Bernard would be allowed to eat with her, but feeling it out of place to voice this.

"'Tis no trouble, Miss Bennet. Master Adolphus will be here soon you say. We must make the house ready for him. Though why he calls himself Adolphus now, I do not know. But he says I must use that name."

Should they tell her that they hoped to get a passage to America as soon as Adolphus arrived? Perhaps not. Perhaps best to say as little as possible.

"How do you know him, Mrs Pepper?"

"I worked for his family and was a nurse to him at one time. But I had to come back to Bristol when my sister was ill and the Fairweathers helped me to get a job here. They know my master here. 'Tis years since I've seen him. But he sends me letters sometimes. He was always a good writer of letters was Master Ju...Adolphus. He would write to me from school where he was sent, and then Cambridge. I wonder what he looks like now."

"Yes, he wrote to me too, from London first and then from...Cambridge."

This was not true, that he had ever sent letters to her from Cambridge. She had been going to say 'America', but decided to discuss with Bernard if they were left alone how much to disclose. The young footman had been listening closely to the conversation. Possibly Mrs Pepper noticed too for she said to him:

"Would you go and see how cook is getting on with the supper, Neville."

"Certainly," he said. "Should I ask Faith to set two places for dinner in here?"

"I suppose you had better," said Mrs Pepper and he left by a side door towards the back of the house.

"Again, I apologise Miss Bennet that you are having to eat in here with me for today. I will go and see how that girl Betty is progressing with opening the rooms and making up a bed for you. I hope you do not mind if I leave you for a time."

"Not at all," Mary said.

Once she was out of the room, Mary addressed Bernard.

"What shall we tell them? Is it safe to mention the name of the Fairweathers although Mrs Pepper did? Or Julius? Or that we are going to leave for America?"

"Probably not. That fellow Neville was looking too interested for my taste."

"I thought so. But if I am to sup with Mrs Pepper and you with the servants in the kitchen, it is going to be difficult. We will have to tell them something."

"Hmm. Let us see what happens."

"How soon do you think Adolphus will get here?"

"Very soon, I should think. Possibly even tonight. It took us only a day. He will have started out as soon as he was told last night that you were being brought here instead of London. He will probably ride like the devil."

"We should alert Mrs Pepper to his possible arrival tonight, should we not?"

"I don't know."

Bernard appeared to be considering some point or other.

"Miss Bennet," he said, "I am thinking that I should go down to the docks and see what vessels may be sailing for America in the next few days. Tonight, even. Yes. That is what I must do. We have no time to lose. If we miss a sailing then there may not be another for days or weeks."

"But…we have spent a day travelling on horseback and in an uncomfortable coach. Surely we should rest for a day."

"No. We must sail if we can. You do not understand. The tides here are reputed to be very variable. If there is a ship leaving, then we must be on it, once Mr Barrant arrives."

Mary was rather starting to regret having embarked upon this adventure. She had never considered that months of discomfort would have to be endured to reach some unfamiliar destination at which it was possible, but only possible, that she could receive some sort of education for which she was, she had to admit, unprepared. She had no grounding in mathematics or science. She had concentrated only on literature, the Bible and music, all pursuits which she could follow perfectly well from England.

She glanced guiltily at Bernard who had apparently risked arrest and deportation or death to bring her here and would now, come what may, have to leave for America with Julius. In that case, if she refused to board the ship, then who would accompany her back to Hertfordshire? She could not with propriety travel alone. Bernard had been a very good and true chaperone and she had come to trust him but he would be gone across the sea if she decided not to go herself.

She was, she told herself, a very silly, selfish girl to have subjected a young man to such danger and her family, her dear Mama and Papa, to the worry of her disappearance. She should return to Hertfordshire somehow and write her stories. It was not as though she was short of material. Her family's doings alone in various ways would provide adequate particulars to fill several volumes. Her father would likely advise and help her. Now that Lizzy and Jane were gone, she sensed that there was a void in his life. Or was she deluding herself about that as well? Would he help her or would he—

"Miss Bennet," Bernard interrupted her thoughts, "I would be obliged if you would make my apologies to Mrs Pepper and tell her that I will be returned very soon."

So saying, he collected his knapsack from a chair where he had stowed it and quickly left the room. Mary distantly heard the sound of the front door slamming and feared that this would bring Neville or Mrs Pepper swiftly to this room, demanding an explanation.

She sat down, in a quandary of indecision. She had to make up her mind for it may be a few hours only before she was required to quit this comfortable little house, board a large sailing vessel, something she had never before undertaken or imagined having to do, and travel half way around the world with a man she had not seen for nearly two years and another whom she had only met yesterday. What she had done, the assumptions she had made, she now told herself, were the height of stupidity and rashness, on a mere whim that life might possibly be better elsewhere, an outcome for which she had no evidence whatsoever.

The door opened but it was not the housekeeper or the footman who entered, but a woman about twenty-five and a boy about eight years old, both neatly dressed in black, the boy as a page. However it was not just their clothes which were black, but everything else about them, the skin of their faces and hands and the woman's arms and the hair of the boy in tight curls. The woman wore a mop cap which itself was white, around the sides of which was visible a fringe of black hair, so thick that it was like a carpet as was the boy's. She curtsied to Mary and the boy bowed.

"If it pleases you, ma'am," said the woman, her voice rich and fruity with an accent which Mary had never heard before, "I have been sent to lay two places at table."

Mary, having never seen an African before, tried hard not to stare. She had seen pictures in books of course and knew of the slave trade, now under threat of abolition in the British territories, but had never glimpsed a real black person.

"Yes, of course," she said.

"Adam," said the woman who Mary assumed was the other maid, Faith, "get the table cloth and cutlery out."

"Yes'm," he said. This must be 'the boy' previously referred to. He opened the drawers of a sideboard and proceeded to extract the necessary items. Faith drew glasses and plates from a set of built-in shelves, and table napkins and rings from one of the drawers beneath the shelves. Between the pair, they laid two places at the table.

"Thank you," said Mary, fascinated to see from the corner of her eye that their fingernails and the undersides of their hands were white. Had not Bernard said that there were many blackamoors living in Bristol? She had never expected, though, to find herself in a house with black servants.

"Will that be all, ma'am?"

"Yes, I am sure it will."

"We must go, then, and continue opening the rooms upstairs. Come, Adam."

The woman nodded, almost bowed and the boy did bow. They met Mrs Pepper coming back in. She looked around the room to see that the table had been laid.

"Off you go then," she said. And to Mary: "Where's your footman?"

"Oh…he has gone back to the…quay I think he said to see if Mr Barrant has arrived."

"Was he coming by packet, then? I assumed he would be riding."

"We are not sure."

"Well, your footman wants to watch he do not get taken by a press gang. He has no employment here. Not that it would make any difference to most press officers if he did."

Mary gasped at the prospect of Bernard simply never coming back to this house and ending up in the Navy on a war ship. This whole escapade was becoming more and more of a disaster and it was her fault. But Mrs Pepper laughed.

"Do not upset yourself, my dear. I expect I was exaggerating. Now, here comes our meal," she said cheerfully as the door to the back of the house opened and Betty and Mrs Blazer, presumably, came in bearing steaming dishes. "Sit yourself down. I will pour the wine."

BERNARD was being careful. He, too, was well aware of the press gangs which lurked in ports like Bristol. He went to Broad Quay and looked for shipping company offices. They were still open as were most businesses despite the relatively late hour. The lamps had been lit and merchants and pedestrians were going about their business as though it was the middle of the day.

Tugboats were navigating through the smooth waters and merchants loaded their wares onto waiting vessels. Commerce and trade were everywhere. He watched the sleds loaded with barrels that were used in place of carts being pulled along by horses.

If Adolphus was here, then he did not see him. The full black beard was perhaps not the best disguise to have adopted, he thought. He would suggest trimming the beard to a neat point and bleaching the beard and his hair as ladies sometimes bleached their hair.

When he enquired, there were sailings before long to Newfoundland, Antigua and New York, but none to Boston. New York would be the closest. And there were many sailings to Ireland which might be a possibility.

At least he had some information and he slipped through the streets back towards Berkeley Square where, on knocking at the front door, he was directed by Neville to the back door and the kitchen where he was expected to have his meal with the other servants and no doubt he would be found a cot for the night in some hole barely bigger than a broom cupboard if he was lucky. The order of things had been determined. Miss Bennet was of the gentry and he was a common man.

He would, he resolved, definitely go to America and make his fortune and no one could thenceforth look down upon him and consign him to a rat-hole for his sleeping quarters.

Chapter 30

ON SATURDAY, Bingley and Harvey had returned with no information. Elizabeth was not surprised but the others were at least perplexed. Where had the girl gone? The Honourable Daniel Barton, when they called upon him in Grosvenor Square, claimed to have no knowledge of Adolphus Barrant's whereabouts or whether he was still in London. He certainly did not know whether his friend Adolphus Barrant had boarded a packet lying in the Pool of London, with or without a young lady by the name of Miss Mary Bennet or otherwise.

He had directed Bingley and Harvey to the Fairweather house, also in Grosvenor Square but the house seemed to be shut up, the curtains drawn, no signs of activity. They had enquired of the shipping agents and packet companies. There had been sailings to Falmouth, a common departure point for Rhode Island, but none had included passengers by the names of Mr Adolphus Barrant or a Miss Mary Bennet. The companies' clerks were dismissive when offered a description of Miss Bennet and told that she may be travelling under an assumed name.

Bingley and Harvey had no idea what Adolphus Barrant looked like, having neglected to obtain a description from the Honourable Daniel Barton. They decided against returning to his house and questioning him further since it was getting late, always assuming that he would still be at home, and turned their horses towards Smithfield Market in order to gain the Great North Road, and travel back to Hertfordshire.

It was a mystery, everyone agreed, where Mary could be. Mrs Bennet gave way to bouts of quiet weeping in her room and Elizabeth and Jane tried to assure their mother that Mary was almost certainly safe somewhere and at or on the way to one of the many other ports from which it was possible to embark for America.

"But, why?" their mother kept repeating.

Mr Bennet declared that he was now convinced that he and Mrs Bennet had managed to bring forth yet another of the silliest girls in the country, the first two being Lydia and Kitty.

"Yes, well," he admitted, "Kitty has shown a marked improvement of late; sadly not Lydia."

No solution to Lydia's further fall from grace had been put forward. Colonel Fitzwilliam had related that a British Army barracks at Waterford in Ireland was in the course of being completed though he did not know whether Wickham was stationed there. He would make enquiries.

To take everyone's minds off the unsatisfactory outcome of Saturday's investigations, it was agreed that another puppet play should be performed by the Gardiner children who had been agitating to show off their hand puppets and had written another of their dramas based on more scandal of the day.

They had been painting scraps of wood to make scenery almost since their arrival at Netherfield, sewing costumes and fashioning puppets' heads out of *papier-mâché*. Hand puppets, they claimed, were easier to make and less troublesome on stage than puppets with strings.

Of more concern to Elizabeth was the non-return yesterday, Sunday, of Darcy. She had spent a good deal of yesterday peering out of windows and starting at any sound which might have been a horse or carriage arriving.

She concealed it as best she could but she was very worried now, not that he was philandering with another woman, Clara Lang or anyone else, but that some dire accident had befallen him. Perhaps he had fallen prey to a footpad or a gang of highwaymen. Bingley stressed that he had taken a carriage to Kent rather than having ridden there. He had, Bingley said, been exceedingly eager to get to this wretched paper mill in Kent, Turkey Mill. He may have stayed even longer than intended to find out as much as possible.

Elizabeth tried to comfort herself that Darcy should be a little safer in a carriage than on horseback, from a footpad at least. But still, he could be lying in a ditch somewhere, injured and helpless and undiscovered.

Early in the day, Harriet came to her.

"Lizzy, I fear we cannot defer any longer our marriage arrangements. Jeremy has spoken to Bingley and he is prepared to act as Jeremy's second bondsman. I, too, must obtain a licence to marry out of my normal place of residence. And Harvey, of course, will act as Jeremy's groomsman."

"Do you really think that is necessary just yet, Harriet? Darcy may return at any time."

"But my parents are due to arrive within a few days."

"Well, I suppose that in the end it will not matter who is second bondsman and who is groomsman," Elizabeth had to admit.

"I hoped that you would see it that way, Lizzy, my kind friend who has brought me together with the man of my dreams."

Yes, yes, Elizabeth wished to say, but in a year's time that too will all be much of a muchness. What I care about is the safe return of my husband.

As though reading her thoughts, Harriet said, "Lizzy, Jeremy says that he knows no one like Darcy for resilience and strength. He knows…we know…that you are worried about him, but Jeremy is quite sure he will be all right."

"Thank you, Harriet." Elizabeth made an effort not to sound too forlorn. It was not easy.

ELIZABETH'S day was enlivened, though not necessarily in a very cordial way, by a letter addressed to her delivered to Netherfield House in the early afternoon. Who could it be from? The seal impressed upon the wax which fastened the folded piece of paper together was European in appearance, an eagle, its head in profile and its wings spread. It had a slightly frightening quality, signifying aggression, arrogance and assumed superiority. Elizabeth experienced an instant and instinctive dislike of the symbol and, by association, what might lie within.

When Price the butler sought her out and handed the letter to her, she looked around to see if anyone had noticed. It appeared not. She immediately secreted the letter in her sleeve and rushed upstairs to her bedroom.

She again scrutinized the fine detail of the seal before pulling it apart and opening up the letter within, noting straightaway that it was a very short missive. As there was no heading, she looked first to the end of the letter to determine its author. It was signed 'Clara Lang'.

She found herself pausing at that. Was it her imagination or was there some hesitancy between the first and last names? There seemed to be a larger space than necessary and, if she was not mistaken, a thickness in the ink at the end of 'Clara'. Why would a woman sign her Christian name and then leave her pen over-long at the end of the name before drawing her pen away from the paper and applying the nib to the paper once again to write the surname? She must know her own name.

But there could be a logical explanation. Perhaps she used more than one name or surname in her dealings and was undecided which to use in this case. Or perhaps she had considered signing only 'Clara' but had decided that it would be too informal. But speculating would get her nowhere, therefore she raised her eyes to the top of the sheet and began to read it.

"8TH APRIL

DEAR MRS DARCY,

It cannot have failed to escape my notice that you have lately been seeking to meet me, leaving several of your cards at the Black Bear in Cambridge and the Shire Hall in Hertford.

Why you would wish to have an audience with me, I can only speculate but of course you have piqued my interest and I must assume that you have some interest in me. Since I shall return to Hertfordshire for a brief further period later this week, it seemed sensible to offer you an interview that we may each assuage our curiosity about the other.

On Friday at noon I will be in the small parlour of the Pheasant Inn at Meryton. If you would care to attend me there, I hope we may be assured of some privacy.

Yours respectfully,

CLARA LANG"

It seemed to Elizabeth that the letter was imperious to a considerable degree, hardly an invitation at all. There was no request for a response, therefore Clara Lang must assume that her wish would be complied with. Elizabeth wondered if she should succumb to this commanding manner, but reflected that this was what she had sought, a chance to speak to Clara Lang and try to discover why Darcy had been so discomfited after having merely seen Clara's son Max perform at an informal soirée in London nearly three weeks ago.

She had all but attempted to ambush the other woman and it would now be, she had to tell herself, perverse to refuse the invitation or fail to attend through a sense of indignation at the woman's phraseology. And she should not overlook the fact that Clara was foreign, Prussian she understood. She may not be skilled at English letter writing, not accustomed to the courtesies the English habitually extended.

Yet the woman had proposed, nay prescribed, Friday for the encounter. She would have to wait until Friday to find out more! A wave of frustration went through her. But it was too bad. It could not be helped. She would have to usefully fill her time before the appointed day.

She again secreted the letter in her sleeve and tripped downstairs to find her father. He was the only person with whom she could discuss a meeting with Clara Lang. He would not need to be told what it was about. He would conceivably be as interested as she was to ascertain the truth about Darcy's past and to know whether there was some continuing connection with Mrs Lang and her son Max. He would, she hoped, offer to drive her to Meryton on Friday in Bingley's curricle and, if need be, make up some excuse for the trip. Perhaps a visit to the library to scour the newspapers for any information about sailings to America.

Against all logic, she started to look forward to the meeting. She was impatient to know the truth and a frisson of excitement passed through her to think that she was on the verge of discovering the answers to the questions which had been plaguing her since her visit to Lucas Lodge on 21st March when Darcy had returned from London.

THE puppet show accordingly went ahead that evening. This time, the children had written a programme listing a cast of characters which included Lady Hamilton, Sir William Hamilton and Nelson, the Duchess of Devonshire, as usual King George, and Queen Charlotte, Prince George and Princess Caroline.

Lady Hamilton was portrayed at first as a nymph, prancing about in diaphanous garments, but later with some sort of large padded bulge in the front of her dress. Aunt Philips screamed with laughter at this. Nelson chased after her. He wore the same sort of hat as Bonaparte, was minus an arm and had an eye patch which flapped up and down.

Nelson was then shown holding a screaming baby with his one arm while Emma Hamilton flounced about and posed for paintings. Sir William Hamilton peeked out from behind furniture and, when the stage was empty, came out and made extravagant gestures of despair, mopping his eyes with a handkerchief.

The Duchess spent much time at card tables losing a great deal of cash represented by mock bills and buttons painted to look as though they were coins made of gold and silver.

Prince George was shown throwing on lavish garments and drinking profusely with the King remonstrating with him. Princess Caroline wept as Prince George gallivanted with mistress after mistress.

After thirty minutes the puppets took their bows.

Music was then played. Elizabeth, Georgiana and Harriet played and sang. Georgiana on the piano accompanied Lieutenant Colonel Harvey's singing and Kitty played sweet tunes on her lute.

As Elizabeth climbed the stairs later, she grieved over the absence of Darcy to accompany her in their usual joyful state. When would he return? Surely it could not be long now.

Chapter 31

BEFORE MID-DAY, another letter was delivered to Netherfield addressed to Colonel Fitzwilliam. Curious glances followed him as he took the letter to Bingley's study with Bingley's agreement.

"I rarely use the room in any case," said Bingley cheerfully, "unless forced to, if I have to look over the household accounts or similar. Jane does most of it," he admitted. "She seems to enjoy adding up figures and inspecting the suppliers' bills and…everything else. It takes a great weight off me, I can tell you. I hope your new wife will be as handy with a ledger as is mine."

"Oh, I have every expectation that Harriet will be the soul of efficiency and industry in the management of a household. I think, indeed, that she keenly anticipates the necessary tasks."

"Upon my word, that is very fortunate. Well, I will leave you to your letter. I hope that it is good news."

"I thank you. It is from my brother, by the seal."

Bingley withdrew and Fitzwilliam sat near the fire to read his letter in comfort. In truth, he was disconcerted and lingered a while before opening the letter. He and Ernest did not correspond frequently. He was fairly often at Pakeleigh Abbey due in part to the ill-health his brother had suffered all his life, rather like their cousin, Lady Catherine's daughter Anne. It seemed to be a strain, some weakness, which ran through some branches of the family and not others. He must hope that his own children were not plagued with illness, nor indeed Darcy's, though in truth his brother's and Anne de Bourgh's respective ailments appeared to be of a totally different order. Yet the result would probably be the same; their days were numbered. He had not told Harriet of his brother's poor constitution. She would find out in due course.

It seemed unnecessary to write to each other as Fitzwilliam

went home when he could. And when they did write, the letters tended to be short, dealing briefly with the matter to be communicated. This letter in his hands, however, was rather more bulky than usual and he doubted that it was filled with eloquence expressing Ernest's rapture at his forthcoming marriage. It must be something else.

He pulled at the seal, opened the sheets and read.

"PAKELEIGH ABBEY

MONDAY, APRIL 8

MY DEAREST JEREMY,

Please allow me to say at the outset how very delighted I was to receive your letter two days ago informing me of your forthcoming marriage to Miss Harriet Layham. I wish you and Miss Layham every happiness, my dear brother, and would have written to you by return had not certain events overtaken the hours between the receipt of your letter and today when I now have an opportunity to reply to you.

You must permit me to first explain why this letter is unable to be written under by own hand. I regret that I have suffered a further episode of the shaking palsy, therefore what I wish to say must be dictated to my secretary, Alan, and I trust that you will excuse my inability to pen this letter of congratulations to you myself as I would so very much have wished to do, although I will attempt my own signature. May this tiresome affliction abate as it cannot do soon enough.

The palsy is having some considerable effect this time and the physician's treatment appears much less efficacious than it has been heretofore. I think I must tell you, my dear brother, that as a result I will be unable to attend the celebration of your marriage during this week or whenever it is exactly to take place as you are unsure on this point. For this, I am more sorry than I can express. I can only be gratified that you appear, from what you say, to be among such cordial company at Netherfield and that Miss Layham's parents, at least, will be present at the wedding despite their home being so far afield as Derbyshire.

You and your new bride and indeed her parents must come here as soon as you may and please extend this invitation to them. Be assured, too, that your house here is being made ready for your arrival though I hope that you and your bride will in the first place wish to repose at the Abbey where every effort will be made for your comfort and pleasure.

My dear brother, I often think of you in your military role and wish you some respite here until you must return to the regiment."

Fitzwilliam had by now become convinced that, despite Ernest's plea for an early recovery, his beloved older brother was going to relate to him that his illness was incurable and progressive and that he had not long to live. Salty tears coursed down Fitzwilliam's cheeks and he was glad that he had chosen to read this letter in private.

"Now, having proffered my apologies for being necessarily absent from your wedding, I must recount to you the events of yesterday. Pray, be not alarmed when I tell you that your cousin and mine, Fitzwilliam Darcy, has suffered injuries during an accident nearby when his carriage overturned soon after leaving Maidstone yesterday morning to return to Hertfordshire. He had been touring the nearby Turkey Mill since last Thursday.

Alas, his journey was cut short. When the carriage in which he was travelling overturned not far out of Maidstone due to the condition of the road early yesterday morning, he asked to be brought here rather than the hospital at Maidstone. A good choice I think. He suffered cuts and severe bruising to his face and body which the physician calls contusions and it was thought initially that his left arm had been fractured but the physician says it is merely a bad sprain. Luckily, his cuts needed no stitches, he being protected by his thick clothing and guarding his face with his arm. His injured arm is in a sling to rest it. My physician says that he will make a full recovery but is unable to travel for about two weeks and, being confined to bed and very stiff about all his person, is unable to write to you all at Netherfield himself. The physician says that the stiffness will likely get worse before it improves.

Fortunately, Bingley's footman who was driving the carriage was thrown clear and suffered only minor bruising. The carriage, which I believe belonged to his friend Bingley, is at a local smith undergoing repairs and the horses are stabled here.

Dear brother, I am obliged to pass on Darcy's wishes which are that you should go ahead with your wedding plans. He is sorry he cannot act as your second bondsman or groomsman, but assumes that his friend Bingley or Lieutenant Colonel Harvey will assume these roles.

He also expresses the wish, I do not know why, that the company at Netherfield attend the dance at Lucas Lodge next Saturday. His sister Georgiana in particular, he says, should not concern herself about him. He will be back in Hertfordshire within a fortnight and he regrets that a return to Pemberley is bound to be delayed for which he asks that his profuse apologies may be extended to Mrs Darcy and Georgiana.

He hopes also that Mrs Darcy will be able to attend your wedding to her friend and should not immediately travel to Kent to attend him.

In short, my brother, he expresses his ardent hope that all your plans at Netherfield will proceed regardless of his accident and injuries. He will be well in reasonably early course and hopes that you will all at Netherfield regard his requests in this light.

And he enquires after Mrs Darcy's sister, Miss Mary Bennet. If word of her wellbeing may be sent to him, he would be obliged.

Again I know not why.

Those are our cousin's stated wishes, my brother, and I feel that we should observe them for he is powerless to act on his own account at this time. Having said which, my physician's opinion is that Darcy will not keep to his bed by any wise as long as has been advised and may attempt to travel back to Netherfield far sooner than he should, which is of course another good reason why none of you from Netherfield should risk travelling here and unknowingly passing Darcy on the road.

I know, dear brother, that you will be amused to learn that Darcy has privately to me described Dr Simmons as an 'old woman'. He is trying to leave his bed today to the doctor's great alarm, but as we know, Darcy always was one to be greatly attached to having his own way.

If you would send me your wedding day when it is known, then I will think of you on the day.

I offer my felicitations to all at Netherfield and my heartfelt thanks to Mr and Mrs Bingley for their hospitality at having received my beloved brother and Miss Layham into their home over the Easter festivities. Indeed, I must offer my most sincere sympathies to Mrs Darcy for the distress which must be caused by the tidings of her husband's injuries which it has been my unpleasant duty to bear but please be heartened, Mrs Darcy, by my physician's assurance of your husband's anticipated recovery in reasonably early course.

I believe that the above is all that I can tell you for now. Should there be any further intelligence to share with you, you may be sure that it will be speedily conveyed to you.

I remain, as ever, your loving brother,

ERNEST"

Colonel Fitzwilliam bowed his head, not in consternation, but as laughter shook his shoulders at the thought of Darcy's waywardness and the doctor's indignation, coupled with relief that there was no immediate reason to believe that his brother was nearly on his death-bed. If he knew Darcy, it would be a matter of a few days only before he boarded another carriage or a stage-coach and attempted the journey to Hertfordshire.

He could relate none of this to the household, apart from Bingley in confidence, until at least he had been able to show the letter to Cousin Elizabeth who was away in Meryton with Harriet, Georgiana and Kitty making purchases of haberdashery, he understood, in readiness for the ball at Lucas Lodge on Saturday and for Harriet to be measured for a new dress for the wedding. That Darcy had been involved in a road accident and suffered injuries could not be made common knowledge until Elizabeth was aware of what had happened. He would tell Bingley because it was his carriage and because he was Darcy's great friend who may wish to send a letter for Darcy back to Kent with Ernest's messenger. Darcy and Bingley had certainly seemed to spend much time together this Easter in quiet, somewhat mysterious, discussions.

Actually, ever since his arrival at Netherfield, he had been conscious of some undercurrent present in the household, or some members of it, something unspoken, but known by a few. From his first contact with Darcy, the other had been distracted for some reason he was not willing to discuss. Fitzwilliam was sure that, whatever the secret was, Bingley had shared it from the outset, the two men frequently whispering to one another and travelling to London a second time from which Bingley returned in some bad humour.

And increasingly, Cousin Elizabeth had become fraught, heavy with some anxiety, and on occasion behaving oddly, irrationally, such as her desire to suddenly visit Cambridge last Wednesday. Now it seemed to him that, more recently, Mr Bennet had also been inducted into the secret, resulting in more quiet chats between Elizabeth and her father.

Harriet was also aware of all this tension and had hoped and expected that her friend would confide in her but she had not.

They had both hoped for a merry time this Easter at Netherfield, with much singing and dancing but this had turned out not to be very frequently the case with Darcy discomposed and he and Bingley being away so much. The evenings when there had been such entertainments had felt rather muted and forced.

Well, at least there would be the ball at Lucas Lodge on Saturday to look forward to. There had been some concern that it might be cancelled or, a terrible thought, that the invitations to the Netherfield party might be withdrawn on some fictitious basis for propriety's sake but, happily, neither had occurred.

He and Harriet both agreed that the Collins-induced unpleasantness at the ball at Meryton was not the cause of the underlying problem, but rather a symptom of it. Darcy, they were sure, would likely not have made so much of Mr Collins's interference had he not already been discomposed, though Fitzwilliam had been quite prepared at the time to support his cousin's stand against the difficult man. The trouble pre-dated the ball and was caused by something else.

He only hoped that the trouble would not cause a rift between Darcy and Elizabeth, whom he had heretofore regarded as the epitome of the perfect love-match, whatever the inferiority of her connections. He valued stability. He would be very disappointed if the trouble led to his cousin's marriage being severely damaged, indeed severed.

He was immeasurably grateful to Cousin Elizabeth for being the means of bringing him together with Harriet, albeit that the making of a match had not been premeditated. He had even sensed that Elizabeth had been cautious and had not necessarily regarded the match with favour initially. Hopefully, the caution was now a thing of the past. He also sensed that Elizabeth was not a woman who would accede to any dilution of her husband's regard for her, would not be prepared to share his affections, if that turned out to be the cause of the trouble with Darcy.

In truth, he had begun to be impatient with the various goings-on this Easter. In addition to the riddle of Darcy's uncertain mood, there had been the debate upon what to do about the atrocious behaviour of Elizabeth's sister, Lydia, compounded by another sister, Mary, absconding on a mission supposedly to improve her education in America. None of these things, he felt, were any of his business, but the whole household had been drawn into the discussions regarding Lydia and Mary. That Harriet was diverted and amused was of some comfort but his main object now was to be married to Harriet, to become better acquainted with her parents and to commence their new life together in Kent. It would be a happy marriage. She was an attractive, affectionate, steady girl and of a good family. She wanted children. She was the perfect partner in life for him.

Despite his irritation over the conduct of Elizabeth's sisters, he found himself examining the problem of Lydia because there was some similarity in their circumstances. He was an army officer about to be married and Lydia was the wife of an army officer. He, Fitzwilliam, would soon be faced with similar choices; where would an officer's wife live? In fact, he had no intention of taking his own wife with him to an army camp or barracks or any town in which he was billeted. Harriet would live in his house in Kent and he would in early course most probably dispose of his commission and leave the army. He thought that Harvey would be interested in buying the commission. He knew that Harvey wished to wait until Kitty was a little older before marrying.

Indeed, the army provided no significant married accommodation even for officers. In some barracks, there was rudimentary provision for wives and children in the form of a curtained-off section of the men's quarters, but it was regarded by most, Fitzwilliam included, as most unsatisfactory. The conditions for wives and children were primitive and their presence was a distraction to the soldiers.

The building of any barracks was a relatively new development. There had been a reluctance to establish a standing army housed in barracks, it being associated with dictators and the intimidation of the people. Troops were generally billeted in inns and other locations. Nevertheless, training and the enforcement of discipline was easier if troops did not live amongst the general population. Accordingly, barracks had become more widespread.

His own most suitable solution to the problem of Lydia,

which he would suggest to Darcy on his return since Elizabeth's family seemed to wish to involve Darcy and seek his opinion and assistance, would be to arrange for Lydia and Wickham to be found lodgings in the town in Ireland where Wickham was serving. Who would pay for the accommodation would, of course, be a matter for the family. Wickham was known to be irresponsible. The family, probably Darcy and Bingley, would have to decide whether it was worth their while in order to remove Lydia from London and her troublesome proximity to the family.

It would only be a temporary solution of course. It seemed to him that the couple would continue to have to be provided with assistance potentially indefinitely. It was not a happy position for the family to be in.

None of it of course was his concern, beyond giving his advice to Darcy. As to Mary, Darcy's enquiry about her in Ernest's letter suggested that Darcy was cognisant of some possible risk to her. Fitzwilliam shook his head. Another mystery! Yet another conundrum for someone else to find an answer to. He just wanted to get on with the wedding and his and Harriet's new life together.

He, Harriet and Bingley were to visit the rector at Meryton later and make arrangements for the licences and set an early date for the wedding.

He got to his feet, threw more wood on the fire and left the room to look out Bingley.

BINGLEY IN turn called for the whereabouts of the rider who had brought the Earl's letter and made it known that he wished to send a response back to Kent. He hurriedly penned a few lines to Darcy and sealed his short letter around that of the lawyer Blake and the report of Matthew Benjamin, ordering the messenger to set out for Pakeleigh Abbey straightaway. He calculated that it would take the rider about eleven or twelve hours and would probably necessitate an overnight stop. In all likelihood, it would not reach Darcy until some time tomorrow, Wednesday. He wondered what Darcy's reaction would be.

WHEN LATER told of Darcy's accident and injuries, everyone agreed that it was most unfortunate. There was much discussion whether those most close to Darcy who might have immediately set out for Kent, Elizabeth in particular of course and perhaps Georgiana to a slightly lesser extent, should do so or should heed Darcy's expressed wish to await his return.

Colonel Fitzwilliam offered his opinion that Darcy would not follow the doctor's advice and would have returned far sooner than a fortnight, therefore the most sensible course would be to wait.

Elizabeth had already read the letter as Colonel Fitzwilliam came to her in private after her return from Meryton. The signature 'Ernest' was unrecognisable as such, and she wondered how ill the Earl actually was. The condition from which he suffered sounded of long-standing, but the Colonel had never spoken of it before.

She must belatedly reply to Mrs Holmes of Frogmore Mill to decline the invitation to their party on Friday evening. She would have a good excuse now.

She was naturally upset and felt that her fears had been justified. Her sisters, her mother, Harriet and Georgiana took turns to comfort her and caution her against rushing off to Kent. With a show of reluctance, she agreed to remain at Netherfield for the time being.

"Yes, Lizzy," said her father, looking over his glasses at her. "You do not want to miss events hereabouts, for example Saturday's ball in particular and the wedding of your cousin and your friend, in order to take part in a wild-goose chase if Darcy is on his way here at the same time, as Fitzwilliam's brother suggests could happen."

"No, Papa."

Colonel Fitzwilliam frowned to himself, feeling that there was some hidden meaning in Mr Bennet's words and knowing expression.

Chapter 32

DARCY eased his legs out of the bed and sat up with a groan. Then he fell back, initially unable to support himself, and his legs ended up in the air in a most undignified pose. The night-shirt into which he had been painfully wrestled on Sunday by a couple of footmen under the direction of Old Woman Simmons had ridden up almost to his manhood enabling him to view the full black and blue effect of his injuries along both legs.

"Oh God," he moaned. But he was determined to get up to-day and catch a stagecoach, stop overnight in London at the Golden Cross and there catch a stagecoach tomorrow which passed through St Albans where he would alight and hire a carriage to carry him back to Meryton and Netherfield.

He would take Bingley's footman with him to help him in and out of the coaches and generally, and to drive the carriage to Netherfield on the last leg of the journey but he would not borrow one of Ernest's carriages for the whole journey. For now, he would avoid long journeys in private carriages.

He had been very effectively reminded on Sunday that private carriages were not so strongly built as stagecoaches. It had been most unpleasant to be thrown about, realising that a wheel had been lost and that the finely balanced structure was going to collapse, to be hurled against the frame of the carriage as it fell to the ground, and the broken glass of the windows coming at him, shards of which would have pierced his skin deeply, his eyes, had he not thrown himself to the floor of the carriage and shielded his face and head with his arms. The horses had dragged the broken carriage farther along the road in their panic and he felt that large parts of his body must have made contact with almost every surface of the inside of the carriage as it bumped along, eventually falling into a ditch which was when Darcy's left arm had been wrenched as the carriage overturned completely and came to a stop.

He had been forced to lie there, largely trapped, blood from his cuts seeping through his torn clothing. He tried moving his arms and legs and thought that nothing was broken. At length, he heard Bingley's footman cursing as he released the horses and got them back up to the road. He came to Darcy, leaning over the window, out of breath.

"I'm not hurt, sir. I was thrown free. I will take one of the horses and get help. I'll be back as soon as possible."

Darcy had croaked his thanks. "Stanforth," he had said, "I do not think I am badly hurt but I seem to be trapped in here. My cousin's estate near Wrotham Heath is but four or five miles away. I would rather be taken there than to any hospital. It is Pakeleigh Abbey. Anyone around here will know of it. My cousin, the Earl of Wareham, will afford you any help necessary. Bring some men, five or six I should think, to help me get out of here. The Earl's men will let you have a carriage."

"Very well, sir." The man stood up and walked away, calling to the horses.

It was several hours before Darcy was eventually delivered into the tender care of Dr Simmons at Pakeleigh Abbey.

IF DARCY was going to be so foolish as to not only leave his bed but also to actually leave Pakeleigh Abbey and make his way back to Hertfordshire, Dr Simmons insisted that he should be provided with a pair of crutches.

"I am not an invalid, you know," Darcy protested.

"Well, actually you are, for now." The physician regarded him gravely. "Upon my word, Mr Darcy, you must realise that getting about by holding onto furniture is all very well inside a house, but outside, you are going to need something else, something you can take with you."

"A walking cane will suffice, surely."

This conversation was taking place in the breakfast room to which Darcy had been helped by two footmen.

"Try it if you must. There is one in the corner."

The doctor and Cousin Ernest watched as Darcy was helped over to the corner by a footman and grasped the cane. He took

251

one confident step out into the room and started to topple forward. The footman caught him.

Ernest laughed as his shaking hand conveyed a spoon of devilled kidneys roughly in the direction of his mouth. He had told Darcy that a spoon was easier these days than a knife or fork. Darcy had been privately horrified at the decline in Ernest's health on first seeing him on Sunday after a year or more.

"You had better take a second footman with you, Darcy." Even his speech was affected. He had to take his time to form his words.

"Thank you, Cousin." And to Dr Simmons: "Very well, I will try out the crutches if you have a pair."

"I will send for them. And you will have to take laudanum for the journey." The doctor left them and Darcy was helped back to his seat.

"I have a sedan chair," said Ernest, "in which I have been carried about the estate at divers times when my balance has failed. I fear that I shall need it again soon. But I suppose you would rather not travel back to Netherfield at running speed." He chuckled.

"Indeed."

"It is possible to obtain a wheelchair I believe, but I have never seen one. I imagine it would be too heavy to take on a stagecoach." He raised his eyebrows in mock innocence, an expression with which Darcy was familiar. Ernest had always been a little childlike, his jokes not at all subtle. Fortunately for his servants and tenants, he was very kind and good-natured. A man-child with a cruel temperament could cause untold misery.

"Thank you, Fitzwilliam. Your suggestions are much valued, but I fear impractical as you say."

"You could think of hiring either contraption once you are back at Netherfield."

"I will consider it."

"Have you had the time to read the letter from Bingley delivered this morning by my servant?"

"Yes. Er, he thinks that the wedding will be next week but will write to you when the precise date is known. No one at Netherfield, on hearing of my accident, has yet indicated an intention to travel here which is fortunate in the circumstances as they would miss me. He sends love from Elizabeth and Georgiana, neither of whom had time to write any note to be included with his own letter. I think that is all."

Ernest appeared to have given up with his kidneys and was chewing on some small biscuits.

"I had written that you were desirous of receiving any news regarding your wife's sister Mary. Did Bingley not supply any report in that regard?"

"He did not. I think there was not time."

"So very little news, therefore, for a letter of such ample proportions."

"Yes, very little. Bingley is not a good letter writer. He is not...economical with words."

Ernest regarded his cousin. He obviously saw that Darcy was holding something back. Darcy smiled, hoping thereby to deflect any further searching enquiries. The ploy seemed to have the desired effect.

"Well," said Ernest, rising from his chair a mite unsteadily himself, "if you are bent on journeying back to Hertfordshire, we had best get you off to The Bull at Wrotham."

Chapter 33

MR BENNET drove the curricle to the back of The Pheasant, tipping a stable boy to look after the horse and handing Elizabeth down onto the cobbled yard.

"Come, my dear," he said and she took his arm.

There was no one in the world she would rather have with her to share her dread and anticipation than her loving, sensible Papa who would guard her secret if she so desired and forebear to exaggerate the crisis of the occasion if a crisis was the outcome. He would support her in whatever course she chose. The prospect of what certain courses might be caused a lump to form in her throat and tears to spring to the corners of her eyes, but she would not show this Teutonic matron, for near-matron she must be to have a child of ten, how hurt and desperate she was.

Mr Bennet examined his watch. She and Papa had made sure not to arrive too early. She did not wish to be found sitting fidgeting and picking at her nails when Mrs Lang swept confidently into the parlour, for that is how Elizabeth imagined her.

He ordered refreshments to be brought to the parlour in about ten minutes and, with a fluttering heart, Elizabeth allowed her father to lead her to the room which they knew to be at the rear of the building. The door was slightly ajar. No sound came from within and Mr Bennet pushed the door open further with his stick, and there she was. A beautiful, well-dressed, flaxen-haired woman, sitting alone, reading a book, the very essence of composure. She did not look up.

Elizabeth and her father were accorded every opportunity to take in her extravagantly dressed hair, piled high and threaded with jewels and decorated with feathers. Her gown, while simple in the Greek classical style, was of the finest beaded material, clinging to her slim figure. Elizabeth found her breast pulsing with envy for this woman. And hatred? She shook her head.

What good would a vile emotion like hatred do?

Their scrutiny was suddenly interrupted.

"I believe, Mrs Darcy, that I prescribed privacy." She might have said "ordered". Her meaning was clear. She liked her own way and did not want the gentleman to stay. She still hadn't raised her eyes from her book. Elizabeth was reminded of Colonel Fitzwilliam's words used last Easter at Rosings to describe Darcy. "He likes to have his own way very well."

Did an eighteen-year-old Darcy at Cambridge and the daughter of a Prussian professor recognise in each other kindred spirits? Did they find themselves irresistibly attracted to one another, unable to avoid a passionate affair of love? Did that congress spawn a love-child, born some nine months later without Darcy's knowledge? Of course, knowing Darcy, if he now found that the child was his, he would wish to acknowledge the boy, make him his heir. And what of Elizabeth and the child she was carrying? What would become of them in Darcy's life?

Elizabeth wanted to scream, to hurl herself at this smug European woman and gouge her eyes out, at the very least. Throw at her some caustic substance which would destroy her beauty forever. To—

"Lizzy," her father said quietly, "I had better retire to the taproom. I can quite see that whatever it is the two of you have to discuss should be done in private. I will find a news sheet to read. Have me called if you need me."

She was looking down, he could not see her face. Had he been able to, he might not have removed himself so readily, but he was gone suddenly and she was left with no alternative but to compose her features, step into the parlour, shut the door and take the seat opposite Mrs Lang.

THE STAGECOACH jogged along, repeatedly jolting and unsettling its two passengers. Before reaching the outskirts of London, there were frequent stops for the traffic was heavy and, on one occasion, a large wagon had lost its load of barrels which cascaded onto the road, holding up vehicles in both directions. Darcy found himself amused rather than annoyed as men charged after the barrels, some of which broke open. The barrels, it turned out, held salted fish which spread over the cobbles, slithering and sliding everywhere, attracting many people and dogs hoping to secure a free meal. He laughed at the chaos. It must be the effect of the laudanum Old Woman Simmons had given him to take 'in moderation'.

"Increase the dose a little at nights," he had been instructed. Thus he had passed a reasonably peaceful night at the Golden Cross, despite the noise from the taproom and the clatter from a variety of sources outside.

As the coach was stationary, Darcy's travelling companion sighed, turned to him, leaned across the carriage and held out his hand.

"Matthew Benjamin, sir, at your service."

Darcy had already recognised him and felt all the irony of the occasion. Benjamin would not know of him therefore he felt safe to take the proffered hand, nod and reply with his name:

"Fitzwilliam Darcy, sir."

"Are you travelling far, Mr Darcy?"

"Only to St Albans where I hope to hire a carriage to take me to Meryton. And you, sir?"

It was unusual for him to respond to strangers, much less to make conversation. But this of course was an amazing twist of fate, quite by chance to be sharing a carriage with the very gentleman whom he had paid, albeit secretly through a third party, to delve into his circumstances in such a private matter. He fingered the letter in his coat pocket and suppressed a smile as Benjamin replied.

"I am going all the way to Liverpool to visit my son, though I propose to stop for a day or two in Northampton where my daughter lives as it is on the route. My son is married to the daughter of a wealthy merchant and I hope to be of some service to him in view of having lately foresworn my life-long...occupation."

"I see." Darcy thought to himself that he would like to ask more, but instead offered a rejoinder about himself.

"Well, I too am hoping to embark on a new venture, that of papermaking, about which I have learned much in the last few weeks in both Hertfordshire and Kent, from the latter of which I am now returning after visiting a large paper mill."

He could see Benjamin looking curiously at the cuts and bruises on his face and he had no doubt noticed Darcy being helped into the carriage by the two footmen who were travelling on a rear-facing seat outside. He had discarded the crutches as too cumbersome.

"Yes, well," said Benjamin, "I suppose that paper mills may hold their dangers as well as any other place of business."

"Paper mills hold no fears for me, Mr Benjamin. My main fear is that someone may mistake me for a war hero and I will have to admit to never having been in combat, being perhaps even a coward."

Benjamin laughed.

"No, I suffered my injuries on Sunday when the carriage in which I was travelling overturned. I have been staying with a relation since then, but felt that I must return to my family in Hertfordshire. The doctor said two weeks' bed rest, but I could not stomach the inactivity any longer."

"Eminently understandable, sir. I must say that I am very keen to get back to my normal profession as a writer. I hope to be able to assist my son and his father-in-law in some way. My other main occupation to which I averred I am sorry to say was an over-fondness for the gaming tables. In addition, I occasionally undertake investigations of one sort or another. I have recently been engaged in one of these…er…enquiries and in the course of it I realised that my predilection was a curse which I must shake off in order to lead a better life, both to benefit myself and others. That is all I will say of the matter and I am sorry to unburden myself in this way. I had not intended to do so. I hope no offence has been caused."

"Not at all."

Darcy found himself examining the man seated opposite him, surprised to be the recipient of a confidence clearly of some import to the man, a rare experience for one who knew himself to often appear to others to be cold and unapproachable. Less so, he hoped, since he had met Lizzy. The coach had moved on, out of the congestion of the London streets and into the countryside, but very soon of course there would be a stop for a change of horses. If he read the other man aright, it must be the case that the assignment which he, Darcy, had caused to be inflicted on the other had resulted in a fundamental change for the better. Should he congratulate himself? A vain man might. He felt pleased of course, but also humbled. The part he had played in the other's redemption was wholly unwitting. Any other experience might have had the same effect.

But perhaps not. He often reflected upon fate and the part it played in people's lives. His own life might now have been so different had it not been for certain events over which he had had no control. Mr Benjamin was scrutinising him in his turn. How long could these two men peer at each other before discomfort overrode them?

BENJAMIN found the man with whom he was sharing a carriage curiously familiar. He had never met the man before but he was an excellent judge of character and discerned that the other man had some peculiar interest in him or was aware of something to do with him. Either that, or he was a man of exceptional composure who judged others in an almost ice-cold way.

Of course, one could not discount the fact that the man had been injured and was possibly under the influence of laudanum. He started to go over his dealings in the last few years. His life was very varied. He met and engaged with many people. His last piece of luck which was very fresh in his mind had involved the paternity of a child. He had earned decent money, enabling him to pay off his debts and take himself off to Liverpool and out of the way of London temptations. He was even able to contemplate a renewal of an affair he had enjoyed with a woman he had loved, that is if he could stay away from the cards.

He fiddled with the paper in his pocket. He had kept a copy of the letter he had written to the lawyer, Blake, who had ultimately, after a struggle and a lot of bluffing on his, Benjamin's, part, paid him the agreed amount. He had almost skipped away from the chambers in Holborn, his pockets full of silver and his heart full of hope and determination for the first time in years. Whoever this rich person was who could afford to lay out such a fabulous sum he had cared not a jot as he hurried away from the attorney's office. Now, he wondered as he thought about the letter he had written which had so changed his fortunes.

"6TH APRIL

DEAR SIR,

It is my pleasure to be able to apprise you of the results of my extensive enquiries on your account in accordance with your instructions of the 3rd inst. on the subject of Mrs Clara Lang and her son, as was put to me, the renowned violin-playing prodigy Maximilian Kohler whose paternity is sought to be revealed. Of the name and position of your client who requires this information, I remain ignorant.

On receiving your instructions I was assured by you that your client's purpose in seeking to establish who may be the child's father is entirely virtuous and free from any malignant intent or motive. In the absence of any facts attaching to your client's desire to have information in respect of the boy's pedigree, I have assumed some suspected family interest on the part of your client.

After establishing Mrs Lang's address while in London in February and March, I proceeded to interview, with every discretion, those with whom Mrs Lang had come into contact during her time in London, be they close or conversely distant acquaintances or business connections. I was unable to identify any persons who might be related to Mrs Lang or Master Kohler. I pride myself that those questioned had no reason to suspect any special interest on my part in Mrs Lang or Master Kohler.

As a consequence of those enquiries, I was able to consult a physician who attended Mrs Lang a number of times during her London residence. I asked for information regarding a good number of patients of his on a pretext which he found entirely plausible, therefore he would be unaware of any special interest in Mrs Lang."

In fact, the doctor being known to him and in view of Benjamin's extensive circle of acquaintance, he already had ample examples of ladies whom the doctor had attended for all manner of female complaints. There had been no need for him to waste his time scouring London for the names of high-born ladies who habitually stooped to common practices with the object of rescuing them from awkward situations and saving their marriages and reputations.

Thereby he had gleaned a fair quantity of intelligence on a good number of society ladies which, though superfluous to him at that time, could be of some use in the future.

"I am confident of the doctor's silence. He was paid a substantial fee for breaching his duties of confidentiality to his patients and will know of the consequences awaiting him should he spread abroad his willingness to disclose his patients' business.

As above, I have assumed some suspected family interest on the part of your client, in all likelihood a man who suspects that Maximilian Kohler is his son following a past liaison with Mrs Lang or less likely a lady who suspects that her husband or other relation is the father for the same reason.

I can cordially assure your client that any past liaison with Mrs Lang did not lead to the birth of Maximilian Kohler because Mrs Lang herself cannot be his mother. The doctor attested to the fact that he had intimately examined Mrs Lang in connection with the matter for which she had consulted him and he was most insistent that Mrs Lang had never given birth to a child.

That being the case, Maximilian Kohler cannot be the child of your client, if a man, as a result of any past liaison of your client with Mrs Lang. Likewise, if your client is a woman, then neither can any past liaison of your client's husband or other male relation have resulted in the birth of Maximilian Kohler.

I hope this information will reassure your client.

I remain, sir, with respectful compliments to your client, your humble and obedient servant,

MATTHEW BENEDICT"

Benjamin determined to hold his tongue for the remainder of the journey until Mr Darcy got off at St Albans. In any case, Mr Darcy already seemed to be dozing off, no doubt due to his injuries and the medicine he would be taking. Pity. He enjoyed talking to people and finding out about them. Darcy was obviously a gentleman, probably wealthy, possibly even the person who had paid so handsomely to ascertain whether Max Kohler was his child. But most likely not!

He should not let his imagination run away with him. Save it for his writing career which he hoped to revive. With a less-pressing need for money, he could write more freely, more professionally, more expansively.

He laid his own head back on the carriage seat and allowed his thoughts to roam. The road was fairly smooth, the sun shone through the window warming the carriage and before long, torpor overtook him.

Chapter 34

Friday 12th April 1799

"WELL, that is better," said Mrs Lang, placing a ribbon in the book she had been reading to mark her place and laying the book on the table between them. Elizabeth eyed the cover of the book and saw that it was in a foreign language, presumably German. How nice it must be to be able to understand and fluently speak more than one language, how accomplished that must make one feel. Far more so than her own school-room French. Indeed, the woman probably spoke French too.

Elizabeth frowned. The book title when she looked more closely *was* in French.

"I am sure," Mrs Lang continued, ignoring Elizabeth's scrutiny of the book, "that you understand that anything I choose to tell you about myself should be for your ears only."

She spoke with a slight accent, whether German or French Elizabeth could not tell.

"It is an arrangement with which I am quite satisfied, Mrs Lang."

The woman examined Elizabeth in a calculating way, but said nothing. If it was intended to discompose Elizabeth, then it had that effect, but Elizabeth would not show it.

"All right, Mrs Lang, you wish to know why I wanted to see you, and of course that is natural. I will tell you what I know, and then I hope that *you* will tell *me* what you can add to the picture I have begun to form of you and my husband, Mr Fitzwilliam Darcy.

"I am aware that you knew him when he was at Cambridge about ten years ago, for how long I do not know nor what exactly was the nature of your relationship with him. You have a son named Max who is about nine or ten years old and is a genius, a prodigy, who has been playing the violin to audiences in London and elsewhere recently. According to your friend Caroline

Bingley, Max has been in America with you performing to audiences.

"My husband attended a private recital in London a little over three weeks ago at which Max was playing. He, my husband, returned home from London a day earlier than expected and was thereafter...not himself. I know that Charles Bingley, my husband's very best friend, refused to allow his sister Caroline to spend Easter at Netherfield, and I think that his refusal had something to do with you and Max, perhaps planning to come to Netherfield with Caroline."

Elizabeth finished there. What else could she say? Mrs Lang's eyes narrowed as she stared at Elizabeth.

"And from these few facts you conclude?"

"There are other things, such as...but I won't go into them as you have the answers, I have only questions. I know my husband, Mrs Lang, and he is much discomposed. I think that he believes, fears perhaps is a better way of putting it, that Max is his child, conceived in Cambridge ten years ago."

"Why do you not ask him, Mrs Darcy?"

"I hoped I had made it clear. He does not know. How can he answer such a question? That is why I am here. To ask *you*. Is Max his child?"

"All right. Then why does *he* not ask me?"

"Well, I can hardly answer for him. And as a matter of fact he is not in Hertfordshire at the moment. Ten days ago, he returned to London with his friend Bingley and then went on alone to Kent to investigate some...commercial possibilities. He may be in the process of returning from Kent now or soon. We at Netherfield are not sure."

There was no reason to tell Mrs Lang of Darcy's accident.

"And I think that he and his friend Bingley while in London may have put in hand some sort of enquiry into the matter of Max, Max being his child."

Mrs Lang laughed.

"How entertaining. So very like the English. Running around, trying to find answers where no clue exists."

"Mrs Lang, maligning the characteristics of another race is one way of trying to keep the upper hand in a discussion, but it is pretty low and not helpful, I would say. You may find this matter amusing, but I do not. I have come to you honestly, hoping to establish some truths about my husband's past and its consequences. And all you do is place verbal obstacles in my path."

The next pause was much longer.

"Why should I tell you anything about myself? I owe you nothing."

"Indeed, you do not. But what about your son? What about Max? Is he not entitled to know who his father is? And is my husband not entitled to know if Max is his child?"

Speaking these words hurt more than Elizabeth could hardly bear, but she had to get at the truth.

Clara seemed to weaken. A sort of shield came down and she suddenly became a human being, not a female Teutonic warrior.

At that moment, there was a knock on the door and a waiter entered bearing a tray of tea and delicacies which he placed on the table, pushing the book aside. Could it have been only ten minutes that she had been in here, verbally sparring with Mrs Lang?

"Thank you," said Elizabeth, looking up at the waiter. "Yes, that will be all. Please shut the door."

The man left.

"Mrs Darcy, it has not been easy bringing up a boy on my own, especially a boy like Max, needing expert tuition, opportunities to perform, instruments of the finest quality. The *expense*!"

"I imagine not," said Elizabeth, fascinated at the change of tone of the woman. What would she say next?

"Mrs Darcy, Max is not my son."

"I beg your pardon?"

"He is my brother's son."

"What do you mean?"

"My brother and his wife came to England with their baby son, Max, to escape the turmoil in Europe, the tyranny of the individual rulers in our homeland, the instability, the threat of civil war. My father and I met with them in Newcastle after my father's lecture tour ended. The lecture tour which included Cambridge in 1788. We were to live together and have a new life in England. My brother and his wife were both brilliant musicians and our ambition was to start a music school.

"And all was well for a time, then my brother and his wife became ill with typhoid. My father and I moved to another house with Max to try to keep him safe. But my brother and his wife died. Not long after, my father died too. And I have been on my own ever since with Max. It seemed easier to tell people that he was my son."

Elizabeth swallowed. The implication of what she said, if true, was inescapable. If Max was not her child, then certainly he couldn't be Darcy's child. This should have been a relief but there was still the lingering image of Clara and Darcy as lovers, and jealousy once again clutched at her heart. It must have shown on her face.

"Mrs Darcy, I do not deny that your husband and I knew each other in Cambridge. You can imagine what a handsome young man he was, dark and brooding, yet charming in his precise Englishness." The jealousy took on a violent tinge. "I cannot help the past, Mrs Darcy, and neither can he."

Elizabeth swallowed and brought herself under control. "Yet you are married. Or were married."

"Yes. Since you know most of my past, I might as well tell you about that. Gerald Lang was an English official in the East India Company which governed large parts of India. He returned to England as many do to seek a wife. I had lived in England for five years by then with my mother and father. I was foolish enough to marry him and travelled to India with him. I stayed a very short time. I discovered on arrival that he already had an Indian mistress and children. My father sent me the money for a passage back to England. While I was away my mother died. This all happened before my brother and his small family came over to England. After my brother's death, the East India Company informed me that Gerald Lang had died of cholera."

"So you are single now."

"Well…"

THE TWO FOOTMEN helped Darcy from the hired carriage at

Netherfield. Two more footmen raced down the steps and after them came Bingley. He embraced his friend and Darcy clasped him round his shoulders, an unusual gesture for either man.

"Thank God you are back," said Bingley and he and the footmen helped Darcy into the house and the large saloon to the general greetings of the assembled company who were enjoying drinks before their meal. They helped him lower himself into a seat and Bingley remained standing by him.

"William," cried Georgiana, rushing up to him. "Cousin Ernest's doctor said you should rest in bed for two weeks. Oh, William." She bent and hugged him. "I am so happy that you are back."

"How is Ernest?" said Colonel Fitzwilliam, coming up to Darcy. "I worry so about him."

Darcy looked up at his cousin. "He is fairly well. In good spirits. I understand your concern. We must try to spend more time with him."

"But his physical condition? How does he appear to you?"

"Not as you or I would wish, I must confess. He…has trouble controlling his movements and his speech. But he is happy, Fitzwilliam."

"Well, that is something."

Darcy peered about the saloon. No Elizabeth had hurried forward to greet him. He frowned.

Colonel Fitzwilliam shrugged. "Elizabeth left the house with her father earlier to apparently visit the library in Meryton! Some alleged mission to find out about recent sailings to America from English ports, if you can believe that."

"And you do not, by the sounds of it. Ah, well."

"Something has been troubling her, Darcy, increasingly so since you left. She is not happy. Perhaps you know what it is, for I do not. She does not confide in Harriet. In her father perhaps."

Darcy sighed. "I see." He cast about. "And Mary?"

Fitzwilliam recounted the events since Adolphus Barrant's footman had brought a manuscript to Netherfield and Mary had disappeared overnight.

Darcy would later explain to some, how in London Adolphus Barrant and Daniel Barton had tried to persuade him to bring a manuscript back to Netherfield himself or give it to Bingley to deliver. He did not wish in Georgiana's presence to allude to Daniel Barton in any way which might sound derogatory.

"I regret," continued Fitzwilliam, "that we do not know where she is. She may be some way into the Atlantic by now. We simply do not know."

Darcy knew he had been away for far too long.

"And Caroline Bingley has been here telling us of *Lydia's*...er...misfortunes in London. Darcy, she needs someone to take control of the situation and carve out a suitable future for her and Wickham. At the moment, she seems destined for a most...*un*suitable fate.

"I am sorry, Darcy, that you return to this unpleasantness. But may I tell you at least that my wedding day with Harriet is set for next Tuesday, and Harvey and I are to stay at Longbourn House from Sunday with Bingley's man-servant. Harriet's parents will arrive on Monday. We will spend a few days here and then travel to Kent to stay at Pakeleigh Abbey."

"I am delighted to hear this, Fitzwilliam."

Darcy was charmed by Mrs Bennet's genuine warmth and pleasure at seeing him. She was seated nearby and had been listening to his exchanges with Colonel Fitzwilliam. She rose from her seat and walked the few paces necessary to reach him. She was not a tall woman and he knew all of a mother's love as she bent over him and kissed his cheek, awkwardly hugging him from the side of his chair. He hid his pain as he twisted his body to stretch out his free arm and clasp her around her shoulder.

"How wonderful that you are back, William. Everything will be all right now that you are here. I am sure that whatever ails Lizzy will disappear immediately she sees you."

Over her shoulder, Darcy caught Bingley's eye at these words.

"And your poor face." Mrs Bennet drew back slightly and touched his cheek, moving her fingers gently over his cuts and bruises. He pulled her to him and found his face buried in the soft pink fabric covering her ample bosom. The extreme comfort which this bestowed made him feel tearful. He sniffed.

"It will be better very soon, Mother."

He was roused by a call from Mrs Philips. "Tell us, William, all about your adventures in Kent."

"Yes," echoed Mr Philips. "We cannot wait to hear."

Darcy smiled and raised his voice to the whole room. "I would be happy to. At risk of boring you all to death, I will tell you all about the Turkey Mill in Kent."

ELIZABETH started as the door to the parlour was pushed open and there stood Max with none other than Viscount Cedric Morley. They moved into the room. Morley had his hand round the boy's shoulder and the boy looked up at him adoringly. Clara rose and went to them, standing on the other side of Max. The three of them formed a tableau framed by the door behind them. The family of Elizabeth's fevered imagination in Cambridge over a week ago, except that the man was not Darcy.

And suddenly, she understood. Morley was rumoured to be recently married. She had assumed to some poor neglected creature left back at his seat in Devon while he enjoyed the delights of London. Clearly not so.

The apparent hesitancy in the signature 'Clara Lang' in the letter inviting her here made more sense now, because of course it was no longer her name, yet she presumably had not wished in the letter to reveal her married name.

As husband and wife, they would also surely have confided particulars of their past lives to one other. Specifically, Morley would know of Darcy's and Clara's affair in Cambridge, and accordingly would possibly have realised that Darcy may fear that Max was his son. Morley knew that Caroline had been prevented from coming to Netherfield. He would have known that Max and Clara were intended to accompany Caroline. Therefore, Elizabeth must assume that Morley already knew it all or, if he did not, then he would soon have it from Clara. Did it matter? She would have to consider the point later.

Evidently, though, he had been sufficiently discreet as to leave Elizabeth with the bare minimum of intelligence during his talk with her just before he and his party left Netherfield. It now appeared that he could have told her much more. And she must consider that his suggestion that she befriend Caroline Bingley was in fact actually genuine and well-meant.

"Mrs Darcy," said Morley. "What a great pleasure it is to see you again."

His face and voice held his usual slightly mocking quality, laced with, she could see, happiness at his situation. She doubted whether she and Darcy could ever be good friends with this man, but she was now willing to believe Caroline's claim that he was a kind man.

Clara made their relationship absolutely clear.

"Meet my husband, Mrs Darcy. We married in Devon after Max and I arrived in England from America. Max has never known a proper father until now." She regarded her husband and Max fondly.

"I wonder, then, why you have not announced it to the world," Elizabeth said.

Morley raised an eyebrow. "My family would not immediately approve, Mrs Darcy. You must know how strictly these things are viewed."

Elizabeth did know. She thought of Lady Catherine.

"But they will come round in due time," Morley continued, "and the fact is that they are all in my gift."

Yes, Elizabeth could imagine the relations who must submit to Morley's will in the end, not to mention the number of fawning sycophants who might be dependent on someone like him for favours.

She was wondering how to bring this meeting to a conclusion, when there was a knock on the door and her father appeared. The Morleys turned and moved aside to make room for him. He appraised them with interest.

"Mr Bennet," said Morley and bowed.

"Lord Morley," her father countered, returning the bow.

"Papa, may I introduce...Lady Morley, formerly Clara Lang, and Max Kohler."

"How do you do." Mr Bennet bowed and then said apologetically:

"Lizzy, I think we should repair to Netherfield soon or we will be sorely missed."

"Yes, of course, Papa." Then to the Morleys. "I wonder, shall we see you again?"

"I think not," said Morley. "Max has engagements and we must leave Hertfordshire today. We will arrive by and by in Devonshire and hope to spend most of our time in Devon thereafter."

The tea and the delicacies had not been touched and Elizabeth saw Max eyeing the food.

"Please," she extended her arm, "we must take our leave, but do partake of the fare ordered by my father when we arrived."

"Yes, please do," said Mr Bennet.

"Thank you," said Clara.

"May I?" Max looked up at his mother and Morley.

"Go on," said Morley, patting the boy's back and he hurried forward.

Good wishes and farewells followed and Elizabeth and Mr Bennet left.

"WELL, that was rather awkward," said Mr Bennet as they waited for the curricle to be brought round to the front of the inn. "No doubt you will enlighten me on our way back to Netherfield."

Chapter 35

Friday 12ᵗʰ April 1799

CHATTER and laughter emerged from the large saloon. Darcy's voice could clearly be heard. Mr Bennet stood, undecided, by the door to the room.

"Will you come in with me, Lizzy?"

"No. I cannot face him, anyone, at the moment." And she ran up the stairs and away along the landing.

Mr Bennet sighed and walked into the room which fell silent. Naturally, he went first to Darcy and placed a hand on his shoulder.

"Well, I am glad you are come back, my boy." He smiled down upon his son-in-law with a mixture of amusement and sympathy. "You look as though you have taken up prize-fighting."

Darcy raised his head to his father-in-law. "Does Lizzy know I am home?"

"She does. Price told us and we heard your voice. She has gone straight upstairs."

"Oh. Then I had better go to her. Would you mind assisting me, Bingley?"

"Of course, or I could ask for her to come to the small parlour. That might be easier for you."

"No, I must go to her. She would not appreciate being summoned to come to me."

"Very well." Bingley rang for a footman.

Darcy addressed the room. "And please do not delay your meal on my account."

ELIZABETH stood at the window.

"Come in," she called at the knock on the door. She did not turn around at the commotion of the door opening and Darcy stumbling to a chair between Bingley and the footman George.

"On second thoughts, could you take me to the bed and prop me up with pillows."

He wanted to be able to hold Lizzy properly if she chose to join him.

The task was performed. Bingley and George went retreated and closed the door.

What could or should he say? The subject had been closed to them for too long. He should have told her straightaway.

"Lizzy, my love, you know, do you not."

"No." She swung round. If she was shocked by his battered face, then she gave no indication. Her beautiful dark blue eyes burned into his brooding brown eyes. She could see into his soul, he felt. "*You* speak the truth. *You* tell me what *you* know."

"I am sorry, Lizzy. The fact is, I thought that Max might be my son, but now I know he is not, cannot be. I should have told you of my fears at the outset, but I was trying to protect you, Lizzy, until I had the opportunity to make enquiries, and initially by stopping Clara and Max from coming here for Easter. I acted as soon as I could. Before my first trip to town, I had no idea of Max's existence. You may be sure that had I become aware of him at any earlier time, I would have made it my business to find out exactly who he was."

"Well, I do not know how you know, but I have just come away from The Pheasant Inn where I met Mrs Lang…" Elizabeth laughed rather hysterically. "Actually, she is Lady Morley now. She, Viscount Morley and Max are a family. Is not that sweet and delightful?"

There was nothing sweet and delightful in her voice or her expression. They spoke the opposite of her words. She looked at that moment like some demon from hell. Had she started to breathe fire, he would not have been surprised.

So Morley *was* married as Bingley thought. And to Clara, it transpired. So be it. Morley would no doubt experience considerable amusement if he thought that he, Darcy, had been troubled over Max's paternity. If so, it would have to be borne, though there were good reasons why Morley would keep it to himself, principally his position now as Max's adopted father and Clara's husband.

I wonder, he thought absently, whether Morley is aware that he may have difficulty getting an heir with Clara.

Lizzy's further words cut into his silence. "I have had to endure over three weeks of the growing realisation of what was wrong with you, grasping at straws until the obvious conclusion became unavoidable. And this morning I have had to go through the ignominy of a meeting with that woman to find out the truth. She told me that Max is the son of her dead brother. Ergo, he cannot be your child."

"The intelligence I received was that Clara has never given birth to a child so I suppose it amounts to the same thing. I caused enquiries to be made and the gentlemen who carried out the investigation spoke to a doctor whom Clara had consulted in London, and the doctor assured the man that, having examined Clara, she had never had a child. I received the report just yesterday morning. The man is unaware of my identity."

"Clara, Clara, Clara," she screamed, almost spitting the words. "*Don't* say that name. I hate the woman. I wish I had taken a dagger with me today and stabbed her to death."

Darcy breathed hard. He had expected tears, recriminations of some kind, but not that his wife would be transformed into a deviless.

"Lizzy, please. Lizzy, listen to —"

He was unable to complete the sentence. Elizabeth flew at him. She was across the room in a second, on top of him on the bed, first beating his chest with her closed fists and then scratching at his face. He stifled a cry at the pain of her attack and quickly held her arms away from him. It was as much as he could do. Every bone and muscle in his body ached, every movement was torture. The laudanum must have worn off.

"Lizzy, stop. Please believe me, I did not love her." But his wife wriggled free of his grasp and sat back on the side of the bed, her eyes wild, her hair in disarray, strands escaping from the pins. Her pose suggested that she might spring at him again any second.

"It is not as though I have been unfaithful to you, Lizzy. I am only sorry that my past has erupted in such a damaging fashion, though as it turns out, unnecessarily so. As I said to you once before, you have a past and I accepted that. If I must speak plainly, I think you were in love with that rector, Mr Wilde. You were meeting him in secret for months. With Clara and me, it was *three days* only. Then she was gone."

At last Elizabeth seemed to have calmed down, was more herself.

"But my relationship with Mr Wilde was completely innocent. Our meetings were for a quite legitimate purpose."

"But were you in love with him? I asked you once before, but I did not receive an answer. As we are on the subject of past liaisons, I would rather like an answer now."

ELIZABETH found that all her anger had suddenly abandoned her. She studied her hands as she turned them in her lap. The subject embarrassed her, she felt like a child who had been caught out. But really why should she? If anyone should feel ashamed, it should be him. Should she evade answering this precise question yet again? Should she respond indignantly that he had created this problem, that he could not now twist everything to make it appear that she was somehow at fault?

But this was, she recognised, an opportunity to hurt him which might not arise again.

"Yes," she answered petulantly. "I was in love with him. He was the kindest, gentlest man in the world. He was charming. He was very handsome. In fact, he was the best man I have ever known."

And she also knew very well that if she ever saw him again, her heart would turn over.

Darcy was watching her. She felt like a traitor, describing Mr Wilde as the best man she had ever known. She had once used the same words about Darcy when speaking to her father.

"And Wickham. You liked him too, did you not, at one time? But I will not ask you about him. He was and remains a most despicable character."

Yes, she had liked him, enough to have discussed with her Aunt Gardiner the possibility of marrying him had the circumstances been more suitable. She shivered at the thought.

In truth, she was in turmoil. She was tempted to ask Darcy

whether there had been other women in his past besides Clara but she felt that it would not help. Thinking back to last Easter at Rosings, she had described Darcy to Colonel Fitzwilliam as a man who had lived in the world. Now what had she meant by that if not that he had experience of life in all its variety?

"Very well, Lizzy, you loved Mr Wilde. I have only ever loved you, in a way that was irresistible practically from the first moment I saw you. But, please tell me whether you still love me at least a little."

Elizabeth put her hand to her mouth. A sob escaped her. Her answer might spell the end of everything if she continued to be resentful and churlish. It was unthinkable.

She dredged up a small voice. "Yes," she said, "of course I do." And then she found herself collapsing in tears on the bed. She had never cried like this. Sobs racked her body. Would she ever be able to stop? Would he forgive her for what she had said?

"Lizzy, will you not come to me, let me put my arms around you. I regret that I can barely move at the moment but I do so want to be close to you."

Keening as she went, she crawled across the bed to him and almost fell on top of him, causing the breath to leave his body for a moment. He gasped and laughed gently.

"Here you are," he said, running his fingers through her hair, undoing the remaining pins as she continued to weep copiously, dampening his shirt.

"Lizzy, we will always be together. I will always be yours. Always."

Epilogue

GEORGIANA sat in her bedroom clutching a letter from Daniel Barton received that morning expressing his great enjoyment of the ball at Lucas Lodge on Saturday and his wish that they may meet again very soon.

"Beautiful Georgiana, you have stolen my heart. I count the minutes until I may see you again."

Her cheeks reddened at these words and a most pleasant shiver went through her body. She thought about him all the time. To know that she was in turn the subject of his thoughts was almost overwhelming and her breath quickened. She pictured him at the end of the evening, standing in the drive of Lucas Lodge waving to her as Bingley's carriage departed to bear her and others back to Netherfield. The lanterns illuminated his tall young figure which her own had once or twice been pressed against earlier in the crush at the supper tables causing her to almost cry out. He had looked at her with naked lust. She had read enough novels to know the look.

His letter spoke of his acquaintance with Caroline Bingley whom he understood she knew and who was the sister of Charles Bingley, the best friend of her guardian Mr Darcy. Miss Bingley, he wrote, frequently attended soirées at his family's home. If she, Georgiana, chanced to be in London at any time, he and his family would warmly welcome her presence.

Would that this could come about in early course. She must talk to William.

But now, she had to ready herself for the wedding of Colonel Fitzwilliam and Lizzy's friend Harriet Layham. The family had started to congregate in the large hall. The wedding must take place before midday in accordance with the law and it was already ten o' clock. There would be a merry party at Netherfield afterwards. It would be a wonderful day. It could, perhaps, form the basis of a letter which she might write to Mr Barton. These country gatherings would not of course be so grand as a London event, but she felt sure that she could make it sound pretty sophisticated on paper.

THE letter being read by Darcy quietly in the dining room after returning from the church was not entirely unrelated to that which had earlier in the day so thrilled his sister. The party following the marriage of his cousin proceeded loudly in the saloon. The sender was Caroline Bingley. Receiving a letter from her was something of a surprise though it was of course entirely proper that she should approach him as Georgiana's guardian since the letter invited Georgiana to visit London and remain there with her and Mr and Mrs Hurst at the Hursts' home for the forthcoming season.

This was very sudden and he had to think about it and discuss it with Lizzy and of course Fitzwilliam as Georgiana's other guardian. Indeed, so far as Fitzwilliam was concerned, there would be little time left to discuss this or indeed anything else. And naturally it depended on whether Georgiana herself wished to remain in London but it seemed like a reasonable idea. She would probably enjoy it immensely. Since his marriage to Lizzy and Georgiana's involvement with her family, Georgiana's shyness had largely dissipated and she probably needed more social opportunities.

He was in no very favourable position himself at the moment to advance her marriage prospects either in general or in particular in the direction of Daniel Barton, whom she obviously liked and the liking seemed to be reciprocated. He frowned to himself however. Georgiana at large in London with an obviously keen suitor in the foreground? He would worry about her. It was to be welcomed at least that Caroline Bingley had made friendly overtures to Lizzy, so Lizzy had told him. That was reassuring. Lizzy and Caroline could more easily keep in contact. That is if a decision was made to —

The door opened, putting an end to his musings for now as

Bingley and a footman entered.

"Come, Darcy," said Bingley. "You must have finished your letter by now. I hope it is reasonable news."

"Yes, indeed. It is certainly not bad news."

"Then come back to the saloon. You cannot dance, I know, but I hate to see you here by yourself."

"Very well, and thank you for coming to my assistance."

At his invitation, Bingley and the footman took an arm each and supported him to the saloon. This dependence on others could not end soon enough!

ONE HUNDRED and thirty miles away, Mary sat examining her notes prior to settling down, feeling rather foolish, to write a letter to her family asking for their assistance to return to Longbourn where she hoped she might pursue a writing career.

Had she been allowed to leave Netherfield for London in the Fairweather's carriage in an orderly fashion as she had expressed in her short letter left in her room at Netherfield for her family, then things might have been very different. She might have been on her way to America now. But the discomforts of the long horse-ride to Bristol, the uncertainty and the fear of being apprehended had caused her to have second thoughts.

Adolphus Barrant and Bernard had boarded a ship, 'The Experiment', for New York. They had spent over a week at the house in Berkeley Square, impatient to be gone. Mary had at last summoned the courage to reveal that she had decided against travelling to America. The response of Adolphus had been quite mild, more so than she deserved, she felt.

"Well if, in the future, you suddenly find that a long and dangerous sea voyage appeals to you, you have only to write to me."

Bernard gave the impression that he could not have cared less whether she accompanied them or not. He was simply eager to leave himself.

In the days spent at the house in Berkeley Square, she has befriended Mrs Pepper and gained her consent to talk at length with the black maid Faith and her son Adam about their lives and experiences, thereby considerably broadening her own knowledge. She has made copious notes. It was, she felt, time well spent.

MRS BENNET tossed and turned alone in her bed wishing, as she not infrequently did these days, that her married life contained more affection or indeed any affection, beyond a gentle pat on her hand or shoulder by her husband or the customary placing of her arm through his when out walking. William had clearly been moved by his physical contact with her the other day, as though he were her son by not only marriage but by blood. It had reminded her how precious love was.

She was not an old woman yet. Only forty-six years of age and she prided herself that she looked well for her years. She sometime yearned for a marriage more akin to those of Lizzy and Jane. As to Kitty, the Lieutenant Colonel was a kind man, a sensible man who was willing to wait for Kitty until she was a little older, and he was a rich man.

But two of her other daughters were presently abroad in the world with no way of knowing where they were or how they fared. It would have been better had she suggested that Lydia be offered a home at Longbourn until Wickham returned, probably not in the same house, but perhaps in a cottage on the estate with a small allowance. However Lydia might behave, it would be less heart-rending than silently worrying about her night and day.

Mrs Bennet was of course mindful of the possible dangers to which Mary had subjected herself, not least of which was a potentially hazardous sea-crossing, but somehow she was far less worried about her third daughter. Mary was three years older. And different from Lydia. She was not flirtatious and did not attract the attention of men. And Adolphus Barrant was willing to look after her. If he was actually Julius Fairweather as Mr Bennet had suggested, then he was very rich. If Mary did find her way to America, then Mrs Bennet was fairly sure that she would be all right.

It was Lydia, who was the problem.

AFTER the party broke up, the house grew silent, apart from the noises of the servants downstairs clearing away the debris of the celebration. Away in the suite of rooms in the east wing, Fitzwilliam found the de-flowering of his new wife both intensely physically exciting and deeply emotionally moving and he had felt overwhelmed by his love for her. Despite his excitement, he had been gentle and careful, knowing from what others had said that if the first night went badly, that side of the marriage sometimes never recovered.

It had been wonderful. They had tumbled between the covers in ecstasy, laughed together, wrapped their bodies around each other's, watched together through the window as a nearly full moon had risen above the trees and shone brightly over the grounds in which their first kisses and embraces had been shared this Easter.

ELIZABETH and Darcy lay together in the near darkness broken only by a single candle and the dying embers of the fire. They were both tired after a day of merriment, in which Darcy had partaken as best he could. He was, he said, beginning to recover, his joints and muscles less sore, his bruises turning yellow and his cuts appearing less livid. They had decided that they should remain at Netherfield for another two weeks and then think about returning to Derbyshire.

They had reached no firm conclusion yet whether Georgiana should remain behind and had not broached the subject with Georgiana, though it had been mentioned to Fitzwilliam who had said he would leave the decision up to Darcy. Elizabeth still had lingering doubts about Caroline but could not imagine what harm she could or would wish to do to Georgiana or her marriage prospects.

If Georgiana did stay in London for the season, Elizabeth decided that she must speak to her sister regarding the folly of becoming too intimate with a gentleman before marriage. Two years ago, she had been almost entirely innocent of the consequences of an unsuitable liaison prior to learning of the fate of the Bennets' kitchen maid. She had been forced to consider what could befall a girl who was not careful. Georgiana had no mother to guide. Nor indeed had Elizabeth received any guidance, but it would have been most helpful if she had.

She must assume the position of Georgiana's mother and caution her in language which would be clear enough to take every care and not let her feelings overwhelm her.

"I will be sad to leave Netherfield," she now said to Darcy. She would not voice it, but the spectre of Max's paternity hanging over her had considerably spoiled her joy at seeing her sisters and her parents, and witnessing the romance grow between her friend and Colonel Fitzwilliam. Darcy would understand this without having it spelled out by her.

"Oh," she suddenly exclaimed, placing a hand on the growing bulge below her umbilicus.

Darcy was all concern, attempting to raise himself up from the pillow. "What is the matter? Is something wrong?"

"No, do not vex yourself. I think that I just felt the baby move."

"Upon my word, how wonderful. May I feel it?"

"Yes, please do try, though it is but a small flutter inside, like a baby bird. I could feel it, but you may not be able to yet."

He kept his hand still where hers had been and waited a minute or two.

"I think I just felt something. Very faint, but it was something."

"Yes, I felt it too."

"Lizzy." He hugged her. "To think that in a few months, we will have a baby. I am so looking forward to it."

"Me, likewise." She yawned.

He kissed her cheek, then turned, licked his fingers and doused the candle.

"Goodnight," he said, but she was already asleep.

THE END

Please turn the page for information about the next novel in the Elizabeth Bennet series and a message from the author.

Author's Note & Sources

I hope you have enjoyed reading *Easter At Netherfield*, my third historical novel based on Jane Austen's acclaimed *Pride & Prejudice*. It is my second sequel and takes place in 1799, unsurprisingly over the Easter period. As you see, we are still in the late eighteenth century.

I chose to set the first novel in the series, *Intrigue At Longbourn*, in 1797 which was when Jane Austen finished her unpublished manuscript, *First Impressions*, later to be published as *Pride & Prejudice* in 1813. No one know how many changes may have been made during the intervening sixteen years, and *Pride & Prejudice* itself contains very little background information to enable any reliable judgement to be made as to the years in which it was intended to be set.

Previously, I haven't described my novels based on *Pride & Prejudice* as 'variations' because they don't interfere with the basic Lizzy/Darcy story covering their romance. There are, of course, many variations which *do* re-write the Lizzy/Darcy story in all sorts of ways.

However, I've chosen this time with *Easter At Netherfield* to describe it as a variation. There are a few departures from the strict background 'facts' of *Pride & Prejudice.* These mainly relate to characters' ages.

I took a liberty by adjusting the ages of the Gardiner children who, in *Pride & Prejudice*, were said to be two girls of six and eight years old and two younger boys. This was in the summer when Elizabeth departed with Mr and Mrs Gardiner to tour Derbyshire and the children were left at Longbourn in the care, principally, of Jane. Using my timescale, this would have been the summer of 1798.

Notwithstanding, in *Menace At Pemberley*, my first sequel, I made the girls twelve (Julia) and seven (Beth). The two boys Anthony and David, were somewhere in between. In *Easter At Netherfield*, Anthony comes over as the older of the two boys and his mother says that he is to be sent away to school soon. Therefore, I have made him about eleven.

A further departure concerns Darcy's and Bingley's ages. Without going into possibly tedious detail, an analysis of *Pride & Prejudice* suggests that Bingley was 4 years younger than Darcy. When Elizabeth and Darcy decided to marry in the autumn of 1798 (according to my timescale), Darcy was 28 and Bingley would have been about 24 (he was nearly 23 when he took Netherfield a year and a bit earlier). However *Menace At Pemberley* and *Easter at Netherfield* both have them at Cambridge (University) at the same time. Therefore they would have to be about the same age so, in that minor respect, both books are variations of *Pride & Prejudice*.

However, I feel that my major variation in *Easter at Netherfield* is possibly Darcy's ambition to start a paper mill on his Pemberley estate. Whether Jane Austen's Darcy would ever have considered going into commerce or trade is possibly arguable, although he did not look down upon Elizabeth's family for having been in trade as did Bingley's sisters, but rather for the behaviour of her mother and sisters. He also interacted respectfully with the Gardiners when he arrived home to Pemberley a day early to find Elizabeth there with her aunt and uncle. Indeed, the last chapter of *Pride & Prejudice* says that Darcy and Elizabeth were always on the most intimate terms with the Gardiners and that Darcy, as well as Elizabeth, really loved them!

Another factor which makes me think that Darcy would not necessarily have found trade or commerce anathema is that it was not unheard of for members of the aristocracy, even, to engage in commerce at the time. The 5th Duke of Devonshire who owned Chatsworth used the profits from his copper mines to develop

Buxton into a resort, including a replica of the Royal Crescent in Bath. Therefore in two respects, the copper mines and the development, he had a hand-hold in commerce.

To further his papermaking ambitions, in *Easter at Netherfield* Darcy visited Frogmore Mill in Hertfordshire and the Turkey Mill near Maidstone in Kent. Frogmore Mill still exists as a heritage site but sadly suffered a serious fire and has ceased to be open to the public. It is expected to re-open in 2024.

As to Turkey Mill, I am very much obliged to Dr Maureen Green who is recognised in the field as a Paper Historian and author. She is associated with the Hayle Mill in Kent which she described to me as the last of the great industrial hand papermaking mills still operating in the late 20th century which closed in the 1980s. I came across her name when I was trawling the internet on the subject of Turkey Mill and found a 2013 piece in the Kent Messenger about the eighteenth century papermaker James Whatman, Turkey Mill and William Balston who worked there. I managed to make contact with her and she helped me enormously with advice, recommended explanatory You Tube videos and also recommended books.

In particular, she recommended two books which fortunately I was able to obtain pretty quickly from Amazon. They are 'James Whatman - Father and Son' and 'William Balston, Paper-Maker 1759-1849' both by Thomas Balston, a descendant of course of William Balston. These two books between them as well as a few church records and other genealogical information sites provided most of the material for Chapter 23 in which Darcy visits the Turkey Mill. It is so important when writing about real people and real places to have access to information about them and the books mentioned massively helped to bring these real eighteenth century people to life.

In Chapter 12, the Gardiners' children during one of their puppet plays have Queen Charlotte addressing Napoleon Bonaparte in relation to the French musician François Couperin using the words: 'But he is dead this last sixty years. Far from playing, he is decaying. You have the wrong century.' In the play, Bonaparte stomps off.

I derived this wording from the story I once heard somewhere about W.S. Gilbert, of Gilbert and Sullivan fame, who, when someone asked him whether his old partner Sir Arthur Sullivan was still composing, replied 'On the contrary, he is decomposing', since Sullivan had died. Whether this actually happened or not, I don't know and, try as I might, I can find no reference to this anywhere on the internet. Some similar wording seems to be connected to Beethoven, but nowhere near so wittily phrased.

Chapter 13 contains the rather mawkish wording used by Darcy when inviting Elizabeth to dance at the Easter ball at the Assembly Rooms at Meryton, hoping to redress his refusal in *Pride & Prejudice* to dance with Lizzy during the first ball he attended at the same venue on first coming to Hertfordshire with Bingley. To repeat the words used in Chapter 13:

'"There is only one woman in the room handsome enough to tempt me. Would you do me the honour, Lizzy?"
Elizabeth blushed as Harriet smiled her puzzlement, not knowing the history of her friend and Darcy's first few meetings. The others could guess. Harvey raised an eyebrow to Kitty.
Bingley laughed.
"You see," Darcy said to him, "it does not take a kingdom."
More confused looks accompanied Elizabeth's reply that she would be honoured and followed them onto the dance floor.'

To explain the passage, in *Pride and Prejudice, Volume the First, Chapter 3*, the following conversation took place between Darcy and Bingley at the first Meryton ball they attended on first coming to Netherfield when Bingley urges Darcy to dance.

'"I certainly shall not. You know how I detest it, unless I am particularly acquainted with my partner. At such an assembly as this, it would be insupportable. Your sisters are engaged, and there is not another woman in the room whom it would not be a punishment to me to stand up with."

"I would not be so fastidious as you are," cried Bingley, "for a kingdom! Upon my honour, I never met with so many pleasant girls in my life as I have this evening; and there are several of them, you see, uncommonly pretty."

"*You* are dancing with the only handsome girl in the room," said Mr. Darcy, looking at the eldest Miss Bennet.

"Oh, she is the most beautiful creature I ever beheld! But there is one of her sisters sitting down just behind you, who is very pretty, and I dare say very agreeable. Do let me ask my partner to introduce you."

"Which do you mean?" and turning round, he looked for a moment at Elizabeth, till, catching her eye, he withdrew his own, and coldly said, "She is tolerable; but not handsome enough to tempt *me*; and I am in no humour at present to give consequence to young ladies who are slighted by other men. You had better return to your partner and enjoy her smiles, for you are wasting your time with me."

Mr. Bingley followed his advice. Mr. Darcy walked off; and Elizabeth remained with no very cordial feelings towards him. She told the story, however, with great spirit among her friends; for she had a lively, playful disposition, which delighted in any thing ridiculous.'

Research into the history of the Port of Bristol was immensely interesting. I had to carry out a great deal of research on many sites on the subject of Bristol and routes to Bristol whither Mary runs off after her father refuses to sign the Deed of Guardianship in favour of Adolphus Barrant. The sites consulted are far too numerous to list. I am not familiar with Bristol and ended up spending several days researching the town, maps of the town, the history of Bristol, its topography, its tides, the phases of the moon (including in relation to the previous intention to sail from London), its coaching inns and other buildings et cetera and also whether it would have been practicable for her family to have applied for a Writ of Habeas Corpus. Probably not seemed to be the answer.

The description of Broad Quay was derived from a piece about Bristol Docks on a site called brisray.com which included a beautiful painting said to be of the late eighteenth century attributed to Philip Vandyke according to the site. Another site, mediastorehouse.com, also included a description of the painting and puts the date circa 1760 by an artist from the British School. The painting is said to be housed at the Bristol Museum and Art Gallery.

I read in a study shortly entitled 'The port of Bristol in the second half of the eighteenth century' by John Gilbert MacMillan that a diary of winds and tides of Bristol from March 1792 to March 1793 showed that on 241 days of the year or 68% of the year ships could not leave the harbour due to the conditions. I had to worry therefore that my small party consisting of Mary Bennet, Adolphus Barrant and Bernard the footman in Bristol in April 1799 in Chapter 29 hoping to board a ship for America might have found it impossible to do so. It was thought to be due mainly to 'neap' tides, (that is tides which occur when the sun, moon, and Earth form a right angle, and this causes the regular high tides and low tides to become much lower than usual) but also the long winding river down to the sea being particularly vulnerable to wind and tide and any strong wind between south and west. Though, as the reader will see, Mary has doubts about emigrating to America.

However, the British Archives Online Bristol Shipping Records: Imports & Exports, 1770 to 1917 (for which I had to pay a temporary subscription) did include details of a few transatlantic sailings from Bristol in April 1799 to Quebec, Jamaica, possibly Charleston (the record isn't very clear), Antigua, Newfoundland and New York so hopefully my small party would not have been stranded in Bristol for too long. But there were a lot of other sailings to Ireland so Adolphus Barrant and Co could possibly have travelled via Ireland in the first instance.

Of course, Bristol, with its high tidal ranges, is a special case. I was also concerned in 'Easter At Netherfield' about the effects of the tides on sailings from the Pool of London and the book refers to a new moon heralding a high tide. In 1799, a new moon fell on Thursday 4th April.

However, a member of my writing group suggested that sailings from London would be largely unaffected by tides and that sailings could take place at any time, though his/her assertion only related to the present day.

I wondered whether to alter 'Easter At Netherfield' to remove the references to a high tide and a new moon. Having carried out a little more research, I find that there have been considerable changes to the river Thames for many centuries, both before and since 1799 the year in which the novel is set, principally the almost continuous embankation to counteract the effects of flooding upstream and downstream, so that in 1799 the Thames in London was considerably wider than it is today. This is clearly shown in the John Rocque 1746 map of London. Hence the Thames would have been shallower than it is today and of course would not have been dredged as it is today. Therefore sailings would have been more dependent on a high tide than today.

Sources for these assertions are:

'Investigation of Thames High Watermark at London' by Rick Bradford, 31/3/22; and

A long Wikipedia piece entitled: Embanking of the River Thames.

The Wikipedia piece, incidentally, contains many wonderful old drawings and paintings of the Thames and extracts from written works.

I have a great respect for the now deceased author Winston Graham and read all his Poldark novels for a taste of the period when attempting to write a historical novel set in the late eighteenth century because the Poldark novels cover the period. In 'The Angry Tide' set in 1798/1799, there is a paragraph in which a vessel carrying Ross Poldark 'left the Pool of London on Easter Monday...sailing on a full tide'. Easter Monday in 1799 was on 1st April. Winston Graham therefore obviously felt that a high tide would be a good time to sail out of the Pool of London in 1799.

As to a new moon, various scientific sources say in effect that coincidentally high tides occur at but are not caused by new and full moons. The new and full moons simply cause high tides to be higher.

On balance, I decided not to alter the wording of 'Easter At Netherfield' in relation to high tides and new moons.

I have found that for all my novels based on *Pride & Prejudice*, it has been necessary to research inns, that is inns which characters might have visited and stayed at en route between various places. This seemed to be especially the case in *Easter At Netherfield*. Rather than make up names for fictional inns, mostly I preferred to find out which inns actually did exist in 1799 and carry out research so as to be able to describe them, checking also their present-day appearances if they still exist and many do.

The journeys undertaken by the characters also involved considerable research using old maps, usually the Faden Map, as well as present-day maps to work out a route, checking towns and villages with coaching inns and looking at sites, papers and articles containing details of coaching routes.

Obviously I had to research many subjects for *Easter at Netherfield*. Much of the general research into the period, language used, et cetera had already been carried out for the previous two novels in the series and some details are given in the Author's Note and Sources at the ends of those books. Also from time to time I post on various Facebook groups items to do with my research on this book and the earlier books. I also include these in a blog on my website and to avoid repeating those bits of research here, I would point those interested in reading my research to the blogs on my website:

https://www.gillmather.com

Please turn the page for information about the next novel in the Elizabeth Bennet series and a message from the author.

The Loves Of Georgiana Darcy

A Pride & Prejudice Variation

The Elizabeth Bennet Series Book 4

To be published shortly

As *Easter At Netherfield* draws to a close in April 1799, the visitors to Netherfield will soon be on their way, returning to their own homes, including Darcy, Elizabeth and Georgiana to Pemberley. But should Georgiana be made to go with Darcy and Elizabeth, who have still to decide whether to accept the invitation of Caroline Bingley for Georgiana to remain behind with her for the London season? Georgiana would reside at the London home of Mr and Mrs Hurst where Caroline lives.

Georgiana, aged nearly eighteen, has not yet been told of the invitation, but it must be expected that she will be very much in favour of staying with Caroline, not only to enjoy the endless round of balls, receptions and social and sporting events of the season, but also to further her infatuation with The Honourable Daniel Barton who lives in Grosvenor Square and whom she has now met at two balls, one held in Meryton and the other at Lucas Lodge.

Darcy is somewhat reluctant to give his consent, concerned for his sister's well-being. He would worry about her being at large in London with an obviously keen suitor in the foreground, especially as the Hurst's own residence is a mere stone's throw from Grosvenor Square. On the other hand, he is in no very favourable position himself at the moment to advance Georgiana's marriage prospects either in general or in particular in the direction of Daniel Barton, whom she obviously likes and the liking seems to be reciprocated. There were his commercial ambitions to pursue and, within a few months, Elizabeth would be giving birth to their first child. There would be little time to devote to his sister. Therefore, on balance, he is minded to accept. He has always found Caroline to be a sensible woman, indeed mindful of every propriety to an almost rigid degree.

Elizabeth knows that she must talk seriously to Georgiana if the girl is to be allowed to stay in London, to warn her not let her feelings for Daniel Barton overwhelm her. Indeed, she must discuss Georgiana's safety in this and other respects with Caroline Bingley since Georgiana will be largely in Caroline's care. Elizabeth's recently forged friendship with Caroline should render this task less daunting.

There will also be the provision of clothes and other arrangements to make with Caroline. As to precisely what social activities Caroline would arrange, Elizabeth knows that she can safely leave all that in Caroline's capable hands. Having so very recently expressed to Elizabeth her sadness at being unable to attract a husband, Caroline will surely relish the additional social opportunities afforded to her by sponsoring Georgiana's coming out.

Caroline, for her part, is indeed enthusiastic about having the opportunity, if it is granted, to chaperone Georgiana about town, to initiate her into all the gossip going around, introduce her to people, attend dress fittings with the girl and advise her on the latest fashions. Her offer is not entirely selfless. She has become somewhat jaded of late. To have a lovely girl like Georgiana in her care for a few months will, she feels, give her the fillip she needs to garner more enjoyment from society again, especially since Mr Darcy will no longer be at Netherfield. Instead, she will have a connection with him through Georgiana.

If Georgiana does stay in London, how will she fare? Will everything go according to her wishes and expectations? Read *The Loves of Georgiana Darcy* to find out!

Thank you for reading *Easter At Netherfield*, the third book in the Elizabeth Bennet series. *Intrigue At Longbourn and* Menace At Pemberley are the first and second.

I hope you enjoyed it and would be delighted if you could spread the word about this book and other books of mine. Online reviews, so important for authors, would be particularly appreciated on Kindle/Amazon, Goodreads, Library Thing, other sites for book readers and/or your favourite book provider's website.

All of my books are available as ebooks and paperbacks all over the world and under the Kindle Unlimited scheme. Just search by my name, Gill Mather, and the book title.

Try out the Roz Benedict Detective Novellas series. The short books are cozy-crime mysteries with more than a dash of romance in some of them. They all feature Roz Benedict, a detective inspector at the outset who becomes a private sleuth, and Guy Attwood who tends to act in an advisory capacity. Roz's neighbour, Kate Sampson, appears in the third and subsequent novellas.

Compromised – A noir tale of love, suspense and guilty secrets

Cut Off – A fascinating cozy crime caper in a country commune

Conflicts of Little Avail – A stunning yarn arising from brotherly love and official arrogance

Conjecture Most Macabre – A cautionary tale of how suspicion can take extreme forms

Subsequent to *Conjecture Most Macabre*, Roz and her friend Kate form a private detective agency carrying on business under the name of Cops & Roz's. Guy continues to act in an advisory capacity. The first two cases for the Cops & Roz's Detective Agency appear in:

Le Frottage – An intricate web of hidden pasts, religious orthodoxy and young love

Confounded – A sophisticated novella about a property fraud causing serial frustrations for a pair of female private sleuths.

Gill's other book series is called the Colchester Law World series. They are all romantic novels and feature crime or criminal activities. One, the second novel, *Threshold*, is an adventure novel too and the last, *Beyond The Realms*, is a paranormal romance. There are five books in the series available as ebooks and paperbacks. All of the novels can be read alone. Here are the titles of the novels:

The Ardent Intern

Threshold

Relatively Innocent

Reasonable Doubts

Beyond The Realms

***

Other novels by Gill are also available as both ebooks and paperbacks. Check them out below, read a sample on Kindle and see what you think.

AS THE CLOCK STRUCK TEN

Have you ever experienced a life-changing event, after which nothing will ever be the same again? Has anything totally out of your control ever happened to you which, within just a few short hours, robbed you of your assumed place in the world and challenged your preconceptions? A person in *As The Clock Struck Ten* was the unlucky object of such an occurrence. It started when the clock struck ten and, by the end of the day, the consequences were irresistible.

This gripping contemporary thriller takes the reader into a dark and murky subject. This is the perfect lockdown, Christmas or holiday read in which secrets accumulate, white lies yield unwanted results, blackmail is ruthlessly employed and family relationships are tested.

Don Morrison has a new live-in girlfriend, Grace Bennett. His eighteen-year-old daughter, Emma, newly arrived home from university for her first summer vacation, isn't happy to have her home invaded, as she sees it, by this other woman, especially so soon after the death of her mother, Carol, who was very ill for many years and was cared for by Don.

Grace's twenty-year-old son, Luke, lives at home with his father, Greg, Grace's husband.

The five main characters progress through the hot, rural East Anglian summer, some rather haphazardly, others with a more definite purpose. A young woman, Alex, known to some of them helps things along.

The law takes over at one point, its effects quite devastating for the unprepared.

THE UNRELIABLE PLACEBO

A hilarious and powerful romantic comedy.

Funnier than Bridget Jones's Diary, more bizarre than Fleabag, Anna Duke's clumsy attempts to re-join the couples club after the Arsehole – sorry, her husband Alfie – has left her, result in various embarrassing events, and lead her to some strange places and into some weird situations.

Her theory is that some foreknowledge of a man she's dating would help to bring about a positive result, like placebos affect medical outcomes. But it doesn't necessarily work out that way.

Is it possible that one person will have the courage to manfully hack through the thorny thicket of Anna's mind, circumventing the muddled hopes, dreams, fears, musings and speculations, to reach the perfect ending?

<u>CLASS OF '97</u>

In the summer of 2019, 'Greta' has fetched up in South Yorkshire on land owned by Francis. They both have secrets, more entrenched and harder to shake off for one of them than the other. Nearly two hundred miles to the south in Ipswich, Oliver continues to labour as a criminal solicitor, unaware of the consequences of earlier events in his life and, as we all are, of what is yet to come.

Francis doesn't put pressure on 'Greta', nevertheless she ups and disappears anyway, returning to her real life. And yet, is that life any more real than her sojourn with Francis?

She becomes friendlier with Oliver and, despite having serial problems of his own, he helps her with a serious and distressing difficulty. While doing so, he discovers something sinister, though he can't quite believe it.

Their romantic entanglements with others don't run entirely smoothly and, for both of them, the past rakes up some unexpected issues. Gradually, and from various sources, the truth emerges, less palatable in some respects than others…

The twists in the plot will keep you guessing right to the end. Class of '97 is the ideal book club novel, providing food for endless questions about the characters' circumstances, difficulties and life-changing events.

Send me a message any time through my website: https://www.gillmather.com and you can follow me on:

twitter @readgillmather

and Facebook https://www.facebook.com/gillmatherauthor

With my best wishes,

Gill

Made in the USA
Middletown, DE
19 January 2024